For my mother, Virginia Stuart,
a writer, editor,
proof-reader extraordinaire, god bless her.
And a pretty damned good mother as well.
Love you, Moo.

ANNE STUART

Breathless

THE HOUSE OF ROHAN

ISBN-13: 978-0-7783-2850-6

BREATHLESS

Copyright © 2010 by Anne Kristine Stuart Ohlrogge.

www.MIRABooks.com

For questions and comments about the quality of this book please contact us at Customer_eCare@Harlequin.ca.

Printed in U.S.A.

Recycling programs for this product may not exist in your area.

THIS PRODUCT IS RECYCLABLE • PLEASE RECYCLE •

Beginning

"I don't think this is a good idea," the honorable Jane Pagett said, wringing her hands. "Mr. St. John isn't very good ton. I don't trust him."

Lady Miranda Rohan looked at her dearest friend with a wicked grin. They were sitting in Miranda's bedroom in the Rohan townhouse on Clarges Street as the young lady of the house prepared for a clandestine night out. "Oh, I don't trust him, either," she said cheerfully. "That's half the fun. Don't lecture me, darling. I've been a very good girl for three seasons now, and this is the first time I've done anything even remotely naughty. They want me to find someone to marry, and I'm just… experimenting."

"I don't think your parents are going to let you marry Christopher St. John," Jane said tartly.

"No, I don't expect they will," she said with a sigh. "I don't think it's fair, though. They'd probably reject him because he has no money, but I have more than enough for both of us. We could live very well on my income."

Jane looked at her strangely. "Would you really want to marry Mr. St. John?"

Miranda shrugged. "He's as good as anyone, I suppose. It's not as if I were a great beauty and could take my pick. Certainly there are a number of men who'd have me, and I expect I'll end up with one of them, but in the meantime I just want to indulge in a tiny bit of wicked flirtation."

"You're very pretty, Miranda!" Jane protested.

"Well, I'm not a complete antidote," Miranda admitted. "I'm just ordinary. I'm neither tall nor short, plump nor thin, my eyes and my hair are a nice boring brown. My face is inoffensive. Nothing for anyone to take a disgust of. But nothing to induce a wild passion, though Christopher St. John seems quite enthusiastic. Though I expect he's probably more enthusiastic about my money than my person," she added in a practical voice.

"Then why risk your reputation by going to Vauxhall with him? Alone!" Jane cried. "I'd be happy to come with you, or you could take your maid..."

"Absolutely not," Miranda said briskly, tying her domino at her neck and pulling it around her. Her clothes were far too discreet and modest for a raucous night at the pleasure gardens, but the domino would be adequate disguise. "I want to dance wildly and drink wine and play cards for high stakes and laugh too loudly. I want to kiss and be kissed until I get tired of it, and I want to do it with the most beautiful man I've ever seen. You have to admit Christopher is beautiful."

"His chin is too weak," Jane said in a grumpy voice.

"Not as far as I'm concerned," Miranda said. "I'm only sorry this just came up, though I doubt I could have made my escape if you weren't here. My sister-in-law takes her duties very seriously since my parents have gone up to Scotland, and she's always asking me what I'm doing. The thing is, I don't want you to have to lie for me if anyone notices I'm gone."

"Well, I'm not going to lie for you," Jane said. "I'll tell them exactly where you went and with who."

"With whom," Miranda corrected absently. "And it won't be a problem. It'll be too late to find me, and my family knows I'm not an idiot. I'll be home around midnight, uncompromised, and no one need ever know. I just want a taste of freedom before I agree to marry one of those boring young men my brothers keep bringing home. Just a few stolen kisses while we watch the fireworks at midnight, and then I'll be safely back and chances are no one will even notice that I went out. And what can they do to me if they find out—beat me?"

"You know you'll manage to charm your entire family out of being angry with you," Jane said. "You'll even manage to charm me."

Miranda pulled the hood over her boring brown hair and reached for her loo mask. "That's because I'm adorable," she said pertly. "Don't worry about me, love. I'll be back before you know it."

Jane looked at her, worried. "I wish you wouldn't go. I don't think Mr. St. John is trustworthy."

"We've already gone over that. I'll marry someone trustworthy. I'll be just a tiny bit wicked with someone beautiful beforehand." She leaned over and planted a kiss on Jane's cheek. "Don't worry about me. I'll be fine." And a moment later she was gone.

There were times, looking back on that night, when Lady Miranda Rohan couldn't believe how stupid she'd been. How gullible, how certain of her own invulnerability that she never considered the danger. Christopher St. John was charming, rakish, ever so slightly dissolute, and spending a few unchaperoned hours with him should have been perfectly safe. He'd been so handsome. Penniless, but that hadn't bothered her. She would inherit more than enough for both of them. And after three years on the marriage mart there'd been no one she'd even considered as a possible husband, until Christopher had glided into her life, with his perfect face and tall, straight body, his white teeth and his charming smile.

She'd laughed when he'd suggested she elope with him. It took her far too long to realize that the closed carriage he was using to return her home was taking too much time, that while Christopher was dozing on the seat opposite her the road was becoming rougher. And when she pushed up the blind she saw only pitch-black night, not the lights of London.

She hadn't succumbed to hysterics, though she'd been tempted. She'd been firm, angry, determined. And in the long run, helpless. He'd maintained his charm throughout her protests. He loved her, he adored her, he couldn't live without her. And yes, without her substantial fortune.

"I won't marry you," she'd said firmly. "You can drag me in front of a minister at Gretna Green and I'll still say no."

"First off, Miranda darling," he'd said in the smooth voice she'd once found enchanting and now found irritating. "Ministers don't have to do the marrying in Scotland. Anyone is qualified. Secondly, you'll say yes, once you realize you have no other choice."

"I'll always have another choice."

"Not once you're ruined. Now, stop fussing. You've been spoiled and willful and now you're going to have to pay the price. We'll deal well enough together. I won't be a demanding husband."

"You won't be my husband at all," she'd said darkly.

"Now that's where you're wrong."

She'd hoped he'd take her to an inn where she could throw herself on the mercy of the innkeeper. Instead he brought her to a small cottage in the country, miles away from anyone else, with one sullen servant who'd ignored her.

It had been her own fault, Miranda told herself, refusing to cry. And St. John was right about one thing: it was up to her to pay the price. Just not the price he thought he'd guaranteed.

Because compromising her was not enough. St. John was a man who cared about the details, and the second night he took her virginity, to ensure his financial future.

It hadn't been rape. Miranda had curled up, holding her stomach afterward. She'd neither screamed nor fought, and when it became clear that it was going to happen she did her best to get into the spirit of the thing.

Vastly overrated. He kissed and slobbered over her breasts, actions that left her entirely unmoved. She'd never seen a penis that hadn't belonged to a baby, but she found the adult version fairly unprepossessing. It was short and squat in a nest of hair and really quite unattractive. It was just as well she didn't intend to seek out any future acquaintance with one.

It hurt, of course. She'd been warned that it would the

first time, but St. John apparently considered her listless response to be arousing, for he repeated the process two more nights, and each night she hurt, each night she bled, and when he told her to prepare for him on the fourth night she'd slammed a water ewer down over his head, watching him slump unconscious at her feet.

It had been an oversight that she hadn't tried that before. If she'd just had the brains to consider brute force the first night she might still have retained at least her physical innocence, if nothing else.

She'd stepped over St. John's body, only slightly concerned that she might have killed him, went downstairs and headed for the stables. The hired carriage had been returned, but Christopher's showy chestnut was there, and it had taken her only a few minutes to saddle and bridle him, thanking God her father had always insisted his children know about horseflesh. Riding astride was its own misery, particularly considering St. John's attentions, but by the time she was an hour away from the cottage she ran into a small army come to rescue her, including her three brothers and her formerly annoying sister-in-law Annis.

"Don't kill him," she'd said calmly as she was bustled into the carriage they'd brought with them.

"Why not?" her brother Benedick grumbled. "Father would tell me to. Don't tell me you're in love with the creature?"

Her expression had answered that ridiculous question. "I just want to forget about it."

"Miranda is right," Annis had said, earning her eternal gratitude. "The more fuss we make, the bigger the scandal, and we'd like this to blow over quickly, would we not? I suggest you horsewhip him and leave him at that."

"He didn't touch you, did he? Didn't force himself on you?" Benedick had demanded.

It wasn't that she wanted to lie. But her fiery-tempered older brother would have gutted St. John if he'd known the truth, and even peers couldn't get away with murder.

"Of course not. He wants to marry me, not make me hate him."

Benedick had believed her calm assertion, and she and Annis had started back for London, while her brothers moved on for revenge. "I don't know if we're going to be able to keep this quiet, Miranda," Annis said in a practical voice. "You know how the gossips are, and I think Mr. St. John might have deliberately dropped a few hints before he absconded with you." Her dark blue eyes swept over Miranda, warm with sympathy. "I'm afraid you might be ruined."

Miranda ignored the sick feeling in the pit of her stomach. It was becoming second nature to her. "There are worse things in this life," she had said.

But in truth, it didn't appear that there were. Her parents had rushed back to England, her mother full of hugs and comfort and not a word of reproach, her father coming up with outrageously intricate plans to remove parts of St. John's anatomy and feed it to the fishes. When her monthly courses had arrived, on time, she had breathed a sigh of relief, and the rest of the family remained safely ignorant of her loss of innocence.

But in the end it hadn't mattered. Miranda was no longer welcome among the ton. Her invitation to Almack's had been politely withdrawn. Mothers and daughters had crossed the street rather than be obliged to speak to her, and when forced, gave her the cut direct. She was a pariah, an outcast, just as Christopher St. John had sworn she'd be.

He'd had the consummate gall to show up at her house and offer to do the honorable thing. He'd sworn that it was his passion for her that had overcome his scruples, that he would marry her and the scandal would soon die down. They loved each other, and his darling Miranda would soon get over her case of the sulks.

Marriage to him was still her only route. If she wished, they could even live in separate establishments, and he'd be certain to see that she received a generous allowance from the money that would now be in his control.

And it had been her father, Adrian Rohan, the Marquess of Haverstoke himself who'd thrown him down the stairs of their vast house on Clarges Street.

Miranda had retired to the country for a few months, until a new scandal occupied the ton's attention. Not for one moment did she believe her sins would be forgiven—she was ruined, now and forever, and nothing would change it. But by the time she returned life had moved on, and so had Miranda.

And she had discovered, to her immense joy, that being ruined was much more fun than being on the marriage mart. She didn't have to simper and flirt with shallow young men, she didn't have to make certain her every move was accompanied by a footman and an abigail. She bought a house of her own, just a pied-a-terre that was nevertheless all hers, and she rode in the parks, ignoring both the cuts and the importunate young men. She went to the theater and the library and

Gunters, and while she enjoyed the companionship of her cousin Louisa, the older lady was mostly deaf, sadly stout and the most indolent creature on the face of the earth.

For the first time in her life Miranda was free, and she reveled in that freedom. She had her staunchly loyal family and she had her dearest friend Jane and the rest of the Pagetts. In truth, she'd lost little and gained everything. Apart from the trouble the whole contretemps had brought upon her family, she didn't regret it. By the following spring she'd happily settled into her new life, and she wouldn't have changed it for the world.

Christopher St. John didn't fare nearly as well.

The house on Cadogan Place had always given him an unpleasant feeling in the pit of his stomach. It wasn't that the place was huge and dark and gloomy, sitting on the edge of the better areas of town, a bit too near the purview of the criminal class that haunted the darkened alleys and side streets. It was the man who owned that house, the man awaiting him and his excuses for failing to do what he'd been paid to do. It was The Scorpion, known more formally as Lucien de Malheur, Earl of Rochdale, who would sit there and look at him with those colorless eyes, his thin lips curling in disdain, one elegant hand gripping the top of his cane as if he'd like to beat a man to death with it.

Christopher St. John shuddered, then shook off his nervousness. A light, icy rain had begun to fall. February in the city was always dismal. Had it been up to him he would have stayed out in the countryside with Lady

Miranda Rohan warming his bed. If the bitch hadn't clocked him one and taken off.

And she and her family were proving most unreasonable, he thought, absently rubbing his bruised shoulder. He had a cracked rib, a broken wrist, several torn muscles and scrapes and bruises over most of his body. No, the Rohans didn't seem likely to become sensible any time soon.

He raised his hand to knock on the massive black door, but it swung open before he reached the knocker, and Leopold, Rochdale's sepulchral majordomo, stood there, staring down at him with strong disapproval.

Leopold was part and parcel of Rochdale's general peculiarity. The servant was immensely tall—possibly six feet seven—and skinny in his black clothes. Someone once likened him to a giraffe in mourning, and St. John agreed. A very unpleasant giraffe. He had some sort of accent that no one could decipher. Rochdale had picked the odd man up during the travels that had occupied him for most of his adult life, and Leopold only added to the mystery surrounding his employer.

"He's waiting for you," Leopold said in an unpromising voice, receiving St. John's wet coat and hat and handing them to the waiting footman, also dressed in funereal black.

St. John grimaced as he straightened his coat of superfine, not made by Weston but a reasonable facsimile if one didn't look too closely. Appearance was paramount in his position. He found that if one looked and acted as if one belonged, then usually one was welcomed.

He followed Leopold down the long dark hallways, ending up in the depressing library where he usually met with the earl. It was deserted, of course. Rochdale always liked to make an entrance.

A small fire burned in one grate, doing little to warm the cavernous room. Why in the world anyone would want so many books was beyond him. And all these books had to have been acquired by the current earl. The previous one had lost almost everything in a short-lived, profligate life.

He heard the familiar approach, that ominous step that wasn't quite even, the bite of Rochdale's walking stick hitting the ground heavier than mere stylistic use, and an unconscious dread filled him. The door opened, and light flooded the room.

"They've quite left you in the dark, dear Christopher," Rochdale purred, moving forward with his barely halting gait. "How remiss of my servants. Or perhaps how prescient. I gather you haven't come to celebrate our success in your little venture?"

Christopher swallowed. "I did everything I could. Those damned Rohans. Any other family would have been begging me to marry the girl. Any other girl would have been besotted and grateful."

Rochdale said nothing, moving to a chair by the fire and sinking down gracefully, his ruined face in shadows. "Ah, but I warned you those Rohans are not like other people. Am I to presume those bruises and cuts on your face are the result of the brothers' attentions?"

"And her father's. My entire body's nothing but bruises and cracked bones."

"Refrain from showing me. I certainly don't doubt the Rohans would take their revenge. You're lucky they didn't spit you like a goose."

"By the time they found out I'd bedded her it was

too late. We were already in London and I refused the younger brother's challenge. I could have bested him easily—he's nothing but a boy—but I decided he wasn't worth having to flee the country for. You know how they've gotten about dueling recently."

"I know," the earl said gently. "I'm surprised the two older didn't challenge you. The oldest in particular—I believe his name might be Benedick? If you'd managed to kill him it might have mitigated this disaster."

"They were both in Scotland, taking the girl with them," Christopher said in a sulky voice. At least this particular interview was going far better than he'd anticipated. It was a balm, after the total failure of his plans for Miranda Rohan.

"Ah, I see. So let me understand this. You were to seduce the Rohans' sister, marry her, and kill the older brother when he challenged you to a duel. Yet you have failed me on every level. Am I correct?"

"I did seduce the girl," Christopher's voice was defensive. "She just refused to marry me."

"Then you clearly must have botched the job. Did you rape her?"

"I didn't have to. Once she knew it was inevitable she stopped fighting."

Rochdale shook his head. "I chose you for your handsome face, your reputation as a lover, and your deadliness with a sword. I'm sorely disappointed in you, St. John. You may leave me."

Initial relief flooded through him, followed by dismay. He'd been half afraid Rochdale would have… He wasn't sure what he'd been afraid of. It had been silly. "But what about the money?" he said, trying not to let the panic show in his voice. "You promised me five hundred pounds to abduct her, and then I'd have her marriage settlement. Since I don't have that I'd think a thousand pounds would be a more reasonable recompense."

Rochdale laughed softly, a sound that sent a chill down St. John's backbone. "You forget who you're dealing with. Your reward for a thoroughly botched job is the knowledge that I won't arrange for you to be gutted in some alleyway when you least expect it. And you know I can. I have a goodly portion of London's criminal class at my beck and call."

A cold sweat broke out on Christopher's forehead. "At least the five hundred pounds." His voice a whine now. "I'm out of pocket for the cottage, the carriage, any number of things…"

"Then you shouldn't have failed." His voice was like silk. "Leopold, see him out."

The servant had appeared silently behind them, and St. John jumped, startled. One look at the man's impassive face and he knew he was bested. He opened his mouth to hurl a threat, a recrimination, but Rochdale's voice stopped him.

"I wouldn't if I were you. Killing you here would be so inconvenient."

Christopher closed his mouth with a snap. And followed Leopold though the dark house, out into the cold, cruel streets of London in the rain.

If you want a job done well you'd best do it yourself. Wasn't that what the old saying was? Not that the Earl of Rochdale listened to old sayings, but in this case it was true. He'd chosen the best weapon he could, and the idiot had failed him.

His wants had been simple. The Rohans had destroyed

his only sister, bringing about her death. He'd wanted to return the favor, with the hopeful side-benefit of killing Benedick Rohan, the architecture of Genevieve's destruction. Though he could have been just as happy at the thought of Benedick living with the knowledge that his precious little sister was trapped in a life of misery with a gazetted fortune hunter and womanizer.

St. John had proven a miserable failure, and with his bungling it was unlikely that another pretty young man would get anywhere near her. Trust the Rohans not to care if one of their own was ruined in the face of society.

Clearly it was time for him to take a hand in the situation himself. He couldn't rush into anything—she would be whip-shy for a bit. He'd have more than enough time to decide exactly what form his revenge would take.

He would wait. Wait until they'd lowered their guard. Wait until he had everything in place. Wait until his prey had no idea that she was simply the pawn in a game of revenge.

And then he would pounce.

2

Two years later

Lady Miranda Rohan stood before the window of her cozy house on Half Moon Street, staring out into the rain. She was restless. She hated to admit it—she'd always prided herself on her ability to find interest under almost any circumstances. At the advanced age of twenty-three she considered herself a resourceful young woman. She'd faced disaster on a social scale and come through the other side, independent and happy, with the support and affection of her large family and closest friends, and, indeed, ostracism had unexpected benefits. She didn't have to attend boring parties, dance with odious men who simply wanted to ogle her and her inheritance. She didn't have to survive miserably crowded gatherings and lukewarm punches and boring conversations filled with salacious gossip and little more. Particularly since nowadays she was more than likely to be the topic of that gossip.

No, that was no longer true. Enough time had passed that her transgressions were no longer half so interesting.

There were always more exciting scandals around. She didn't have to spend time with those judgmental wags who'd tell her she was simply reaping the rewards of her foolish behavior two years ago. Foolish, not truly wicked, but in a society where those two words were interchangeable, Miranda Rohan was living with the results.

Normally she didn't care—she found life to be full of interesting things. She read everything she could get her hands on, from treatises on animal husbandry to paeans to the classical poets. She found nature to be boundlessly fascinating, and while her own efforts at the pianoforte and singing were decidedly lackluster, she still found great enjoyment in pursuing those two disciplines. She was an exceptional horsewoman, both as a whip and a rider; she had a limitless capacity for affection for both dogs and their haughtier cousins, cats. She had a gift with children and according to her dear companion Louisa she readily sank to their level.

She followed politics, gossip, science, the sciences, the arts.

And at that particular moment she was ready to weep with boredom when she swore she would never be bored.

"This winter is lasting forever," she announced disconsolately, staring into the dark, dismal afternoon. Half Moon Street was a mere two streets over from the Rohan family manse, which, unfortunately, did her no good. It was deserted, as the rest of her noisy, sprawling family had gone up to Yorkshire to await the birth of her newest niece or nephew.

"It will last just as long as it always does," Cousin Louisa said placidly. Louisa was in truth the most stolid creature alive, and therefore the perfect match for an outcast like Miranda Rohan. Her great girth allowed her no more than the least taxing of social venues, and her calm, placid nature was a balm to Miranda's rare emotional outbursts.

"I should have gone to Yorkshire with the family," Miranda said, swinging one foot disconsolately.

"And why didn't you? Granted, the thought of traveling that far brings on a most severe case of the vapors in an invalid such as myself, but if you'd been with your family there would have been no need for me to accompany you on such an arduous journey, and you wouldn't be pacing this house like one of those lions they show at the Bartholomew Fair."

Miranda forbore to point out that, in fact, none of Cousin Louisa's duties had been strictly necessary. After all, ruined was ruined, and even the presence of a middle-aged cousin of impeccable lineage and reputation couldn't do anything to lift Miranda's banishment.

Not that she wanted it to, she thought defiantly. It was just that she was…restless.

It was distressing. She wouldn't have thought she needed anyone's company to make her happy, and she'd always been perversely pleased that ruination meant she no longer had to spend her life trying to attract a suitable husband.

But that was before she knew what true isolation was. Before her world narrowed down to her boisterous family, her dearest friend Jane and the rest of the Pagetts, and the indolent and comfortable Cousin Louisa.

And right now everyone was out of town. Her brother Charles's wife was just about to give birth to her second child, Benedick's new bride was increasing, and their parents were thrilled.

They'd begged her to accompany them, but she'd refused, making up a believable excuse when the truth was far simpler. When Lady Miranda Rohan was a member of the household the social invitations dwindled to a trickle. Society had already accepted that the wild Rohans were prone to misbehavior, but when it came to young ladies of the ton, rules were rules. Miranda was an outcast, and the Rohans, proud and loyal to a fault, didn't leave their daughter behind, no matter how great the opprobrium of the ton. Miranda's best choice was to simply absent herself, allowing her family to enjoy themselves without second thoughts.

Unfortunately Cousin Louisa could scarcely make up for the energetic Rohans, given her tendency to fall asleep at unlikely moments. Normally this would have been no problem, but in March even the few members of the ton who did recognize her were still out of town, including dearest Jane.

"You need to do something to stop that appalling fidgeting," Cousin Louisa said with the small, catlike yawn she seldom bothered to disguise. "Why don't you go to the library and see if there are any new French novels? Something saucy to take your mind off things?"

"I went yesterday. I've already read everything that interests me, saucy and otherwise," she said in a disconsolate voice. She kicked at her skirts. "Listen to me! I sound like a nursery brat who's lost her favorite toy. Forgive me, Cousin Louisa. I'm not usually so tedious."

Cousin Louisa yawned behind her fan. "What about a walk?"

"It's raining," Miranda said in mournful accents.

"Is it?" her companion said sleepily, not bothering to turn her head to look out the window into the dark afternoon. "I hadn't noticed. Go to the theater."

"I've seen everything, and my problem is right now——" Miranda made a sound of disgust. "I can't imagine what's wrong with me! I'm not usually so ill-tempered."

"You're usually so good-natured you exhaust me. In truth, child, you're wearing me out at this very minute. I'd suggest you go practice on the pianoforte but you're always a bit too enthusiastic, and I need my nap without music thumping through the house. Go for a drive. Take the curricle. It looks as if the rain has stopped for now, but if it begins again you can simply have the groom raise the hood."

Miranda seized the notion like a lifeline thrown a drowning man. "That's exactly what I shall do, minus the groom. I'm entirely capable of driving myself, and if the rain begins again I'm sure I won't melt."

Cousin Louisa uttered a long-suffering sigh. "I do wish you wouldn't insist on flying in the face of conventions. Society has a long memory, but I'm certain there are any number of people, short of the most proper, who'd eventually overlook your...er...fall from grace if you'd just give them proper reason to."

It was an old argument, one Miranda had given up on ages ago. She could spend the rest of her life doing penance and being grateful for the scraps of acceptance tossed her way, or she could embrace her new life on the outskirts of polite society, no more apologies to anyone. The choice was simple and she'd made it without a second thought.

"No."

Cousin Louisa was too good-natured to argue. "Enjoy your drive, my dear, and try not to wake me when you return. I sleep so dreadfully that my little naps are crucial."

In fact Louisa slept at least twelve hours each night, aided by her admitted fondness for the French brandy Benedick provided for them. And since she found the trip up the stairs to her bedroom too exhausting to accomplish more than once a day, she tended to nap in the salon.

By the time Miranda had changed into driving clothes the horses had been put to and she could hear faint snores drifting from the drawing room. In fact, Louisa slept like the dead. The house could fall down around her and she wouldn't notice, she thought with an affectionate smile.

One of the great joys in Miranda's altered life was her curricle and horses. She loved driving, and owning her own carriage and pair delighted her to no end. In truth, she would have loved a phaeton, in particular a high-perch one, but she'd resisted temptation, deciding her family already had enough censure to deal with.

She never confided this particular concern to her brothers; Benedick would have immediately purchased the most outrageous equipage he could find for her. They were loyal to a fault. She adored them all, but in truth they'd been through enough, and she'd discovered that an insult to a family member was always more painful than an insult to oneself. And the pain that she caused them was far harder to deal with than her own censure.

She headed for Hyde Park, perversely enjoying the cold, damp air. She could feel her hair escaping the confines of her bonnet, and she knew her cheeks would be flushed and healthy, rather than the fashionably pale, but she didn't care.

She let the horses out a bit, enjoying the sensation as they pounded through the park. Perhaps she ought to go out to the countryside, to the family estate in Dorset, but that would scarcely solve her problem with her family away in the north. She would still be kicking her heels in frustration, bereft of any kind of stimulation apart from the solitary enjoyment of books and the theater. She had no one to talk with, no one to laugh with, to fight with. And it looked as if it would continue that way for the rest of her life.

An unexpected fit of melancholia settled down around her, and she bit her lip. She made it a rule never to cry about her situation. She was simply reaping the rewards of her own foolishness.

But after endless days of rain and gloom she could feel waves of obnoxious self-pity begin to well up. The damp wind had pulled some of her hair loose, and she reached up a gloved hand to push it out of her face.

The swiftness of the accident was astonishing. One moment she was bowling along the road, in the next the carriage lurched violently and she just barely held on to the reins, controlling the horses as she kept them from trying to bolt.

She knew immediately that something must have happened to one of the wheels, and she hauled back on the reins, trying to stop the frightened beasts, trying to maintain her seat and not be tossed into the road, just as a huge black carriage came up from behind her. Within moments two of the grooms had jumped down, pulling her frightened animals to a halt.

It had begun to rain again, and Miranda was getting soaked. The carriage had stopped just ahead of hers on the road, a crest on the door, but she didn't recognize whose it was, and she was too busy castigating herself as an absolute idiot, a total noddy for letting the horses panic like that. Her curricle was tilted at a strange angle, and she scrambled down before anyone could come to her aid, passing the broken wheel and moving to the leader's head, taking the bridle in her hand and stroking his nose, murmuring soothing words.

The footman she'd displaced went back to the dark carriage and let down the steps, opening the door, holding a muffled conversation with someone inside before returning to her. "His lordship wonders if you would do him the honor of allowing him to assist you," the groom said politely.

Bloody hell, Miranda thought, having been taught to curse by her brothers. "I thank him, but he's already come to my rescue."

A voice emerged from the darkened interior of the carriage, a smooth, sinuous voice. "Dear child, you're getting drenched. Pray allow me to at least give you a ride home while my servants see to your horses and carriage."

She bit her lip, glancing around her in the rain. There was no one else in sight, and she certainly couldn't handle this on her own. Besides, he was of the peerage—he was unlikely to be terribly dangerous. Most of the titled men she'd known were elderly and gout-ridden. And if he offered her any insult she was quite adept at kicking, biting and gouging, all skills that would have stopped Christopher St. John two years ago…if she'd possessed them then. Her father and three brothers had seen to it that she would never again be at the mercy of any man.

"You are very kind." Giving up the fight, she handed the reins back to one groom as she allowed the other one to hand her up into the darkened carriage. A moment later the door shut, closing her in with her mysterious rescuer.

He was nothing more than a shadowy figure on the opposite seat of the large, opulent carriage. The cushions beneath her were soft, there was a heated coal box near her feet and a moment later a fur throw was covering her, though she hadn't seen him move.

"You're Lady Miranda Rohan, are you not?" came the smooth voice from the darkness.

Miranda stiffened, glancing toward the door. If need be she could always push it open and leap to safety—they weren't moving that fast.

He must have read her thoughts. "I mean you no harm, Lady Miranda, and no insult. I simply wish to be of service."

It was a lovely thought, but she still wasn't certain that she trusted him. She glanced out the window. "Where are you taking me?"

"To your house on Half Moon Street, of course. No, don't look so distrustful. The sad fact is that London society is a hotbed of gossip, as I've discovered to my own detriment. Everyone knows of your...ah...unique lifestyle." His voice was gentle, unnervingly so.

"Of course," she said with a grimace. "You would think polite society had better things to do than concern itself with me, but apparently not. There is nothing worse than having the world judging you, making up outrageous stories and even worse, believing them."

"In fact, there are any number of things that are a great deal worse." His voice was dry. "But I do understand what you mean. I've been the victim of the same sort of malicious gossip for most of my life."

Miranda was trying to tuck her wet hair back inside her bonnet when she paused. She imagined she looked like a rain-swept slattern, but perhaps her odd rescuer could no more see her than she could see him.

"You have?" she said, curious, her own misery banished.

"I beg pardon—I've been most remiss. Allow me to introduce myself. I'm Lucien de Malheur." He paused for a moment. "You may have heard of me."

Miranda didn't blink. So this was the notorious Scorpion, the fifth earl of Rochdale. She peered through the darkness with renewed fascination. "You're right," she said with her usual frankness. "Even in *my* cloistered existence I've heard the stories. Compared to you, I'm St. Joan."

His soft laugh was oddly beguiling. "But we both know that gossip is seldom true."

"Seldom?"

"Occasionally an element of truth colors a story. Doubtless you've heard that I consort with criminals, that I'm debauched and evil and lead young men to their financial ruin and consort with the notorious Heavenly Host. Don't look so shocked—I realize people seldom admit the organization even exists anymore, but it's a very badly kept secret. And you would have heard of my deformities, doubtless exaggerated to the point where I'm better suited to Astley's Circus and its objects of Wonder and Horror."

He'd been described in exactly that way, but she

wasn't about to admit it. "And what is the truth?" She didn't have to look out the window. She recognized the sound of the pavement beneath the carriage, the pattern of cobblestones on the narrow street. They were already on Half Moon Street. Too soon, she thought, frustrated. This was the most interesting thing that had happened to her in weeks, perhaps months.

For a moment he said nothing, and she had the odd sense that he was weighing something, considering something new and unlikely.

"The truth is, Lady Miranda, that I am an ugly brute with a lame leg and I prefer not to impose my ugliness on unsuspecting strangers."

She wanted to see him. For some reason she was quite desperate to set eyes on the notorious, reputedly villainous earl, and she suspected his words had been formed with just that intent.

They had pulled up outside her small, immaculate house. "I've been warned," she said with humor in her voice. "You can show me and I promise not to scream or faint."

His soft laugh was her answer. "I'm afraid I don't know you well enough yet, Lady Miranda. I would never trespass on so short an acquaintance."

She picked up the important word. "Yet?" she echoed warily.

"Please," he protested, once again reading her doubts. "I do only wish to be your friend."

"A friend I can't see?"

"I'll make a bargain with you, Lady Miranda. You're fond of music, are you not? If you agree to attend a musical evening at my house in Cadogan Place you'll have no choice but to look at my unfortunate face. And no, don't go jumping to conclusions again. The twenty-four people who've been invited have all accepted with flattering alacrity. I would be honored if you joined us."

She probably shouldn't, but the risk sounded so tempting, and in faith, what did she have to lose?

"I was planning to go out of town, my lord...."

"But surely you can put your departure off for a few days? London has been so devoid of company you must be bored to tears. Indulge yourself, and me."

"I shall have to see." It was tempting. It had been so long since she'd held a conversation with anyone outside her small circle, and she was strangely drawn to him, another outsider. She'd be a fool to walk into trouble again. Still, there was always the chance that common sense would reappear as needed.

He seemed to take her pause for acquiescence. "I'll send my carriage round for you, since I expect it will be a while before your curricle is repaired. Wednesday next, at nine."

"I shall see," she said again, being careful. The servants had opened the door to the carriage but the gray, dismal light penetrated no deeper than his shiny black boots.

He took her lack of agreement in stride. "You can come or not as you please. In either case, my men will have your horses back in no time, and I'll see to the return of your carriage, as well. In the meantime I'm most delighted to have met you, and honored to have been of some minor assistance."

To her surprise he took her hand, bringing it to his lips in the dark of the carriage. The touch of his mouth was light, but against her bare skin it was oddly...disturbing. What in the world had she done with her gloves?

She practically scrambled away, almost falling down the lowered carriage steps. She might have heard a soft laugh from the shadows, but realized that was absurd.

"À bientôt," her mysterious rescuer murmured.

And a moment later he was gone.

Lucien de Malheur, the Earl of Rochdale, sank back against the well-cushioned squabs, tapping his long pale fingers against his bad leg. He was feeling meditative— he always prided himself on his ability to shift with the changing winds, and having spent a mere ten minutes in Miranda Rohan's company had changed those winds quite significantly.

She was lovely. He didn't know why he should be surprised—no one had ever referred to her as anything less than presentable. To be sure, she had brown hair when the current fashion was for blondes, but her eyes were extraordinary. She had a low, melodious voice and her soft mouth, when it wasn't set in a tight line, was full of good humor.

Which frankly surprised him, given that she'd spent the last two years in isolation, without much hope of having anything change in the near future. He would have thought she'd be a bit more subdued, even crushed.

Lady Miranda Rohan struck him as someone extremely difficult to crush. Thus, the challenge was immediately appealing. The Rohan family had a debt to pay, and so far they'd gotten off too easily. Even their only daughter's fall from grace had failed to disturb their equanimity.

That would soon change.

All her watchdogs had finally left town. Every single one of the notorious Rohans were in Yorkshire, days away, leaving her behind. Alone. Unguarded. Vulnerable.

It had been simple enough to have one of Jacob Donnelly's men sabotage the young woman's curricle. He'd run the risk of a dangerous accident, but it was a chance worth taking, and he'd come to her rescue like the proper gentleman he was. She hadn't suspected a thing.

And now he was very glad he'd decided to do something about the soiled dove. So far the Rohans had faced disgrace with total hauteur and defiance. As he would have, had he ever been fool enough to get caught in his various illegal and immoral activities.

Lady Miranda's brother Benedick had no idea his former fiancée had a half brother living in the tropical islands of Jamaica. A half brother determined to gain revenge no matter the price. Taking Benedick's sister had perfect symmetry, and Lucien liked symmetry.

Besides, Lady Miranda had quite caught his fancy. His original plan had been simply to meet her, so he could better decide the best way to continue his vendetta. *Vendetta*—he rather fancied the word. The raging fury of old Italian families wiping each other out over an imagined slight—*that* was a similar, albeit more well-bred, version of what drove him.

One look at her windblown countenance and he knew he'd be a fool to leave it to anyone else to ruin her.

He should have known better than to delegate the task the first time. But then, he'd never realized that there could be all sorts of added delight in drawing Miranda Rohan into his web.

He was halfway to his home on Cadogan Place when the idea came to him, and he laughed out loud.

He knew exactly how to crush the Rohans, to leave them unable to rescue their sweet, ruined little girl this time, unable to do anything at all about it.

He would marry her.

The thought of Lady Miranda in the Scorpion's hands would drive them mad once they knew who and what he was. They'd protected her from everything, even her foolish disgrace. But they wouldn't be able to protect her from her lawful husband.

The more he thought about it the more delightful it seemed. He had no intention of hurting the chit. If he was desirous of inflicting pain there were always the infrequent meetings of the Heavenly Host where like-minded people could happily while away an hour or so.

No, Miranda would survive the marriage bed with no more than her spirit beaten down. He would drive the laughter from her eyes and from those of all the Rohans.

It was a very practical solution to a number of issues. He'd been meaning to find a bride these last few years. He was halfway between thirty and forty—more than time to find a wife. Miranda Rohan would do admirably.

He'd get a couple of children on her, quickly, and if she survived childbirth he'd keep her at his estates in the Lake District, as far away from her family as he could manage. Pawlfrey House was a cold, grim place deep in one of those shadowed valleys that abounded in the Lake District, and he doubted even a woman's touch could make it more appealing. It would be a difficult life for any brats she might happen to bear him; he'd most likely bring them to a warmer climate to be raised.

Miranda, however, would remain at the house. She would never see her family again, and his familial debt would be repaid. Genevieve would at last rest in peace, knowing he'd avenged her, and he might very well return to his travels. Even the sunnier areas of this blighted island were a little too raw and cold for his liking.

He remembered the taste of Lady Miranda's skin when he'd kissed her hand. Oh, this was going to be quite delightful. He could indulge his taste for villainy and no one would know what he planned until it was too late.

No shoddy abductions or protestations of love. He would propose their union as a business venture, though he certainly didn't plan to start out that way. He suspected she wouldn't be wooed, which was just as well. It would take time to fix his interest with her, and time was his enemy. As soon as the Rohans learned who he was they'd be on their guard, and he hated the thought of being forced to do anything clumsily.

No, the advantage was definitely on his side, and when had he ever failed to take full use of such a boon? He would have her eating out of his hand well before her family even caught wind of it.

She would probably view the thought of him as a lover with extreme distaste. *Tant pis.* She would learn to like, if not him, at least the things he could do to her. He was a most accomplished lover when he cared to be. And she just might be worth the effort.

The rain was pounding down by the time he reached his house, but rushing made him clumsy, and he mounted his front steps leisurely, ignoring the drenching. Indeed, he was a man who relished storms over insipid blue skies. And they were in for tumultuous weather.

3

Of course she wouldn't think of accepting his invitation, Miranda told herself regretfully. Once she'd made certain her horses were returned and none the worse for her near disaster, she retired to her rooms and a hot bath to take the chill from her bones, during which she had ample time to review her strange encounter. An encounter that left her feeling oddly breathless.

In truth most of what she knew about Lucien de Malheur was rumor, innuendo and conjecture. For one thing, despite the French name, his family was as Norman English as they came. The de Malheurs could trace their lineage back to the Domesday Book, and no one dared sneer at them, no matter how low the last few generations of that name had fallen. Fortunately the one thing that could exert Cousin Louisa was gossip and scandal, and Miranda had little doubt her companion could be counted on to provide every salacious on-dit imaginable.

"Ah, the de Malheurs!" the lady said with a gusty sigh. "Did I ever tell you I was quite enamored of the current earl's uncle? It would never serve, of course, even with such an illustrious title. At that point they were desperately poor, most of their holdings were sold off to pay their gaming debts, and I was without a sufficient dowry. It was just as well. They were quite mad—the stories I heard were so disturbing I shan't even share them with you, for I do not scruple to inform you, dear Miranda, that you really are appallingly innocent despite your own less than spotless past. Of course, I paid those stories about the de Malheurs no heed—after all, I was merely a girl and aux anges by the sight of a handsome face and a dark and dramatic history. And Lord, that family was a handsome one." She said this last part with a sound that was disturbingly akin to smacking her lips.

"Not the current bearer of the title, of course, though I doubt he's quite the monster he's painted to be."

"Haven't you ever seen him?" Miranda asked.

"Lord, no, child! He never came to London. When the de Malheurs lost all their money they retreated to one of those islands in the new world, full of slaves and such like, and the current earl was raised there after his father died. He hasn't been back in this country for long, and alas, my poor health has kept me a prisoner.... He rarely goes out, even now. It's the most strange luck, that you should have happened to meet up with him today."

Miranda felt a faint trickling of uneasiness, but she shoved it away. "Wouldn't you like to see him yourself? We needn't stay very long if you mislike it."

"Alas, my poor health!" Cousin Louisa wheezed.

"But I see no reason why *you* shouldn't go."

Miranda looked at her doubtfully. While neither of them were privy to the latest gossip, the Scorpion had a reputation that reached even to their isolated circumstances, one that hinted of darkness. But then, as he'd pointed out, society was full of lies and innuendo, of harsh judgments and rigid strictures.

Besides, she received most of her information from members of her family and no one had ever said a word about the man. He could scarcely be that bad if her family hadn't passed along any entertaining on-dits or warnings.

She would go. How long had it been since she'd enjoyed a musical evening in someone's home? It could scarcely damage her reputation any more than it already was.

She would stay where she was. A friendship with Lucien de Malheur was probably not a good idea. She had no idea why he was known as the Scorpion, but clearly that was a warning sign. It wasn't as if he was known as Lucien de Malheur, the Wooly Lamb.

But at half past nine on Wednesday evening when the front knocker was heard, Miranda was dressed and ready. Her very proper sister-in-law Annis had once helpfully suggested that she go into demimourning after the debacle. Pale mauves and lavenders, dove-grays and taupes would be more fitting to her changed circumstances than the innocent pastels she'd been forced to wear, Annis had said.

"She's not in mourning for anything," her strong-minded mother had snapped, and from then onward Miranda had indulged her taste in rich, deep colors. She was wearing a forest-green accompanied by emeralds that evening when Lord and Lady Calvert were announced.

"My dear Lady Miranda, what a pleasure it is to meet you!" Lady Calvert, adrift on a cloud of the finest

French perfume, greeted her. "Dear Lucien thought you might be more comfortable attending his little soiree if we fetched you. Of course he couldn't come himself—his duties as host preclude that. And I'm sorry we were late. I absolutely couldn't find a thing to wear! But truly, we shall have a lovely time. He has Signor Tebaldi from the opera house, quite the best tenor London has known in an age, and Mr. Kean will be on hand to regale us with some readings from Shakespeare. Indeed, you cannot miss it!" Her breathy voice was wildly aflutter. "But I see you have no intention of reneging. You look lovely, my dear. You quite cast my aging charms in the shade."

Since Lady Calvert was breathtakingly beautiful Miranda took leave to doubt it, and she made the proper demurral. It had taken her but a moment to recognize Eugenia Calvert, a woman who'd done the unthinkable and left her first husband to run away with Sir Anthony Calvert. They were on the outskirts of society just as she was, and yet apart from that blot on Lady Calvert's reputation she was as well-born and gracious as any member of the ton.

She was also commanding. In no time at all Miranda found herself ensconced in a comfortable carriage, warm bricks at her feet, a fur throw across her lap, being regaled by Lady Calvert's clever on-dits, mostly at the expense of the people who'd shunned her. Sir Anthony said very little, content to gaze adoringly at his wife and murmur any required pleasantries, not a bad sort of husband, Miranda thought mischievously, also remembering that Sir Anthony was quite plump in the pocket.

Rochdale House was on the very edge of the fashionable district, on a street she failed to recognize. While it wasn't quite the blaze of light Miranda remembered from soirees of old, it was well-enough lit that she could see the dark, prepossessing outlines of the large house, and her initial misgivings returned. Had she been foolish once more?

She was still trying to come up with a graceful excuse when she was swept up the broad steps into a blaze of light, and she readied herself for her first view of the so-called monster who'd unaccountably befriended her.

He wasn't there. As she handed her cloak to one of the waiting servants she looked about her in surprise. In a gathering this small the host usually greeted his guests, but the foyer was empty, and the music drifted down the broad marble stairs from the first floor.

"We're a bit late," Lady Calvert said apologetically. "He probably thought we weren't coming."

An unaccustomed nervousness swept over her. Miranda was someone who took jumps headlong, who, to her detriment, never showed fear or even reasoned hesitation. And yet something swept over her, a sense that there would be no coming back from this step across his threshold.

"I wouldn't want to disturb them," she said, looking behind her for her relinquished cloak. But the maid had already disappeared. Lady Calvert threaded her arm through Miranda's and began herding her up the staircase, chattering gaily so that Miranda couldn't manage another faint protest, so she instead straightened her shoulders in preparation. She'd never shied away from a challenge in all her life. She could hardly run away at this point.

Signor Tebaldi was singing quite loudly, and no one

heard them arrive at the entrance of the large salon. It was redolent of candle wax and perfume and hothouse flowers, and the heat was stifling. There were about two dozen guests, as he'd promised, all watching the tenor with rapt attention, except for one man.

One man, sitting in the shadows at the back of the room, and she felt his eyes on her. Lucien de Malheur.

Lady Calvert had melted away, her duty done, and Signor Tebaldi launched into another lengthy aria with scarcely a pause for breath or applause. And Miranda's choices were clear.

Her host, and she knew it was he, hadn't moved. He watched her from the shadows, and she wondered for a moment if he was unable to walk. She could move ahead, slip into one of the empty seats, as far away from him as possible. She could turn and leave. She would scarcely be blamed—his failure to rise and greet her was a social solecism of the first order.

Instead she started toward him, unable to see him clearly in the shadows. He was sitting alone, which struck her as odd, but she kept moving, when suddenly her view was blocked by a broad male chest, and it took her good balance to keep from barreling into him.

She looked up into a handsome face, dark eyes and a winning smile. He looked vaguely familiar, and for a moment she wondered if she'd been mistaken, if Lucien de Malheur, the Earl of Rochdale, was this magnificent male specimen.

"Lady Miranda!" he breathed, and she knew immediately that this wasn't her host. The Scorpion's voice had been soft, sinuous, unforgettable, a far cry from this man's hearty tones. "It's been an age since we've met, but I'd been told you might be joining us tonight and I must confess I've been watching the door. I flatter myself to think you haven't forgotten me."

"Of course I haven't," she lied promptly.

He laughed heartily. "Not that I should ever dare to question a young lady's veracity, but I suspect you can't possibly remember who I am. I'm Gregory Panelle, a friend of your brother Benedick's. You and I met several years ago, even stood up together."

She could feel her smile warm slightly. "Of course I remember you, Mr. Panelle," she said, still not placing him. However, her brother would never have introduced her to any kind of loose fish, so she could assume there was nothing untoward if she was in his company.

He was very large, blocking her vision, and she leaned past him to glance at the now-deserted seat in the shadows. Her intended target had vanished. "I don't suppose you could tell me where I might find my host? I'm afraid we were delayed, and I haven't had a chance to greet him."

"We? Have I trespassed on some gentleman's previous claim? I saw no one with you when you floated through the door like a radiant angel."

She didn't like him, she decided abruptly. In the past she usually made an effort, but she was no longer willing to spend her time with flirtatious buffoons. "No one has any claim on me," she said with a soft edge.

He leaned forward, too close, and murmured in a heated voice, "Then may I stake mine?" There was no missing the double entendre, but Miranda simply blinked up at him innocently.

"I'm afraid I do need to see Lord Rochdale. Perhaps we might talk later."

He took her hand in his thick one and brought it to

his mouth, pressing his lips against the soft kidskin, dampening the leather before pulling it into the crook of his arm. "It would be my honor to take you to him. I don't know why you would want to, but one must do the pretty, eh? Come with me."

He started toward the far side of the room, the row of French doors that presumably led to some sort of balcony, and short of getting into a public brawl there was nothing she could do but go along with him. "Did he ask you to bring me to him?"

"Certainly," Mr. Panelle said immediately. "It's devilish hot in here, isn't it? He'll be waiting outside on the terrace."

Bloody hell, Miranda thought, not believing him for one moment. He was a big man, but she was more than capable of getting away from him if it came to that. And perhaps she was wrong and he *was* acting on his host's behalf.

The night was blissfully cool after the overheated room, and the moon was bright overhead, almost full. And there was no one out on the terrace at all.

"Lord Rochdale must have changed his mind," she said, glancing about her. "We should go back…"

Gregory Panelle swooped her into his arms, clasping her to his manly bosom with surprising clumsiness as he leaned down to kiss her. "You know as well as I do that Lucien's not out here. Damn, but you're a sweet little piece of crumpet. I never realized it before." He aimed for her mouth, but she jerked her head to one side and his wet, blubbery lips landed on her chin. His grip was quite strong, and she stood still, frozen in his arms, awaiting her chance.

"Come on now, don't be missish," he complained.

He moved one hand and clamped it over her breast, squeezing tightly, still imprisoning her with his strong arm. "You and I both know you're not too good for this. Treat me nicely and I may see about setting you up somewhere with a place of your own."

"I have a place of my own," she said icily. "And if you don't take your bloody hands off me you'll regret it."

He made the mistake of laughing. "I like a girl with spirit. Trust me, you don't want anything to do with the likes of the Scorpion. He's a Very Bad Man."

"And you're a good one?" she said derisively, biding her time, carefully choosing her target.

"Well, not nearly so bad as Lucien, if truth be told, and a hell of a lot handsomer. He's as ugly as sin and twice as mean when he gets riled. The man's ruthless," he said, pinching her breast so hard it was all she could do not to squeak with pain.

"Then do you think you ought to manhandle his guests and risk his wrath?" a silken voice came out of the darkness.

Miranda made her move. It was far from ladylike, but so very effective. She brought her knee up, very hard, between his legs, slamming into that male part of him she had particular cause to dislike, and his high-pitched scream was much prettier than Signor Tebaldi's most measured cadences. He fell away from her, collapsing on the stone terrace as he made agonized, whistling noises, curling in on himself like a baby.

If she'd been alone she would have kicked him for good measure. Instead, she looked up at the man who'd appeared from the shadows, and by the light of the clear March moon had her first good look at the Scorpion.

She didn't blink. He was a tall man, and lean, almost gaunt. The scars across his face were old but nonetheless vicious, and she couldn't quite identify their origins. Something had raked across his face, leaving furrows, and there were other deeper, neater lines from something else even more cutting. He was dressed in the first degree of elegance, all in funeral black, and he leaned on a gold-headed cane.

"Look your fill, Lady Miranda," he said softly in that well-remembered voice. "I owe you at least that much for failing to protect you from an oaf like Panelle. Would you care to see me walk? You don't get the full effect of my monstrousness until you see me move." He turned around slowly, leaning heavily on the cane, and she could see that one leg was bent slightly, twisted, as if broken and never set properly.

He had long dark hair, but he'd tied it back from his face rather than use it to shield himself, and when he faced her she looked more closely, past the scars. He had a narrow, clever face with high cheekbones, and his eyes looked faintly exotic, tilted. She couldn't see their color in the moon-washed landscape, but they were very pale, unusually so. His nose was thin, strong, with a slight twist to it. Oddly enough, his mouth had scarcely been touched by whatever horror had befallen the rest of him. His upper lip was narrow, thoughtful. His lower one full and sensuous. What did it feel like to kiss that mouth? she thought with distant, shocking curiosity.

"As you see, I'm quite appalling," he said in that gentle, seductive voice. "I thought it better if you were warned. Doubtless any number of people told you not to come tonight, not to allow my friendship."

"No," she said calmly. "No one said anything at all."

For a moment he looked surprised. "Dear me... All that effort in building a terrifying reputation and it fails me completely."

"Well, to be sure, I don't go out much in society, so there wasn't much of a chance for anyone to head me off," she said in a placating voice. "I'm sure if any of my friends or family knew I'd made the acquaintance of such a hardened villain they would have warned me away, but they're all out of town."

For a moment an odd expression crossed his face. "Then I can only be glad for your absence of company," he said in that soft, drawling voice. "This way we can get to know each other without helpful relatives interfering." His expression was just on the very edge of a smile, one that didn't reach his eyes. "I've bespoke dinner for the two of us in my study. I would hope you'd agree to join me."

"But what about your guests?"

"Signor Tebaldi will doubtless sing until at least half the guests are asleep or drunk, and then Mr. Kean will attempt to wake them up with some stunning orations, and no one will notice whether I am there or not. In fact, I quite often fail to attend my own parties. It's part of my delightful eccentricity."

"Oh, I *would* like to be delightfully eccentric," she said, unguarded. "It seems that only men can get away with it."

"I will give you lessons, child. Join me for supper and we won't even have to think about those people."

In for a penny, in for a pound. She glanced down at Mr. Panelle, who was still making whistling noises between his teeth. "What shall we do about him?"

"The servants can dispose of him. Unless you'd like

to hit him again. I doubt he'd even notice a sharp kick in the kidneys if you were so inclined."

Had he read her thoughts? "I think he's suffering quite sufficiently," she finally pronounced, ignoring the temptation.

"I would offer you my arm but I'm afraid my gait is quite clumsy and it would be uncomfortable for you," he murmured. "There's a servant at the end of the terrace with a candelabrum in his hand. He'll see you to my study while I make arrangements to rid us of this piece of detritus."

She'd already spent half the night hesitating. She could do the safe, boring thing, go back to listen to Signor Tebaldi and take a hackney home.

But she'd never been fond of tenors.

Lucien de Malheur leaned over the agonized body, and the tip of his cane caressed the man's pale, sweating face. "Well done, Gregory. You acquitted yourself admirably. It's too bad that's she's so effective at defending her honor, but in truth I expect I might have hurt you more. And I think it's better that I don't come off as a gallant rescuer. Not yet."

Gregory didn't say anything. He couldn't—he was still making high-pitched noises through his nose. "Don't worry, I'll take excellent care of her," Lucien continued. "I know you have enough sense not to speak of this night's work, lest you end up unable to speak ever again." His voice was soft, like that of a lover.

"Girl…deserves to be schooled…" Gregory gasped out. "Beaten."

"She'll be schooled, Gregory. Broken to my bridle most effectively, I promise you, though I find there are much more effective ways than brute force. Now go home and avail yourself of some ice if you can procure it. All your parts should be working well enough in a week or so."

As he followed his guest across the broad terrace he heard the belated, muffled shriek of his Judas goat, and he smiled.

4

The door led to a study, bathed in warm candlelight, mercifully quiet after Signor Tebaldi's famous fortissimo, and Miranda stepped inside, breathing a sigh of relief. There was a table set for two, a blazing fire taking the chill out of the air, and some of her apprehension began to fade.

She'd felt the eyes on her as she'd headed out onto the terrace. She would have hoped that a similar outcast like the earl would have fewer gossip-minded guests, but even among the demi-ton curiosity seemed to run rampant.

She should never have come. And she would tell her host that she should leave—he could send her home in his carriage, or at the very least have one of his servants call her a hackney.

She heard him approach—the steady strike of his cane, the faint drag of his leg. She supposed she should feel a sense of dread; the stories about this man were legend. But she didn't. The brief glimpse of him on the shadowed terrace had been enough of a forewarning.

She would sit across from him over a candlelit dinner and view his ruined beauty without blinking.

Because beneath the scoring across his face he was indeed beautiful, and she wondered what or who could have caused such cruel damage.

He moved into the room, a peculiar grace to his broken gait. But then, he struck her as a man who was never less than graceful. He sank down into the chair opposite and she met his gaze calmly.

"Most women keep their eyes in the general area of my shoulder, Lady Miranda. Do you have a particular fascination for horrors?"

She couldn't help it, she laughed, and he looked genuinely startled. "Hardly a horror, my lord. You had me expecting something out of a Gothic romance."

"I've disappointed you?" His voice was silky, his sangfroid back in place. "You continue to surprise me. Would there be a difference in your response if I were the deformed creature you were expecting?"

"I imagine I'd be compassionate, understanding. But all you've got is some scarring and a bad leg. Hardly the stuff of nightmares."

He seemed to have gotten over his initial surprise, and he simply looked at her coolly. He poured her a glass of wine, then one for himself. "So I have no call on your compassion and patience as I am?"

"Of course you do, if you need it. I must say, you don't seem to be particularly needy."

"Very astute. I have most of what I need in this life, save one thing, and I imagine it's something you could do with, as well." He leaned back in the chair, languid and elegant, and yet beneath his light tone she sensed a truth. "I have business partners, enemies, lovers and social acquaintances. I need a friend."

It was, of course, the one thing he could say that would move her, but she kept her own face as impassive as his. "You think we can be friends? I must admit friends have been in very short supply recently. But simple friendship between a man and a woman tends to be misinterpreted. Would society approve?" The last trace of her wariness had vanished.

"I doubt it, and I doubt you care. It does seem like we don't have a large pool of prospective friends to pick from. Tolerant people are fairly thin on the ground around here. I don't think one should dismiss possibilities too swiftly without due consideration."

She looked at him for a long, meditative moment. In some ways he seemed like a little boy, cherishing his differences even as he hated them. And yet it wouldn't do to underestimate him. Despite his scarred face and wounded body he seemed oddly...potent. Masculine. And after her wretched mistake, she'd learned to beware of that trait.

But still, his offer of friendship felt genuine. As if he actually cared about her empty life. And he was right—there hadn't been many other options.

"I would be honored to count you my friend," she said abruptly, surprising even herself.

His answering smile was a revelation. Lucien de Malheur would have been an Adonis if it weren't for the scarring. When he smiled everything else disappeared.

She smiled back.

To her astonishment the hours slipped by as they talked, and she realized he was someone she had dreamed about. A friend, rather than a lover. Someone who saw things the way she did, slightly askew. He made her laugh, particularly when he was doing his best to sound tortured and villainous, and she loved puncturing his perverted vanity.

"I can see you as some plucky Shakespearian heroine," he said at one point. "Not quite a Miranda—you're no wizard's daughter. More likely someone who dresses in boy's clothes and runs into the forest, like Rosalind or Viola, and tricks the poor young hero into being fool enough to think he's fallen in love with another man."

"Perhaps. I'm sure you'd like to think of yourself as Othello, all broody and tortured, but I see you as more of a Caliban, not nearly so monstrous as you'd like to believe."

He looked at her for a long moment, and she met his gaze fearlessly. "No, my lady," He said gently. "Wrong play. I'm Richard the Third, determined to prove a villain."

She laughed, because there was no other response, and his answering smile was faint enough that she felt some lingering unease surface again. He was joking, of course. But looking into his pale eyes she wasn't quite certain.

She was still thinking about that moment as she rode home, comfortably ensconced in his elegant carriage, the same one that had carried her in the rain. It had been brought to a side door, and he'd accompanied her out there, away from the guests, tucking her in, catching her hand in his and holding it for a breathless moment while he looked up at her in the darkness, and she'd waited for his mouth to touch her skin.

But instead, he released it, and she immediately

pulled her gloves on, knowing to her shame that she'd paused there because she'd wanted to feel his mouth against her hand. A moment later he'd closed the carriage door and she was bowling down the narrow alley away from his huge, dark house, and she sank back against the tufted cushions and closed her eyes.

Good God. What was wrong with her? Was it simply because she'd been so isolated for so long, that even a reputed monster would arouse her banked interest? Not that he was a monster at all. Within moments she'd looked past the scars and only seen his face, the beautiful bones, the pale, watchful eyes, the mouth that kept drawing her gaze. He had beautiful hands, as well—long fingers, hands that looked capable of great strength and elegant tenderness.

Indeed, he was neither Richard the Third nor Caliban. He was a dark prince under an enchantment, and she was...

Out of her bloody mind. She laughed out loud. She'd had too much of his wonderful wine, even though her family had taught her how to hold her liquor. She'd had too much of his wonderful voice, his attention, his intelligence and sly humor, the faint, bewitching malice that was irresistible. She was drunk on Lucien de Malheur.

Indeed, it was a safe enough attraction. No one would ever guess she'd become enamored of the Scorpion, certainly not the man himself. It seemed as if it had been forever since she'd indulged in daydreams and fantasies, and now she had a perfectly safe subject for them. She could dream of rescuing him from his darkness, taking away his bitterness. She could dream of happy endings. For him, if not for her.

***

Lucien de Malheur moved through the halls of his townhouse, well-pleased with his night's work. He had her. She'd been ridiculously easy, falling into his hands with only the most delicate of lures. She'd been so isolated she had become enamored of the first man who knew how to play her, even a damaged creature such as himself.

Caliban. He laughed beneath his breath. She certainly was fearless, mocking his melodramatic airs. He'd thought playing the wounded spirit would draw her sympathy. Instead she'd laughed at him, seeing right through him, and he found himself unwittingly caught by her, as well.

It was going to make the whole endeavor so much more interesting. Miranda Rohan looked at him directly and felt no pity or fear. By midnight he'd felt her first stirrings of attraction. By the time he saw her to his carriage it was after three, and she was already trapped in his web, caught in his snare.

It should have bored him. He thought she'd be silly and emotional and missish and he'd have to patiently work through her childish fussing. Instead she'd been direct and challenging.

She would make an excellent wife for the short period he planned.

The house wasn't yet devoid of guests. He was known for his openness to misbehavior, and couples had found hidden places to indulge in more than flirtation. He could hear the occasional sounds of passion filter through as he moved down the corridor, and he felt a faint stirring in his own body. Miranda Rohan had skin like cream touched with honey. He was going to enjoy discovering all of it.

He went straight to his study, his real study, the one he used for business and nothing else. As he expected, his guest was waiting, sitting by the fire, his booted feet propped on the brass fender, a glass of French brandy in his hand.

Lucien could hardly begrudge him the brandy—Jacob Donnelly was in full control of the trade that brought smuggled brandy into London, and he kept the house well-supplied.

"To what do I owe this honor?" Lucien drawled, pouring himself a glass. His servants knew better than to come anywhere near this room, and he was used to waiting on himself.

Jacob glanced up at him from beneath his shaggy hair. He was an extraordinarily handsome man. He was tall and long-limbed, with the kind of face that won scullery maids and whores and countesses. The two of them couldn't have been more different—the maimed aristocrat and the handsome king of London thieves. It was little wonder they worked so well together.

Donnelly leaned back, casting a look up at him. "I heard some things on the street," he said, his deep voice a strange mishmash of Irish, street slang and the aristocratic phrasings he'd picked up. The man was a born mimic, who'd made his life on his own since he'd run away from wealthy male planters who used him as a slave. Donnelly had been eight years old, and Lucien had no illusions about what the boy had done to survive. One could see it in his dark, dark eyes.

"I expect you hear a great many things on the street," Lucien said, moving to stand by the fire. It was a cold night, and his bad leg ached. "Is it anything that would interest me?"

"It may. Apparently the Duke of Carrimore and his pretty young wife are coming to town. Complete with the diamonds she drapes herself with, I think she needs to be relieved of some of them.... They...distract from her natural beauty."

Lucien laughed. "The idea has merit. The old man is so besotted he'd simply buy her more, and she'd enjoy the chance to shop. Eugenia is easily bored, as I know only too well, and she's probably tired of her jewelry by now. Were you interested in all of them or just a measured selection?"

"Oh, I think we should take them all," Jacob said idly. "Why go to all that trouble for half measures?"

"Indeed. If things follow as they usually do then they'll hold a ball to celebrate their return to London. Who did you want to play my servant for the night? I know that Billy Banks is your best cracksman, and he's excellent at playing the bored footman, but I think we may have used him too much. Have you got someone else who could handle it?"

"I was thinking of doing it myself?"

He'd managed to surprise Lucien. "Yourself? Do you think that's wise? A general doesn't join the ranks of the soldiers—he gives the orders. Surely you have an army of able thieves who can come in as my footman, make their way upstairs and relieve Lady Carrimore of her excess diamonds."

"Of course I do. Perhaps I just want to see if I my skills are still sharp. They can grow stale from lack of use, and I want to make certain I can still support myself if the whole organization goes belly up. Besides, I've got my share of enemies, men who want to take over my part of London, and I suspect it wouldn't do me harm to show everyone I can still handle a simple job. Though who knows, I may even retire. I've been feeling the urge to travel of late."

"Don't be ridiculous. You're barely in your thirties—how could you possibly have grown stale? I say it's much too great a risk. If you get caught your entire empire is ruined and I lose a very nice bit of my income. Not that I need it, but as you know, I rather like the game."

"I know you do. We've shared many schemes since we first met, and we both enjoy the challenge. In truth, neither of us really need those diamonds, and Carrimore is damned protective of them. Last I heard he had a servant dedicated to keeping guard over them night and day."

"A challenge you'd have no trouble dealing with, old friend, but why risk it?" Lucien said. And then he laughed. "What an absurd question—you'll risk it for the same reasons I would." He laughed again. "You're a little tall for a footman."

"I can stoop."

Lucien took the seat opposite him, stretching out his bad leg gingerly. "I don't know that I have anyone in my service who's quite your strapping size, and I'm certainly not about to let someone who works for me dress in an ill-fitting coat."

"I've got people who can see to it faster and won't ask any questions."

"Dear boy, are you suggesting that people dare ask me questions?" Lucien said, affronted.

"No, but they'll talk behind your back. My people wouldn't even dare do that."

"Clearly you have better control over your employees." He eyed him lazily. "If you're willing to run the risk, then I suppose I am, as well. After all, I can pretend I've never seen you in my life if they catch you."

"If they snabble me I'm not going to wait around to answer questions, and I'm not letting them send me away. I have an aversion to cramped quarters."

"And who can blame you? Then it's settled. I'll send word to you as soon as I receive an invitation." Lucien paused. "Was there something else?"

Donnelly brought his booted feet down to the floor. They were brown leather, scuffed, a far cry from the shiny black Hessians preferred by the ton. "I heard you might be getting married."

Lucien raised one eyebrow. He shouldn't be surprised at the speed of Donnelly's information. He hadn't said a word to anyone, but he'd made a few inquiries, and the King of Thieves had informers everywhere. He was more than adept at putting two and two together. If Jacob had been born a gentleman there would have been nothing he couldn't do. As it was, even with his hazy forebears, he'd risen high enough that there was little out of his reach.

"How prescient of you. I suppose you wish to congratulate me?" he said in a lazy tone. "There's no hurry: I'm afraid the lady has no idea what's in store for her."

Jacob's laugh was mirthless. "I don't think it's a wise idea. I know who you're after, and why, and you should let it alone. Revenge is the enemy of good business sense, and I'm your business partner. I don't like it. Haven't you done enough? Forget about her."

"As my business partner it's none of your damned business what I do with my life," Lucien said in a silky voice. "I've decided it's time I married and produced an heir, and Lady Miranda Rohan will suit me very well."

"Marriage has never been part of your plans before. Why now?"

"Dear boy," he said in his haughtiest voice. "Do you really think I would discuss my nuptial issues with the likes of you?"

Donnelly simply laughed. "Yes, you would. I'm the only man you trust. Slightly."

"I trust you as much as you trust me."

Donnelly grinned. "As I said. Slightly. Though in truth I trust you as much as I trust anyone. It's just that I'm not by nature a trusting man."

"Which is why we're so well-suited. Don't worry about Lady Miranda. She'll have no regrets. At least, not in the beginning. And who can say that her life would be any better with another choice?"

"Thanks to you she doesn't have many choices, now does she?"

"So now I'm making up for it," Lucien said with a sweet smile. "She'll get to be a countess."

Donnelly shook his head, rising. "She doesn't strike me as the kind of woman who'd care about such things. I'd think twice about it if I were you."

"All women care about such things, Jacob. Don't worry about me. We all do things that are perhaps unwise. I should keep away from Lady Miranda. You should keep away from practicing your thieving skills and let your associates do the job. But what's the fun in that?"

Donnelly laughed. "You have a point. Except you stand to benefit with a tidy portion of the proceeds from my little gamble. Whereas if you marry that girl I'll get nothing but headaches."

"You'll get a business partner who's more versed in dealing with revenge and business at the same time. Now go away and let me get some sleep."

"It's only four. The shank of the evening," Donnelly mocked, heading for the French doors that led directly to the gardens, bypassing curious servants. "Don't let that girl tire you out."

"It will be the other way around, as soon as I can manage it. I expect I will be taking her away once I have her, rather than let her family interfere with our so-happy honeymoon. So you can count on my presence in London being sporadic for several months. I trust our business can survive without me?"

"Course it can, guv'nor," he said, letting his voice drop into a thick cockney drawl. "Just be careful it don't survive so well that we don't need you back."

Lucien smiled thinly at him, the expression that could put the fear of God into his servants, his associates and anyone he happened to run across. It left Donnelly completely unmoved. "I'm not about to give up my investments that easily."

Donnelly snorted. "Then I'll be wishing you many felicitations. Maybe I'll have to give your blushing bride some of Lady Carrimore's diamonds as a wedding present."

"If my wife needs diamonds, I'll see to it."

"I'll come up with something."

A moment later he was gone, into the shadows with the same grace that he'd used since he was a boy, Lucien thought. Theirs was a strange business arrangement, complicated by an unlikely friendship.

They had known each other for many years. Young Jacob had found his way onto a ship borne for the tropics, indentured to a pair of wealthy male planters, and he'd run away, ending up at the decaying ruins of La Briere, the plantation house of the de Malheurs. Lucien had been living there alone, the only survivor of a virulent outbreak of cholera, and the two young men, barely more than boys, had bonded together, determined to escape.

Escape they had. Jacob had ended up back in London, and within a decade was responsible for the thieving kens and smuggling imports controlling half of the city. He no longer had to do the dirty work himself—he had scores of eager underlings.

And Lucien had gone on to Italy, where he'd made his first fortune at the gaming tables, and a second, as well. By the time he made his first appearance in London he was wealthier than his family had ever been, due to a gift with the cards and a willingness to cheat when need be. His partnership with his old friend Jacob only profited his overflowing coffers.

He'd lied to Lady Miranda, of course. He studied his enemies well and she was, by dint of her family, his enemy. He knew asking for friendship would touch her as nothing else could.

Friendship wasn't exactly what he had in mind. If he needed one, Jacob would do.

But if anyone was going to be draping diamonds on Miranda Rohan's beautiful white flesh it was going to be the Scorpion.

And it would drive her family mad.

5

The white vellum envelope lay on the silver salver, her name written with a perfect hand, a delicate, feminine one. Miranda looked at it in surprise when her butler brought it in, and Jane, who was sitting on the floor amidst a welter of brightly colored ribbons, looked up.

The arrival of Jane Paget had almost broken Miranda free from the doldrums that had assailed her after her brief taste of friendship. Jane was engaged to marry Mr. George Bothwell, a worthy gentleman indeed, and she'd come to town for a visit and a bit of early wedding shopping. Her mood, however, had been almost as glum as Miranda's.

"That's an invitation," Jane said, stating the obvious. "I didn't think you ever got any. Do you think you've finally paid enough penance to be allowed back in society?"

"I doubt it," Miranda replied. She was loath to open it. The obvious source would be Lucien de Malheur. It had been more than a week since she'd been to his house, and she hadn't heard a word from him. She'd expected at least a note, perhaps flowers, some recognition of the wonderful evening they'd spent together, but so far there'd been nothing.

She'd come to the conclusion that it was not nearly as wonderful for him as it had been for her. Which shouldn't surprise her. It had been her first adult, intelligent conversation in weeks, and the first with someone outside her family in almost a year, not counting Jane, who really was family.

She tapped the envelope against her other hand, reluctant. If it was the note she'd expected it was both overdue and something she wanted to savor in private. Jane knew her too well, and Miranda wasn't even sure of her own feelings and reactions to Lucien de Malheur. She certainly wasn't ready to share them.

"Aren't you going to open it?" Jane demanded, rising and leaving the ribbons behind. Jane was tall, dark-haired like her mother, but lacking Evangelina Pagett's extraordinary beauty or her father's cynical grace. She was a little thin, a little plain and the best and dearest friend in the world.

"I'll open it later." Miranda set the note back down on the salver.

"Oh, no, you won't," Jane said, lunging for it, grabbing it before Miranda could stop her. "I'm the one with the stultifying life. At least I can live through you vicariously."

Miranda leaped to her feet, reaching for the letter, which Jane laughingly held over her head, and fixed her with a stern look. "You're about to marry a good man who adores you, and you'll live in a lovely house and have wonderful children and…what's that face for? Don't tell me you're not happy?" Miranda stopped reaching for the invitation, falling back to look at her troubled friend.

Jane tried for her usual smile, but Miranda could see the pain behind it, the pain she should have recognized before, and she forgot about the letter.

"Things are never quite what they seem," Jane said carefully. "Mr. Bothwell feels that I'll make a suitable wife and that I should breed quite easily. He's most desirous of an heir. He likes that I'm quiet and well-behaved and conduct myself just as I ought, and he thinks I'll do very well."

"*You'll do very well?*" Miranda echoed, incensed. "And you agreed to this affecting proposal?"

"I'm three and twenty, Miranda. I'd had five seasons and no other offers, and Mr. Bothwell is a gentleman with a significant income." There was a faint wobble in her voice.

"And your parents agreed to this iniquitous match?"

"Don't be absurd. I told them I was madly in love with the man. I can't live with them forever, and I want children. I want a life of my own. Mr. Bothwell will do very well, I'm sure."

For a long moment Miranda said nothing. And then she put her arms around Jane's waist. "Dearest, you should have told him no. You could come and live with me, and we can become two strange old ladies who keep a great deal too many cats and wear eccentric clothes and say things we shouldn't. It would be grand fun."

Jane shook her head. "No, it wouldn't. You can't convince me you're any happier than I am."

"I do well enough. And besides, I deserve my banishment. I'm a lightskirt, remember? You deserve a man who adores you."

"You aren't a lightskirt. And we all deserve a man who adores us. Haven't you yet learned we don't always get what we deserve?" Jane said. She handed her the vellum envelope. "Why don't we see your invitation? It might be something diverting."

Miranda cast one last troubled glance at her dearest friend and then turned her attention to the envelope. It was addressed with a feminine hand—she knew it hadn't come from de Malheur, but she was nevertheless disappointed when she tore open the envelope to find a card inviting her to attend a ridotto given by the Duke and Duchess of Carrimore, in honor of their fifth wedding anniversary. She showed it to Jane, then tossed it back onto the salver with a negligent air, taking her seat by the fire.

"It was very sweet of them," she said. "At least, sweet of his grace. He was in awe of my shocking grandfather when he was young, and he's always gone out of his way to be kind to me no matter what. I won't go, of course."

"You will go," Jane said firmly. "I'm invited, as well. You know it's impossible to drag my parents back to town and I could scarcely go alone. If Mr. Bothwell was in town he'd refuse on the grounds of propriety—he doesn't hold with masked balls. If I don't go with you I'll never have the chance to attend one again, and besides, I'm dying to see Lady Carrimore's diamonds. Apparently she has one the size of a pigeon's egg."

"They'll have other parties that aren't shocking to your fiancé's delicate sensibilities. Bothwell can accompany you."

"Bothwell doesn't approve of the Carrimores at all.

Says they're bad ton and he doesn't want to associate with them."

"And what does he say about me?"

"He wouldn't dare criticize you," Jane said, a little too swiftly, and Miranda knew he'd done just that. "Please, Miranda. It's been ages since you've been out. And if anyone dares cut you I'll kick them. You're acting like it's something shocking, like, like an orgy given by the Heavenly Host."

"Assuming they give orgies," Miranda pointed out.

"No one really knows what they do."

"Orgies," Jane said flatly. "I would be too disappointed if they indulged in something tame, given their atrocious reputation. But that's neither here nor there. It *isn't* the Heavenly Host, it's a perfectly respectable gathering hosted by a duke and a duchess. Besides, most people will wear a mask and domino. They needn't have any idea who we actually are. We'll show up, wander around and laugh at all the ridiculous people, and then come back here and drink too much champagne and thank God we don't live like that. Mr. Bothwell says diamonds are much too gaudy. He prefers me in something more subdued, like jet."

"Something cheaper, more likely," Miranda muttered. She'd always confided everything to Jane, her dearest friend since childhood, just as her mother had been best friends with Jane's stunning mother. But it suddenly occurred to her that she hadn't breathed a word about her midnight rendezvous with Lucien de Malheur, and she wasn't quite sure why. She hesitated for another moment. If the Carrimores had lowered their standards enough to invite her, then she had little doubt they'd invited Lucien de Malheur, as well. And since he seemed to have forgotten her existence her best chance might be simply to arrive at a place he was likely to be. She was used to being ignored by the ton. She wasn't going to accept being ignored by a fellow outcast like the Scorpion, not if she could help it.

"I'll do it. As long as we leave before any planned unmasking. People will be incensed if they find out they've been polite to a shameless whore."

"Stop it! You're no such thing! This isn't like you, Miranda. You know it's going to be fun. Like old times. No one will have any idea who we are, and we can behave very badly indeed."

"I think most people will attest to the fact that I've behaved badly enough for one lifetime, precious," she said wryly.

"Oh, I don't mean that," Jane said in a dismissive voice. "I was thinking more along the lines of going places we shouldn't go, ignoring people we don't want to see. I'm about to be trapped in a dutiful marriage when there are so many places I want to visit, things I want to do. Grant me this much, Miranda."

"You should have been born a sailor, love." It was too tempting, what with the promise of a cape and mask to disguise even her gender if she so chose. And the sadness had momentarily left Jane's eyes, which were sparkling now with excitement. "When is this going to be?" she asked, wondering if she could come up with a sudden trip out to the countryside. That would be the wise thing to do, remove herself from temptation. But then, when had she ever been wise?

"Didn't you read the invitation? In three days. We got our invitation weeks ago—yours must have been delayed."

"Or it took them that long to make up their minds whether to invite me," Miranda said. Or had someone talked them into it? Someone powerful and mysterious who seemed to have disappeared out of her life as suddenly as he had entered it.

"I can arrange for the dominos and masks," Jane said eagerly.

It would be a mistake, as surely as attending Lucien de Malheur's salon had been a mistake. And she was going to do it anyway—and to hell with all the old biddies who'd be horrified at who was lurking beneath the domino. "Get me a red one," she said firmly. And the last bit of shadow left Jane's warm brown eyes.

It was the evening of the Duke and Duchess of Carrimore's ball and Miranda was angry. Not that she was willing to admit it—after all, why should she care about the likes of Lucien de Malheur? He'd rescued her from a disaster with her carriage, invited her to a musical evening, spent hours alone with her, talking to her, his acid wit and his eccentric charm beguiling her until she half fancied herself attracted to him. And then nothing.

At one point she thought he might have left town, but she'd overheard two stout matrons discussing the latest scandal concerning his appearance at the opera and a certain dancer, and Miranda couldn't acquit him of the unspeakable crime of simply forgetting about her. He'd been polite, he'd done his duty, but he must have found her deadly dull. *Tant pis.* She had no interest in entertaining the likes of him. All she wanted was the quiet of their Dorset home near the high cliffs. It wasn't as if she was running away. Clearly there was nothing to run from.

Jane was almost feverish with excitement when she arrived at the house wearing a pale blue domino, the scarlet one Miranda had requested over one arm. The street outside the Carrimore mansion was thronged with carriages, and by the time Jane's hired hackney carriage brought them to the front portico Miranda was regretting her impulsive decision. It was too late to do anything; the footmen were already opening the door and letting down the steps, and Miranda pulled her hood up over her head, made certain her loo mask was carefully in place and followed her friend into the brightly lit gaiety.

But her bad mood had begun to lift as she heard the sound of music floating down the stairs from the second-floor ballroom. It had been so very long since she'd danced, and she'd always loved dancing. Tonight she wouldn't have to worry about who was good ton or bad, who was a proper partner and who was a bad hat. Since she'd come, she'd enjoy herself, and stop worrying about it.

She met Jane's mischievous eyes. Her friend was almost her old self, the wicked behavior stripping away the layers of restraint Mr. Bothwell had heaped upon her. If Miranda had been around she could have done something to forestall the match, but it had been made in the drawing rooms where Miranda was no longer welcome, and it was too late. Jane would never cry off.

A moment later Jane had disappeared, swung into the arms of a dashing young man in uniform, a half mask over his handsome face, and Miranda wanted to laugh at her startled expression. And then she did laugh, as an older gentleman bowed before her, and she moved into his arms smoothly, sailing onto the crowded dance floor for the first time in years.

It was glorious, it was breathtaking, and she felt as if she were flying. Her hood fell back as she whirled around the floor, but it didn't matter. With her plain brown hair sedately dressed and the loo mask firmly in place no one would have any idea who she was. She could dance, she could flirt, she could laugh and pretend there wasn't a cloud of shame hanging over her head. A cloud of shame she refused to give in to.

The Carrimores were casual: no one solicited dances ahead of time, and Miranda moved from one partner to another, her feet flying on the polished wood floor. She danced until she could dance no more. Dinner was announced, people were pairing up and heading into the heavy-laden tables, but Miranda backed away. Her loo mask covered a good two-thirds of her face—there was no way she could eat without getting food on its silk, and the brighter lights of the dining room might be dangerous.

She faded back into the shadows, pulling her hood back over her head. She'd been silly to ask for a scarlet cape, but it was hardly as gaudy as some of the other outfits that night. She glanced over to the row of dowagers who sat against the wall, most of them unmasked, watching their charges with disapproval.

These were the ladies who despised her the most, and it gave Miranda a certain pleasure to join their ranks, keeping her disguise firmly in place. They nodded a tentative greeting in her direction, clearly not sure about anyone who wore a red domino, and she nodded back, sinking gracefully into one of the small, straight-backed chairs that creaked dangerously beneath some of the other women's bulk, grateful to rest her feet. She sat back, listening to their malicious gossip, trying to catch a glimpse of Jane to see if she still danced or had gone in for supper. As long as she sat with the dowagers no one would try to entice her into the dining room, and it was safer that way. Even though all her exercise had worked up an appetite.

But the dowagers began to annoy her as they found fault with everyone they could recognize, and with their attempts to draw her into their disdain, and eventually Miranda rose, drifting farther into the shadows, away from everyone. The room was too warm, and she longed for the cool night air, but there was no terrace outside the Carrimore ballroom, and no place to escape to. She simply moved back into the deepest shadows, where her bright red domino turned black in the absence of light, and found a delicate table and chair. If Jane remembered she might sneak a cake or something that Miranda could devour when no one was looking. In the meantime she would simply wait.

She didn't hear him approach, but then, the room was noisy, filled with the orchestra playing at top volume, the chatter of voices trying to drown out the music, the sounds of feet on the dance floor, the clink of glasses.

One moment she was blessedly, peacefully alone.

In the next, she wasn't.

"Did you tire of dancing, Lady Miranda?"

There was no mistaking Lucien de Malheur's sinuous voice. It came as such a surprise she jerked her head up, then wished to God she hadn't. It would have been so much better if she'd simply ignored him, but it was already too late for that. So she blundered her way through it. "Lord Rochdale," she murmured with cool courtesy. "I didn't expect to see you here."

"Didn't you? The Carrimores are known for their open hospitality. Even a damaged rogue like me is included."

"As well as damaged goods like me," she said in a sweet voice. "Don't let me keep you, my lord. I'm certain you have more important things to attend to."

He grew very still, looking down at her. "I seem to have offended the lady. Pray, what did I do to earn your ire?"

She could hardly tell him, not without sounding ridiculous. "Not a thing," she said breezily.

She didn't like the smile that played around his mouth. He hadn't bothered with a loo mask, which would have covered a great deal of his scarred face. Instead he was dressed in the height of elegance, all black and silver, and the walking stick he carried had a huge ruby on the top of it. "I rejoice to hear it. May I join you?"

"I'm waiting for someone."

"Are you indeed?" There was a note in his voice she couldn't quite recognize.

"Yes," she said firmly. "The person who accompanied me."

"Ah." He sank into the chair opposite her anyway. "You wouldn't deprive a cripple of a moment of rest, would you? Even though I couldn't indulge in the riotous dancing I find my leg is paining me damnably."

"You're hardly a cripple," she said, not interested in playing his games.

He ignored her statement. "So tell me, my child, are you awaiting a man or a woman? Who brought you to this party, because I'm certain you wouldn't have come on your own."

"I was invited, my lord."

"Of course you were. I saw to it."

He'd managed to surprise her. She'd suspected as much, but not that he'd admit it. "Why?"

His smile was secretive. "I'll tell you when you answer my question. Who brought you here, a man or a woman?"

"Why should it matter?"

"Because if you came with another man I'd have to have him killed." The words were spoken with the lightest touch, accompanied by a faint smile, and she wondered why she wanted to shiver.

"I believe the crown frowns on dueling."

"Oh, I rarely duel. I'm not light enough on my feet. I'd have him set upon by Mohocks and stabbed. It would be expensive, but, fortunately, easy enough to arrange."

"Really? If I gave you a name could you see to it?"

"I believe Christopher St. John is no longer in England, or I'd be more than happy to have him killed for you."

She froze. She should have known he'd be aware of all the intimate details of her fall from grace and the man who engineered it. "Too bad," she said calmly. "That would have suited my amour propre very well."

"Who brought you?" There was steel in his persistent question beneath the pleasant smile, and she was tempted to lie, just to see what would happen.

"My dearest friend Jane and I came together. We thought no one would recognize us in our dominos and masks, and Jane is about to be trapped into an unpleasant marriage. She wanted to enjoy herself before that happened."

"I knew you the instant I saw you, Lady Miranda. But, pray tell me, isn't that how you got into such trouble in the first place? Indulging in one last evening of harmless fun?"

She looked at him. "How is that you're so intimately aware of the details of my downfall?"

"The entire ton knows the details of your downfall, child. Could you doubt it?"

"A gentleman wouldn't mention that."

"I'm not particularly a gentleman."

She didn't bother arguing. "If Jane causes a scandal and her husband-to-be cries off then it would be all to the good. She'd be better living life as a spinster than marrying someone she doesn't love."

"You're still so young," he murmured fondly. "Tell me this man's name and I'll get rid of him."

"Why are you so bloodthirsty tonight?"

"I wasn't going to have him killed, Miranda." This time his voice faintly caressed her name without the title. "I was just going to throw a roadblock in the way of this marriage, since you seem so set against it."

"Jane thinks she wants it."

"And you think Jane's wrong. I trust your judgment. What's his name?"

She finally laughed. He was being absurd and charming, and he hadn't forgotten her after all. "George Bothwell, but you're not to do anything about it. Jane would never forgive me."

"Jane need never know." He rose, towering over her, leaning on his cane. In the shadows his scars were barely discernible. "Come with me, Lady Miranda. You need to admire her grace's extraordinarily vulgar jewels. You need to get some fresh air. You need to stop hiding in the shadows like some kind of leper. Not that I don't prefer you with me, but you need to be back out there dancing as your friend is. You looked…luminous." He nodded as Jane waltzed by, too busy to notice anyone around her. Miranda wondered how he happened to recognize her friend, but she decided not to ask.

"Are you asking me to dance?"

His smile was twisted. "Hardly. You would find the effect quite gruesome. But I could find you any number of eligible partners who know better than to presume. Or we could simply go for a walk. Carrimore House is huge and possessed of mile upon mile of hallways. We could find someplace quiet to sit and talk."

"You haven't made any effort at all to talk with me in the last week." It came out unexpectedly, and she could have bit her tongue.

"Did you miss me? I thought you would prefer not to be besieged. Had I known you were pining for me, I would have sought you out sooner."

"I was hardly pining for you!" she snapped.

"Of course not, my child." He held out his arm. "Shall we walk?"

And like a fool she rose and threaded her arm through his.

6

In fact, Jane was not having a particularly good time. She should have known better than to badger Miranda into coming to this ball. She hadn't really expected to have fun, but Miranda had been isolated for so long she thought it would do her good, with no risk of anyone giving her the cut direct.

And indeed, things had started out well enough. Miranda had danced, and even as Jane suffered the clumsy feet of her slightly inebriated partner she could see Miranda's joy as she'd moved across the dance floor, and Jane had put on the appearance of having a grand time while she was tossed around like a sack of potatoes. But, in truth, balls were excruciating. She was shy; there was no way around it, and to make conversation with strangers while trying to remember the intricate steps of a country dance was her idea of hell.

It was her fault they were there, of course. She had a very bad tendency to try to fix things, Jane thought, and she'd always felt guilty that she'd let Miranda go out that night so long ago and not run screaming to her brothers. Because she'd kept quiet Miranda's life had been ruined, and there'd been nothing Jane could do to make up for it.

Miranda would have laughed at her if she knew how guilty she felt. No, she wouldn't—Miranda never laughed at her megrims. She was the best, dearest friend a girl could have, and Jane just wished she could give back even a tiny portion of all Miranda had given her.

She'd made her brave when she wanted to cower. She'd made her laugh when she wanted to weep. She made her dance when she wanted to sit in the corner, and now Jane had finally been able to do the same thing for Miranda.

Until she'd disappeared.

It took some doing to extricate herself from the dance floor. With the mask covering her plain, unremarkable face she suddenly had limitless partners, and she was exhausted from trying to sound like someone she wasn't. It wasn't that she didn't like to dance. She loved to, with the right partner, but she seldom found anyone willing to stand up with her and to put the right attention and energy into the production. Mr. Bothwell was stiff as a board, and disliked dancing, and as an engaged woman she could scarcely stand up with anyone else. She'd hoped to have a lovely time even as she helped Miranda, but the anonymous dancing had been unsatisfactory, and if Miranda had decided to hide out then Jane was more than ready to leave. She simply had to find her first.

Escaping from the ballroom was her first task, and easier said than done. When she tried the open doors someone would catch her arm and spin her back onto the dance floor, and her demurrals were swallowed up by the noise of the crowd and the vigor of the orchestra.

Eventually she gave up, moving instead toward the back of the massive ballroom. If Carrimore House were anything like the houses she grew up in, there was most likely a hidden door near the back to allow the servants to come and go.

She slipped into a corner near the back of the room, waiting, and eventually her patience was rewarded when a door opened in the wall. She darted through, startling the servant who'd opened it, and found herself in one of the back hallways, clearly meant only for the staff. No rugs on the floor, no pictures on the grim walls, and she panicked, looking for a way back. There must be a trick to the door, because it wouldn't move. She looked to her right and to her left, but she had no idea which would be the best way to go, and she was frozen with indecision. She thought the grand staircase was to the left, and she headed in that direction. Not that she could actually leave—she had to find Miranda first. God willing, she might be there waiting for her.

Jane was dying from the heat. She slipped off the enveloping domino and mask, draping both over one arm as she made her way down the narrow hallway as swiftly as she could. If she were home she'd take the dancing slippers off her aching feet, as well. But she could hardly do that in the Carrimore's house, so she persevered, until she came to the end of the hallway, with no obvious way out.

She stared around her for a moment, then recognized the outline of a door beside her. She pushed, and it opened, silently, into a dark, deserted room.

At least, she thought it was deserted. She heard the noise first, a quiet, scratching sound, and a faint light was coming from across the room. As her eyes adjusted, she could just determine the outlines of a huge bed, and she flushed with embarrassment, reaching behind her for the door to make her escape before whoever was in there realized their privacy had been breached. But the door had already swung closed again, and she turned, desperately trying to find the edge of it. Her fingers finally caught the slight rim, and she had just managed to pry it open when something loomed up behind her, and the door was pushed shut again.

Jane wasn't the kind of girl who screamed, though she couldn't help a smothered yelp of surprise. Smothered, because whoever had come up behind her had hauled her away from the door, back against a hard male body and one hand was clamped across her mouth.

They stood that way for a long moment, while she struggled to catch her breath. Her heart was beating wildly, there was no way she could disguise it. It was a far cry from the man behind her. His heartbeat was slow and steady, completely calm, as if sneaking up on young ladies and imprisoning them was something he did every day.

"Now what in the world is a lass like you doing wandering around the bedrooms, alone?" The voice in her ear was low, faintly amused. It wasn't the voice of an aristocrat, but she knew a servant would never dare put his hands on her. "If I move my hand are you going to scream?"

She shook her head, as much as his imprisoning hand would allow. As he pulled it away he murmured, "Good girl."

Of course she ought to scream for help, but she was so frightened she doubted she could make more than a squeak. Besides, the man hadn't threatened her, and she'd told him she wouldn't shriek. It would feel as if she'd broken a promise. She tried to clear her throat, struggling for her voice. "I was looking for someone," she managed to whisper.

"Now what fool left you to find a bedroom all by yourself? If it had been me I wouldn't have given you a chance to get lost. I would have had you tucked away beneath the sheets before anyone noticed we were gone."

Color flamed her face. He was being absurd, she thought, saying such things to her. He wouldn't have done it if he'd gotten a clear look at her. Men didn't put their hands on her, risk their livelihood, whatever it might be, by assaulting a member of the ton. It was clear by his voice that he was not a member of the ruling class, but what was he?

"I was looking for my friend," she said in a stiff voice.

"My female friend."

"Oh, do not say so, lass!" he crooned. "I hate to see you wasting yourself on another woman when there are so many men who would worship at your feet."

All right, she was getting annoyed, enough that it overshadowed her usual timidity. "The room is dark, whoever you are. If you got a good look at me you'd know that no one is worshipping at my feet."

He was still pressed against her, and his body was warm in the cool room. She realized suddenly that one of the tall windows leading out onto the tiny balconies that adorned Carrimore House was open.

"Ah, but I saw you quite clearly. I have eyes like a cat—I can see in the dark."

She wasn't quite sure how to respond to that, particularly since he didn't let her move. "I don't imagine you're here for any good reason."

"I'm afraid not." He sounded almost apologetic. "I'm here for Lady Carrimore's diamonds."

She breathed in, shocked. "She's wearing them."

"Oh, that's only a very small part of her diamonds. She has cases of them. Or she did. They now reside in a silk bag, and they're damned heavy."

"You're a thief!" she gasped. "That's awful."

"Not particularly," he said in a cheerful voice. "I make a good living at it. And you needn't cry for the poor duchess. Her husband makes his money in the slave trade—those stones don't belong to her."

"Then who do they belong to? Are you going to send them back to Africa along with the stolen natives?"

"Of course not. They belong to me, as of fifteen minutes ago. I would have been long gone but I heard you fumbling about behind the walls and I wanted to make certain I was safe. And I am safe, aren't I, me darling?"

She wanted to deny it. "Why would you think you were?"

To her amazement he turned her in his arms, suddenly, still keeping her tight against his body, and she looked up, trying to see him. "Because you're a pirate at heart, lass. I can feel it. You aren't going to turn me in. Are you?" His voice was low, his face so close. His fingers caught her chin and tilted it up to his face. "Are you?"

"I...I ought to," she stammered.

To her amazement he turned her in his arms, suddenly, still keeping her tight against his body, and she looked up, trying to see him. "Because you're a pirate at heart, lass. I can feel it. You aren't going to turn me in. Are you?" His voice was low, his face so close. His fingers caught her chin and tilted it up to his face. "Are you?"

"I...I ought to," she stammered.

She couldn't see much of him. Just a broad smile, and the glitter of his eyes. "You know I'm going to kiss you, don't you? I shouldn't. But I can't resist. And you're going to kiss me back."

She was more shocked by that than by discovering he was a jewel thief. "I most certainly am not! I'm engaged to be married."

"I hope he appreciates you. That's not much of a ring on your finger—you deserve far better."

She hid her hand and the pathetic ring in her skirts.

"It's good enough for me."

"No, it's not. He's not. But there's nothing I can do about that. Brace yourself, lass." His mouth covered hers, and she jerked in surprise.

It wasn't an indiscreet pressure of his lips against hers. It was his mouth, hot and wet and open, and the fingers that held her chin stroked her, tugging it, and she tasted his tongue.

She froze, not certain what she should do. This was ridiculous, it was bizarre, it was shocking. She couldn't scream, and she didn't want to fight. He slowly seduced her with his tongue, sliding it against hers with a steady, sinuous rhythm that she felt in her breasts, the pit of her stomach, between her legs. It was a kiss that caught her soul, wrapped it up and stole it away from her, and when he finally lifted his head she was breathless. And so was he.

"He doesn't even know how to kiss you," he said, a mixture of regret and laughter in his voice. "Such a waste, lass."

She looked up at him in the darkness. And then said something she never would have thought she'd utter, not in a million years. "Kiss me again."

And he did. She was clamped against his hard body, and he was very strong. She was clamped against his hard body, and he was very strong, and he lifted her, with seeming effortlessness, carried her, and she thought he was taking her to the bed, and she didn't care. He moved her across the room, kissing her so deeply her brain was whirling, and they came up against a solid surface, and she wondered if he was going to take her there.

He moved his mouth, trailing kisses along her cheek. "Goodbye, lass," he whispered, his lips against her ear. And a moment later she was out in a hallway, alone, no sign of a door in the damask-covered walls.

She was shaking. She realized with shock that he'd managed to fasten her domino back around her neck, though he hadn't bothered with the loo mask, and she quickly reached for the hood and pulled it low over her flaming face. She rested her forehead against the wall, trying to catch her breath, waiting for the pounding of her heart to slow. She could hear the noise and music from the ballroom, and she pushed away, moving toward it in a daze, walking until she came upon some of the guests, until she found a cushioned chair near a window. She sank into it, sitting there in breathless shock. And it was there Miranda found her.

She shouldn't be going off with him, Miranda thought, her hand on his arm, her gloved fingers resting on the superfine of his black coat. She could feel the eyes on them as they moved through the halls, but for once she knew those guarded, disapproving eyes weren't meant for her. The Scorpion put the strumpet's sins in the shade.

"Where are we going?" she demanded.

"Someplace where we can talk. I have a small task to perform and I thought you could bear me company while I did it."

"A task?" That seemed absurd. What kind of task did one have in the middle of a ball? And Lucien de Malheur had people to perform his tasks—she couldn't imagine him exerting himself for anything less than monumental.

"I think it would probably be better if I didn't explain too much. We simply need to keep guard in a hallway, keep anyone from going into any of the bedrooms."

"Why would people go into the bedrooms?"

"Oh, child, how can you be a fallen woman and still such an innocent! The Carrimores are very liberal hosts. They make certain there are bedrooms available for couples who feel the need to fornicate."

The word startled her, but she was determined not to show it. "Why should they?" she said in a caustic voice.

"Why can't they just go home?"

"Because most of them have a husband or wife they have to take home with them, not the one they want to fuck."

She ripped her arm from his, moving away from him. "You disappoint me, Lord Rochdale," she said in a shaky voice. "I hadn't realized you had the same low opinion of me that others have."

"Now why would you say that? Haven't you ever heard that word before? It's what those guests are doing, and using prettier words for it is being disingenuous. I meant no offense."

She stared at him. "Now who's being disingenuous? You can't use a word like that without expecting a reaction, not to a young lady of the ton. But then, you know I'm not a proper young lady. The truth is when I was part of polite society I was protected from such harsh realities. Once I was considered persona non grata I had no idea how people conducted themselves. So why use such words with me? Were you planning on seducing me? Oh, excuse me. Were you planning on *fucking* me?" She'd never spoken that word out loud, and the very utterance of it made her faintly breathless, but she was too angry to care. She'd trusted him, fool that she was.

"I've made you very angry," he said, sounding sorrowful. "I didn't mean to. It's only a word, Lady Miranda."

"So is whore. Lightskirt. Trollop. Outcast. All only words."

He appeared unchastened. "Not to mention monster. Abomination. Villain. You can be assured I know a great deal about the power of words. I hadn't thought you were so vulnerable."

She stiffened. "I'm not."

"Of course you are. I apologize. I wouldn't want anything to hurt our friendship." He took her arm, and his hand covered hers, stroking her reassuringly.

She knew she should pull away again. But he was looking down at her, his pale eyes were like ice, sharp and hypnotic, and she'd given up so much already. She didn't want to give him up as well, even though she knew she should. This man was truly like a scorpion, a poisonous sting when one least expected it.

And then, to her amazement, his fingers brushed her cheek, turning her stubborn face to his. "Forgive me?" he said softly, and she felt herself slipping again, under his spell.

No wonder they called him the scarred devil. The Scorpion, who hypnotized its victim before delivering that lethal sting. When he touched her face she felt more than Christopher St. John had ever managed to elicit from her. It was dangerous, it was seductive and it shocked her, but she couldn't move. She stood perfectly still, staring up into his ravaged face, and he moved closer, and she wanted him to kiss her.

"Ooops, sorry, old man," someone said from the end of the hallway, and the couple disappeared in a welter of giggles and whispered comments, but he'd already moved back from her, and the moment was over.

"Don't worry," he said in the soft, seductive voice. "They didn't recognize you. They're talking about me and what poor victim I'd lured up here."

She took a deep breath. "Did you lure me up here?"

"Not at all. I asked you to accompany me while I helped a friend. Nothing secretive about it." He nodded toward a pair of chairs tucked into the embrasure. "Do you mind if we sit while I continue to abase myself? I find it difficult to stand for too long."

The last bit of offense vanished as concern flooded her. "Of course," she said. "I should have thought of that. I'm sorry—when I'm with you I forget about…"

"Forget that I'm a monster?" He sounded amused but also faintly surprised. "If so, then you're the only one." He waited until she sat down, and took the chair opposite her. "While I, on the other hand, have to stare at that loo mask and wonder exactly what you're thinking."

She glanced at the empty hallway, then reached up and untied it, letting it drop into her lap before she raised her chin to meet his gaze.

"Ah, that's much better. You're quite lovely, you know."

"I hadn't realized your vision was impaired, as well,"

she replied quite fearlessly. "I'm perfectly ordinary and you know it. Ordinary brown hair, ordinary shape and height, ordinary brown eyes."

She startled him for a moment, and then he laughed. "I like it that you're almost impossible to intimidate, Lady Miranda. My vision is perfect, and she felt his gaze like a touch, running from her dark hair, down her face and slender neck, over her breasts and her waist, down her legs to her feet and then back up again. It was a thorough examination, and if she'd been missish she would have blushed, but she withstood it calmly. And then he smiled.

"Someday," he murmured, "I'll tell you about yourself. But this is neither the time nor place."

She opened her mouth to speak, when heard a sudden thump against the wall of the bedroom opposite them, and a frown crossed her companion's face.

"What was that?"

"A very clumsy mouse," he grumbled. Another inebriated couple appeared at the end of the hallway, and he glared at them, so swiftly that they practically ran the other way. It happened too quickly for her to replace her mask. She could only hope it was too quickly for them to get a good look at her.

"A mouse?" she said dryly. He must be keeping guard for one of those illicit dalliances he'd talked about, making sure no one walked in on a friend who was in bed with someone else's wife. But he had no friends, he'd said, no true friends. And he was hardly the type of man to do a favor for an acquaintance.

"A slow, clumsy mouse," he said, leaning back. "Who needs to hurry up. In the meantime, why don't you tell me about your family. You have brothers, do you not? Any sisters?"

She shook her head. "Just the three brothers. Benedick, the oldest, is the heir. He and his wife are expecting their second child. Charles is the middle brother, just returned from Italy with his new wife. And there's my younger brother Brandon, whom I adore. He's in Yorkshire right now with the rest of my family, but when he returns I'll introduce you. I think he would love to meet you. I think my entire family would."

A faint, cold smile crossed his face. "I imagine they would."

She heard a muffled sigh from beyond the thin walls, the low murmur of voices, and she smiled. "Someone is clearly enjoying themselves. Is that why we're standing guard?"

He blinked. "What makes you think we're standing guard?"

"A favor for a friend, you said. I imagine you're making sure no one interferes with his tryst. I'm guessing one party or the other is someone so well-placed that the shock of exposure would topple the government, and therefore for the sake of the kingdom we're here to make certain no one walks in on them."

He was clearly amused. "You think I care about the safety of the kingdom? Not likely, but I suppose that's as good an explanation as any. If people come in search of an empty bedroom they'll see us sitting here and head in another direction, making life a great deal simpler. But don't we have more interesting things to discuss? For instance, why you greeted me with icy reproach? Have I done something to offend you?"

For a long moment she said nothing. And then she met his gaze fearlessly. "You're playing the game…and I'm well out of it. I can simper and smile and say 'of course not' and you'd pursue it and I'd laugh and hide my face behind my fan. But I don't have to do that any-more. I spent four hours alone in your company ten days ago, having a wonderful time, the best I've had since I can remember. We talked about everything, and I thought we became friends. Good friends. And then I heard nothing from you for ten days. I was left to assume that the feelings of friendship were one-sided and I'd been foolishly optimistic, and then you stroll into my life again as if nothing had happened."

"I assure you, I don't stroll," he said, his voice cool. "So you're angry that I haven't paid enough attention to you?"

It sounded so petty. She should have simply lied, as everyone else did. "Yes."

He surveyed her for a long moment. "Honesty is a very unsettling trait. It's not something I'm used to."

"I'm sorry. You have many friends, I only have one. I put too much importance on a simple conversation and…"

"Stop it!" he said sharply, his silken voice becom-ing harsh. He took a deep breath. "I didn't pursue our acquaintance because I was afraid your family would get wind of it and interfere. And I didn't want to embark on a friendship that would be terminated abruptly."

"But why should my family object to our friendship?"

"My reputation precedes me. I'm afraid I'm quite notorious, and I'm known to have some most unsavory acquaintances. Most families bar me from the door."

"My family doesn't tell me what to do. I live my own life, independently. If we choose to be friends, then they have nothing to say in the matter."

"Are you certain?"

"Of course I am."

"Then ride with me tomorrow. In full view of everyone. At four in the afternoon, we'll ride down Rotten Row and give the old biddies something to talk about."

"Absolutely."

There was an odd look in his pale eyes, one almost of triumph, but at that moment there was a muffled double knock on the wall, and the earl rose, leaning heavily on his cane. "Then that's settled. May I drive you home?"

Miranda shook her head. "I came with my friend, and I need to find her."

"Ah, yes. Miss Pagett with the miserable fiancé." He was leading her away from the mysterious room, chatting amiably. "I'm afraid you're having a very deleterious effect on your friends, Lady Miranda. You're leading Miss Pagett astray."

Miranda flushed. "I tried to stop her."

"And yet, here you are, and for that I'm indescribably grateful. Shall we go in search of her?"

"No need," she said as they turned the corner. Jane was sitting in a corner, her loo mask gone, an odd expression on her face. And then she saw Miranda and her relief was plain as she rose on unsteady feet.

"You go to her," Lucien said, releasing her arm. "I doubt Mr. Bothwell would appreciate his future wife being introduced to the Scorpion. I'll pick you up at four tomorrow. Be ready."

"But…" He'd already walked away, disappearing into the crowds, and Miranda moved ahead, catching Jane's trembling arms in hers.

"Jane, dearest, did something happen? You look upset."

Jane's laugh was a little shaky. "You won't believe it when I tell you, but you'll have to wait until we get back to the house. Let's get out of here."

Miranda cast one last look behind her, but Lucien de Malheur had disappeared. She turned back to her friend with deep foreboding. Jane was looking just as she ought to look—happy and excited and in love.

And Miranda knew that something was very wrong.

7

"You did *what?*" Miranda demanded, staring at her friend in astonishment.

They were back in Miranda's cozy little house, the dominos discarded, the dancing slippers gone as well, sitting by a fire in the small dancing salon where Cousin Louisa usually held court. That stout lady had retired to bed, and they were entirely alone.

"I didn't do it! He's the one who kissed me." She blushed. "And I have to say it was quite delightful. You never told me men use their tongues when they kiss."

"They do?" Miranda said doubtfully. "I don't remember St. John doing anything like that, but he was fairly abrupt and practical about the whole horrid business. So you're telling me you were thoroughly kissed by a jewel thief and you didn't scream for help?"

"I promised I wouldn't," she said with a weak smile. "He definitely wasn't a gentleman—I could tell that by his voice. But he was very tall, and very strong, and yet quite gentle when he kissed me." She had a faraway look in her eyes, and Miranda's heart sank.

"Love, I don't want you to marry a stiff, prosing bore

like Bothwell, but you simply can't fall in love with a member of the criminal class. You know that, don't you?"

For a moment Jane looked deflated, and she nodded. "But you managed to change your life by running away."

"Not necessarily for the better. I enjoy my life tremendously, but I wouldn't wish it on you. And did this ruffian ask you to run away with him?"

"Of course not," she said, sounding disappointed. "And if he had, I certainly wouldn't have gone. It was just so...so..."

"Exciting?" Miranda suggested, but Jane shook her head. "Frightening? Distracting? Entertaining? Tempting?"

"Delicious," she said with a shy smile, brushing her hair away from her face.

Miranda froze. "What the bloody hell is *that*?"

"*What*?" Jane said, confused.

"On your finger. That's not Bothwell's tiny little ring."

Jane looked at her hand, and jumped, uttering a distressed squeak. A very large, very handsome diamond now rested on the ring finger of her left hand, and she yanked at it, trying to pull it off. It wouldn't budge.

"Oh, no," she moaned.

"Where's Bothwell's ring?"

She held out both hands, but the plain, cheap little ring was nowhere in sight. "Oh, God, what am I going to do, Miranda? How will I ever explain this to him?"

"Try your pockets."

She did, hurriedly reaching into the pockets sewn

into her dress, and breathed an audible sigh of relief.
"It's here."

"Now all you have to worry about is getting the other
one off."

"And returning it to its rightful owner," she said,
yanking at it.

"Don't do that—you'll make your finger swell and
it'll be even worse. We'll use warm water and soap and
it will slip right off. I presume it belongs to the duchess
of Carrimore?"

"Of course it does. What else would draw a jewel
thief in the middle of a party? We have to get it back to
her!" Jane looked as if she wanted to cry.

"That'll teach you to go kissing jewel thieves in the
middle of the night," Miranda said cheerfully.

"Don't laugh! This is a serious problem."

"You meet a quixotic jewel thief who kisses you and
slips a diamond ring on your finger. Next thing we know
he'll be asking you to marry him."

"Don't be ridiculous." She stopped fretting at the
ring. "I'm marrying Mr. Bothwell."

"Of course you are.... Unfortunately. But aren't you
glad you at least had a taste of adventure?"

Jane absently put her hand to her mouth, and the diamond ring sparkled in the candlelight. Miranda watched,
and an unexpected spark of jealousy danced through
her. The dreamy expression still lingered in Jane's deep
brown eyes, and the fingers that touched her slightly
swollen lips were a subtle caress. Miranda had never
been kissed like that, and it was more than likely she
never would. She'd never know that swept-away feeling,
that tender, almost painful longing for something you

could never have. She had been ruined in more ways than one.

"I think," said Jane sadly, "I might have been better off without it."

Miranda could feel the pain in her voice. "The good thing is, no one knows about it. No one but the thief, and he's hardly likely to start talking. You'll forget all about this once you're happily married."

"I thought you didn't want me to marry Mr. Bothwell."

"I don't, but it's better than running off with a jewel thief," she said frankly. "And don't worry about the ring. I'll ask the earl what we should do about it."

"You aren't going to tell him what happened!" Jane protested, horrified.

"Of course not. I'll tell him I found it. But he's a very clever man—I expect he'll figure out a way to return it with no one the wiser." She couldn't rid herself of the sudden suspicion that the earl knew far too much about the jewel thief and the Carrimore diamonds. But that was absurd—he was a peer of the realm. With a worse reputation than she enjoyed. But still, it was ridiculous.

Jane glanced down at the ring, a wistful expression on her face. "That would be for best...wouldn't it?"

"Yes, dearest," Miranda said, tucking her arm around Jane's waist. "You can't keep it, as gorgeous as it is. Don't fret about it. You just get a good night's sleep and tomorrow everything will be resolved."

But she knew Jane would do no such thing. She would lie in bed, and touch her mouth again, and remember what her mysterious admirer had said and done. And the sooner she got married off to the odious Mr. Bothwell, the safer she would be.

It was a great deal too bad that safety no longer looked so appealing.

"You did what?" Lucien de Malheur demanded of his criminal confederate.

"I kissed a proper young lady who happened to stumble in on me while I was gathering the duchess's extra diamonds. I don't know how she got there—probably the servants' access. One moment I was alone in the room, scooping up the diamonds, in the next she was there. What else was I to do but kiss her?"

"Break her neck?" Lucien suggested dryly.

"You know I wouldn't do that. Not to an innocent. Besides, she was such a shy, sweet little thing. Though not so little, if I recall. Clearly she needed kissing."

"You're just lucky she didn't scream her head off." The earl's voice was sour; he'd been thinking too much about Miranda Rohan and it had put him in a foul mood. Jacob's romantic dalliances didn't help.

"Oh, I made sure she couldn't," Jacob said. "And even if she had it wouldn't have been a problem. I could have just dove out the window and be off before she managed to raise the wind on me. You would have been perfectly safe."

"I wasn't worried. I just think you're being a little reckless. You had half a dozen men who could have done your job tonight, and yet you chose to endanger yourself and me."

Jacob Donnelly shrugged his wide shoulders and began using his aristocratic accents. "Don't worry,

I won't be seeing her again. I don't even know her name."

"I do. It's Jane Pagett. She's engaged to marry some dull stick named George Bothwell, and she happens to be Miranda Rohan's closest friend."

Jacob looked undaunted. "Too bad we can't have a double wedding."

Lucien swore. "How many wives do you have at this point, Jacob? Half a dozen?"

"None of them legal," Jacob said cheerfully. "And there's none that calls themselves that at the moment. I'm fancy free."

"Keep it that way," Lucien said in a chilly voice. "My life is complicated enough."

"And how are your plans working out? Is the lady enamored?"

"Completely. She's a great deal more outspoken than I expected, but in the end that will serve me well, I think. I'll just move things up a little faster than I planned."

"You were seen with her tonight—I heard the servants talking. It won't take long for word to get to her family, and then all hell will break loose."

"I know what I'm doing. I wish I could say the same for you."

"Jesus, Lucien, it was only a kiss."

"Just so long as you keep your distance in the future. You're sure she didn't get a good look at you?"

"It was black as night. I saw her, she couldn't see me. Ah, but Lucien…" he said, shaking his head, leaning back in his chair. "She tasted…delicious."

The next few days were almost too lovely, Miranda thought in retrospect. That in itself should have been a warning—after twenty years of a singularly blessed life she'd learned that things could turn ugly very quickly. Who would have thought falling in love with Christopher St. John would have led to such disaster?

She'd accepted she would spend the rest of her life as a disgraced nun, shunned by former friends, living a secluded life empty of love and life and joy. A calm life.

But now, suddenly, there was Lucien De Malheur. Not so handsome, not so charming, and yet he totally bewitched her, with his soft, lazy voice, his wit, the faint tinge of malice directed toward those who deserved it. The way he moved, despite the limp, the way he mocked the prudes who looked down on them both. And there was something in the pale eyes that watched her, something she refused to define, that nonetheless filled her with the kind of longing she thought she would forever be impervious to.

They rode together, laughing, knowing disapproving eyes were watching them. He joined her for tea, much to Cousin Louisa's fascination and Jane's astonishment. He teased her into calling him Lucien, he flattered her so extravagantly all she could do was laugh. He took her to the opera and kissed her hand decorously and she wondered if it were possible that after all she had been through, after all this time, she was capable of falling in love.

She hoped not. She knew perfectly well that those hopes were doomed.

8

Miranda was sound asleep when she heard the pounding on her bedroom door. She sat up, disoriented, pulling the covers to her neck.

No one in the world would come storming into her house and beat on her door, unless the Bow Street Runners were after the stolen ring, which Jane, after more than a week, still hadn't been able to remove from her finger...in which case she was just going to hide under the covers and pretend she couldn't hear a thing.

"Open up the door, sister!" Her younger brother Brandon bellowed from the other side. "I can't stand here all day."

Miranda would have been more than happy to have left him there all day, but he was making far too much noise to allow any continued sleep. She dragged herself out of bed, shivering slightly when her bare feet met the cold floor, and she crossed the chilly room to the door, flinging it open just as he was about to pound on it again.

"It wasn't locked," she said in a deliberately mild tone.

"I don't just barge into a lady's bedroom uninvited," he said stiffly, doing just that. "You might be dressing."

"I might be sleeping."

"I wouldn't be surprised, with you out and about at all hours...damn, it's cold in here! Why don't you have your maid set a fire?"

"Because I'm trying to be careful with money," she said.

"Why? The family has plenty..."

"I've put you all through enough as it is," she said stubbornly, wishing she'd thought to put on her slippers. It was hard to be noble when her feet were like blocks of ice.

"That's what I'm here to talk to you about, Miranda," he began. "You can't..."

"You can't stand there and lecture me while I'm freezing," she interrupted him, knowing instinctively what was coming. "Go downstairs and eat a large breakfast and Jane and I will join you as soon as we're dressed."

"Jane?" He perked up. "What's she doing here? I thought she'd be busy getting ready for her wedding to old Bore-well."

"He's not old. And his name's *Both*well, and that's exactly what she's doing. Her parents are travelling, and she's here in London choosing fabrics for her trousseau and keeping me company."

Brandon looked at her critically. He was young—a mere seventeen and a half—but he knew her well. "I thought you disliked Bore-well as much as the rest of us did. What made you change your mind?"

She took his arm and dragged him to the open door,

shoving him through. "Allow me time to get dressed and then we'll talk, you reprobate."

"All right. But don't think you're going to weasel out of this. I'm just the first advance—the rest of the family are going to descend on you the moment they hear about what you've been doing."

She knew. Without asking, she knew what had put her family into an uproar. Lucien had warned her. Friendship, with the Scorpion, even for one such as her, was out of the question.

"We'll talk about it once I'm dressed," she said and slammed the door shut in his earnest young face.

She turned and caught sight of her reflection in the mirror. She hadn't been ruthlessly kissed by a criminal last night, but she had the same vibrant look on her face that Jane had had after the masked ball. Every day she spent with Lucien she ended up looking just like that. The flush of color, the shining eyes. Damn.

Miranda's was an entirely different matter, of course. Lucien was her friend, her first friend in a long, long time, and she wasn't about to give him up without a fight. Brandon could lecture her about how awful he was, but it wasn't going to stop her.

She rang for Martha, who helped her dress for battle in dove-gray with faux military trim, gray leather boots and her brown hair tightly pinned and pulled back from her face. As the moments passed her determination grew—her family had been wonderful to her, supporting her foolish choices, and she owed them everything. But she just couldn't give him up.

By the time she walked into the dining room her heart was pounding and her hands were sweaty, which was ridiculous. It was her darling baby brother she was facing, not some ogre. Jane was already up, sitting beside Brandon at the table, picking at her food while he plowed through a heaping plate of eggs and kippers, and she could only hope food had moderated his stern frame of mind.

"There you are," he said, rising automatically like the exquisitely polite young man that he was. "What took you so long?"

She waved him back down into his chair, heading for the sideboard. The sight of food made her stomach lurch in rebellion, but she filled her plate determinedly before turning to join the two of them. "Give me a moment, darling. If you're going to scold I need to fortify myself." She took a piece of dried toast and began to munch on it, trying to delay things.

"I most certainly am going to scold." Brandon had abandoned his plate at the sight of her, convincing Miranda of the seriousness of the matter. It took a great deal for Brandon to ignore food. "What in God's name do you think you're doing? How long has this been going on? Jane says at least two weeks."

She cast Jane a reproachful look, and her friend had the grace to flush guiltily. "I had to tell him, Miranda. You don't realize what a close call you've had."

Miranda resisted the temptation to tell Jane her own close call was a great deal worse. "All right," she said wearily, picking up her cup of tea. "Tell me how evil I've been."

"Not evil, Miranda," Brandon said earnestly. "Just thickheaded. You didn't know what you were doing".

"You do realize that I'd rather be evil than stupid, don't you?"

He grinned at her. "No, you wouldn't. And I know

you'd hate letting another man make a fool of you. But the truth is, you can't go anywhere near the Scorpion, and someone should have told you earlier. Our family has an unfortunate history with the man, and even I don't know all of it. Back when it happened they decided that you should be spared the sordid details, and everything was hushed up, and even Jane didn't know."

"Back when what happened?" she echoed. "What in the world are you talking about?"

"I told you, I don't know the details, I just know he's trouble. Particular trouble for the Rohans. You need to take my word for it."

"Well, I'm *not* taking your word for it. What mysterious connection is there between our family and Lucien?"

"*Lucien?*" Brandon practically spat his tea across the table. "You call him *Lucien?*"

"We're friends. And why do you know about this history at all when I'm six years older than you are?"

"I'm a man," he said simply.

"You were a boy."

"Don't try to distract me. You can't go anywhere near Lucien de Malheur, and if you happen to see him in public you need to cut him dead."

"I'm not going to do that." She set down the dry piece of bread, untouched. "I've been cut dead by people I counted my loyal friends, people I've known all my life. I would never do that to another human being. Not without a very good reason, and you have yet to give me one."

"He's not a human being, he's the Scorpion."

"Oh, for heaven's sake, why is he called that?" she said, annoyed.

"Because he's elegant, slithery and lethal. He stings without warning and his stings can kill you."

Miranda made a rude noise. "Someone's been reading too many Gothic stories. What evil thing did he ever do to our family that makes him so dangerous?"

For a moment Brandon looked blank. "I told you, I don't exactly know details. I do know he's reputed to be hand in hand with King Donnelly."

"Who's King Donnelly?" At least the tea was soothing her. She added more sugar for sustenance.

"Jacob Donnelly is the king of the London underworld. He rules the thieves and the fences, the smugglers and the pickpockets. He can arrange a murder at the drop of a hat, steal a diamond ring off your finger, all with a smile and an 'if you please.' Rochdale has a hand in his criminal activities, so they say, and that's part of how he's built his family fortune back up."

Jane had turned an alarming shade of white, but Brandon hadn't noticed, still intent on his sister. Miranda rose, ostensibly heading for more food, and put a reassuring hand on Jane's shoulder as she passed her. "Well, Lucien would hardly bring such a man into society, now would he?"

"There's nothing he wouldn't dare."

"I don't care, Brandon. He could be running prostitutes from out of his house and it wouldn't matter to me. I find him a pleasant, charming companion who certainly means me no ill, and I intend to keep seeing him."

"If you do, I'll be forced to call him out."

She couldn't help it, she laughed, a blow to Brandon's somewhat shaky amour-propre. "You can't," she said. "He has a bad leg."

Brandon immediately retreated into sulks. "He's a cripple? No one told me that."

"I don't know that I'd call him a cripple, exactly," Miranda said. She turned to Jane. "Do you know anything about our family and the earl?"

"Of course not," Jane said as she nervously tore her bread into tiny pieces that fluttered down onto her untouched plate like snowflakes. The immovable diamond ring flashed on her hand. "If I had I certainly would have told you. I tell you everything, I *trust* you." There was no missing the subtext in her pleading eyes.

"True, we would never betray each other," Miranda assured her. She glanced across at her brother. "Then clearly there's only one answer for it. I'll have to ask him myself."

Brandon was in the midst of taking a sip of coffee and proceeded to choke on it. She rose to her feet, determination washing away her doubts. "I'm certain you're making a great deal of fuss over nothing, and I despise seeing someone else treated as I have been, for an error in judgment. If you could simply tell me what Lucien de Malheur had ever done to harm our family then perhaps I might be willing to listen."

"He hasn't," Brandon said.

She froze on her way out the door. "He hasn't done anything to harm our family?" she repeated in a dangerous voice.

"The fear is that he might."

She allowed her disgust to show on her face. "I would have thought better of you, Brandon," she said in stern accents and swept from the room.

The day was overcast and chilly, but Miranda was in a white-hot rage, with no patience to wait for either a horse or a carriage to be summoned. It took her but a moment to acquire a pale gray pelisse and bonnet, and she was out on Half Moon Street, striding forward with determination, her footman valiantly trying to keep up with her.

Cadogan Place was a fair distance, but no farther than she'd walked in the country almost daily. And she needed the exercise, needed the fresh air and the time to recover her temper. How dare her family try to interfere with her life? It seemed she had their full support when she lived a cloistered existence. Make one new friend and she was suddenly beyond the pale.

If Brandon wouldn't tell her then she knew where she could get the answers. And it wasn't as if the man had done anything to her family—it was the ridiculous fear that he *might*. Just as society feared she *might* corrupt the morals of the young ladies who had once been her dearest friends. Only Lord and Lady Montague had stood by their daughters' friendship, with Lady Montague insisting that whatever Miranda had done, she'd done ten times worse and twice on Sundays, making Miranda laugh.

Evangelina Montague wouldn't order her away from Lucien over any ridiculous *might*. Neither, she was sure, would her parents. It was only her interfering brothers who'd suddenly gotten the alarm up, and she was going to nip this whole thing in the bud. Lucien meant her no ill, and to assume otherwise was absurd.

The Scorpion. What an utterly absurd name for him. He was no more venomous than a field mouse. Well, perhaps that was putting it too gently. No more venomous than a fox. In truth, the whole thing was ridiculous and cruel, and she refused to listen to it.

The brisk hike through the cool morning air put color in her cheeks but did little to dampen the blaze in her eyes. By the time she reached the huge, dark house on Cadogan Place she was still in a fine stage of outrage, and her footman was sweating profusely and trying to catch his breath. "You need to exercise more, Jennings," she said as she marched up the front steps to the shiny black door. He wheezed his agreement as he stood a decorous pace behind her as she used the heavy brass knocker.

The door was opened promptly, and the servant who stood there was tall, lugubrious, cadaverously thin and dressed in funereal black, clearly the Scorpion's preferred color for livery. And for the first time Miranda began to feel conspicuous. Young ladies, even ruined ones, didn't call at a gentleman's house unannounced. "Is his lordship at home? Would you tell him…tell him a lady is here to see him?" She should have had enough sense to wear a veil, she thought belatedly. She'd just been too angry to think clearly.

For a long moment she was afraid the man would have her wait on the doorstep, but he opened the door wide, silently inviting them in. "I am Leopold, Lady Miranda. Lord Rochdale's majordomo. He told me to expect you one day. If your ladyship would follow me I'll find a place for you to wait while I see if the earl is receiving. He often doesn't arise until noon."

Now that was an embarrassing image, she thought, following him down the dark, faintly foreboding corridor. The thought of Lucien in bed, asleep amidst snowy-white sheets, was disturbing, though she wasn't sure why.

And why was the servant told to expect her? And

recognize her? The room he left her in was dark and cold. What windows it had were covered with heavy black fabric, and there'd been no fire laid in the grate. The furniture was stiff and uncomfortable, and Miranda was glad no one had bothered to take her cloak and gloves. She needed all the covering she could get in that icy, dark little dungeon.

She waited a very long time. There was no way she could really tell, though. The room boasted no clock that she could see in the gloomy shadows, and her fury was finally beginning to drain away, to be replaced by a touch of embarrassment. Any apprehension that slid into her consciousness she swiftly banished. She simply needed to clarify things, to find out why her family found the earl so unacceptable. And then she could stuff it down Brandon's throat.

After all, the Rohans were hardly the epitome of respectability. Though her loving but stern mother had made certain her sons had never succumbed to the lure of such depraved activities as the Heavenly Host provided, she had accepted that young men were bound to kick up the occasional fuss. And Miranda knew the shocking truth. Her own darling father and his father before him had been active in the Host. In fact, her father said his knowledge of them gave him particular reason to make certain his sons kept their distance.

But still, she vaguely remembered the occasional scandals. Benedick had once been engaged to a woman so unstable she'd threatened him with a gun at a public rout, and then she'd continue to behave so strangely she would have ended in Bedlam if she hadn't died.

Charles, stuffy Charles, had had a great fondness for opera dancers until he'd fallen in love with Kitty

Marsden, the surprisingly down to earth daughter of a country squire.

And Brandon was doing his best to follow in the family tradition. It was no wonder they'd been so forgiving of her lapse.

So the Rohans were scarcely high-sticklers. Why should they kick up a fuss about a simple friendship with a man of bad reputation? It made no sense.

She rose and strolled nervously around the cramped confines of the room. She peered through the window that looked out over the mews, then turned and walked back around the crowded room. What was taking him so long?

Eventually she sat again, back on the hard sofa. If it had been at all warm she would have fallen asleep, but as it was she had to pull her pelisse closer about her in a vain effort to keep warm. She began to worry that the majordomo had forgotten her existence, or that his disapproval of a young lady visiting a gentleman so offended his proprieties that he thought to teach her a lesson, which was far-fetched, but servants could at times be even stuffier than their masters. Except that he'd looked almost embarrassed when he'd shown her into the dismal room.

She'd just about given up hope when the door opened, and the gloomy butler reappeared. "His lordship will see you now," he announced, and she could sense his disapproval. Presumably with her, though he looked around the grim room with disapprobation. Miranda rose as gracefully as she could with frozen joints, giving the man a pleasant smile as she preceded him out the door.

She hadn't realized how big the house was as she

followed the gloomy Leopold through the darkened corridors. She expected to be brought to the cozy little parlor where she and Lucien had shared so many pleasant hours, but the room he brought her to was a great deal different. Warmer, thank God, with a good fire blazing in the grate, but with dark, almost severe furnishings and heavy draperies.

Lucien de Malheur was sitting behind a desk, writing. He glanced up as she approached, but in the darkness she couldn't see his expression. Just his face surrounded by a mane of long dark hair. He made no effort to rise.

"Oh, thank God," she said briskly, heading straight for the fire. "I'm absolutely freezing! Don't you have fires in any of your parlors?"

He raised an eyebrow. "Leopold put you in an unheated room."

It wasn't exactly a question. "He did. He probably didn't expect it to take you so long to see me."

"Is that a note of reproach I hear?"

There was something wrong. His voice was light, faintly teasing, but there was something between them that hadn't been there before. Some odd constraint that made her uneasiness deepen.

But she refused to give in to it. "It is," she said in a cheerful voice. "I come racing across town in a desperate hurry because I had to see you at once, and you keep me locked up in an icebox for hours."

"One hour," he corrected her, and he gave her no answering smile. "Things have moved a little faster than I expected, and I needed to make a few arrangements, marshal my forces before we met."

Her flippant response died on her tongue as she looked at him. He might have been a stranger. Not the man she'd laughed with, talked with. The scandal-mongers had been right after all. This was the Scorpion who faced her, cold and deadly.

"Did I do something wrong?" she asked in a quiet voice. "Have I somehow offended you?"

"No. Have a seat, Lady Miranda. I'm still waiting confirmation on a small issue, and then we'll talk."

She turned slowly, facing him. He hadn't risen, when he always had before. Perhaps his leg was paining him, and that was why everything was so stiff and strange...

No. She wasn't going to lie to herself, and she wasn't going to sit patiently like a good girl. She moved closer. "I think not. I think you should explain what's going on now."

"Sit down."

She sat.

She sat, hating herself for doing so, but there was something in his voice, an icy chill, that hit her knees, and she sank into the chair behind her.

She watched him, her face composed, even as her heart raced beneath the stern trappings of her day dress. "I've been a very great fool, haven't I?" she said in a conversational voice.

He was scribbling something on a piece of paper, and he didn't bother to look up. "More than once, Lady Miranda," he said. And then his pale, empty eyes met hers. "To which time were you referring?"

"Our friendship is far from accidental, isn't it?"

"Our friendship?" he echoed, and there was only the slightest trace of mockery in his voice. "It was planned."

"But how did you know I'd have a carriage accident?

Or was that simply good luck on your part?" She kept her hands clasped in her lap. She didn't want him to see how tightly she was gripping her fingers, and she buried them in the folds of her pelisse.

"I never count on luck, child. One of my men tampered with your carriage, ensuring the wheel would come off."

This was a nightmare, she thought, not blinking. This was some horrid bad dream and she was back home in bed, sleeping soundly.

But she knew it wasn't. "I could have been killed."

Her voice was steady.

He showed no remorse. "That would have been highly unlikely, given that you are a notable whip. I expected you'd be able to control your cattle under even more dire circumstances. And of course we were right there waiting. If my calculations had been off it still would have accomplished what I hoped."

"And what is it you wished to accomplish?"

He set the pen down and leaned back. "Your family's misery," he said frankly. "In particular your older brother's, but I'd be happy if the entire family suffered the torments of the damned."

It felt like a knife to her heart, she thought dazedly, trying to compose herself. Her friend, her lover, the lover who'd never touched her, never said anything but who was, nevertheless, her love. "Me included?" She managed to keep her voice steady even as she was breaking inside.

His eyes met hers. "Actually not," he said. Watching her, and there was an odd expression in his pale eyes. "I thought I'd marry you."

His arrogance took her breath away, and her grief vanished, replaced by a cleansing anger. "I think not."

"Do you? You forget: I always get what I want, sooner or later. Call it payback for what happened to my sister."

"I didn't know you had a sister."

"She was my half sister and my only living relative. Genevieve Compton." He said it as if he expected it to mean something to her, but she simply shook her head.

"I've never heard of Genevieve Compton."

"Your brother Benedick's fiancée? Granted, you were a child at the time, but I can't believe you weren't aware of the scandal."

"Our family is always embroiled in scandal. My parents did their best to shield me from some of the more salacious stories. What did my brother do to your sister?"

"He cried off from the engagement and she killed herself." The words were flat, emotionless, and Miranda stared at him in shock. The stories of the mad fiancée she vaguely remembered now made sense. "He told her he was going to break the engagement, so she arranged to meet him at Temple Bar to discuss it with their lawyers, and when he arrived she took a gun and blew her brains out in front of them all."

"That is truly tragic," she said, horrified. "But your sister was said to have been mad—she threatened him with the very same gun."

His mouth thinned. "It's of no consequence. He took my sister. I thought I'd return the favor."

She didn't move, afraid if she did that she'd attack

him. She'd never been so angry in her life—she almost trembled with it. "No."

His smile, the one that she'd found so charming, now infuriated her. "Yes."

"This isn't medieval England, you lying skunk," she said with something close to a snarl. "You can't marry an unwilling bride."

"You'll be willing."

"And what miracle or force of nature would ensure that?" she snapped.

His voice was simple and direct. "If you don't I will challenge your brother Brandon to a duel, and I will kill him."

Automatically her eyes fell to his leg. "You can't..."

"I will arrange it so that your brother is the one who calls me out, and it will be my choice of weapons. I'm an expert marksman—I will put a bullet directly between his eyes with no effort at all." He rose, moving around the desk, holding his cane but barely leaning on it. "You see, I can do anything I want. I'm giving you a chance to save your brother, but I'm just as happy slaughtering him. Anything to take a beloved sibling away from the Rohan family. Taking a sister has better symmetry, and the advantage with you would be that the pain would be lifelong. Once you marry me you'll never see them again."

She wanted to throw up. The thought of her darling baby brother lying cold and dead in the predawn light horrified her, and she didn't doubt for a moment that this vile man meant it.

She couldn't show weakness. "I think your brain must be as disordered as your sister's, my lord," she said with a foolish lack of tact. Except she didn't believe he was mad at all. Cruel, determined, but perfectly rational. "Why in the world would you want to be saddled with a wife you despise?"

He laughed. "Oh, I don't despise you, my precious. I find you quite...irresistible. My original plan had nothing to do with marriage at all, but a few minutes in your delightful company and I decided you were just what I needed. I need an heir, after all, and I have to marry sooner or later, and if I marry you it will be forever. You'll never be free." His smile was positively angelic. "At least with you I won't have to worry about foolish conventions."

"Such as pretending to be in love?"

"Exactly. I rather thought we'd present your family with a fait accompli. There will be nothing they can do about it—they certainly can't kill their brother-in-law in a duel. All they can do is...miss you." There was no pain beneath his smooth voice, and yet for a moment she thought she had a glimpse of what drove him.

"No."

He looked at her tenderly. "The ton will be astonished. Who would have thought a soiled dove would make such an excellent match?"

"You bastard."

"Not in fact, but in nature, absolutely. I have a special license already in hand. I think distance would be a wise idea when your family hears about our elopement. We don't want our honeymoon interrupted by a brawl."

"I won't marry you."

He came toward her, and she noticed his limp was far less apparent than it had been. He came close and she wanted to flinch, but she held herself still. She gripped the seat of the chair as his fingers ran down her cheek and along the side of her neck, dipping inside her collar for a brief, shocking moment. "Oh, my precious," he said softly, "of course you will."

She shivered. Shivered because he was touching her, shivered because she reacted to it, to the caress. But she didn't move, and her eyes flashed fire.

"You wouldn't do it."

"You think not? I had no qualms about endangering your life with a carriage accident. Trust me, the name *Scorpion* isn't an accident. I'm cold and lethal—society shuns me for good reason." He leaned his face down, and brushed his lips against her cheekbone. "I'm sorry I'm such an ugly brute, my precious, but you can always close your eyes and pretend I'm someone else."

She did close her eyes then. Not because of the scars—those she'd ceased to notice long ago. The sight of his betrayal was new, though, and she couldn't stand it.

"So what's it to be, my darling? Your brother's life or marriage to me? I do promise that I'll grow bored of you very quickly and you will live a pleasant life out in the country, with more than enough money to indulge your every whim. Look at it this way—your life will be very much like it is here. You'll be free to do what you want without a thought to the ton. You'll simply be a bit more isolated. Make your choice." The soft, caressing voice ended on a note of steel.

He'd won, as he'd known he would. She knew Brandon too well—he'd rush into a confrontation and Lucien would kill him without hesitation.

"Yes." Her voice was cold.

He laughed softly beneath his breath. "I warned you I was 'determined to be a villain.' I may look like foolish

Caliban, but my soul is far blacker. You just refused to see it." He pulled back. "I'll have the horses put to."

"*What?* I have no clothes, and my servants will have no idea where I'm gone…"

"Leopold will see to your servants. In fact, he'll see to everything. As for clothes, you won't be needing any. You've been dancing on the edge for long enough—we may as well seal our devil's bargain immediately."

"But where are we going?"

He shook his head. "I think you're better off not knowing. But you'll be pleased to know I'll ride while you have the carriage to yourself. I think I'd find the trip a bit too…arousing. And I certainly don't want this to remind you of your last elopement."

"It's *exactly* like my last elopement," she spat. "I was abducted against my will that time, as well."

"But at least I'll marry you," he said in a silken voice.

"Whether you want me to or not."

And a moment later he was gone.

9

Lady Jane Pagett was not having a good day. Ever since the night at the Carrimores' ball she'd been in a terrible state of upheaval. Half the time she didn't want to get out of bed in the morning. Despite Miranda's warnings, all she wanted to do was think of the tall man who'd kissed her, and wrong as it was, she wanted to lie in bed and touch herself through her fine lawn nightdress and pretend they were his hands on her body. She didn't want to think about Mr. Bothwell and his chaste, dry kisses, she didn't want to think about her future life in the dreary north. She wanted to dream of pirates and smugglers and wicked licentiousness that nevertheless felt so good.

Because the truth was, all her life, beneath her timid exterior, beat the heart of an adventuress. She wanted to travel to strange and distant places, she wanted wild adventures and passionate love. Instead she was marrying Mr. Bothwell because no one else had wanted her.

She was tall and thin and plain and shy, doomed to an ordinary life with an ordinary man, and just once she wished she was brave enough to have even the mildest of adventures. The kiss in the dark had been a taste of all the richness life offered and she was denied.

The fact that she hadn't been able to get the blasted diamond ring off her finger didn't help matters. Nothing worked, not soap or duck grease or sheer force. It seemed stuck for good, and she didn't dare return home to her family with it adorning her hand like a blazing sign of her wickedness.

She'd summoned up enough courage to have Miranda ask the Earl of Rochdale about it but he'd denied any knowledge of jewel thieves, and she was half tempted to believe him, if he weren't known as the Scorpion, with the reputation to match. A pirate indeed, but a little too frightening even for Jane's wild fantasies. She wanted the man in the dark.

On top of everything else, she had the beginnings of a putrid sore throat, and she planned to spend the day in bed, nursed by Miranda's most excellent lady's maid.

But Brandon Rohan had made such a row she'd had no choice but to get up and put her best face on, listening to him as he stalked around the dining room, ranting about some wicked crime that Lucien de Malheur *hadn't* done. To be sure, the scarred man unnerved her, and she would have warned Miranda to beware. If she hadn't seen the way he looked at her, when he thought no one would notice. It didn't matter how much Brandon ranted and raved—Jane knew people, and always had. She'd seen the way the earl looked at Miranda and known she was safe.

Of course, hours later she was rethinking that. It had been a dark, gloomy day, and Miranda had taken off on foot, anger vibrating through her, gone before Jane could offer to accompany her. Brandon had finally taken himself off to his club, but Jane had no idea whether he was coming back to spend the night or, having delivered his warning, considered his duty done and was devoting himself to the pleasures of town the way any normal seventeen-year-old male would.

And there was the damned ring. Trust Brandon to notice it. "Did old Bore-well give you that diamond?" he'd asked with an appreciative whistle. "He must not be the nip-farthing, cold fish he seemed to be."

She'd said nothing, of course. What were the chances a boy like Brandon would remember what ring his sister's friend was wearing? Normally nil, but the way her luck had been running there was no guarantee.

It was getting late, and there was no sign of Miranda. Apparently the footman had returned hours ago, alone. Cousin Louisa lay ensconced on the divan in the morning room, nibbling on fresh-baked almond biscuits and trying to convince Jane there was absolutely nothing to worry about. As long as Louisa didn't have to move she was the most placid creature in the world.

It took Jane another hour to screw up her courage. Something was wrong, something was off, though Jennings assured her that Miranda had arrived safely. She was probably worrying about nothing. Jane had joined the earl and Miranda on several occasions, having wonderful conversations, and Jane hadn't seen her friend that animated, that happy, in years. Everything was perfectly fine.

But it was late, cold and dark, and Jane could either think about her mysterious encounter in the darkened bedroom or she could worry about Miranda. Miranda won.

She was going to go about it in a perfectly respectable

way. No haring across town in a rage, she would have the carriage brought round, be driven to the earl's house on Cadogan Place, keep Jennings and perhaps even a maid with her for propriety's sake. But just as she was about to order the carriage Brandon came stomping back in, and she had no choice, grabbing her coat and her reticule and sneaking out a side door into the garden, then through the gate into the rain-slick street.

She'd never hailed her own hackney before, but luck was on her side, though the driver expressed doubts about taking a "nice young lady like yourself" to *that* part of town. She wasn't quite sure how to depress his pretension since he was clearly just an overprotective male, but after his first warning he drove in silence, through the darkening evening.

The first thing that met her eye wasn't the dark, gloomy house. It was the large traveling carriage that was standing in the front portico, a matched set of six black horses, no less, waiting and ready. She told the driver to let her down at the end of the square, which he did after expressing one more warning, and then she started back toward the house, keeping to the shadows, astonished at her own bravery. She was half tempted to call the hackney back, but he'd already disappeared in the fog.

Jane straightened her shoulders. She had to be brave. This was for Miranda, after all, and Miranda would face an army for her.

Her nose was beginning to run from the cold, wet air, and she struggled in her reticule for a handkerchief. Her throat was worse, and she wasn't sure whether she was cold or hot. She only knew she'd probably been an idiot to come out in weather like this when she was clearly coming down with something.

Two uniformed servants came up the side alley that lay next to the earl's townhouse, so busy talking they didn't notice her hasty move back against the wall. "Wish 'e'd give us some warning. Why would 'e want to go off on a night like this, when he's got a nice warm bed at home if he wants to tumble her?"

"Don't let 'im hear you talkin' like that. This ain't one of his society whores, mark my words. If I were you I'd keep me trap shut and do what 'e says."

The other man responded with a cheerful profanity that nevertheless seemed to signify agreement. They moved past the coach to where three other men stood talking amidst themselves. There was a beautiful thoroughbred horse, saddled and ready, and she assumed Lord Rochdale was going to be riding. So who was traveling in the carriage? And where the hell was Miranda?

She straightened her spine, starting for the front door, when it opened, and panic swept over her. The door to the carriage stood open and waiting, the steps were already down, and she didn't stop to think. She simply scrambled inside, crouching down in a far corner and pulling a heavy fur throw over her. With luck no one would notice.

It took her only a moment to realize her instinctive movement was mad. The earl had most assuredly sent Miranda home, and right now was planning on an assignation with his current mistress, who would find a strange young woman hiding in the carriage and Jane's embarrassment would be monumental. She started to push the throw aside when she heard voices, the earl's deep one, warm and caressing. "Try to sleep," he was saying, and Jane felt the coach sway as someone climbed up into it. "You're going to need your rest to keep fighting me."

"I'm not fighting you," came Miranda's calm voice, and Jane almost swooned with relief. "I have no choice."

"Very true, sweetheart," he murmured. "Have a peaceful journey. We won't be making many stops." And she heard the door close, plunging the interior of the carriage into darkness.

Jane didn't move. If she did she might startle Miranda into making a sound, and then they might drag her out of the carriage, and she couldn't allow them to be separated. She held herself very still, barely breathing as she felt the carriage begin to move forward, smoothly with the skill of an experienced driver.

Miranda wasn't making any sound at all, and Jane scrunched down in the corner, trying to decide when to announce her presence. Her body took care of that decision, with a loud, uncontrollable sneeze.

"Who's there?" Miranda demanded, her voice edgy but calm. "Please show yourself. I've had a very difficult day and I'm not in the mood for playing games."

Jane pushed the cover off her head. The interior of the carriage was very dark, but she could see Miranda quite clearly, and the expression on her face terrified her. "Just me," she said brightly, sneezing again, and she climbed onto the seat next to her dearest friend. "So… are we being abducted?"

Miranda didn't know whether to laugh or cry. She did both, hauling Jane into her arms and then giving her a shake. "You idiot. It's bad enough that I made a thorough mess of things. I didn't want to destroy your life, as well."

"We're best friends," Jane said with barely a tremor. "And I haven't noticed that your life has been destroyed."

Miranda shook her head, leaning back against the squabs. "It is now." Jane was doing her best to look fearless and failing, and Miranda realized it was up to her to calm her fears. "What in heaven's name made you come here? You sound like you should be home in bed, not chasing after me. And why did you hide in the carriage?"

"I had every intention of marching right up to the front door and demanding to see you," she said, her voice wobbling slightly. "But at the last minute I panicked and hid in the carriage. You know what a coward I am. As for what made me do it—Brandon. He came home acting like a bear with a sore paw, and I decided it was better to sneak out and see what was keeping you than have him start badgering me."

Miranda thought fast. The last thing she wanted to do was bring Jane into this horrific mess she'd brought upon herself. "We need to get you home before we go much farther," she said, leaning forward to rap on the roof of the coach.

"As long as you come with me."

Miranda shook her head. "I'm afraid not. I'm eloping, dearest, and much as I love you, I really don't want you on my honeymoon." She thought she'd done a creditable job of it, but Jane was giving her a peculiar look.

"Miranda, you've always been my dearest friend, but you've never been a terribly good liar, and it's a waste of time trying that with me. I know you too well. What in the world is going on?"

"I'm in love." She tried not to choke on the vile words.

"Surely that comes as no surprise? I've been obsessed with the man since he first…rescued me after my accident." Her voice sounded strained even to her own ears, and she leaned forward and rapped on the roof again, doing her best to look properly besotted when she was vibrating with anger and pain.

No response, of course. The driver would have orders to ignore her. Miranda sank back against the seat. They were moving swiftly, and in no time they'd be past the limits of town, though in which direction she could only guess.

Jane was looking at her doubtfully. "He said something to you about fighting."

Bloody hell, Miranda thought. At that point she'd lost the ability to judge. She had absolutely no idea how terrible Lucien de Malheur was capable of being. If he'd been willing to risk a stranger's life in a carriage accident, if he would murder her younger brother in cold blood, then there was no guarantee that Jane would be safe anywhere around him.

The safest route was to lie to her, and keep lying. Surely she could manage. "We have a tendency to argue," she said in brisk tones. "It's nothing you need to worry about. I'm hardly likely to be abducted twice in one lifetime. Trust me, I want to be with Lucien. I'm simply worried about you. As soon as we stop to change horses we'll make arrangements for you to travel back to London, none the worse for wear. You shouldn't be out and about when you're sick, dearest Jane. I can't imagine what possessed you to come out after me."

"Can't you?" Jane said, sounding absurdly brave.

Miranda sighed. She should have known she'd drag others down with her. She simply had to make sure Jane was left in good hands before they continued onward. "I love you, too. And Lucien will take care of things when we stop. In the meantime we may as well make the best of it. I expect I won't be visiting London for quite a while, so we need to enjoy our time together."

"But, Miranda, my wedding is only three months away! You were to be my maid of honor—now I suppose my matron of honor. We'll have lots of time then, won't we?" She was looking worried again.

"Assuming you don't run off with your brigand in the meantime," Miranda said in a light, teasing voice.

Jane frowned. "I'm no longer finding the memory quite so delightful. It really was quite shocking of me to enjoy it so, wasn't it?"

"Quite shocking. And perfectly understandable. Don't worry, love. Mr. Bothwell never need find out anything about it. You'll be counting yourself lucky to have made such a close escape."

Jane's small, cold hand slipped into Miranda's. "Are you certain you know what you're doing, Miranda?"

"Quite," she said firmly, squeezing her hand reassuringly. Perhaps practice made perfect in the art of lying.

At least the earl made certain his hostages traveled in style. The coach was magnificent—well sprung, with warm bricks, several magnificent throws, pillows, a basket of food and wine. Poor Jane was feeling more and more miserable, and Miranda would have soon eaten snakes than touched anything provided by her host, so they simply curled up together under the shared blankets and talked, not about the present or the future, but about the past and the happiness of shared childhoods and doting parents. Jane drifted off to sleep first, and slowly, slowly Miranda forced herself to release her fury enough to get some rest herself.

She awoke with a start, a bright light momentarily blinding her, and she realized the coach had come to a stop and someone was standing in the open door of the carriage.

"What have we here?" Lucien's voice was silken. "Did we pick up an uninvited passenger along the way?"

Miranda could feel the fear that swept through her friend, and she put a protective arm around her. "Lord Rochdale, I believe you are acquainted with my dear friend Jane, are you not?"

"Indeed," he said gravely, though she could sense the damnable amusement in his voice. "Though I scarcely expected to renew my acquaintance under these circumstances. I've bespoken a room and a meal while we change horses—why don't we continue this conversation by the fire?" He held out a hand to her, and there was a mocking light in his eyes.

To continue any hope of keeping Jane ignorant of the true basis of this marriage, she had no choice but to accept his hand, letting him lift her down onto the ground, bypassing the steps entirely. For a moment she swayed, automatically reaching for Lucien, and then she drew her hand back swiftly, using the carriage for momentary support rather than willingly touch him again.

Unfortunately he was already seeing to Jane, and couldn't appreciate her cold reaction. And then she stopped thinking about him entirely when she saw the pinched, miserable expression on Jane's piquant face, and her anger toward the man flared up once more.

He didn't relinquish Jane's arm, and in truth it didn't look as if she would have made the trip across the cobbled stable yard without his support. He didn't look back at Miranda, leaving her to follow in their wake, and at least then some of her anger dissipated. Jane must be taken care of first. Once she was dealt with there would be time enough to figure a way out of this mess.

Because there had to be a way out. If he thought she would simply acquiesce then he had very little notion of who she really was. The first thing she had to do was forestall the wedding. A stomach complaint would do to begin with, and then anything else she could come up with. As long as Jane was safe.

The inn was small but neat, and she followed the two of them into the private dining room, glancing about her curiously as Lucien settled Jane into a chair by the fire. He glanced back at Miranda. "I imagine you both will wish to refresh yourself before we eat, but I'm afraid my curiosity will not withstand another minute. Why are you here, Miss Paget?"

"She didn't realize we were eloping," Miranda spoke up. "She was concerned about my reputation and thought to accompany me."

He had an ironic expression on his face. "Alas, I'm afraid I prefer my honeymoons à deux."

"I'm certain you do. For some untoward reason the driver ignored my attempts to gain his attention. We will simply have to turn around and go back to London at once."

"Will *we?*" Why had she ever thought his smile to be charming? It didn't meet his cool, pale eyes.

"Jane," Miranda said in a firm voice. "Why don't you go upstairs and lie down for a bit while I have a conversation with my...affianced husband?"

"Oh, dear," Lucien said with a note of laughter in his voice. "Are we about to have our first quarrel, love? By all means, Miss Pagett, go and make yourself comfortable while Miranda and I come to blows."

Jane didn't move, bravely stubborn for the first time in her life. "I don't think..."

"Go ahead, Jane," Miranda said firmly. "Leave this to me."

He waited until Jane had left the room, then sank down gracefully on the recently abandoned chair. Miranda stood by the fire, rigid with fury and fear, but he simply nested his fingers and prepared to give her his full attention. "You can't do this," she said.

"Don't be tiresome. I can do anything I please. Indeed, it's a shame your friends are equally as headstrong as you are, but that is scarcely my concern."

"She's not headstrong at all, she's very timid and right now she's terrified. You need to send her back home. It's one thing to run off with me. My reputation is already in shreds, and you have some misguided reason for taking out your anger on me. So be it. Jane is an innocent, and her family will hardly let you get away with this."

"I hesitate to correct you, but you are wrong on several counts. One, I have no anger toward you. You're simply a means to an end, and a quite delicious one. As for Miss Pagett, I will have a doctor see her before we continue on our journey, to set your mind at ease, and then I will have her write a letter to her family telling them she chose to accompany you on your bride trip."

"My family won't believe it."

"I don't expect them to. But they're unlikely to frighten Miss Paget's family. Now why don't you come over here and sit?"

"I'm not coming anywhere near you."

He shouldn't have been able to move that swiftly. She didn't even see his cane anywhere near him. At one moment she was stiff and defiant, in the next he'd crossed the room, scooped her up and carried her back to the chair, sinking down with her imprisoned in his arms.

Without thinking she fought back, and he tightened his grip, painfully, so that her struggles abated and she held very still. "That's better. . . . Once you cease fighting I think you'll realize we'll do quite well together."

"Once I cease fighting you'll lose interest in me."

He laughed. "That is always a possibility. In which case, why keep fighting me? Or do you want me to lust after you?"

In a day full of shocks he'd somehow managed to shock her further. The thought that he might actually desire her was so bizarre that it had never occurred to her. She jerked her head to look at him, startled, and he laughed at her astonishment. "Why in the world does that surprise you, my pet? I would hardly decide to marry you if I didn't want you. There are any number of ways this particular game could play out. I happen to prefer it in my bed."

She managed to recover from her shock. "God knows why," she said. "I'm no great beauty, I'm no longer innocent and I have it on the word of an accomplished rake that my skills in the bedchamber are lacking."

"Now you're fishing for compliments." His grip had loosened, marginally, and she wondered if she could take him off guard, as she had Christopher St. John, so long ago. But then, she could hardly run. For one thing, Jane was upstairs, and she couldn't leave her behind. For another, she had not the faintest idea where they were, how far from London they'd traveled. Until she discovered that much any escape plan would be a waste of time. "I'm not particularly concerned about your skill in bed," he continued. "I have more than enough for both of us. To make up for my appearance I'm quite adept at performance, and you'll get the way of it before long."

"Now who is fishing for compliments?" she shot back.

She'd managed to surprise him. "Don't be ridiculous. You're a very pretty child, if not perhaps a flamboyant beauty, whereas I'm an ugly brute with a soul to match."

"Don't be ridiculous," she mocked him. "Your soul may be the epitome of putrescent decay, but apart from minor scarring you know perfectly well that you are quite decadently appealing."

His pale eyes widened, and then he exploded in laughter. "I don't know which enchants me more, putrescent decay or decadently appealing. You can't decide whether to insult me or flatter me into releasing you. In honor of your fighting spirit I'll make a wager, my pet. I'll offer you a chance of escape."

He meant it. She held her breath. "Anything you choose."

"It's quite simple. We have yet to seal this devil's

bargain with a kiss. If you can let me kiss you and not respond in any way then I'll send you home with your friend, leave your brothers in peace and do my best to ruin your family *financially*. That will require more effort, but I'm more than capable of succeeding. What do you say to that?"

The tight knot of fear that had lodged beneath her breastbone loosened at his light words. "That's too easy. I'm not certain I trust you to keep your word."

"Again, more insults," he said with a sigh. "I swear on my sister's soul that if you do not kiss me back I will release you. Immediately."

At that she believed him. "Yes," she said immediately, her eyes glowing. "Oh, most definitely yes. Though I fail to see why you're giving up so easily."

"I'm not giving up. I'm winning." Tucking one long finger beneath her stubborn chin, he drew her face up to his. She looked into his pale eyes and felt the first trickle of misgivings. This was impossible, wasn't it? He ran his thumb across her lips, pulling them apart. And then he settled his mouth against hers.

10

This was going to be so easy, Miranda thought, the moment his mouth touched hers. She'd never been fond of kissing, at least, not when it didn't involve young babies or family members, and this was a wager she was preordained to win. She'd gone from defeat to certain victory, and she held very still, waiting for him to be done with it.

She expected brutality. She expected force. She didn't expect the featherlight brush of his mouth against hers, a whisper of a touch. His hand cupped her chin, holding her loosely, knowing she wouldn't, couldn't pull away, and he moved his mouth to the side of her cheek, his warm breath in her ear, down the line of her jaw, and she squirmed.

And realized she was sitting on his lap, his arms around her, and she was no longer a virgin. She knew exactly what was beneath her bum, hard and growing harder, and she told herself it was one more reminder of how little she liked any of this. But his mouth tickled her eyelids, closing them, and she felt an odd little shiver dance down her spine, and she squirmed again. And he grew harder.

He moved his other hand up to the back of her neck, his fingers playing gently with her hair as it was coming loose, barely grazing the skin. His mouth brushed her temple, then moved down the other side of her face. He brought his other hand down to cradle her throat, stroking gently, and he pressed his mouth against her pulse, which for some strange reason was pounding.

"I thought you were just going to kiss me," she said in a tight voice.

"Hush," he whispered against her skin. "I'm taking my time. You're not an easy conquest."

She was tempted to bite him, but she resisted. "I'm not a conquest at all—" she started to say, but he covered her lips with his long fingers, silencing her.

"If you're impervious then you can be patient." He slid his hand down to the high neckline of her dress, and she felt a button pop open. And then another. She preferred dresses she could get herself in and out of—she hated being at the mercy of a lady's maid, but he was having far too easy a time unfastening the top of her dress.

"I don't . . ." He silenced her by covering her mouth again, and his lips were soft, damp, brushing against hers, and if he were any other man she thought she might even enjoy it. He hadn't lied. He knew how to kiss, a great deal better than Christopher St. John, and she could feel an uncomfortable warmth between her legs. She tried to harden her mouth, but he caught her chin again. "That's cheating," he admonished her.

She wondered if he'd use his tongue. That would guarantee her disgust, she told herself. No one had ever kissed her that way. Jane had insisted it was wonderful, but Miranda took leave to doubt it. Nothing this man did to her would bring her pleasure.

Not when his hand pushed open the front of her dress, baring her skin, the tops of her breasts to the warmth of the fire, the warmth of his hand. Not when he slid his fingers inside her chemise, cupping her small, bare breast, but when she felt her nipple harden against them, felt that unfamiliar heat build, she tried to move.

"I really don't think you should do that, my dove. I failed to bring my valet, and I must confess I'm at about the limit of my self-control. I would certainly hate to embarrass myself before I claimed victory, and I don't have many changes of clothes."

It took her a moment to realize what he was talking about, and she froze. "Kiss me and get it over with," she said, ignoring the fact that she wanted to press down against him, she wanted to slide her fingers through his long, dark hair.

"Then open your mouth for me, darling."

His tongue was a shock, its intimacy astonishing considering he was pressing her bare breast against his fingers. She held utterly still as he tasted her, with deep, sensuous thrusts that should have reminded her of the unpleasantness of mating but instead only turned the heat to dampness, and her other breast pebbled against the cloth, wanting his hand, wanting his mouth, as he kissed her with such slow, deep deliberation that she closed her eyes and let her head sink back against the support of his long, stroking fingers.

Jane was right. The touch of a man's tongue was intimate and arousing, and she had never known this. She didn't want to think anymore—her body was on fire, and she wanted more of this decadent sweetness. She couldn't have it, she told herself dazedly. If she was to win this battle she needed to stay cold, reserved, but how could she do that when she was burning from the inside out?

She wasn't even aware of raising her arms to slide them around his neck, to cradle his head as her tongue reached out for his. And she was lost.

He put his hands on her legs, lifted her and swung her around so that she was astride him, her skirts up high around her thighs, and he was pressing her against his erection, pressing that damp, aching part of her against the hardness that she despised, and she made a soft, moaning sound as he rubbed against her. His hand slid down beneath her skirts, touching her, and this time she tried to pull away, but his arm held her fast, and in truth she didn't want to escape. She wanted his hand on her dampness, his long fingers parting the secret folds of her body, and when his thumb brushed against her she jerked as a rush of pleasure washed through her, and for once in her life she wanted more.

He stopped.

They stared at each other for a long, frozen moment, and then he pulled his hand away, swung her back around and settled her skirts down around her legs, as if nothing had happened. His eyes were narrow slits in the candlelit room, and she could feel his heart pounding against her, his breath slightly labored.

"I won," he said plainly. "You're wet. Even in this heated room your nipples are hard. And you kissed me back."

She pulled out of his arms, stumbling across the room and collapsing in a chair. She was shocked that her shaking legs had carried her that far. "You're disgusting. And I didn't kiss you back."

"Your tongue was in my mouth, precious." He sounded bored. He reached down and adjusted himself, drawing her eyes to the part she didn't want to think about. "No one forced you to do that. You were aroused, and in another minute I would have had you in that chair. I do promise to make up for it eventually—we have any number of excellent chairs in my house upon which to experiment."

She couldn't find the words. She'd wagered and lost, though she couldn't quite believe it. In truth, her skin still longed for his touch, her mouth for his kiss. Perhaps he'd drugged her. Perhaps she'd gone mad. It didn't matter: she had lost.

She realized then that her dress was gaping open, and she swiftly began to button it again. "It is a great deal unfortunate that I didn't wear something a bit more difficult for you to deal with," she said in what she hoped was an icy voice. She couldn't ignore the raw undertone to it.

"My precious, I could get you out of full court dress in seconds flat if I so desired," he said, pouring himself a glass of wine. It was as if those hot, fevered moments in the chair hadn't existed. If she hadn't felt the evidence of his arousal she would have thought this was all a game to him. "But I think we'll wait to consummate our grand passion until we're legally wed. In the meantime we still have the problem of your friend. And I must confess I've never found threesomes to be particularly satisfying. I do a much better job concentrating on one woman at a time."

How did he still manage to shock her? she wondered.

"She's sick. Send her back home with an escort," she said, then paused. "Do that much for me."

"But, darling Miranda, have I ever expressed any desire to do anything for you?" he said mildly.

"It would make life easier for you."

"And have I ever expressed an interest in doing things the easy way? If I preferred simple efficiency I would have killed your brother Benedick the moment I arrived in England. He was lucky I was in the tropics when my sister died—it gave me time for my initial rage to pass and for me to come up with a plan."

She stared at him, hating him, hating the fact that her breasts still tingled and she wanted to rub them against him. She kept her hands fisted in her lap. "I made a very great mistake with Christopher St. John," she said. "I didn't fight him. I knew he was going to bed me and there was no way I could stop him, so I didn't struggle. Not until later, when I couldn't stand it anymore. That's not going to happen this time. I won't lie down for you, and I won't let you rape me."

"Haven't I just demonstrated that it won't be rape?" He almost purred the words. "Don't worry, your nonvirginal body is safe from me for the time being. When I take you the first time I intend to do a proper job of it. You've only had a taste of what I can do."

She wanted to cry. He'd taken unfair advantage— he knew far more about women's bodies than she did, even though she lived in one. He knew how to touch and where, how to kiss, how to arouse, when she had been so certain she'd be impervious.

She pulled together what little dignity she had left.

"Are we continuing our journey tonight?"

"We are. I will be joining you and Miss Pagett in the

carriage. My leg is beginning to pain me, and I prefer to begin my wedded life in good health. Don't worry, precious. I won't tell Miss Pagett that I almost made you climax."

Nearly anything could be used as a weapon. But there was nothing around for her.

He rose, and she realized he'd left his walking stick behind. He favored one leg, but he still managed to move with a sinuous grace that belied his usual appearance.

"Just how bad is your leg? You're scarcely as crippled as you pretend."

"You'll find, my sweet, that little about me is as it appears. I broke my leg when I was younger and it was set badly. I don't let it trouble me."

"Then why don't you continue the journey on horseback?"

"Because I don't wish to," he said in the softest, sweetest voice. "Accept it, Miranda. You lost the wager, and you're wasting time fighting me."

"It's not in my nature to give up."

He had come even with her, and he paused, looking down at her. "And that's why you're so irresistible," he said.

Lucien walked out into the cool night air, breathing deeply. It was astonishing how much Miranda Rohan aroused him. His hands were shaking with the need to touch her, and controlling himself a few minutes ago had required more strength than he knew he had.

He should have just taken her. She was no shy virgin—he could thank Christopher St. John for his bungled part in that. She had rubbed against him, instinctively, helplessly, as he kissed her, and she was wet with longing. It would have taken a moment to release himself, and he could have plunged up into her, burying himself in her welcoming heat, holding her hips as he bucked and fucked and lost himself.

Bloody hell, he had to stop thinking about it. He couldn't walk around with a perpetual hard-on. And yet, there was something wickedly enjoyable about being physically aroused and anticipating Miranda's eventual surrender. Tonight had been a delicious taste of it.

There was an old saying: revenge is a dish that is best served cold. Who would have thought his revenge would be so deliciously hot and yielding?

Jane Pagett was a complication, but one he could deal with. Right now he was bone tired and ready to sleep in his expensive carriage. It was a long way to go, up into the Lake District to his secluded home by Ripton Waters, but once they reached it he could count on time to complete the coup de grace of this particular revenge. For now, he was ready to rest.

Miranda climbed back into the carriage, stifling her instinctive moan. No matter how comfortable a carriage, how gifted and smooth a driver, being cramped up in a small space for so long made her bones ache. Jane was already curled up in one corner, her sweet face creased with misery, her nose and eyes red. She'd finally realized just what a mess she was in, and there was nothing Miranda could do to reassure her. She took her hand and squeezed it as she took the seat beside her, and Jane managed a weak smile in return. Until the carriage dipped slightly and Lucien climbed in, taking the seat opposite them and stretching out his long legs with a sigh.

The door was closed, plunging them into darkness, and a moment later they were moving once more.

"Miranda, my love," his voice came through the darkness like a seductive snake. "Come join me and give your dear friend more room."

"I'm quite fine where I am."

"But I'm not." With luck Jane wouldn't recognize the hint of steel in his voice. She wanted to continue the charade that this was a voluntary elopement for as long as possible, and refusing would be to call his bluff.

With an audible sigh she rose, just as the carriage hit a stone, tossing her against Lucien. He caught her easily, and even in the darkness she could see a glint of his smile. "That's one of the many things I love about you, my darling. Your reluctance and your enthusiasm." He settled her onto the seat next to him, his arm around her shoulder, clamping her body against his, his heat pouring through her. "That's right," he whispered in her ear. And then, to her shock, he bit it, not hard, catching the lobe between his teeth lightly, and she jerked in reaction.

"Thank God Jane couldn't see what he'd done. "Miss Pagett, are you comfortable?" he asked, all solicitude, as he pulled the capacious fur throw over them.

"Yes, thank you," Jane said sleepily. Jane was looking decidedly unwell, and Miranda had the uncharitable wish that Jane's stomach would erupt, as well. Please, Jane, cast up your accounts all over his elegant Hessian boots.

Jane sniffled, coughing a little, but the ride was smooth enough to keep nausea at bay. She would be asleep in moments, Miranda thought, and that was all for the best.

Perhaps she could induce nausea on her own. She could think back to Christopher's hands on her, the ugliness of his member, the pain of his penetration, the sheer awfulness of lying beneath his naked, hairy, sweating body as he pumped away at her.

But unbidden came the memory of Lucien's erection, planted at the juncture of her thighs, and even through the layers of clothes he seemed substantially bigger than her erstwhile lover. Christopher had hurt her—Lucien would tear her apart. What in God's name was she going to do?

"Stop twitching," he murmured sleepily in the ear he'd just nipped. "We've got a long way to go, and I, for one, would like to pass some of it in sleep."

"What about Jane?" she fretted.

"She's already asleep, and it's clearly nothing more than a slight cold. I've sent word to her family that she's accompanying you on a visit to a dear friend and will return in a few days. It should set their minds at ease, at least for a time."

"They'll be terrified. Jane and I always had the capacity for getting into trouble."

"Then when the truth comes out they won't be that surprised." He pressed her head against his shoulder, and while she wanted to pull away she knew he'd simply force her, and in truth it settled there quite comfortably. "Go to sleep, my angel. It will give you strength to fight me in the morning."

And with that sage advice, she did.

11

She dreamed, of course. Curled up beside her enemy, she dreamed of Christopher St. John, his handsome face with its weak chin and his ugly hands. He was chasing her through a forest, and she was naked, nothing but her hip-length hair as covering. And as she ran she tried to pick leaves to hide her nakedness, but they fell off, and she kept running, toward some mysterious safety in the distance. She could feel Christopher gaining on her, smell the ugly sweat-smell of his body, and she knew his thick hands were reaching out for her, catching her hair with a painful yank, and then suddenly she was free, hurtling forward against safety, a warm body with arms that enclosed her. He smelled of leather and spices and warm male skin that was a far cry from Christopher's foul odor, and she looked up with love into Lucien's scarred face.

Her eyes flew open in shock, wide-awake. He was asleep beside her, thankfully unaware of her insane dreams, and his arm was loose around her. She tried to edge away, certain he slept on, but his short, sharp "don't" disabused her of that notion.

"I need to stretch," she whispered. "And I want to check on Jane."

He moved his arm then, releasing her, but she had no illusions that it would be more than a brief respite.

Her eyes had grown accustomed to the darkness, and Jane was curled up on the opposite seat, a lump in the shadows. She reached over and touched her forehead, careful not to wake her. It was blessedly cool—she had no fever, despite her sniffles.

She glanced instinctively toward the door. She couldn't leave Jane, and they were traveling too fast for her to attempt a leap to freedom. She sat back on the seat, reluctantly accepting her fate. For now.

"Why do you think I brought your friend along and didn't send her straight back to town?" Lucien said in a soft voice that wouldn't disturb Jane. "You can hardly try to escape as long as she's with me. Indeed, I'm aware of the closeness of your two families. If you ran off and left her with me I suppose I could make do with her. It might serve as an adequate revenge."

"If you touch her I'll cut off your hands," Miranda said fiercely.

He laughed. "In truth, it's you I want to touch, my precious. I'm simply a practical man who'll make do what I have to in order to attain my ends. You have no idea just how ruthless I can be. I suggest you don't force me to show you."

He wouldn't be able to see the hatred on her face. Which was just as well. What did they say—revenge is a dish best served cold? If she let the heat of her rage take hold she'd be helpless. She needed to be cool and calculating if there was any chance of besting him.

No, she thought. Besting the Scorpion was unlikely.

Holding her own, refusing to let him win, was a more reasonable goal.

Why had she dreamed of him as safety? Safety from Christopher St. John? What madness was that? Lucien's kiss, his hands on her body, had brought back all sorts of memories of Christopher's assault on her body, all of them unpleasant. She had survived that, and survived it well, left with nothing but an aversion to that intimate act between men and women, that thing she didn't even like to name.

So why had Lucien won? Why had she twined her arms around his neck and kissed him back? Why had her body, that most intimate part betrayed her to his knowing hands?

He was even more devious than she'd given him credit for. He was no scorpion; he was a snake, a lying, treacherous…

"And what lovely thoughts are you thinking, my darling?" he murmured softly, pulling her back against him, where she settled easily enough. Damnably easy. "Looking forward to your wedding night?"

She let him feel her instinctive shudder, but he simply laughed. "I was thinking you were more a snake in the grass than a scorpion."

"Then you know little of scorpions, my precious. Scorpions are deceptively lethal. They avoid sunlight, and they poison their prey before the victims realize what's going on."

"So why are you called the Scorpion? Are you a poisoner?"

"Oh, there's little I won't do if the need arises. But in fact the name came from the pet scorpion I brought with me from Jamaica when I finally returned to England.

I brought it as a pet, and my traveling companion took to calling me Scorpion as a term of affection."

"A female, no doubt."

"The scorpion? Yes. The traveling companion was not. He was a friend."

"And where is your deadly little pet? Are you planning to unleash it on me?"

"I'm afraid Desdemona died. I was staying at an inn outside of Paris and she got loose. The landlord panicked and stomped her to death." His voice was cool and detached, but Miranda wasn't fooled.

"And what happened to the landlord?"

"He met with a fatal accident. On my sword."

She shivered. Again, he could doubtless feel her reaction, but he said nothing. He enjoyed thinking he'd cowed her, she realized. That was his goal—to shatter and destroy her, not physically, but in every other way. A suitable revenge for the sister that Miranda knew nothing about.

And with sudden blazing insight she realized her one defense. She could weep and cower and moan, and ensure his victory.

Or she could embrace the adventure. She had taken social ostracism and made it a joyous life. She had reacted to abduction with calm fortitude. She was sadly lacking in the frail sensibilities most young women were prone to. She was practical, adaptable, and not one to waste too much time bemoaning her fate.

She glanced over at Jane. So he'd brought her along to keep her in line. She could think of one way to handle that. "In truth," she said in a conversational voice, "I'm glad you brought Jane along, particularly if she's not truly unwell. Her companionship makes things much more bearable."

She felt him stiffen, and she almost wanted to giggle. "That's hardly a charitable way of looking at things," he said. "Don't you think she's frightened? Worried about what her parents would think?"

"As long as she's with me she'll be fine, and her parents have complete faith in my ability to keep her safe. We've gotten into a number of scrapes in the past and I've always looked out for her." She smiled in the darkness, enjoying his discomfiture. "I'll keep her safe this time, and thoroughly enjoy her company. It was indeed very kind of you to keep her with us."

"I didn't do it as a kindness," he snapped, then took a deep breath, regaining his self-control. "Though of course I rejoice in my ability to bring you pleasure." There was silence for a moment, and Miranda held her breath, waiting to see if her ploy worked.

She felt his body relax. Strange, that she had grown so accustomed to his body so quickly, that she could read his reactions. "But I'm afraid that Miss Pagett won't be continuing our journey. I've made arrangements for someone to escort her back to London. She'll be leaving us at...ah, but I think you're better off not knowing where we're going. I wouldn't want to ruin the surprise."

Miranda let her shoulders slump in a good show of defeat as she grinned into the darkness. She'd done it! Her first ploy had worked, and Jane would be returned, safe.

And then all she had to worry about was herself. And she knew exactly how she was going to do it.

She snuggled against him, pressing her face against

the superfine of his coat. In fact, he did smell good. Leather and wool and spice and warm male skin. The battle was on. And she was not without weapons after all.

The sky was growing lighter when they stopped to change horses again, and Miranda peered out the window, trying to gauge where they were. The posting house gave no clue—how many Cock and Swallow taverns would there be scattered around England? The landscape was no help at all, either. They were in the countryside, and through the early morning mist she thought she could see mountains, but that was useless, as well. The Pennines ran up the center of England; their carriage could be on either side of them. She tried to see if she could smell the salt tang of the ocean, but there was nothing in the air but the earthy smell of early spring.

Jane had emerged from her fog and was looking about her with vague alarm. "Do you have the faintest idea where we are?" she asked nervously. "My parents are going to explode."

"Lord Rochdale sent a note to your parents. They'll be appeased at least for a while, and then you'll be back home, safe and sound. They may scold, of course, but you know your parents could never be too harsh."

Jane smiled ruefully. "But what are they going to say when they see this?" She'd pulled off her glove, and the extravagant diamond glowed even in the dim carriage light.

"You still can't get it off?"

Jane tugged at it, but it stayed where it was, as if glued. "I was hoping a day without eating would make a difference but it seems to be there for good." She glanced at her right hand, where Bothwell's pitiful ring resided. "I suppose I could cut off my finger."

"Don't even joke about such things. Do you think Bothwell is worthy of self-mutilation?"

Jane's face suddenly lightened, and she looked like her old self, something Miranda hadn't seen in months.

"I don't think he's worthy of one finger, much less my entire hand in marriage."

"Much less your entire body," Miranda added. "Good. I'm glad that's settled. I was afraid I was going to have to abduct you so you wouldn't marry such a prosing old bore."

"He's not that much older than we are," Jane pointed out fairly.

"He's old. And Brandon would have helped me carry you off. He calls him Bore-well."

"And instead the Scorpion is the one to carry both of us off," Jane sighed. "He's an odd man, isn't he? If I weren't certain he was besotted with you I'd worry."

Besotted, Miranda thought. She was a means to an end and nothing more. She smiled, hoping she could continue to trick her friend. "He's promised to have people waiting to escort you back to London, though he refuses to say when. We probably won't have much warning, but I wanted to assure you how happy I am." The lying words were like bile on her tongue, but she forced a serene smile on her face, and to her relief Jane appeared to believe it.

"It's all right to be nervous, Miranda," she said, mis-reading the edge in her voice. "You like to pretend you know everything about…about sex and men, but really, you only have experience of an absolute rotter. I just thank God St. John is not accepted in good company anymore. I don't know what I would have done if I'd been forced to face him."

"At least he's had to go to ground," Miranda said, happy to talk about anything but Lucien.

"And no one could be further from Christopher St. John than your future husband," Jane said, absently toying with the diamond ring. "I suspect you'll be very happy."

"A match made in heaven, in fact."

Jane laughed. "Well, hardly. You forget—I know you too well. I imagine you'll have your battles. But I think you will...."

The door opened, and Lucien stood there, blocking the early morning light. "Miss Paget," he said in his smooth, charming, scorpion-voice, "this is where we part ways."

"Already?" Miranda couldn't keep the initial squeak of pain from her voice, and she was rewarded with Lucien's damnable smile.

"I'm afraid so. We have an oh-so-respectable dame to keep her company, one of my light traveling coaches with my second-best driver, and he's an excellent shot, as well. He'll keep her safe and sound until he returns her home. Come along, Miss Paget. You'll...." His words trailed off as his gaze fell on her ungloved hand. "That's quite a lovely ring you have, Miss Paget. Your affianced husband must be quite besotted with you."

Jane turned bright pink as she tried to hide her hand in her skirts, but he was reaching out for her, to let her down, and she had no choice but to put her hands in his.

And Miranda knew a moment, a merest flash, of irrational jealousy. She started after them, but Lucien closed the door. "You'll be staying in the coach, my darling."

"I can't," she said flatly. There were a thousand things she hadn't said to Jane, warnings, messages…

"You can."

"I have to use the necessary." She didn't even blush. She would use anything as a weapon against him, and he could hardly argue. They'd been riding a long time.

"I'll have one of the chambermaids bring you a pot, my love. You'll stay put."

She wanted to snarl at him. Instead she leaned out the window and called to Jane. "Tell my parents I love them. And tell them I'm blissfully happy."

"Blissfully?" Lucien echoed with a soft laugh. "I'm honored."

She glanced at him, and he couldn't see her hands curled into fists in her lap. "Blissfully, my love," she said firmly. And sat back, rather than burst into tears at Jane's retreating back.

Jane sat in the private parlor of the coaching inn, drinking her tea. She was uneasy, though she wasn't quite sure why. She had complete faith that the coach and chaperone the earl had summoned would be there momentarily—she couldn't imagine anyone daring to do less than Rochdale demanded. She was going home, which was a good, thing, wasn't it? With luck she'd be back before Mr. Bothwell even noticed she had gone.

Not that she particularly cared. She just hoped she had the courage to break off the engagement that was now looking like a living death.

Back in her ordinary world, though, it would probably seem like the wise thing to do. Marry the man, and she'd have her own house and children. Surely she could tolerate him for that much.

She'd rather concentrate on Miranda and her husband-to-be. Something was wrong, Jane thought, though she couldn't put her finger on it. She had no doubt at all that Miranda was in love with Lucien de Malheur, but there was something in the way of it, and she couldn't imagine what. As for the earl, he was harder to read. If it weren't for the way his strange, pale eyes followed Miranda wherever she was, she might have refused to leave.

And fat lot that would have done, she thought, staring into the fire as she awaited her own carriage. Lucien de Malheur didn't strike her as the kind of man who accepted refusal any more than Miranda was the kind who meekly did as she was bid. They would have a fiery marriage. Full of adventure, Jane thought dismally. She had Mr. Bothwell.

She availed herself of her crumpled handkerchief, dabbing her eyes and her nose. It and she were in fairly bedraggled condition by now, and the thought of climbing into another carriage was her personal idea of hell. She loved to travel, but she definitely preferred a more leisurely pace, and this time she'd simply be heading back home. She had watched as the earl's carriage pulled away, and slow tears began to slide down her cheeks. When next she saw Miranda she'd be a married woman, while Jane had little doubt that Mr. Bothwell would take one look at the huge diamond on her finger and promptly renounce her. Perhaps she'd be ruined. Miranda's house on Half Moon Street would be vacant—she could take up residence there and become eccentric.

Or so she could only hope. In truth, she wasn't sure

she wanted to get the diamond off her hand. Once she did so, and disposed of it, then Mr. Bothwell would have every right to kiss her with his hard, dry mouth. He could continue to criticize her dress and her behavior, and even if he gave her children he would doubtless be the kind of man with strong opinions on child-rearing, ones that were ridiculous and the opposite of her own.

Two extremes stood before her: the life of an outcast or the life of Mrs. George Bothwell. It was little wonder the diamond wouldn't come off.

She brought her handkerchief up to her eyes again, not sure if she was crying for herself or for Miranda as she disappeared on her strange bride trip. All she knew was that she hurt, inside, and her tears, instead of abating, were flowing more freely, and her disgusting handkerchief was useless against the flow....

A snowy-white handkerchief appeared in her blurred vision, and she took it gratefully, wiping her streaming eyes and blowing her nose before looking up at her savior. And for a moment she froze.

It was one of the earl's servants—she could recognize the deep black livery. Though, he was quite tall for someone who worked with horses. Most people preferred their grooms to be small but strong, keeping the burden on the horses light. This man must weigh fourteen stone at the least.

Before he could say anything he stepped back into the shadows, replaced by the plump, cozy figure of a woman dressed in neat black clothes with a dark blue shawl around her shoulders. "Miss Pagett, I'm Mrs. Grudge. The Earl of Rochdale has hired me to escort you home. I promise Jacobs and I will take good care of you while we're on the road."

Jane wanted to crane her head around, to look at the man who'd given her the handkerchief, but he was gone, and she tried to school her reaction. "Who was that?" she found herself asking, when she should have been much more polite.

But Mrs. Grudge clearly didn't live up to her unfriendly name. She smiled at her. "That? Oh, that's Jacobs, our driver. He's one of the grooms. Quite the likely lad, isn't he? All the servant girls are mad for him, of course. I believe he's married to Cook's daughter, but that doesn't keep him from looking about, if you know what I mean."

"Yes," Jane said in a hollow voice, thoroughly appalled. What was wrong with her? She'd barely had a glance at him and yet she'd felt this instinctive leap inside her, an odd sense of recognition. As if she'd recognize some womanizing servant of a man like the Scorpion.

"We only just arrived, miss," the older lady continued, "and the horses need a rest. I've ordered you a good breakfast. I gather you've been sick, and I promise you we'll take our time getting back."

"We're not that far from London, are we? I think I would prefer to return as soon as possible."

"Bless you, miss, we're up near the Lake District, a good two and a half days away from London."

"We've only been gone overnight!" she protested.

"His lordship travels very fast, with the best horses. We'll be needing to be a bit more careful. But not to worry, miss. Jacobs took your note to your parents himself and they were unalarmed. You needn't fret if it takes us a few days to get back."

And if she didn't eat anything for those days the ring

was bound to come off. That was what she wanted, wasn't it?

No, it wasn't. She wanted rashers of bacon and coddled eggs and toast and butter, she wanted thick cream and strawberry jam, she wanted hot chocolate and biscuits to nibble on.

And she wasn't in the mood to face her fiancé, who doubtless would be less likely to accept her absence than her indulgent parents. Her parents knew their daughter and trusted her intelligence. Mr. Bothwell seemed to think she had only half a brain and needed to be led around like a prize calf, lest she get lost.

She yanked at the ring again, but her knuckle was getting red and swollen, so she let it be.

"Oh, what a pretty ring! May I see it?"

It was a surprisingly impertinent question from little more than a servant, but Jane would have been more than happy to have given her the damned thing. "It won't come off. I don't suppose you have any remedy for that, do you?"

"Duck grease!" the woman said triumphantly. "I'll go ask the kitchen…"

"Tried it," Jane said flatly. "Also soap, butter, hot compresses, cold compresses, yanking, pulling. It won't come off."

There was a speculative expression in Mrs. Grudge's eyes. "We'll see about that, miss. In the meantime, what can I get you for breakfast? The cook's just made up a fresh batch of muffins, and there's the usual—bacon and eggs, beefsteak and fried sausage and tripe."

"Just dry toast and tea, thank you," she said, ignoring the lovely smells wafting from what was probably the taproom.

"That's not enough to keep a mouse alive!"

"I'll be fine. Please see to it, Mrs. Grudge." She could feel the tears welling up again, and she dabbed the wicked groom's handkerchief to her eyes.

It wasn't until Mrs. Grudge had left that she stopped to look at the cloth in her hand. It was of a finer weave than a servant usually carried, and she expected to see Lucien's initials in one corner. Instead the man had his own initials there—J.D. Except that his last name was Jacobs. He must have stolen it from someone.

What a bold, wicked man, she thought dismally. Why had she suddenly become attracted to the saucy, totally inappropriate ones? Like the jewel thief who'd effectively married her with this damned ring. And now the cook's womanizing son-in-law.

She shook her head. The sooner she was back home, the ring safely stowed, or tossed, or whatever seemed the best fate for something of such intrinsic value and inestimable trouble, the better she'd be. Mr. Bothwell was a good man, and she was lucky to have attracted him. Maybe he reserved real kisses for the marriage bed, and he would put all thought of jewel thieves out of her wayward mind.

She could only hope.

12

When Miranda awoke it was bright daylight and she was blessedly alone. Lucien hadn't rejoined the carriage after the last change. They had driven on into what appeared to be a dark, mountainous landscape, and she racked her brain, trying to remember what she knew of England's geography. They hadn't traveled far enough to reach Scotland, but these might be the fells of Yorkshire, or the brooding mountains of Northern Wales. She knew for certain they'd headed north; to the south there was only the sea. She wished she could reason how far they'd traveled, but Lucien's coach moved so smoothly, so swiftly, that she really had no idea.

The sun was out only fitfully, peeping from behind dark, ominous clouds. The Scorpion had ordered the weather to fit with his evil plans. And the question was, exactly how evil was this man? What was he capable of?

He'd forced her to come with him. Brandon had warned her he was capable of evil things, and she hadn't believed him. He'd threatened to kill her brother in cold blood, and she had no choice but to believe him. She couldn't risk Brandon's life on the chance that Lucien was merely bluffing. And in truth, she didn't think he was. He was determined to gain revenge for his sister's death, of that there was no doubt.

But what was he planning for her? Not rape, not murder, not a vicious beating. His brutal plan was to marry her. Hardly the stuff of epic villainy.

No, he was no Richard the Third, no matter how much he wished to be. And he had her pegged right. She *was* a woman who'd dress in men's clothes and take off into the forest to find her future. She wasn't one to curl up in the corner of the carriage and weep.

Though she was ready to weep from sheer achiness. Her family tended to travel at a more leisurely pace, with lengthy stops for meals and walks to work out the kinks in one's muscles, and they tended to spend the night at a comfortable inn or with friends along the way, rather than risk the danger of driving in the dark. Right now Miranda felt as if she'd been locked inside a box for days, and every muscle, every joint hurt.

The last of the sun disappeared, and a soft mist enveloped the coach, making the intimidating landscape even gloomier. There was a basket of food on the opposite bench, something she'd steadfastly ignored, but hunger finally got the best of her, and she opened it, discovering fresh bread and cheese, a tart of dried apples, and even a bottle of wine.

She devoured everything, washing it down with the wine. It was much more than she usually drank, and she knew she was probably a bit tipsy, but it would help her sleep during this interminable journey and—

The coach came to a stop again, and she sighed. This time she was going to leave the carriage whether

he liked it or not. Assuming she could walk without wobbling.

The door opened, and Lucien stood there in the light rain, looking none the worse for it. "We've arrived," he said. "Welcome to your new home."

He would have expected anger and despair. She could play this game as well, and the last thing she intended to do was what he expected. She gave him a dazzling smile, taking his hand, and his ironic expression faltered for a moment. "How delightful. I'm afraid I drank a bit too much wine—I didn't realize we were so close to our destination." She managed to climb down the steps well enough with the support of his arm, and she looked up at the grim edifice that was to be her home. And wished she'd had a second bottle of wine.

It was huge, dark and dismal. No light shone from the myriad of windows that looked out over the overgrown driveway, and there was a sharp chill in the air. "Am I allowed to know where we are?"

"Of course, my love. This is Pawfrey House. It's been in my family for generations, and indeed, it's the only place left from our original estate. The rest were sold to pay my grandfather's and father's gaming debts, but apparently no one was interested in buying this, so it remained in the family."

"I wonder why," Miranda said in an undertone. It looked truly dreadful—a pile of dark, wet stones that no one, not even money-lenders and creditors, wanted. And this was where he intended to keep her. "And where are we?"

"In the Lake District. A particularly remote part of it, I'm afraid. We're tucked in a valley with mountains all around, and the house is extremely difficult to find."

"Lovely!" she said with breathless delight. "And such a very large house! I know I'm going to enjoy it tremendously."

"Exactly how much wine did you drink?" Lucien asked suspiciously.

"Enough," she said sweetly. "Shall we stand in the rain or will you show me my new home?"

Indeed, the rain was coming down more heavily now, soaking through Miranda's pelisse, and she only hoped there was at least a fire laid in the mausoleum that confronted her.

"Of course," he said immediately, taking her arm and leading her up the front steps. "Mind your step. Some of the stones are broken."

The front door opened, and Miranda felt a surge of relief. A woman was standing there, a branch of candles in her hand, and she could see light coming from behind her. "Welcome home, Master Lucien." The woman cast her eyes over Miranda with clear disapproval.

"Thank you, Mrs. Humber. And this is my new bride. Or shall be, as soon as the vicar can be found." He glanced down at Miranda, and she tried to control the chill that had sunk into her body, from the cold, damp air, the gloomy household, and the decidedly unfriendly housekeeper. Not to mention her future husband, assuming she couldn't change his mind.

"Oh, it all looks lovely!" she said in breathless accents. "But, darling, I could do with a nice warm fire and a cup of tea." She started forward but Lucien caught her arm, halting her.

"This is a bit precipitate, but we may as well follow custom," he said, and before she realized what he was going to do he'd scooped her up in his arms and carried

her across the threshold of the old mansion, setting her down inside a cavernous and chilly hallway.

He easily read the surprise she couldn't hide. "My leg is really quite strong, my love. I've adapted very well to its limitations."

"Indeed," she managed to come up with. Being picked up by him had been an unnerving experience, reminding her of those clandestine moments on his lap at the inn, as well as reinforcing how strong he really was. Strong and warm and hard.

"I assume you have rooms that are habitable for my bride," he said in his silken tone, and the sour woman in her starchy black nodded, clearly under his spell, as most women seemed to be. Even Jane had shown signs of blind obedience.

"There's a fire in the green saloon, as well as one in your study, your lordship. I've also had the girls in from the village to clean and dust your bedroom and the brown bedroom in the east wing. I hope you'll find that acceptable."

His lip curved. "That will be quite a walk to my wife's bed when I choose to join her."

"Oh, don't worry about it, darling," Miranda said cheerfully. "Just open your door and give a shout and I'll come running. Now where is this green salon? I'm chilled to the bone." She unfastened her pelisse and dumped it in Mrs. Humber's unwelcoming hands, handing over her gloves and bonnet, as well. The woman just looked at her, a solid lump like the house she oversaw. No help there, Miranda thought.

Lucien looked at her as if wondering who was this alien creature. "I'll take her, Mrs. Humber. And tea would be an excellent idea. I think she's had a surfeit of wine for one day."

Miranda smiled up at him, wanting to kick him in the shins. Preferably in his bad leg. "You take such good care of me," she crooned.

"And you're quite drunk." Taking her arm he led her down the dark, gloomy hallway to a small room that was so blissfully warm she ignored its other imperfections. She sank down in a chair by the fire, holding out her chilled hands and breathing a sigh of relief. Lucien was standing a ways away from her, staring at her.

"Don't you want to come closer to the fire?" she said.

"You must be absolutely frozen."

"I don't pay much attention to the weather.... What are you doing?" he demanded.

"Taking off my shoes. They're wet." She'd pulled off the demiboots, then wiggled her stocking-clad toes in front of the fire. She glanced up at him. "Don't look so shocked. We're going to be married, after all. And I've decided that suits me very well indeed. I was growing quite tired of my own company and that of the few who visited, and I hardly thought I'd achieve a marriage, particularly such a good one. You're quite a prize, you know, despite your physical imperfections," she said lightly. "You're wealthy, you're relatively young, though not quite in the first bloom of youth, and you're an earl. The main thing that's bothering me is will I be Countess Rochdale, or will I continue as Lady Miranda? I believe the hereditary title takes precedence, and I'm the daughter of a marquess, but I never paid much attention to these things. I'm certain my sister-in-law will know— she's a stickler for details like this. I'll write her...."

"The wine makes you talkative," he observed,

coming to sit opposite her, his pale eyes hooded and predatory.

"Oh, I suppose I'm a bit nervous." She was actually finding this quite easy. The cheerful, prattling bride, finding roses in a dung heap. And Pawlfrey House was most certainly a dung heap—it smelled of mold and dry rot and layers of dust. She beamed at him. "After all, I'm to be married. I would like to bathe and change my clothes first, if you don't mind. I'd like to look my best for you."

"I doubt the vicar will be located today, my love," he said, watching her as one might watch a rabid dog, waiting for it to attack.

"What a shame. And I was so looking forward to my wedding night." She pouted, making it as provocative as she could.

He laughed at that, and she wondered if she'd over-played her hand. "Of course you are, my pet. If wine makes you this affable I'll have to see you get a regular supply of it."

"That would be delightful."

He rose. "I'll have Mrs. Humber arrange for your bath. In the meantime I have duties to attend to."

"And what will I wear after I bathe? I didn't have a chance to pack."

"I made arrangements for a suitable wardrobe. It was simple enough to contact your dressmaker. Madame Clotilde on St. James Street, am I right?"

"Oh, you think of everything!" she said with perfect, breathless delight.

He gave her a slight, ironic bow. "I try. In the meantime I'll leave you to Mrs. Humber's good graces. She's been in my family all her life. In fact I believe she's a third cousin or something, and we're all very fond of her. Treat her with respect."

Miranda controlled her instinctive growl. "But of course, darling! I always treat underlings with kindness and respect."

"Mrs. Humber doesn't consider herself an underling."

"No, I imagine she doesn't. Nevertheless, she's your housekeeper, and therefore an upper servant. Or is she your mistress?"

He laughed. "She's my housekeeper. Tread warily, dear Miranda. She would make a formidable enemy, like all of my family."

She already was, Miranda thought, still managing her idiot smile. At this rate her cheeks were going to hurt and she'd have premature wrinkles around her eyes. Go away, she thought. Give me some quiet moments by the fire.

And thank God, he did.

His careful plans had suddenly become upended, Lucien thought as he limped down the hall to his study. It had been an act of sheer bravado, carrying her over the threshold like that, and his leg was paying for it. He did well enough in the best of circumstances, but the incessant rain always made his old wounds act up, and Miranda had been too tipsy to notice one way or another.

She was really quite ridiculous, staring at this dismal pile of stones and cooing. She didn't like Elsie Humber, that much was certain. They'd have a royal battle once he left them alone, and he was only sorry he wouldn't be there to see it.

So she was happy to be getting married, was she? He took leave to doubt that, and she most certainly was not looking forward to the marriage bed. She'd been nervous as a kitten in his arms. That idiot St. John must have been clumsy indeed.

He'd expected her to be in tears. Pleading for escape. Instead she was settling in by the fire, taking off her shoes, of all things, and demanding baths and cups of tea instead of rescue.

He shook his head. She was playing some game, and he wasn't sure what the rules were. But he was a seasoned gamester, and he knew how to adapt. She was happy to be getting married, was she?

Maybe marriage was a bad idea. She was already a disgraced woman. He could keep her as his mistress and there was nothing the Rohans could do about it. They'd never find their way through these tortuous roads.

And if they weren't to be married, why then he could have her tonight. If he wanted to hold to a sham of a ceremony it would be at least tomorrow before they could lawfully be joined.

She said she was delighted to be married. Perhaps he would have to disappoint her.

And see how much wine she needed to keep that calm, annoying smile.

Miss Jane Pagett was safely stowed in the post-chaise, with Long Molly by her side, Jacob thought, climbing into the driver's seat and taking the reins. Molly was a good old soul. She'd worked her way up from the streets to run her own very expensive brothel, which she kept with an iron hand. But she'd always had a hankering for the stage, and Jacob knew she'd jump at the chance to play a motherly soul.

Besides, in truth she did have a strong maternal streak. She looked after her girls, keeping them safe and clean, banishing any gentleman who didn't know to follow the rules or dared to hurt any of her little chickies. He had no doubt she'd be just as protective of Miss Jane Pagett, and a good thing, that. When he'd received Lucien's note he should have done as requested and sent one of his best men along with Molly to see Miss Jane safely back to the bosom of her family. But he hadn't been able to resist the chance to see her in full daylight, to see if her mouth was as kissable. Lucien was going to be very annoyed with him.

He didn't care. Her mouth was just as kissable as he'd thought. Even more so. She had a cold, her nose and eyes were red and swollen, and she was still the prettiest morsel he'd seen in God knew how long. He couldn't quite understand why he was so infatuated. It wasn't as if he'd suddenly developed a taste for quality—he'd had any number of titled ladies and they'd been no better than one of Molly's doxies. Sometimes even less honest with their favors.

She was no particular beauty, but he'd had plainer girls, prettier girls, taller girls, shorter girls, thinner girls, fatter girls. He'd long ago lost count of the women he'd had—when he'd had the itch there had always been someone available to scratch it.

So why was he suddenly so interested in a little bit of fluff from the upper classes?

She was still wearing the ring. That had been a devilish impulse on his part. He'd known the ring was too small but he'd still managed to get it on her when he'd been busy seducing her with his mouth. A treat like Miss Jane Paget shouldn't have to settle for that miserable little piece of shit her fiancé had provided for her.

She was still wearing that as well, though on the wrong hand. Not that he'd given her any choice. If she wanted his ring off she'd have to stop thinking about it, and he could think of only one way to do that.

Scorpion had been right mad at him for tossing away such a valuable piece of glimmer. Too bad. A sad little girl like that needed diamonds more than some over-bred whore like the Duchess of Carrimore. If he got the chance he'd take it off her finger, but he'd do it for her sake and no one else's.

It looked pretty on her hand. A big, brassy, tacky diamond on her elegant bone structure. He looked at it and thought *mine*, in a totally irrational spurt of emotion. But she wasn't, and he certainly didn't want her to be. He'd just really like to get a better taste of her.

That wasn't going to happen. She was engaged to someone worthy, and he made it a rule never to interfere with someone's life simply because he was hungry. She'd be safely deposited at her family home in London, still a virgin, minus the telltale ring, and she could forget all about the blackguard who kissed her in the darkness as he stole diamonds.

And if he had to kiss her to do it, so be it.

Molly was probably telling her all sorts of stories about him. Lies, of course, but he doubted he was going to come off in a good light. It didn't matter. She'd given him a good long look and hadn't recognized him, which didn't surprise him. That room had been pitch-dark, but he had eyes like a cat, and he'd seen her very clearly. She definitely wouldn't have seen him, and today he'd kept his head down, the cap pulled low so that even if she remembered him she'd have a hard time thinking of her jewel thief as the driver with a rough Yorkshire accent.

It would be a longer trip back. He wasn't going to change cattle, and there was a limit to which he would push his horses.

And to be entirely truthful, which wasn't like him, he wanted more time with Miss Jane Paget. No, he wasn't going to touch her. That one kiss had been dangerous enough, and he couldn't afford to get tangled with a young lady of quality. He made it a habit not to despoil virgins or people who didn't have it coming. Not out of any essential goodness, he told himself. Such things were just more trouble than they were worth.

It was a cold night, and he wondered if Long Molly had remembered to get some warm bricks for their feet. Probably not. He jumped down off the driver's seat, headed back into the inn, and a moment later came back out with two warm bricks wrapped in wool shawls that he'd had to pay dearly for, opened the carriage door and found himself looking up, directly into Jane Paget's face.

He quickly ducked his head, shoving the hot bricks toward her. "These mun keep tha warm," he said in his thick Yorkshire accent before backing out and closing the door behind him. He cursed. She'd had a good look at him, but that meant nothing. She'd never seen him before in the clear light.

Worse was the good look he'd had of her. Her soft, kissable mouth, her huge brown eyes, his diamond ring flashing on her finger.

He vaulted into the driver's seat, grabbed the reins

and started forward with a sudden jerk, no doubt throwing his passengers into disarray. It was nothing compared to his state of mind.

Maybe he'd better not take his time. He had a certain love of danger, but Miss Jane Pagett put the fear of God into him.

13

Pawlfrey House was a disaster, Miranda thought as she followed Mrs. Humber's sturdy figure up the first wide staircase, then another, down one long hall until the surly woman finally stopped, turning to look at her out of mean little eyes.

"We don't employ many servants here, Lady Miranda," she said in starched accents. "I've told the upstairs maid to bring up bathwater but of course the master's needs come first, and he always requests a hot bath on arrival. It may be some time before your bath is ready."

Miranda smiled at her sweetly. "Then perhaps you ought to show me to the master's room and I'll avail myself of his bath." She said it mainly to see the shock on Mrs. Humber's face, but in truth it seemed an excellent idea.

"Your bathwater will be up directly," Mrs. Humber growled, pushing open the door to the bedroom. "Make yourself at home."

Miranda stood in the doorway for a long, miserable moment. She could hear the housekeeper's heavy footsteps thudding down the corridor—she was willing to bet the old besom walked with a lighter tread when Lucien could hear.

She laughed beneath her breath. She could just imagine his reaction if he came up to his room and found her disporting in his bath.

No, she wasn't quite ready to fight this war on that level. Because she'd be naked, and she had every intention of putting that particular battle off as long as possible, if not forever. Would revenge against the Rohans be worth living with a cheerful idiot? She wasn't certain Lucien would think so.

She was loath to step across her threshold. The room was dark and gloomy, even with the fire. It smelled like mouse droppings and mildew, and she sighed. The first thing this place needed was a good cleaning, and if Mrs. Humber didn't employ enough servants she'd have to see that they found more.

She crossed to the tall windows, pushing open the faded curtains to look out into the rainy afternoon. A cloud of dust rewarded her efforts, and she began to cough, waving away the motes. She glanced over at her bed, wondering if it were equally untended, but it appeared that at least there were fresh sheets and pillowcases. Probably because Mrs. Humber expected Lucien to share that bed with her.

Fat lot she knew.

The room was damp and chilly despite the fire, and she doubted she'd find any help from the limited servants. At least there was wood piled beside the fireplace, and she leaned down and loaded more logs onto the grate. Really, they ought to be burning coal. It was easier to load and lasted a great deal longer, but perhaps the wretched old house wasn't equipped for it. After a moment she was rewarded with a merry blaze, and she dragged a chair closer, warming her hands and bare feet.

The look on Lucien's face when she'd taken off her shoes had been priceless. He'd hidden it almost immediately, but she'd been looking for it, and she'd almost crowed in triumph.

It was nearly pitch-dark when two burly men carried the copper bathtub into the room, followed by a maid with a bucket of hot water. If she was going to have to rely on the one maid and that small bucket the tub would be filled by next Christmas, but she gave them her best smile and thanked them, and was rewarded, at least by the young maid, with a shy smile.

"Should I close the curtains, miss?"

One of the older men cuffed her. "She's called 'my lady,' you dimwit."

The girl's face flooded with color. "Oh, miss...my lady, I beg pardon. I'm just the kitchen maid—I've never been called to serve a real lady before."

"Never mind," Miranda said kindly. "What's your name?"

"Bridget, my lady."

"Well, Bridget, why don't you help me sort through my clothes while these strong men bring up the rest of the hot water."

"That's not our job," the bully began, but then he saw the look on her face and swallowed. "Yes, your ladyship," he said, and practically bowed out of the room, closing the door behind them.

Bridget laughed. "He's a right brute, is Ferdy. He's Mrs. Humber's cousin, and he thinks he's in charge around here, when he's only a groom. But he's strong, and she uses him for the heavy work."

"Then he's perfectly suited for hauling heavy tins of water."

"Should I close the curtains, my lady? It's an ugly night out there."

"Very carefully. They're full of dust and I almost choked to death when I opened them."

Bridget looked horrified. "Oh, miss…er, your ladyship, I'm so sorry! We hadn't much notice you were coming, and Mrs. Humber is that difficult. She doesn't like it when his lordship brings a female up here."

There was no reason that should feel like a blow, and Miranda weathered it beautifully. "Does she disapprove on moral grounds? Because his lordship and I plan to be married."

Bridget shook her head, and Miranda could see a nasty bruise on the side of her neck. Probably thanks either to Mrs. Humber or her henchman, Ferdy. "That's not it. I think she fancies him herself."

"Mrs. Humber?" Miranda echoed, astonished. "She's twice his age, and his housekeeper, as well."

"No one says that love has to be practical, my lady."

The thought that the stern, sturdy Mrs. Humber could be in love with Lucien was so bizarre that Miranda left the subject for the one that was more troubling. "So he's brought other ladies up here?" she asked, toying with a loose thread on her bedraggled dress.

"No, miss. Not ladies, exactly. You know how gentlemen are—they like a bit of fun now and then."

"I doubt Lord Rochdale knows the meaning of fun," Miranda said dryly. "Well, I suppose I should be happy to hear he's brought whores up here on occasion. At least the place isn't totally unused to female inhabitants."

"They haven't stayed long, miss. His lordship tires of things very quickly."

"Let's hope so," Miranda said sweetly. With any luck he'd tire of her and the battle long before he'd won. In the end he was the stronger, and for some odd reason she was abominably vulnerable when he touched her. So, she simply had to avoid letting him touch her until he grew weary of the game. It had to happen, sooner or later.

"I beg your pardon, my lady?" Bridget said, carefully pulling the heavy brown velvet curtains without disturbing the dust.

"Just talking to myself."

Her bath was filled with steaming water within half an hour. Bridget took over the feeding of the fire, and was even bold enough to tell the bully to bring more logs and a tea tray with something solid to eat.

When Miranda slid into the copper tub she moaned with sheer ecstasy. The heat on her stiff muscles was better than any physical sensation she'd ever enjoyed, and the thought of being clean as well, after two days in that wretched gray dress, was dizzying. Bridget did a decent job of washing her long hair, then pulled out a beautiful nightdress and robe from the wardrobe.

Miranda had a normal woman's interest in new clothes, but at that point Father Christmas himself couldn't have raised her attention. She stepped out of the bath and into the large Turkish towel that Bridget held for her, looking at the nightclothes.

"I won't be dining with his lordship?" she inquired.

It couldn't be that late. It was still light when they'd arrived.

"He's gone out, miss, and there's no telling when he'll be back. He told them not to hold supper for him but to send you a tray in your room."

"You don't suppose he's gone to find the minister?" Miranda said, pulling the lacy wrapper around her. The clothes were gorgeous, elegant, even better than what she was used to. Lucien had expensive tastes.

"I wouldn't know, miss. When he goes out like that he's often gone for days."

"One can only hope." She tied the lacy combing jacket around her. It wasn't nearly enough protection against the cold, unfriendly house, but she was loath to climb into that big bed and await her seducer.

Because she strongly doubted he had any intention of waiting for the marriage vows.

And she had no intention of giving in, ever.

But at least the tray they brought her had a sensible amount of food, even if it was bland and overcooked. This household needed some serious sorting out. If she could just get rid of Lucien she could enjoy herself tremendously. She'd always had an affection for decorating things—even her surly brother Charles said she had a real gift. This house was like a huge, dirty, smelly, moth-eaten blank canvas, and if she was going to be trapped here she was going to do her best to have fun.

She dismissed Bridget for the night, propped a chair under the door handle and climbed up into the big bed. The large, shabby chamber was sufficiently warm now, but as she lay back among the pillows she realized she had absolutely nothing to do. Nothing to read, no one to talk to, no piano—did this wretched place even come

with a piano? If so, it was no doubt dreadfully out of tune. How many bedrooms were there? And how many public rooms? There was the dank salon she'd first come to, and Lucien had disappeared to his study. There'd be a large formal dining room, perhaps a morning room, and…

Bloody hell, she wasn't going to lie there, wide-awake, wondering. She slid out of bed and into the slippers Bridget had set out for her, lit her candle with the fire, moved the chair out of the way and began to explore.

It wasn't until she reached the ground floor that she realized she was more vulnerable, wandering around like this. He'd said he wasn't interested, and she was counting on that. If he changed his mind she was going to be in a more precarious position, and she almost headed back. But the house was still and silent, and she was the only one moving around in the darkness. She and the mice.

The pianoforte was in what was likely called the music room. There were plaster images of cherubs playing instruments along the cornices, and a harp stood in the corner as well as the pianoforte. She dusted off the seat and sat down, playing a quick Mozart piece she'd memorized. To her astonishment the instrument was in almost perfect tune. Someone here must play, but she couldn't imagine who.

There were three salons of varying sizes, a breakfast room, an office clearly meant for the estate manager but now covered with dust. There were stuffed heads of moth-eaten stags, and more ancient armaments adorning the walls than they had in the British Museum, one of her favorite haunts. If she ever decided she had to defend

her honor she had more than enough weapons at hand to make efficient work of her fiancé. It was reassuring.

Lucien's study was the only room that looked relatively clean and comfortable, and the servants knew better than to let his fire die down. There was a rich wool throw tossed carelessly over one chair, and Miranda immediately claimed it, wrapping it around her slender shoulders.

She moved on. There was a set of double doors at the end of the room, and she pushed them open, expecting to see a ballroom. Instead she found the largest library she'd ever seen in her life, and for the first time since she'd discovered Lucien's perfidy she was absolutely, perfectly happy. It took no time at all to find a book to her liking, a French novel short on improving aspects and long on entertainment. The room had no fewer than six window seats, each partially enclosed by heavy curtains, and she took the nearest one, setting her candle down on a convenient shelf as she curled up to read, the woolen throw wrapped tightly around her.

Lucien de Malheur was in a very ugly mood when he returned to the cold, miserable confines of Pawlfrey House. When he'd imagined imprisoning his unwilling bride here he'd forgotten that he'd have to put up with it himself. Not that he didn't have a certain fondness for the place, and he cherished the isolation.

But winter and early spring were both miserable times to be up there. Snow could trap one quite easily. The rain was so cold it could freeze your very bones, and Pawlfrey House was made for consequence, not comfort.

Not the best place to take a new bride, but then, he

wasn't looking for her comfort. In truth, quite the opposite. He needed to bed her and get it done with, then leave her to molder in the old place while her family went mad with fury.

It was enough to warm his cold, cold heart. It was well past midnight when he returned to the last ancestral home the poor de Malheurs had managed to hold on to, and even Mrs. Humber was in bed. He let himself in, just as glad not to deal with servants, and went upstairs to his new plaything.

She wasn't in her room. He even looked under the bed and in the wardrobe, in case she was hiding, and then felt utterly silly doing so. He could raise a search party, but that would make him feel like a complete fool. If she'd run off in this cold, wintry rain she'd be in trouble, but they might as well wait for morning to go in search of her. If she was hiding somewhere in the house he'd deal with it later.

He let the anger simmer in the pit of his stomach. He'd had mixed feelings about bedding her; he hadn't decided which would be worse, with or without marriage. He wanted a warm house, a warm bed and a warm, willing woman, and he was going to find none of those things at Pawlfrey House.

He headed down to his study for a late night glass of brandy. He sat at his desk, telling himself he was annoyed, not worried, when he noticed the doors to the library were slightly ajar. He rose, going over to them, about to close them, when he noticed the faint light over in one corner.

Aha, he thought. He crossed the large room on silent feet, coming to stand over Lady Miranda Rohan. She was sound asleep. Her hair was loosely braided, and he was astonished to see how long it was. It must go down past her hips. How unexpectedly erotic. She had a racy French novel in her lap, but even the remarkable doings of Mme. Lapine weren't enough to keep her awake. She'd wrapped herself up in his best throw, and she looked so peaceful he couldn't bring himself to wake her.

Besides, he reminded himself, his leg was throbbing, he still had a chill running through his body, and his reluctant fiancée looked far too peaceful to disturb. If he did he'd have to get her upstairs, either to his or her bedroom, and have at her.

She looked so innocent, asleep like that. She wasn't—he knew that. Thanks to him and his elaborate schemes. That first one had failed, due to the idiocy and inadequacies of his representative. He wasn't so easily distracted.

On impulse he reached out and touched her hair, brushing it back from her smooth, silken cheek. She didn't stir, deep in slumber, and he found himself smiling. Tomorrow would be time enough. For now she could sleep, thinking she'd outwitted him.

He leaned over and blew out the candle, brushing her skin as he did. She made a sound, a low moan of protest or pleasure, and he was immediately aroused. Which annoyed him—he'd decided to wait until she was really frightened, but his body seemed to have other ideas.

He pulled the curtains around her, closing her into her little nest. The morning sun would wake and warm her.

And the battle would begin again.

14

The library windows faced east, and the first brief glimpse of morning sun awoke Miranda from her delightful slumber. She sat up with a start—she'd slid down onto the seat, curled up under the blanket and had a wonderful, dreamless sleep. She'd left the candle burning—a good thing she hadn't burned the house down. Not that the house didn't deserve to be leveled, but she preferred not to be in it when it happened.

But when she picked up her candlestick from the small shelf she discovered it was only half burned. Something or someone must have blown it out.

The thought unnerved her. It couldn't have been Lucien—he'd have woken her up to torment and tease her or even worse. The thought of Mrs. Humber looming over her was even more unnerving. Perhaps she'd blown it out at the last minute and been too sleepy to remember. That, or this drafty house had taken care of it.

She pushed open the curtains, holding her breath so she wouldn't breathe in the dust. She couldn't remember closing them, either. How very odd. Perhaps Bridget had come looking for her.

She got to her feet, heading back toward the double doors, not even considering that the study might now be occupied. She took one look at his bowed head and froze.

He was busy writing something, and he didn't bother to look up. "I hadn't realized you were quite such a devoted reader, my darling." He looked up at her lazily, and his pale eyes were cool and dismissive. "You do realize it's dangerous to wander around the house in the dark? I think I'd better keep the library locked so you aren't tempted."

It took her a moment to remember that she wasn't going to hit him. She flashed him a bright smile. "Oh, that's an excellent idea, *my love*. When there are books around I never get anything done. Do keep it locked."

The look he cast her was sardonic. "It's not going to work, you know."

She came farther into the room, dropping down into the chair opposite the desk. "What isn't going to work, *my love*?"

"This cheery acceptance and enthusiasm. You may pretend all you like, though I can't imagine what you think you'll gain by it. All I'll gain is a compliant mistress, which makes things a great deal easier."

"I'm a mistress, *my love*?" she said sweetly. "I thought we were to be married."

"I was thinking it might be more effective if I simply made you a kept woman. Marriage vows are damnably eternal, and I'm not convinced you're worth it."

"Delightful! I gather from your servants that you're easily bored, and it would be so awkward for you if you were tired of me but unable to publicly court another woman."

"I don't publicly court women. They come to me. As you did."

"And you're so good at it, dearest," she cooed. "Living in sin suits me, as well. After all, I haven't given up on the idea of true love and happy endings. Once we part ways I might go to the continent if there aren't any blasted wars going on. Set myself up in Paris."

He leaned back in his chair, surveying her out of narrowed eyes. "Do you mean to tell me you're not in love with me, my angel?" he said in cool tones.

She furrowed her brow, trying to look adorable and presumably failing. "Did you want me to be, my darling? I'm certain I can manage it if you'd like. I thought you preferred a reluctant partner."

"You're not doing a very good job of being reluctant," he grumbled, his annoyance breaking through.

She sighed. "I know. I have a terrible habit of being adaptable. Do remember that I have experience with being abducted. With Christopher St. John I never shed a tear. I told him what I thought of him, for what good it did, and when it came time to bed me I did my best to enjoy it."

"Did you really?" He was now fascinated.

"Alas, I found the entire business messy, painful and almost comical. Those odd little appendages men have are so ridiculous."

"Little?"

She remembered those moments at the inn, when whatever was beneath her was far from tiny. Perhaps it might be a good idea to change the subject.

"When I realized he was just going to keep doing it,

I hit him over the head with a ewer and took off. I only wish I'd thought of that sooner and saved myself a lot of bother. But my point is: I'm very good at accepting things that are beyond my control. One would think ostracism from the ton would be the end of the world, but in fact I've been far happier in my little house, doing what I want, not having to think about the balls and parties and Almack's and husbands. No one can tell me what to do, though my family does try, and I'm quite delightfully free. So if you choose to simply despoil me it will give me a great many more choices, including going back to Half Moon Street." She smiled brightly, taking a breath after so much prattle.

"And what was this about love? I presume you were in love with Christopher St. John, weren't you?"

Miranda pulled her feet up under her, getting comfortable. "The terrible truth is, I wasn't in love with him at all. We weren't supposed to run off together—I was simply going for a clandestine few hours at Vauxhall, just a little bit of masked adventure, and Christopher was very handsome, very attentive, and just a little bit wicked. What girl could resist wicked?"

"What girl could resist wicked?" he echoed, astonished. "Are you suggesting women love villains?"

"Well, we do find them terribly appealing. We keep thinking we can save them. It's no wonder women flock around you. It can't be for your charm of manner." She batted her eyes at him.

His sharp bark of laughter surprised her. "I hope you aren't equally enamored of villains, Lady Miranda."

"Why? You're clearly a villain. Don't you want me to be madly in love with you?"

He considered it for a moment. "I'll let you know," he said finally.

"Lovely," she said, rising. "I'm going to go discover my new wardrobe—what a delightful thing for you to do, darling. You know how women love new clothes. I glanced at them last night and I swear I'm going to have a hard time deciding what to wear."

"Just as long as you wear nothing tonight when I come to you."

She paused by the door, a slightly worried expression on her face. "Well, I'll have to wear something. My monthly courses just began, and it's awfully messy if I don't...darling, are you ill?" She was all solicitude.

"Hardly," he said amiably. "And how long do your monthly courses last?"

"Oh, a week or ten days," she said airily. "And I'm afraid I'm blessed with a very heavy flow, but I assume you don't mind. You're such a man of the world you've doubtless dealt with this sort of thing before."

She was gambling on his squeamishness, and she was more than willing to go into greater detail about her imaginary menses, but he simply nodded, not looking the slightest bit bothered. "I don't have any particular problem with it, but I expect you'll be happier if we wait."

Ew, she thought. But then, everything about the entire process of mating seemed rather vile. "As you wish, my darling."

"*Stop* calling me that," he snapped, finally nettled.

"Darling"? Then what would you like me to call you?"

"Lucien will do."

Lucien was the name she used when she trusted

him. Lucien was the way she still thought of him, unfortunately.

"I was planning on being formal and calling you husband, or Rochdale in public, but then, if we don't marry that won't do. Endearments are so charming. If you call someone darling long enough you'll start to believe it. And wouldn't you just love to have me adore you?"

He raised an eyebrow. "I was under the impression that you already did."

One to him, she thought, keeping her smile firmly fixed on her face. "Of course I do. Will I see you at luncheon?"

He surveyed her for a long, contemplative moment. "I think I might find I have other things to do. I expect being around you and unable to touch you will be very difficult for me, and I might get snappish. I would hate to wound my sweet girl."

Miranda almost gagged on the endearment. Oh, he was good at this. She simpered. "Nature has a way of being so inconvenient," she said soulfully.

"Then again… there's always your mouth."

Rat scum bastard, she thought with a loving smile, trying to ignore the color that rose to her cheeks. She knew exactly what he was talking about—Christopher had tried to get her to do that on the second night. It was a revolting thought, and Lucien knew it.

"I worship and adore you, dearest, but if you think you're doing *that* to me you're sadly mistaken." She accompanied her statement with an affectionate beam.

"No, love. You'll be doing *that* to me, and I quite expect you'll want to. Would you care to wager?"

Son of a bitch, she thought. "I think it's probably

not a good idea to wager with my...what are you? My *clandestine lover?*"

He shrugged. "I haven't decided. It might be marriage after all. I simply have to figure out which you'd prefer."

"And then do the opposite."

"Exactly."

She looked at him, determined not to call him by name. "Dearest," she began, "you really have the most mischievous nature. I'll do my best to keep you guessing."

He rose then, coming to the door, and she wished she'd gotten the hell out of there a little faster. She'd been a fool to sit and banter with him.

He was limping more than he had, and he was using his cane. That didn't prevent him from putting his hand on her arm and turning her around to face him.

She didn't resist. She wasn't going to resist anything; she was going to smile and laugh and refuse to let him make her miserable.

He released her arm and slid his hand up her throat, to cup her chin, and she was suddenly terrified that he might kiss her. His kisses were dangerous, intoxicating, and she hadn't quite discovered how to inure herself to them.

"My love," he murmured, "I have the dreadful feeling that I probably never will tire of you. We may as well be married."

She held very still. "A charming proposal."

"And do you accept?"

"Do I have a choice, my darling?" she said through slightly clenched teeth.

"Not at all." And he covered her mouth with his.

It was a light kiss, playful, his tongue running along the tight seam of her mouth, his long fingers stroking her throat. She wanted to open her mouth for him, but she kept her jaw clamped shut. Later, when she came up with a plan, she'd let him kiss her. She'd come up with something ridiculous to think about when he touched her, so she wouldn't start to tremble and melt as she was right now, and she was parting her lips, ready for more, when he pulled away.

There was a strange look in his eyes. "A week to ten days, you say?"

"I'm afraid so."

"Then clearly I'll have to find something else to do."

Miss Jane Pagett smelled like violets, Jacob thought miserably. If there was one fragrance that brought him to his knees, it was violets. It all went back to a sunny afternoon in Jamaica, with those wildflowers all around, crushed beneath their bodies as they made love. And now he couldn't even remember the girl. All he could remember was the sense of peace, of rightness on that cloudless afternoon.

He was already having a hard enough time with Miss Jane Pagett. Every time they stopped to rest the horses and she walked by him he caught the scent, and it made him crazy. He'd already promised they weren't driving through the night, or he would have damned well paid for the change of horses himself in order to get temptation away from him. At least she was safely ensconced in a bedroom upstairs, neat and clean in her little bed. Scorpion had arranged for fresh clothes for his bride's friend, and he'd brought them with him when he'd taken the coachman's place. They didn't fit half badly, though he'd estimated she'd had a bit more in the rump and less in chest. Either way, she was too damned tempting for his peace of mind, he thought, sitting in the almost deserted taproom, listening to her move around overhead.

He'd taken a very circuitous route—he didn't want to risk running smack into an army of rescuers—and the inn was almost deserted. Long Molly still managed to find a likely prospect and was at that moment with her toes to Jesus, having a wonderful time.

And it wasn't as if there weren't prospects for him, as well. The barmaid was a buxom blonde, with a pretty face and a saucy smile, and he knew he could have her without trying.

She'd be enough to take his mind off Miss Jane Pagett. Maybe he could see if she could sneak into Miss Jane's room and steal her violet perfume.

But the fact of the matter was, he didn't want Nancy, or Betty, or whatever her name was. He wanted Jane. He wanted to see if that kiss was anywhere near what he remembered.

He sat for a long time, nursing his beer. It wouldn't do to get too drunk the first night out—he'd have a hell of a headache the next day. Though maybe that would help take his mind off his passenger.

The problem was, the more he drank, the more amorous he became, and if he got truly foxed he might very well go up and introduce himself, or at least a good hard part of himself, to Miss Jane Pagett.

The barmaid flounced off to the bed, alone. He had a bed in the stable, clean and warm, but he wasn't going there. He was going to spend the night beneath Jane, more fool he.

The fire burned down, and Jacob didn't bother to replenish it. He leaned back, propping his long legs on the brass fender, and contemplated the ridiculousness of life.

And it was there Jane found him, just as the clock on the landing struck two.

15

Miranda was in her room for no more than a few minutes when Bridget appeared, looking slightly nervous as she helped her out of her nightclothes. "I'm that sorry I wasn't here earlier, my lady. Mrs. Humber kept coming up with things to keep me busy, and then she forgot to make you a breakfast tray, and then his lordship stopped me on my way here, so it's no wonder it took me that long to get here." She looked nervous. "I'm talking too much, aren't I? Mrs. Humber says a proper ladies' maid never speaks unless spoken to, never volunteers information, and she says I'll be a ladies' maid when hell freezes over, begging your pardon, my lady."

"You'll be fine," Miranda said in a soothing voice, ignoring her sudden uneasiness. "What did his lordship want to talk to you about?"

Bridget blushed a fiery red, and Miranda thought, *oh merde.* She should have known he wouldn't take her word for things.

"Uh…he wanted to make sure you were comfortable up here, that you had everything you needed…."

"Such as?" Bridget was doing up her corset, pulling

the laces tight, and Miranda took a deep breath, holding it in.

"He wanted to make certain you had everything you need," Bridget mumbled again.

"You already said that. Exactly what did he ask you about, Bridget?" Miranda turned and caught Bridget by the arms, forcing her to meet her gaze even though she was fiery red.

"He wanted to make sure I could find rags for your monthlies. I was that embarrassed, my lady! That a gentleman would be asking about such things! But I couldn't very well not answer, and I told him that you said you'd just finished and wouldn't be needing anything for at least three weeks, possibly more because you were never certain and he just nodded and said 'I thought as much' and I thought I might have said something wrong but it was the master and…"

"Don't worry about it, Bridget," Miranda said calmly. She should have known he'd check. She was simply going to have to come up with some new excuse, like Scheherazade putting off her execution. The chair under the door handle might work, at least for one night. He wouldn't rouse the household by banging the door down.

She would come up with an inventive mind. She was blessed with an inventive mind, and if she could avoid doing *that* with Lucien de Malheur she would. At least for as long as possible. If she had to, she could lie there and take it. Recite poetry or poems in her head. Count to one hundred in Latin. Anything to take her mind off what was happening to her body.

In fact, that would be a most excellent way to avoid the deleterious effect of his kisses. Of the way her skin warmed when he put his hands on her. Latin was the perfect antidote to desire.

She was forced to admit the clothes he'd provided were beautiful, and fit perfectly. How long had he been planning this that he had an entire wardrobe made up by her own modiste? It would have taken a while. When, if, she ever got back to London she was going to have to find a new dressmaker. One who didn't accept orders from strange gentlemen without the lady's consent.

She wondered what a proper young lady would do in the circumstances. Not that she'd ever been a proper young lady, but she'd tried. An innocent young miss would refuse to wear clothes a gentleman paid for. She should probably insist that Bridget clean her soiled dress and wear that all the time.

But that could present its own set of problems, particularly if she had to wait around in skimpy night rail. In fact, should she have slept naked rather than worn those clothes?

Behaving in a decorous manner was long gone for her, and it would be foolish to ignore the lovely clothes. As long as she was going to be here she may as well be decently dressed.

He must have enjoyed his evil machinations. All the while he'd been gentle and charming and flirtatious he'd been a lying snake. No, a lying Scorpion. She only wished she could stomp him as effectively as the French landlord had stomped his pet.

And yet...the thought of his pet, no matter how strange a creature it was, being killed by a stranger was somehow heartbreaking. She knew little boys. She had many cousins, and boys had an absurd affection for the least cuddly of creatures. It was always possible that Lucien had kept his scorpion with him as a murder weapon, but she doubted it. He'd even named her.

He was a man who refused to show true emotion, empathy, feeling. And yet she knew he'd mourned that blasted scorpion.

She was quite hungry, and she ate everything on the tray—fruit and toast and lukewarm eggs. Bridget had no knowledge of a lady's hair, so she made do with hip-length plaits, then tucking them into a bun at the back of her neck. Wisps of curls had an unfortunate tendency to frame her face, ruining the severe look, but she was determined not to let anyone get in her way.

The first to try would be Mrs. Humber. She found that redoubtable lady in the kitchens of the big house, and she paused, momentarily appalled.

The huge room smelled of rotting meat, moldy cabbage and things she didn't want to identify. Mrs. Humber was sitting at one end of a long, scarred table, a cup of tea in her hand, next to a smaller woman who looked even less welcoming. She wore a white apron stained with all sorts of nasty things, and Miranda guessed she was the cook.

The two of them looked up at her, and Miranda stood her ground, waiting, her foot tapping softly beneath the hem of her skirt, and finally the two of them rose to their feet, their reluctance both arrogant and insulting. Miranda gave them a polite smile.

"Good morning, Mrs. Humber. I'd like a tour of the house, if you please. I'll be interested in seeing just how bad the condition of the place is."

"I'm very busy this morning," Mrs. Humber said.

Miranda gave a speaking glance to the cup of tea.

"I'm certain you can find the time," she said in a civil voice. "Now would be good for me."

"I can't right now, I've got…"

"Now would be best," she reiterated gently. Mrs. Humber glared at her, but made no more demurrals, and Miranda turned to her companion. "You must be Cook. When we come back I'll be interested in looking at menus for the next few days. I may want to make a few changes. For instance, I have a particular dislike of beets, and small birds distress me."

"The master never questions my menus," the woman said in a hostile voice.

"No, that's your mistress's business, isn't it? And please change your apron before we return. That one has seen better days. If you need to order more, then see to it."

Cook might have hated her even more than Mrs. Humber, Miranda thought cheerfully, but short of outright rebellion there was nothing she could do about it. She made one attempt. "I'll talk to his lordship about this," she said in a sullen voice.

"I have little doubt he'll insist you change your apron, as well. If you wish to waste his time with domestic squabbles you may certainly attempt it. In my experience the earl is easily irritated, but if you think he will find this of interest be sure to go ahead, and let me know the results."

There was pure hatred in the woman's beady eyes, reflected in Mrs. Humber's eyes, as well. A good beginning, Miranda decided, unruffled.

"Come on, then," the woman said. "I haven't got all day."

Miranda had been prepared for the absolute worst,

but in the end she was pleasantly surprised. The house was very old, built sometime in the latter half of the sixteenth century, but it appeared basically sound, the roof intact, though there was clearly a problem of rising damp in several areas. As far as she could see the most pressing problem was neglect. No one had cleaned or dusted the majority of the rooms in what appeared to be decades, and the smell of mouse and moth was an unappetizing undernote to the wood and wool of the old house and its hangings. It appeared that Mrs. Humber saw to it that only the rooms Lucien needed were kept clean. The rest were simply closed up and forgotten about.

She counted seventeen bedrooms, a number with modern powder closets. Hers was far from the largest, and at least one was cleaner, doubtless the bedroom used by whatever doxy Lucien had brought with him in the past. She wasn't sure whether to be offended or relieved.

Mrs. Humber stopped at Lucien's door. "It's not my place to show you in there," she said.

"Why? Is it full of skeletons and murdered brides?"

Mrs. Humber was not amused. "It's the master's suite."

"Is it as filthy as the rest of the house? I would think the earl would insist that at least this room be cleaned."

"We clean it."

"Then what are you afraid of? I gather his lordship has gone out for a ride, so we shan't run into him."

"If you wish to go in then I won't stop you, my lady," Mrs. Humber said in a low voice. "But I only enter when the master requests it."

"I'm not so cow-hearted," Miranda replied, and pushed open the door to Bluebeard's chamber.

Indeed, the room was dark and dreary enough to have held the remains of a score of dead wives, if the old fairy tale were true. It only had a light layer of dust, but the walls had dark, worm-eaten paneling, the curtains the same heavy brown velvet. She looked around her, assiduously avoiding the bed for as long as she could. It was a massive thing, with dark hangings and heavy linen sheets. She could imagine him lying there. She could imagine him there, naked, with a woman, his pale eyes intent, his long, clever hands stroking, touching, arousing...

She shivered, turning away. He had a small dressing room with a cot for his valet, a powdering closet and even a small sitting room, all relatively clean, if dark and depressing. It was little wonder he had such a dark soul, living as he did in such gloomy places. The house in London wasn't much cheerier, at least as far as she could see.

She was surprised to find Mrs. Humber still waiting for her when she emerged. "Well, my lady?" she said in a frosty tone.

"We'll need, as a conservative guess, at least twelve women. Four to serve as chambermaids, four as parlor maids for the public rooms and the remaining four to do laundry and scullery service. Bridget says you have her doing both, which might work out very well with no one in the house, but with it being opened we'll need a great deal more help."

"And what about Bridget?" Mrs. Humber demanded "She's slovenly but I have need of her..."

"I'm training Bridget to be my personal maid."

Mrs. Humber snorted with laughter. "That girl is lazy and disrespectful. I was about to turn her off."

"Then you won't be missing her. Twelve maids, Mrs. Humber. Plus I think at least four footmen for the heavy work."

"My Ferdy can handle that just fine."

Miranda controlled her instinctive shudder at the memory of the unprepossessing Ferdy. "That was when the house was deserted."

"I don't think he's planning on filling the place with anyone but you, my lady."

"And are you privy to Lord Rochdale's plans, Mrs. Humber?"

The woman subsided. She knew too much—she probably listened at keyholes. "What's Cook's name?" Miranda started back toward the kitchens, and the old woman had no choice but to follow her.

"Mrs. Carver."

Miranda chortled. "A perfect name."

"Why?"

Clearly Mrs. Humber was totally devoid of a sense of humor, and Miranda knew better than to try to explain it to her. By the time they reached the kitchen the place was marginally cleaner. Someone had managed to wash the dishes, she suspected it was Bridget, and Mrs. Carver had indeed donned a fresh apron and even a tasteful cap for her flyaway gray hair.

"You'll be getting two new helpers, Mrs. Carver, at the very least," Miranda announced. "Plus two for the laundry as well, who can help out when needed. And that will be apart from the maids who actually serve the meals and tend to the needs of the owner. In the meantime, what were your plans for dinner tonight?"

Mrs. Carver had more malice but less courage than Mrs. Humber. "A consommé of veal and potato, followed by roasted pheasant stuffed with mushrooms. The fish course would be trout from his lordship's own waters, a brisket of beef with a remove of winter squash and asparagus, with lemon pie for dessert."

"It sounds heavenly. I hope you can manage all that without Bridget's help. She'll be busy with me. If you're forced to pull back on the magnificence I'm sure we'll survive with fewer courses."

Mrs. Carver gave her a look of intense dislike. "I take my orders from the earl."

"Of course," Miranda was all affability. "Be certain to let me know his response."

What a treacherous little darling she was, Lucien thought coolly. Prattling on about such wholly feminine matters as if she were discussing gardening, all without a blush, over the subject matter or the lie.

He was becoming quite in awe of her. When he'd first begun to lure her into his net he'd found he had a reluctant admiration for her, for her ability to turn her back on the ton as effectively as they turned their back on her. He'd enjoyed conversing with her, flirting with her so discreetly that she hadn't even realized that was what he was doing, she'd simply responded in kind.

And there was something about her smooth, pale skin, her rich brown hair, her warm brown eyes that unexpectedly aroused him.

In fact, despite St. John's clumsiness, he found he didn't regret her initial ruination one bit. Granted, he'd hoped to accomplish his revenge and still keep a distance, but that was before he'd seen her.

He was quite grateful for the fact that she wasn't a virgin, no matter how badly St. John had botched it. Deflowering was a tedious business, never worth the trouble. He liked the fact that she found sexual congress tedious, and the thought of any kind of variation quite unsupportable. He could just imagine her reaction when he used his mouth on her, which, of course, he intended to do.

And she would do the same to him. Of her own accord, eventually. He had little doubt he could arouse her to such a fever pitch that she'd do absolutely anything if he gave her a slight nudge in that direction. He was going to enjoy this immensely.

He was, admittedly, concerned about Jacob Donnelly, Jane Pagett and the Carrimore diamonds. It would be a wise idea to get that solitaire off the girl's hand, and soon, before anyone else saw it and recognized it. Once it was removed from its setting and recut no one would ever know where it came from, but in the meantime she was wearing the equivalent of gunpowder on her hand. Jacob might find it amusing to play with fire. He himself was less entranced.

And who the hell did the man think he was, some damned romantic hero? It wasn't like Jacob to have slipped the bloody thing on her finger. He'd always been extremely hardheaded when it came to business.

He needed to make certain that Miss Pagett had been returned to the bosom of her family. Then and only then could Jacob arrange for one of his minions to steal it. He needed to make certain the Rohans hadn't begun a call to arms. He needed to take his time with Lady Miranda—the slower, more measured her downfall the greater pleasure it would accord him.

He would begin tonight, but by tomorrow he'd be gone, leaving her to rattle around this old place with Mrs. Humber. He had no doubt that by the time he returned she'd be at least a bit more cowed. Pawlfrey House was enough to pull the joy out of anyone.

He had his horse saddled, heading out into the misty afternoon, pleased that Miranda would once more be denied sunshine. She would learn to live like a mole. Her eyes would narrow as she peered through the gloom. Though that would be a shame, with such deliberately enchanting brown eyes.

He would come up with the coup de grace. He always did, when life was looking woefully tedious.

In the meantime, things were simple. Tonight he would begin the total ruination and subjugation of Lady Miranda Rohan. Tomorrow he would be gone.

16

Jane wasn't quite sure why she'd ventured downstairs in the middle of the night in this deserted inn. To be sure, she'd been sleeping so much in the carriage that she was having trouble closing her eyes. But it was something more, some mystery that she wasn't sure she wanted to consider, and it had to do with their driver, the tall groom that dear Mrs. Grudge had warned her against.

She pulled a loose dress over her nightgown and crept down the staircase, loath to wake anyone, including her temporary companion. Her room at the inn was small, the bed was lumpy and if she couldn't sleep she'd rather be sitting in a chair. Anything to ease the ache at the small of her back.

The ground floor of the Cross and Crown Tavern consisted of the front room for the riffraff, a private salon for hire and the taproom. The fire had died out in both the salon and the large room, but she could see the warm glow from the taproom in the distance, and she headed toward it, drawn like a moth to the flame.

A wing chair had been drawn up to the blaze; the perfect spot. She headed straight for it and then stopped, panicked. It was occupied. She saw the long legs first, propped on the fender, and she tried to back up, but she'd already managed to wake him, and he rose to his feet, still half asleep.

It was the groom. Without his cumbersome cap she could see his face and head quite clearly, and she could see why he wreaked havoc among all the women of the household. He was utterly, wickedly handsome, with guinea-gold hair, the bluest of eyes and a mouth made for sin.

His long, lean body, clad in de Malheur's dark livery, was just delightful. He loomed over her, and she thought she could see a peculiar light in his eyes. They were surprisingly merry as they surveyed her, from her loose, tousled hair to her feet, and she gasped as she realized just how improper this all was. She should turn and run back upstairs. But for the moment she was frozen.

"I'm so sorry," she said nervously, trying to act as if she held conversations with strange men in the middle of the night all the time. When there was only one other time she could remember. Indeed, that she couldn't forget. "I didn't mean to wake you. I thought you'd be sleeping in the stables." Oh, no, that sounded terrible, she thought. Like she thought he was one of the horses. But where did drivers sleep?

But he smiled down at her, that slow, lazy smile. "Aye, yer ladyship," he said. "They said they had a bed for me, but like as not it's that cold, and the bed might have bugs or I'd need share it with another 'ostler, and I figger a chair in front of a good fire won't do no harm, and it'd be a right treat for me, after such a long, rainy drive."

"That's true—you were out in this awful weather," she

said, immediately feeling guilty. While they'd bowled along in relative comfort he'd been up on the box getting drenched. Her practical side came into play immediately. "You could have caught your death. Have your clothes dried properly? Sitting around in wet clothes is a certain way to catch pneumonia. I hope you had something warm to drink?"

His charming smile turned wicked. "Are you asking me to take off me clothes, yer ladyship? Because I'll gladly oblige, just to see if they're still wet, don't you know, though I'm not sure what I'll do while I wait..."

Jane stepped back, not bothering to keep the look of shock from her face. "Mrs. Grudge warned me that you weren't to be trusted."

The groom didn't look the slightest bit chagrined. "Did she now?" He moved toward her, just a bit. "I didn't mean no harm, your ladyship. There's no need to get on yer high ropes about it. I was just having a wee bit of fun with you."

There was something odd about the man, something strangely familiar. It was the kind of face a girl wouldn't forget, particularly a shy, romantic, love-starved girl about to settle for a stultifying marriage. She stared at him, her outrage fading slightly, turning to curiosity. "You didn't talk like that before."

She could tell she'd startled him, and he fell back a pace, looking troubled. "Aw, my lady. I've lived a great many places and I talks like a lot of different people. Don't mean no harm by it, I don't."

No, there was something definitely havey-cavey about this man, and her curiosity overwhelmed her good sense. "Do I know you? You seem familiar."

It was only fleeting, the look of discomfiture in

his bright blue eyes, and then his expression changed, almost like one putting on a loo mask, and he leered at her. "I wouldn't forgets a pretty lady like you."

She looked at him, anger stronger than her discomfiture. "You needn't bother, Jacobs," she said, though her voice shook slightly. "Perhaps you think you're required to flatter your employers, or perhaps it simply comes naturally to you, but I know perfectly well that I'm not a pretty lady and never have been, so leave off, please."

"You need a mirror." His voice was different, without the wheedling, servile accent, and she looked at him with suspicion.

"Begging your pardon, your ladyship," he continued, and the accent was back, part Yorkshire, part Irish, with a bit of cockney thrown in. He truly was the mongrel he'd said. "And what can I be doing for you this foine evening?"

On impulse she held out her hand, the one with the diamond. "Do you have any idea how do I get this off?"

He stared down at it for a long moment, but surprisingly there was no acquisitive gleam in his eye. "How should I know, miss? You might ask Mrs. Grudge."

"I did. She was thinking axle grease. Since you're the driver you'd be the the one to have access to such."

"Lord love you, my lady, it's in the middle of the night and it's cold as a witch's tit out there, begging your pardon. I'll get you some in the morning before we leave. But why would you be wanting to get rid of a fine piece of the sparklies like that?"

"It's stolen," she said nervously. "And my fiancé might have a problem with it."

"Happen as he might," he allowed. "You know, you

ought to be up in bed, my lady. We've a long day on the road tomorrow. And you shouldn't be down here alone with the likes of me."

"I'm too stiff to sleep," she confessed.

"So am I," he said, looking oddly amused.

Poor man. It didn't matter how disreputable he was—he'd spent the day out in the pouring rain and she could hardly kick him out. She took a deep breath. "Well, then, Jacobs, why don't you bring me another chair and we can both stay down here?"

He didn't move, looking down at her.

Oh, God, that was a terrible idea, Jane thought belatedly, feeling the color flood her face. She knew better than to suggest such a thing. He was a womanizer and it sounded like she'd just issued an invitation for dalliance. "I mean..." she began nervously. "That is..."

He simply smiled down at her, and there was none of the leering aggression. "No worries, my lady. I knew what you meant. I was just about to find my own bed over the stable. I'll leave you in sole possession of this very fine chair and this very fine fire, and tomorrow I'll bring you the best axle grease to be had."

She breathed a sigh of relief. "That sounds like an excellent idea, Jacobs," she said gratefully and she settled into his recently abandoned seat. It was still warm from his backside, and the whole thing felt completely improper, but she could hardly jump up again. She had to pretend she was entirely comfortable with this bizarre, midnight encounter. She'd been avoiding looking at him, keeping her eyes focused on his shoulder when necessary, but now she looked up, into his handsome, reckless face, into his blue, blue eyes and she *knew*.

Impossible, she told herself. Absolutely impossible.

"G'night, yer ladyship," he said, bobbing his head. And he backed out of the room, disappearing into the night.

Bloody hell, that was a close call, Jacob thought, heading out into the rainy night. When she'd said he sounded different he was certain she'd recognized him, that she was referring to the Carrimores' ball and the kiss in the dark.

But no, she hadn't meant that at all; she'd meant when he first took over driving. He'd slipped into a bit of Irish when he was flirting with her. It always happened that way. He'd better watch it—the Irish was just a little too close to his voice when he was rubbing up against her in the midst of a jewel robbery.

He should have left the moment she walked in the room. But she smelled like violets, and he couldn't let it be.

At least she didn't suspect him, he thought in relief, ignoring his irritation at her mention of her fiancé. He shouldn't have said he was *stiff*. But she, poor wee lamb, had no idea what he was talking about. What a randy, improper soul he was, particularly when she was around.

And she'd smiled at him. Bloody hell, he wished she wouldn't smile like that. It had been all he could do not to pull her into his arms and kiss her again, the way he'd been dreaming of for the last week.

He still could see her in his chair, her slippered feet propped up on the brass fender. She had long legs, and he could just imagine them wrapped around him. He could see her ankles, and they were so beautiful he

wanted to sink to his knees and start working his way up from them with his mouth.

But instead he'd bowed his way out of the room and into the cold night rain.

And it was a damned good thing. He wouldn't be surprised if the rain hissed against his skin, he was that heated up.

Not for the likes of him. He needed to get her safely home, get the damned ring off her finger and then forget all about her while she went on with her life and married her worthy fiancé.

He just wasn't sure he could do it.

It was a bleak, rainy day at Pawlfrey House, and there was still no sign of Lucien. Miranda, after having survived a thoroughly depressing tour of the place, chose the tiny drawing room near the library. It was painted in drab colors that had once been soft pastels of some sort, and the furniture was delicate, indicating that at one point it must have been the ladies' parlor. She held her fine lawn handkerchief, one of a dozen monogrammed ones that had been provided, up to her face as she took an errant pillow and used it to brush several layers of dust off the desk and chair. She mended the nib of the brittle pen, found a bottle of ink that hadn't yet dried up and began her inventory.

Some of the rooms needed little more than a robust cleaning. Even some of the curtains could be saved once they'd survived a thorough beating to get the thick, choking dust out of them, and while most of the bedding was sadly moth-eaten and worm-chewed, there was enough in sturdy shape for the time being.

A number of the rooms hadn't fared so well. The

mold and damp had spread up the wall in several of the back bedrooms, necessitating a carpenter and the removal of some fine medieval paneling, and paint was peeling in several of the bedrooms, including Lucien's. There was broken furniture in almost every room that needed to be hauled away and either repaired or discarded, windows to be washed and reglazed, floors to be scrubbed. It would take an army of servants, possibly more than she'd already told Mrs. Humber to hire. Half a dozen men would be useful as well, for the heavier work.

Her captor didn't return for the midday meal. She told herself that was a relief, had a tray in her withdrawing room and continued with her lists.

She would start with her room. Get rid of those dusty curtains, which were drab and depressing. She would see if the local seamstress could come up with something suitable rather than order window hangings from London, which would take forever. She didn't like the idea of sleeping with curtainless windows—it would feel like blank eyes staring in at her while she slept.

Her fireplace needed to be cleaned and scrubbed, not to mention all the chimneys of the house, which had to number in the dozens. The rug was beginning to unravel, and sooner or later she'd catch her foot in it and go sprawling. There were any number of rugs throughout the place that were still in one piece that she could have cleaned and moved.

Her villain didn't return for dinner. Not that she minded, she told herself, stretching to ease the ache in her shoulders. She'd been cooped up too long, both in the carriage and now in the house. Tomorrow she would go for a good long hike, rain or no rain. She was no frail

flower likely to melt. Growing up with three brothers tended to make one sturdy.

Bridget had done what she could in the bedroom, beating some of the dust out of the curtains and opening the windows to receive it. She'd scrubbed the fireplace as well, and the room looked almost welcoming when she finally gave up and headed upstairs. It was after ten, the book she'd taken from the library had ceased to interest her and clearly her heartless rat of a seducer wasn't coming home at all.

Bridget had removed the bed curtains, and a lovely coolness lingered in the air from the open windows. She hummed beneath her breath as Bridget helped her out of her clothes and into her nightdress, to prove to herself and her maid that she wasn't the slightest bit nervous. He'd chosen to spend the night abroad—he could be blown away in the winds for all she cared.

She waited until Bridget left, then climbed out of bed and took the straight-backed chair, slipping it beneath the door handle. There was absolutely no need, of course. The door itself had a very efficient lock on it, and he'd shown no interest in her after that moment in the wayside inn. If his only desire to have…relations with her was out of revenge, he probably had to work up interest in the entire procedure. Which was a depressing proposition, but better for her in the long run. He might never get in the mood.

The rain stopped sometime after midnight. The sudden silence woke her, accompanied by a pop and hiss from her fire. She glanced out the uncurtained windows. The moon was peeping from behind fast-moving clouds, shining through the rivulets of rainwater on the windows, and she lay in bed, unmoving, watching each little stream slither down the glass.

She wasn't one easily given to tears, and she wasn't about to succumb at that particular moment. But she doubted if she'd ever felt so alone in her entire life. Off in the middle of nowhere, and no one, not family nor friends, would know where to find her. Tomorrow she'd face her altered world with energy and determination. Here in the midnight hours things felt relatively hopeless.

"You think a chair would keep me out?"

She shrieked, bolting up in bed, slamming a hand to her racing heart and then turned and cast a bitter expression at Lucien de Malheur. "You almost gave me apoplexy!" she said. "You shouldn't sneak up on people like that!"

"I didn't sneak up on you. I've been standing here watching you for the last five minutes, listening to you snore."

"I do not snore!"

He shrugged. "Perhaps it's more like a purr. I trust it won't keep me awake at night."

"I doubt it will, since we're not likely to be anywhere near each other when we sleep," she snapped. And then belatedly remembered her strategy. It was with huge reluctance that she plastered a smile on her face. "Unless you've changed your mind about marrying me."

She had the unpleasant suspicion that he could see right through her, but he replied in a civil enough manner. "Which would you prefer, my precious? Living in sin or holy matrimony?"

She knew perfectly well he'd go with the opposite of whatever she picked. She'd already survived one clandestine elopement against her will. A second one could hardly make things worse.

"I think above all things I should love to be married," she said in a nauseatingly breathless voice. "I do realize we can't have a large wedding—most likely only the two of us at the local church—but every girl dreams about being married. Besides, that would make me a countess, and think how lovely that would be!" She smiled brightly.

He looked at her for a long moment. "Marriage it is," he said, and then he laughed. "Don't look so crestfallen, dear Miranda. We'll have our small private marriage ceremony, but then I promise you a full-blown wedding with lots of guests."

"Really?" she said doubtfully.

"Trust me," he said in a charming voice. "Now move over. And don't annoy me with any more lies about your menses. Yes, I'm in awe of the lengths you're willing to go to manipulate me."

Miranda stayed exactly where she was. "Why? Don't you want to wait for our wedding night?"

"Perhaps. At this point I don't know if I want more than a taste. Just to make certain I'm still interested."

"And how will you discover that?"

"It will depend on how much I want to continue what I'm doing. Whether your responses bore or inspire me. Mind you, I'm perfectly capable of handling the business whether I find you attractive or not, and I will do so. I'm just curious to see whether you're still as attracted to me as you were initially."

She couldn't help her derisive snort of laughter. "La, sir, you do think highly of yourself. Why would you presume I'd be attracted to you?"

"You mean because I'm scarred and lame?" he asked mildly, entirely at ease.

Color flooded her face. "I'm sorry, I didn't even think of *that*. I don't really notice it."

His face was unreadable. "That's quite touching, my angel. If I were a foolish man I'd believe you."

She managed to regain her composure. "And you are certainly not a foolish man," she said, hoping the color would fade from her cheeks. "What exactly did you want? Another kiss?"

"No, my love," he said easily. "I want to get between your legs." And he reached out and began to pull the covers down.

17

Lucien de Malheur was amused. Lady Miranda Rohan was looking at him as if he had suggested he was going to sprout wings and fly. Did she seriously think he was going to leave her alone in her chaste, albeit not virginal bed? He wondered if she'd grow angry or burst into tears.

Instead, to his momentary discomfort, she let out a trill of laughter. "Oh, heavens, my lord, you had me worried for a moment. Of course you aren't serious." She'd grabbed for the covers and was trying to yank them back up over her, but he was a great deal stronger and had no intention of letting her pull them up.

"Of course I am, dear lady. Are you cold? Perhaps I should build up the fire?"

"W-w-why?" she said, stammering only slightly.

"Because you aren't going to have anything covering you. Except me."

She gulped. And somehow managed to reach inside herself and pull out that flashing smile of hers. "You're extremely saucy, my lord. I don't think so."

He'd moved away from her. His leg was giving him

trouble, but he didn't bother to disguise it. He was still bothered by her artless statement. She'd meant it. She didn't see his scars or lameness. In fact, she was embarrassed that she hadn't been more aware. When she looked at him she saw him, not his scars, and that was rare and oddly disturbing. He felt as if he'd been thrown off balance.

It was a shock, when he was so used to keeping to the shadows. He was acutely aware of his own dragging walk whenever his leg pained him too much. And he'd never been fond of mirrors. He didn't like to be reminded of the claw marks on his skin, those permanent memories of a barbed whip brandished by a madwoman. His back was worse, a horror. Even Jacob Donnelly had been shocked the first time he'd seen it, and Jacob knew nightmares beyond measure.

Lucien rose from the bed to put wood on the fire, watching her out of the corner of one eye to make certain she didn't try to run. There were hardly enough servants to keep this place going, and he was more than capable of loading a fire himself. Mrs. Humber had already complained that his future bride was insisting she hire more servants, and she maintained there weren't any available, but he knew she lied. Most women lied, including the one in bed watching him with warm brown eyes.

"Why don't you start by taking off that oh so fetching nightgown, my pet?" he murmured, moving back toward her. "After all, why should there be any secrets between us? We're to be man and wife, after all. You're getting a title and a considerably advantageous marriage, given that you managed to ruin yourself. I may as well see what I'm getting out of the bargain."

"Alas, nothing very exciting, my lord, I assure you," Miranda said in her mock cheerful voice. "I'm nothing above ordinary. Some might even consider me a little plump, but they'd be rude."

"And I would never be rude," he murmured, watching her. She was making no move to unfasten her clothing. "Tell me more."

He took a seat at the foot of her bed and she let out a little squeak of dismay as she pulled her feet out of the way. And then she laughed, with almost all trace of nervousness vanished. "I'm not very tall and not very short. In truth, average. My breasts are too small, my hips a little too generous, I have excellent teeth and skin and while my hair is a boring brown its length and texture are to be admired."

"I haven't seen it down yet. Why don't you unfasten your plaits and show me?"

She shook a playfully admonishing finger. She really had no idea this was a losing battle. "If I did my hair would be a mare's nest of tangles and I'd spend the better part of the day combing them out. It's not that interesting——it's simply long and brown."

"Is it long enough to cover you like Lady Godiva?"

"I have no idea. The idea of being naked on a horse never appealed to me."

"That's a great deal too bad. I find the notion quite entrancing."

Just a flicker of a glare, and then she gave him her sunny smile once more. "Indeed, I can't fathom why you'd want to bother with me, my lord. I know perfectly well that you've had some of the great beauties of the world as your mistresses."

"And haven't you wondered why?"

Her lovely forehead furrowed. "Why?" she echoed, puzzled. And then she remembered. "Oh. Well, I expect you make love in the dark," she said naively. "Christopher St. John always did."

He couldn't stop himself; he laughed. "No, my love, my soon-to-discover wife, I do not make love in the dark. I like to see what I'm enjoying. If women have objections to my appearance I soon make them forget about them."

"Well, you see!" she said, faintly exasperated. "You sounded as if you didn't believe me when I said I forgot about your scars. But you wander around like Lord Byron, all broody and interesting and romantical and it's no wonder women fall at your feet like...like things that fall at your feet. And Byron's almost as lame as you are."

He stared at her in real horror. "Romantical?" he echoed in total disgust. "Broody? Like that ass Byron? My dear Miranda, you have a tongue like a barbed whip." He used the phrase deliberately, like prodding a sore tooth to see if it still hurt.

It did.

This time her smile was genuine, a pleased grin that she'd managed to wound his amour propre. "Well, if you don't want to be a mysterious, romantic hero you need to gain at least two or three stone, talk about finance and belch. Your clothes are too dramatic, as well. I think colors would suit you rather than the funereal black you mope around in. Perhaps a nice puce, or a pale chartreuse. And you could cut your hair. It's too long for fashion nowadays. Something à la Brutus would make you very much more ordinary."

"My hair covers my scarring."

"But we've agreed that no one notices your scarring once they're around you. You woo them like a big, fat hairy black spider, and no matter how much they struggle they're helpless."

"For some reason I can't quite imagine a spider wooing." He didn't even bother trying to hide his amusement. "And I haven't noticed you being particularly helpless. The top button if you please."

"I don't please. The room is cold and we're not yet married and…"

"The top button, or I'll do it myself."

She reached for the top button of her high-necked nightdress. The buttons were small and delicate, mother-of-pearl, and there were far too many of them. He was going to enjoy the slow unveiling, unless she argued too much. In which case he was simply going to rip them open, letting buttons fly everywhere.

The first button came undone, and he could see the hollow at the base of her throat. Such an erotic spot, he thought absently.

"Isn't it rather late for a social call, my lord?" she said, putting her hands back in her lap and clasping them firmly.

"This isn't a social call. It's a conjugal one. Next button."

"Not likely."

"The next button."

There was the briefest hint of a glare, and then that sunny smile. She unfastened it, and he could see the lovely little indent where her collarbones met. "I presume you aren't a practitioner of rape, my lord," she said in a tranquil voice.

"You presume correctly."

"So no matter how many buttons I unfasten you aren't about to force yourself upon me, are you?"

"No. You may strip down naked and dance around the room like a houri and I won't take you unless you ask me to."

She considered him for a moment. "I would feel more secure if not for the occasion of our wager in the coaching inn. You're uncommonly skillful in the manipulation of women."

"I've studied the art quite thoroughly." He crossed his knees. "Toss me a pillow, love, before you undo the next button. I want to be comfortable."

He could read her mind so easily. She wanted to tell him she needed all her pillows, but that would give him the excuse to move up on the bed and she certainly didn't want that. She pulled a soft pillow from behind her back and tossed it to him, then unfastened the third button.

He pushed back his hair, his long, Byronic hair, damn her, and watched her. He liked this part the best, the slow, steady arousal that would become overwhelming until he spent himself in her soft, sweet body. Only her feet were still under the covers, and he wanted to rip the sheets away and toss them on the floor, then put his hands on her calves, spreading her legs for him. This was going to be a challenge, getting her to let go, but he'd always enjoyed challenges. He stayed very still.

"One more," he said softly. That button would open the white nightgown to the tops of her breasts, the ones she said were too small. They seemed quite lovely to him, beneath their virginal covering. He was looking forward to seeing them. Tasting them. Sucking on them as he slowly thrust in and out of her body.

"Don't look at me like that," she said, forgetting to hide the nervousness in her voice.

"Like what, my sweet?"

"Like a predator." And then she pulled herself together, letting out a little trill of laughter that normally would have annoyed him. He knew Miranda too well, knew the nervousness beneath her insouciant behavior, and he recognized it for the paltry defense it was. He was going to be interested to see how long she could keep it up. If she would smile and chatter even as he pushed inside her.

"Listen to me! What a fanciful creature I have become," she said gaily. "No doubt it is due to our very Gothic mansion, my lord."

"You're about to undo another button on your night-gown. You should call me Lucien. You did before."

Her eyes met his for a moment, devoid of artifice, and then she batted her eyelashes at him. "That was a different man, I'm afraid. You weren't who I thought you were."

It shouldn't *bother* him. It didn't *bother* him. It was too bad she wanted a Caliban to her Miranda. How simplistic. He was a villain, and he would be a fool to pretend otherwise. "I can always unfasten that button for you."

She undid it. Her nightgown was now open partway down the valley between her breasts. They were small, but as far as he could tell, quite perfect. "Pull your gown apart," he said lazily.

She looked at him in utter stillness. "You're going to lie with me tonight, aren't you?"

"I already told you, yes. And it won't be rape."

And to his surprise she let out a huge, long-suffering

sigh. "Very well, if you insist," she said in a bored tone of voice. "I do think we should wait till we're married but if you're that eager I can hardly deny you." She pushed the gown toward her shoulders, exposing the swell of her breasts, the valley between them.

"You aren't going to fight me?"

"It would be a waste of time. I've told you more than once, I'm pragmatic. Why make something even more unpleasant than it already is?"

"I do believe my lovemaking is not generally considered to be unpleasant," he murmured.

"Well, they'd hardly tell you the truth, would they?"

Such an innocent! Such a delightfully untried innocent, who still blessedly had gotten rid of her infernal hymen so he didn't have to bother with that part, the blood and the pain and the tears. He'd only taken one virgin in his life, when he himself had been untried, and he swore he would never do it again.

But someone who was almost totally unaware of what actually could lie between a man and a woman was delightful beyond belief.

"I believe there are ways to tell, my darling Miranda."

She looked doubtful, but she lay back against the pillows, her long brown plaits making her look absurdly young. "If you say so. Are you certain I can't change your mind about this?"

"Absolutely certain." And he started toward her, moving up the bed like the stalking beast she'd likened him to.

She could smash a ewer over his head, Miranda thought. But there were none in reach. She could get up, tell him she must use the necessary, but he'd probably insist on accompanying her. She'd tried arguing, she'd tried charming him, and nothing had worked.

She had really hoped to get out of this predicament without having to endure lovemaking again, but that had always been an unlikely goal. And in truth, it would be no epic disaster. She had no maidenhead or reputation to lose. He could do whatever he wanted with her and it would make no difference.

The worst thing that could happen is that she'd respond to his touch, his kiss, assuming he was going to kiss her as part of the whole act. Christopher hadn't, but then, he hadn't liked kissing.

Miranda had discovered that she did. At least, unfortunately, she liked kissing Lucien, no matter what a snake in the grass he was. Whether she wanted to or not, her body reacted to his mouth and hands on her. Which might make the invasion and pain and humiliation of the sex act all the worse. Not that it would matter to him. He was too intent on getting what he wanted.

He was moving toward her like the predator he was, and she lay very still, watching him approach. She could do this if she had to. And clearly she must.

"Do you mind blowing out the candles?" she asked politely. "I think I'd be more comfortable in the dark."

"I imagine you would be. Then you could pretend I'm someone else." He was leaning over her, and she felt very small and helpless. She didn't like that feeling, not one bit. "Tell me, my precious, is there anyone who's taken your fancy over the last few years? Some stalwart young man you could have taken to husband if you hadn't had your fall from grace?"

She wondered what he'd do if he knew the truth.

"Only you, my dove," she said with facetious sweetness to hide her honesty. He would assume she was taunting him, and she was happy with that. Perhaps she could even convince him that her helpless response was all part of the game.

Because, in fact, he was the only man she'd ever thought about willingly bedding, about marrying. About loving.

He had a beautiful mouth. Some of the scarring reached down across the corner of it, and without thinking she reached up and touched it with the tips of her fingers, very softly, a caress that he wouldn't recognize as such.

"What happened to you?" she asked softly.

His pale eyes turned cold. "Is that supposed to drive me away, my sweet? I'm afraid I'm made of sterner stuff than that. A woman with a whip did that to me."

She let her fingers touch the shallow furrows across his temple and brow, gentle, soothing. She wanted to keep touching him, to brush away the pain. "But why? Why would anyone want to hurt you like that?"

His mouth curved in a cynical smile. "Wouldn't you?"

She brought up her other hand to cradle his face, her thumbs brushing against his lips. "No." She couldn't help it. "At times I may want to kill you. But I'd never want to hurt you."

"You realize how ridiculous that sounds?" His voice was low, hypnotic, his mouth very near hers now.

"Yes," she whispered. And she brought his face to hers, and kissed him.

She felt his body jerk in astonishment, and for a moment she was afraid she'd done it wrong, or that he didn't like kissing. She tried to pull back, but he pulled her against him and kissed her back, full, hard and deep, kissing her so thoroughly she was breathless, trembling. This was the way he would have kissed her if he cared about her, if he loved her. She could always pretend, couldn't she?

He rolled her back upon the pillows, his mouth still clinging to hers. She closed her eyes, absorbed in the touch, the flavor of his mouth, letting herself dance into the kiss, reach its center, let the pleasure pour out around her like rays of sunlight, and she wanted to sing with wordless delight.

He lifted his head, and his eyes were glittering in the candlelight as he looked down at her. His long hair fell about his face, hiding the scars, and she wanted to brush it away, but her hands were trapped beneath their bodies as he ran his mouth down the center of her neck, tasting, biting the soft skin, and she felt tiny shivers suffuse her. He kissed the hollow at the base of her throat, and she felt his tongue against her skin. She felt his mouth against the hammering pulse at the side of her neck, as he seemed to inhale the rapid beat, and then he moved to lie down beside her, one hand still capturing her shoulder, turning her to face him.

That was when she realized he'd finished undoing the buttons and the nightgown was halfway down her shoulders. Her breasts were exposed in the cool night air, and she reached up try to cover them, but he took care of that with one strong hand. "No need to be shy, my Miranda," he whispered. "We always knew it would get to this sooner or later."

She didn't answer. She couldn't. She could no more continue with her cheery good-nature than she could give in to the tears that seemed to be forming at the back of her throat for absolutely no reason. She hadn't cried over Christopher St. John—there was absolutely no reason to cry over Lucien.

He was right. It was always coming to this, from the first moment she saw him. No, from the first moment she heard his voice and felt that incredible pull, she knew this man would be someone different in her life. He would take her, claim her, and then she supposed he'd abandon her as he'd threatened. It didn't matter. She didn't even like sex, but she wanted his body on top of hers, pushing inside her. She wanted to put her arms around him and hold him close while he sweated and strained and found his completion. She wanted to give everything she could to him, when she should have wanted to cut his throat.

It made no sense, but his hand had slid down her body to her small breasts, and he was cupping one gently, learning the textures of it, his fingers playing with the hardened nipple, and she could feel a strange surge of response lower down, between her legs.

He leaned over and put his mouth on her breast, sucking her nipple into his mouth, and she arched off the bed, only her amazing self-control keeping her from crying out.

It was an astonishing feeling. The slow, steady tug of his mouth at her breast, while his hand toyed with her other nipple. She'd been determined not to say anything, but somehow a tiny squeak of reaction broke through.

He pulled his mouth away, licking her, and she needed him to move to her other breast, but he didn't, he seemed happy enough, placed closemouthed kisses against her collarbone, and she made a small, whimpering sound, one that couldn't be of need, could it?

He raised his head, and his expression was cool, controlling, though his pale eyes were filled with heat. "Ask me," he said.

She closed her mouth tightly, biting down on her lip. She wouldn't give him that satisfaction—he couldn't just make her give up that easily.

He moved his head down, and his nose brushed against the side of her breast. "Just say please, Miranda. That's all you have to do." He used his tongue, gently lapping her skin, the valley between her breasts, moving no closer, and she bit down, hard, to keep from crying out.

His tongue just danced across the top of her nipple, a featherlight touch, and she couldn't help it, she writhed, wanting more. "Just ask, Miranda," he whispered in a light, singsong voice.

His hand slid beneath the gown to touch her belly, holding her still as she twisted against him, trying to get more of him. A thousand different curses came to mind, the angry, violent things she wanted to rain down on his head, but his hand splayed out across her belly, long, warm fingers, and she couldn't stand it anymore.

"Please," she gasped out, and she heard his damnable chuckle. But then it didn't matter, for his mouth latched onto her other breast, and her back arched as he drew her into his mouth, his tongue dancing across the pebbled nub, as he sucked at her, hard. His fingers slid lower, and she felt a tiny explosion rocket through her, making her jerk against his restraining hand.

She fell back, panting, confused, dizzy. He was pulling her gown completely off, but she no longer cared. She could barely move, but she could see him quite well.

"My, you *are* responsive, my pet... Now what do you think you might like next? I have all sorts of interesting ideas."

She was managing to focus again, and she looked up at him dazedly. He was slowly unfastening his cravat, and he looked at the length of silk for a long, contemplative moment, and that dangerous smile curved his lips.

"We'll leave this for later, shall we?" he murmured, carefully draping it around the bedpost. He leaned back, that animal smile dancing around his mouth. In the darkness the scarring on his face was invisible, and she found she missed it. It was part of him, nothing she needed to hide from, and she wanted to reach her fingers up to touch the hardened furrows across his cheek. She didn't. "You really have extraordinary breasts, and I would happily suckle you all night long, but I'm afraid I'm getting too needy for the business at hand. It's surprising how little self-control I have right now. Perhaps revenge is an aphrodisiac."

Her eyes flew open. She'd forgotten. Forgotten this was simply an act of revenge, not of choice on his part.

And the damnable thing was, it didn't matter. His hand was on her stomach, moving lower, stroking lower, and she felt his fingers touch her triangle of hair, and she tried to clamp her legs together, embarrassed.

"It doesn't work that way, Miranda. Don't you remember?" he said softly. "Spread your legs for me or I'll make you."

She found her voice. "You said you wouldn't force me."

"I lied. At this point I'd do anything to take you."

"Including rape?"

He was unmoved. "Precious, I just made you climax simply by sucking on your breasts. It won't be rape." His fingers moved lower, touching her intimately, and she felt another lightning-like shimmer of reaction. "Will it, my love?"

In answer she spread her legs, closing her eyes so she wouldn't see his triumphant smile.

18

Lucien knew exactly what he should do. She was lying in front of him, legs spread for him, acquiescent...no, more than acquiescent. Wanting. He'd made her come, so simply it astonished him.

He should walk away. He should get up from the bed and walk away, for a thousand reasons, not the least of which was how much he wanted her. So much that it made him vulnerable, and he despised being vulnerable. He had no illusions that once he took her it would be enough. Once he took her he would want more, and more.

Oh, eventually he would tire of her. He tired of everything, truly cared about nothing. But before that happened he would be driven by a need for her, and he hated that.

And indeed, walking away would be perfect. He would leave her trembling on the brink of total sexual surrender, and her physical frustration would shake her badly. She would have offered herself, and he could reject her, mirroring the pain that had driven his half sister to kill herself. He could walk away...

She'd opened her eyes again, looking at him through the dim shadows, almost as if she'd read his mind. She knew him too well, which was part of what drew him to her. She could anticipate his moves, and counter them.

A faint smile curved her mouth, the mouth he needed to feel on his body. Her pale body lay spread out in front of him, and this time she made no maidenly move to cover herself. "Have you changed your mind, my lord? What a shame. Could you retrieve my covers on your way out—I'm a bit chilled." Her voice was calm, cheerful, unmoved, and mentally he saluted her. She'd recovered from what was undoubtedly the first climax of her life with resolute aplomb and was ready to battle again.

And he could no more walk away than he could stop breathing.

He slid his hand over the sweet mound, letting his fingers dance against her clitoris, and she arched in reaction. She was hot and damp and ready for him, and he slid one long finger inside her, testing her.

She was tight, very tight. Why wouldn't she be—it had been two years since she'd made love. He pulled out the one finger and pushed two inside, and she made a faint sound of discomfort, quickly swallowed. She didn't want him to know anything about her reactions, and he knew she would say nothing more. It was up to him to read her body. Fortunately he was an expert at just that.

He moved over her, and for a moment she tried to sit up, to push him away, and then she remembered and laid back, the perfect nonvirgin sacrifice to the monster.

He released himself, simply because it was getting

too painful. He could smell the faint scent of her arousal, and he wanted to bury himself inside her, thrust until he reached his own satisfaction. He needn't bother with withdrawal, or French letters, or any form of protection. He could spend himself inside her, endlessly.

But if he took her now he would most likely tear her, or at the very least bring her discomfort. He had to put off his own release for just a few minutes longer.

He withdrew his fingers, putting his hands on her waist, pulling her down on the bed as he knelt between her legs, and he could see by her shallow breathing that she was frightened, no matter how much she wanted to hide it. St. John had really botched things to an extraordinary extent, but Lucien found he could be glad of it. There was something aphrodisiacal about making a frightened woman climax, and he slid his hands over her lovely hips, down her thighs, pulling them further apart. And then he put his mouth on her.

She made noise then, a horrified, muffled protest that was then silenced as he cradled her hips and brought her closer to his hungry mouth. He let his tongue dart, learning her, teasing her clitoris, opening her with his mouth to taste her fully, his tongue thrusting inside her, and the dampness followed, lovely waves of creamy desire, and the almost climaxed against the bedsheets as she writhed beneath him. He slid his fingers inside her again, more easily this time, as he tongued her, and he thrust with his fingers, opening her for him, stretching her when she was too aroused to notice, too caught up in the sensations he was coaxing from her.

Her climax surprised him, as she arched off the bed with a helpless cry, and he lifted up, seeing that she had her hand on her mouth to silence her sounds of pleasure, and he could wait no more. He wiped his mouth against his sleeve, placed his cock where his fingers had been and pushed.

She was wet enough, aroused enough that he slid in fairly easily, but not as deep as he needed to go. He moved over her, and her eyes were filled with fear.

"I'm not going to hurt you." He wondered why he was bothering to reassure her. "Your body will adjust itself to mine."

She shook her head in distress, soundless, not believing him, and he could feel her tightening around him, trying to keep him out.

But he'd reached his tipping point, and he could play no more erotic games with her. If he touched her again she'd come once more, closing up against him.

He kissed her. Long and hard and deep, but her fear was too great, and he couldn't reach her that way. So he simply did the next best thing.

He bit her. Hard, on the soft flesh between her neck and her shoulder, and the pain shocked her so much she forgot to keep her body stiff, and he slid in, sheathing himself fully in her clinging body, and she arched off the bed, making a muffled sound of distress and pleasure.

He could have spilled at that very moment, but he fought back, holding himself very still, resting his forehead against hers as he tried to master his breathing. "Don't move," he whispered, afraid she was going to try to buck him off. Any movement, any ripple on her part would start his climax, and he needed to hold off.

He needed to bring her to completion. At that point he wasn't thinking too clearly, drugged by the scent and the taste and the feel of her, but leaving her without her experiencing the ultimate of pleasure would somehow compromise his revenge. He lay motionless on top of her, fully clothed, waiting for her panicked tightness to relax.

It seemed to take an eternity, but slowly, slowly her short, frightened gasps slowed. She took a deep breath, and he drew her legs up around his hips. "It will hurt less like this," he murmured in her ear, and she obeyed silently, letting his hands touch and place her, doing what he could to relieve the pressure of his heavy invasion.

And then he could wait no more. He pulled her hands away from her mouth, holding them over her head, twining his fingers with hers, and began to move.

Her first whimper of discomfort almost made him stop. Almost. He pulled partway out and thrust again, slowly, and her dampness covered them both, easing the way.

So tight. So sweet. Had he said those words out loud, or simply thought them? It didn't matter. He was caught up in her skin, the perfume of her body, the soft dampness of her breath against the side of his face. He could feel every hitch in her breathing, the slight changes when he moved just right, his cock hitting the spot that seemed to make women mad, and she let out a satisfying cry when he did so. He would have loved to concentrate on it, but his own climax was fast approaching, and he was determined not to leave her behind.

He whispered in her ear, unguarded sex words, and her warmed breasts pebbled against his chest, as she caught his rhythm, moving with him, oh, so sweetly. The sturdy old bed shook beneath them, and he released her hands, bracing himself against the mattress as he thrust into her, feeling her tightness, the waves of response, the sudden shock of her physical climax, and he let himself go, emptying himself into her, a rush of completion like nothing he'd ever felt before.

His body went rigid in the shadows, his skin alive with a thousand pinpricks, and he threw back his head and cried out.

He kept his weight on his elbows, just barely, trying to catch his breath, as shudder after shudder danced through her body. It took him a moment before he could focus, and when he looked down into her face he almost wished he hadn't.

Her eyes were closed, and tears were pouring down her face. Great, silent tears, and he knew not if they were from the force of her release or something less flattering. Had he hurt her after all? He could barely catch his breath, and her own was fast and shallow, and he could see the pounding of her heart beneath her pale skin.

He started to pull out of her, but her arms came up suddenly, twining around his neck and pulling him down against her. He quickly rolled onto his side with her, so as not to crush her beneath him, and his semierect cock was still inside her. As if they were unwilling to let go of each other.

She buried her face against his shoulder, and he could feel the silent sobs rack her body. He pulled her closer still, wishing he'd had time to remove his clothes, instead of taking her like one takes a doxy. His hand went up to her disordered plaits. One had come loose with a curtain of hair partly around them. He stroked her head gently as she hid her face against his shoulder. She was trying to hide from him, hide her tear-damp face, and he let her. He wanted to hide, as well.

He must have drifted off to sleep. When he awoke

it was light, and he was alone in her bed, still fully dressed, and there was no sign of her.

He lay there and cursed beneath his breath. "Bloody hell!" he said out loud, sitting up amidst the welter of covers, his disordered clothes around him. Had she tried to run? None of the servants should be under any misapprehension that this was a love match, or that their master was in any way a good man. But he couldn't very well have her floating facedown in the lake. He cursed under his breath again, trying to shake off the damnable sense of languor.

He wanted more. He'd slept, deeply, wrapped around her, and he could still smell her on his skin, the sweet, erotic scent of her. She was probably somewhere in the house, crying.

He fastened his breeches and made his way to his rooms, not particularly caring who saw him. He'd bedded his affianced wife. Out in the countryside they were more liberal about such things, believing in handfasting and all sorts of ridiculousness. She was going to get a wedding all right, though not the one she dreamed of. Unless it was in her nightmares.

For some reason he found he was in an utterly foul mood. He shouldn't be. While the sex had been straightforward and far more work than he was used to, it had been worth it in the end. It had been quite... stimulating.

Until he'd seen she was crying, and he'd ended up holding her until he'd fallen asleep. He wasn't quite sure what was fueling his nasty temper, so nasty that even his valet, who was quite used to him, retreated in offended silence. It was a shame he'd left Leopold back in London. Or perhaps not—his old servant had been deeply disapproving of the way he'd treated her, even though he'd said nothing. And Lucien wasn't interested in the opinions of servants, even those who knew him better than he knew himself.

Indeed, things were moving along quite well. His plan had been relatively simple, and each step, though not without its problems, had been completed. He'd managed to win her trust, to abscond with her, and seduce her. All he had left to do was marry her and leave her prisoner in this drafty old place, and there was nothing her family could do about it.

He strode down the dark, drafty halls in a rare temper. He'd been meaning to start back for London, but now he was going to have to waste time looking for Miranda, who was doubtless sobbing her heart out…

Music came from the end of the hallway. Someone was playing the piano, rather badly, and he winced at a wrong note. Whoever was torturing the instrument continued unabated, and he changed direction, moving toward the music room and thrusting the doors open.

His fiancée was sitting at the piano, dressed in a frock of rose-pink. Her brown hair had been simply arranged around her face, and he could see the bite mark on her shoulder and was instantly aroused.

She looked up at him, and there wasn't a tear, not a shadow in her eye. She beamed at him. "That was absolutely lovely, darling," she said brightly. "When can we do it again?"

He stood motionless, looking at her. Her color was high, making her look even prettier, and her mouth was slightly swollen from the pressure of his. But it was the bite mark on her neck that was most arousing, most disturbing. He couldn't believe he'd been so out of control that he'd done that. It was primal, animalistic, something he wasn't used to feeling. Except when he looked at her.

He was half tempted to cross the room, lift her up onto the piano, shove up her skirts and take her there. But he didn't move, giving her a faint, cool smile that belied that turmoil inside him. The sheer, barely controlled lust that would doubtless terrify her. "I'm so glad you enjoyed it, my precious. I'm afraid we'll have to wait for an encore until I return from London."

Her mouth pouted in disappointment, the look in her eyes less easy to read. "Must you go?"

"I'm afraid so. I have a very special house party planned, and I must see to the arrangements."

Her eyebrows rose. "A house party? Here?"

"Not this time. My friends don't mind the dust and decay—in fact, I rather think they enjoy it. But it's not my turn to play host. I simply promised to see that our main event takes place as ordered. Our wedding, my dear."

She blinked. "We're getting married at a house party? That's scarcely legal, is it? And who might the guests be, dearest? Jewel thieves?"

"Among others. You'll find all sorts of guests at these house parties. From royal dukes to anarchists, in fact. I think you'll be quite entertained. As for legalities, we can always deal with that later."

"How entertaining," she said in an unaltered voice. "And do we have a date on this momentous gathering?"

"Friday next, my love. I'll be gone until then—I find you much too distracting, but in my absence you may do anything you please. This house is yours, and my finances are at your disposal. You'll have to entertain yourself as best you can without me."

She rose, and he saw another mark at the side of her neck, from his mouth, not his teeth, and he wondered if he dared wait a few hours just so that he might have her again. He wanted to see what other marks he had left on her pale, beautiful flesh.

"I will be devastated without you, my darling, but I expect I'll manage to contrive."

There was his sweet Miranda, hiding the barb of sarcasm beneath her limpid smile. That was almost more arousing than the love marks, he thought absently. "I'm sure you will. My factor is Robert Johnson. He'll see to whatever expenses you incur."

"I can be very expensive, my love," she purred.

"I imagine you can. I have a very great deal of money." He cocked his head, surveying her. "Come and kiss your lover goodbye."

It wasn't a suggestion and she knew it. She moved across the floor with the perfect simulation of eagerness, standing before him with an overbright smile on her face. "Do you want me to kiss you, my darling?" she inquired limpidly. "Or will you kiss me?"

But he was no longer interested in games. He simply pulled her against him, kissing her, putting his mouth on hers in raw, elemental demand. Then realized with surprise that her arms had slid around his waist, holding on, as she kissed him back.

She probably hadn't meant to. There was a distressed expression in her eyes before she quickly shuttered it, and she took a step back the moment he released her.

"Goodbye, Lucien."

Lucien. She was calling him by his name again, or

perhaps it had only been a slip. But how could you stay formal with a man when you'd had him pumping away between your legs?

He could give her that same courtesy, that same trace of vulnerability. "Goodbye, Miranda. I'm happy that you were pleased with my poor efforts last night." And he brushed a last kiss across her forehead, his lips feathering her pale, composed face.

Poor efforts, Miranda thought, watching as the door closed behind him. If those were poor efforts, she wouldn't survive.

He hadn't hurt her, at least not much, and she'd been braced for it. He was much bigger than Christopher had been, so big that she wondered if he was misshapen. She only had the two men to judge by, and she'd assumed that Christopher had been the norm.

She went back to the piano and sat, gingerly. She didn't know what was wrong with her. Why had she kissed him back? Did she really not want him to go? Her breasts tingled, and when she tightened her legs together odd tremors rippled through her. What in God's name had he done to her?

No, it wasn't in God's name. More like the devil's. He touched her in ways she hadn't imagined, put his mouth between her legs, and when he'd pushed inside her she'd felt…she'd felt…complete. As if she'd found her other half. She'd been naked, he'd still been fully clothed except for his open breeches, and she hadn't seen him, hadn't been able to touch his skin. She was already suffused with a dangerous arousal—what would it be like when he did it again? When his clothes were off, and the candles were lit, and it wasn't such a new and shocking pleasure.

She should be happy he was going away. It would give her time to regain her self-control, to understand what he'd done to her body. It gave him complete power over her, and she couldn't let that happen.

Oh, bloody hell, of course she could, she thought, impatient with herself. If she ended up married to the man she was duty bound to be in his bed, and she'd be an idiot not to take any pleasure she could. Even if it left her weak, helpless, vulnerable, it was really too wonderful to deny. What had been foul with Lucien de Malheur. John was glorious with Christopher St.

And she wanted more.

19

Miss Jane Paget stepped out into the early morning air. Jacobs the randy coachman was already mounted on the driver's box of the landaulet, his heavy greatcoat on, his hat pulled low, and he stayed put, waiting for the hostler from the inn to help them board the small carriage.

At least it wasn't raining today, and it was warmer. If Jane were to be wildly optimistic she might even say she could sense spring in the air, but she was too busy worrying about what her family, and even more importantly, Mr. Bothwell, were going to say when she reappeared. At least the redoubtable Mrs. Grudge would set their minds at ease once they saw her. With a friendly, proper companion like Mrs. Grudge they would hardly suspect anything untoward.

And in fact there had been nothing untoward, at least as far as she was concerned. She'd simply gone for a journey with her dearest friend to see her married, even if that marriage hadn't, in fact, taken place as yet. Not that they needed to know that. And what was the harm in going on a journey with Miranda to keep her bridal nerves at bay'? Even the censorious Mr. Bothwell couldn't have any objections. Could he'?

Of course he probably knew perfectly well that if anyone needed her nerves soothed it was Jane herself, not Miranda, who sailed through disaster with admirable calm. She could only hope her dear friend wasn't heading into disaster with the Earl of Rochdale.

"You look tired, lass," Mrs. Grudge said comfortably. "Did you na' sleep well last night?"

"Not too well. Too long in the carriage, I think. I woke up at two and couldn't get back to sleep. I even went down and slept in front of the fire for a while."

"Tha' did?" Mrs. Grudge was looking disturbed at the notion. "And where was yon coachman? Last I saw Jacobs was in a chair by the fire hisself. Happen he might ha' found companionship for the night."

Jane didn't know whether to defend him or not. Her companion was looking so disturbed that she thought it might be better not to mention their odd meeting.

She'd only slept in the chair for an hour or two, returning to her lumpy bed before the inn came to life, and by the time she woke up she realized how absurd her suspicions had been. Jacobs reminded her of the mysterious man who'd kissed her. And the reason was quite simple—they were both men who knew how to flatter and seduce women. She'd experienced the coachman's easy charm and recognized its familiarity.

In truth, no one flattered and charmed her at the parties she attended. Not even Mr. Bothwell, who had addressed her father before she even knew he was interested.

Simon Pagett was an enlightened man, and he told him it was up to his daughter, a fact Mr. Bothwell found distasteful but not offensive enough to turn him away. And she'd said yes, though now she wasn't quite sure why. She was twenty-three and no one had shown the slightest bit of interest in her. When her father had inherited his cousin Montague's estate there'd been little money left, though her mother had a comfortable amount from her first, miserable marriage. Neither of them liked Mr. Bothwell very much, but Jane insisted she was in love, and they gave in after much arguing. She wanted a home of her own. She wanted children. She wanted a husband, and Mr. Bothwell was tall and handsome, if a bit severe. So she'd lied.

It was astonishing what a few days away could do. Astonishing to have a man kiss her with real passion, astonishing to have another man flirt with her. Granted, the second would have flirted with a tree stump if nothing else had been around, and the first was a criminal, but still.

She looked down at the diamond ring on her finger. It really was astonishingly beautiful. Her mother had jewels that were as valuable, jewels to suit her glorious beauty. But there was something about this ring that she loved. Perhaps because it felt as if it was hers. Which of course it wasn't.

"You certain you want to take that ring off, Miss Jane?" Mrs. Grudge said, eyeing it with only a trace of covetousness. And who could blame her—any woman would want a ring like this one. "Must be at least two carats."

Mrs. Grudge would have been quite striking in her youth, and even in drab clothes she was still more than attractive. How she knew the weight of diamonds was beyond Jane's comprehension, but perhaps she'd had a misspent youth before she married the unfortunate Mr. Grudge. She wore no jewels of any kind, but Jane could almost imagine her dressed in something glorious, bedecked with rubies.

And then she laughed. Her imagination was really going wild nowadays. She looked down at the ring. "I have my reasons."

"Your fiancé must love you very much to give you a ring like that. I wouldn't toss him over without a good reason."

That was the same thing Brandon had said. Why did people equate love with expensive jewels? If that were the case then the stranger with the midnight kiss loved her very much indeed, and he didn't even know her name.

And how did Mrs. Grudge know she was having second thoughts about Mr. Bothwell? Though it was a logical leap, if she was trying to remove an engagement ring, and Jane was hardly about to explain that the diamond came from someone else altogether.

She folded her hands, hiding the diamond from her own sight and that of Mrs. Grudge. She would have to give it up sooner or later, and the truth was, she wouldn't need axle grease. It came off quite easily this morning when she was washing her hands, and she was going to have to do something about it before long.

But not right now. Right now it was hers. A gift from a fantasy lover.

She turned her attention back to Mrs. Grudge. "When do you think we'll reach London?"

"I should think one more night on tha' road and happen we'll be there," she said in her comfortable voice. "We'll try to find you a better bed tonight. Jacobs has been keeping to back roads, but I'll tell him to find a place better suited to the gentry."

Where she wouldn't run across a handsome driver in the middle of the night. "Oh, I like the smaller inns," she found herself saying. One more night of freedom. One more night before she had to face Mr. Bothwell and make up her mind when she thought she'd done that long ago.

Well, she'd wanted adventure, and she'd gotten it. Midnight kisses, elopements, raffish carriage drivers with charming smiles, and it had thrown her safely ordered future in disarray. And she was glad of it. It was simply getting through the shifts in circumstance that were uncomfortable.

"I'll tell Jacobs when we stop for lunch," Mrs. Grudge murmured, closing her eyes. "I had such a night ma' self, Miss Jane. Tossed and turned." A faint smile curved her full mouth.

"Oh, then maybe we should push on ahead," Jane said, feeling guilty. The sooner she faced Mr. Bothwell the sooner she could move on. She was being a coward.

"Nah, there's na reason ta hurry, Miss Jane. I like a bit of the countryside meself. Tomorrow we'll arrive early, all right and tight, with no harm to anyone. Does tha' suit you?"

She should hurry home. She should get rid of the diamond ring; she should be a dutiful wife to Mr. Bothwell.

And she would. Tomorrow. One more night, she promised herself. One more night to indulge the wild child who was trapped inside her ordinary body, and then she'd once more be what people expected her to be.

* * *

One more night, Jacob thought. God knew what was going on in his thieves' ken—there were any number of people willing to take over at the first sign of weakness. He'd done the job at the Carrimores', to make a point, that he could do anything any one of them could do, and do it better. He was a dead shot, wicked with a knife and always ready with his fists, which he preferred. He didn't fancy killing people, though at times it was necessary. Some people just needed killing, and he wasn't a man to shy away from doing what had to be done.

He just hoped that Marley hadn't decided it was time to make his move while the King of Thieves was out of town on what was the most ridiculous, trumped-up excuse he could imagine.

Scorpion wasn't going to be happy with him, taking over like this, but he should have known he could never resist Miss Jane. Besides, Scorpion wanted him to get the bloody ring back, and this was as good a way as any. Except that he didn't care about the damned ring, and neither did Scorpion. He just liked loose ends dealt with.

He would hardly be surprised once he found Jacob had taken over. They knew each other too well.

He didn't know if a man like Lucien de Malheur was capable of falling in love, but he was coming damned close with his unwilling bride. Jacob had known him for more than half his life, and he'd never seen him so wound up, so angry, so twisted. It must be love, he thought with a grin.

Lucien wouldn't have his head for taking over the job, simply because he wanted his best friend in the same rotten condition. That was Scorpion, out to share the misery. What he'd failed to take into account was that Jacob loved easily. He loved them and left them, making the entire process much less onerous.

He wasn't about to love and leave Miss Jane Pagett. He wasn't about to love her in the first place. There was trouble in a tall, sweet package, and he was smart enough to avoid it in the first place. His taking over as driver was simply a way of proving to himself and to Scorpion that he wasn't going to weaken. That kiss had been irresistible, but he wouldn't do it again. If he could manage it, he wouldn't even talk to her again. She looked at him out of her sweet brown eyes and he fancied she could see right through him.

Which of course, is exactly what her type would do. Look straight through their inferiors, not even noticing they were human. Except...she'd been concerned about him riding in the rain. She hadn't wanted to take his chair by the fire. Foolish girl, she'd even suggested they sit side by side.

Lord, he could get under her skirts in no time flat, she was that innocent and trusting. He liked his women wise and experienced. What did he need with a chit who trusted everyone and had a mouth that tasted like magic?

One more night at some small, out-of-the-way inn. He'd survive just fine.

The army of maidservants arrived the next day, and Miranda set them all to work, Mrs. Humber and Bridget included. She herself tied a scarf around her head, rolled up her sleeves and donned an apron. She could dust as well as the next one, and she wanted to make certain the place was cleaned to her specifications, which were exacting, after so many years of neglect.

It took five days to get everything swept and scrubbed and dusted. Each night Miranda would fall into bed, too tired to ring for a bath, too softhearted to make her already overworked servants lug the water for her. On the fifth day, when everything was finally clean and smelling of lemon oil, she twirled around the large front hall with its walls of medieval weapons, laughing.

Mrs. Humber observed her with a grim expression on her face. She'd taken the flurry of cleaning badly, but after one or two weak attempts at intimidation she gave in, following Miranda's orders with an ill grace.

"He won't even notice. We've done all this work for nothing."

"I notice," Miranda said in a tranquil voice. "The next thing we need are painters."

"Painters, my lady? You'll be wanting your portrait done?" Her tone suggested that was a waste of time.

"No, to paint Lord Rochdale's bedroom. It's much too dark and dingy in there. I'm surprised he can see his way at all. We'll need new curtains as well—where's the nearest mercer?"

"The master prefers his bedroom dark."

"The master prefers his life dark. That was before he made the mistake of proposing to me," she said in the sweet voice she usually reserved for Lucien. Calling it a proposal was stretching the truth just a tiny bit, but life with Mrs. Humber was an ongoing struggle and she needed to keep her in line. "I hope to have everything finished by the time he returns, so clearly we must waste no time."

Mrs. Humber stared at her. "It would be a very great

mistake to interfere with the master's rooms. I told you we shouldn't even be cleaning it. He's given strict orders that we weren't to go in there without his express permission."

"Well, we did, and we didn't find anything the slightest bit interesting or romantic. I was expecting the bodies of seven brides, but there was nary a one to be seen. Find me painters and have them here in the morning, Mrs. Humber." Her voice left no room for argument.

"And what color would you be wanting to paint his rooms, my lady?"

Miranda considered it for a long moment, and then a smile lit her face.

"Pink."

Jacob leaned against the railing, drinking his mug of ale, thinking about the woman he couldn't see. The inn, a small but clean establishment with a motherly landlady and a jocular master of the house, had a private room for the gentry, one with a closed door so he couldn't get a glimpse of her.

Which was a good thing. He'd been too long without a woman—since the night of the Carrimores' ball, in fact, and he wasn't a man made for celibacy. He should have taken the barmaid up on her offer last night. That would have settled things.

But he'd been a right idiot and said no and here he was, needy, with the only tapmaid some forty years old and bearing a mustache. No, he wouldn't be enjoying anything but his own hand tonight, more's the pity.

Long Molly would be more than happy to take care of his needs, but they'd been lovers a long time ago, and the friendship they had now was too important to risk on a casual tup.

Besides, if truth be told, he didn't want Long Molly or the buxom maid at the last tavern. He didn't want Lady Blanche Carlisle, whom he'd been bedding on a regular basis when her husband was out of town, and he didn't want Gracie, who ran Beggar's Ken with an iron fist and a lovely smile. Everyone wanted Gracie, and she was right generous with her favors, but she was partial to him, and he enjoyed that partiality.

And he hadn't touched either of them in more than a week. Bloody hell, a woman was a woman, at least when it came to sex. He could have taken either of them, and if he was longing for someone else he could close his eyes and pretend he was smelling violets.

He pushed away from the bar, the beer sloshing a little bit. He'd had too much to drink and he knew it. They would be in London by noon tomorrow, thank God, and he'd never have to see Miss Jane Pagett again. She'd marry her worthy fiancé, have babies and a good life and he'd continue to raise hell.

He could pretend to be drunk, stumble into her private dining room and maybe she'd invite him in, talk to him in that soft, charming voice that he sometimes dreamed about.

He could…

He could head out to the stables and forget all about Miss Jane Pagett. She'd know better than to come traipsing down in her nightgown in the middle of the night this time. She could come across Jacobs the womanizing groom, and there was no telling what might happen.

The truth was, he didn't want to return to London. He was sick of the city, the smell and the smoke, the noise. He'd been a traveling man since he first ran away from his master who'd beat him when he grew too big to climb up the chimneys. He wished he knew where that mangy old bastard was. He'd gotten right big, well over six feet, and it would give him a great deal of pleasure to loom over the old man and show him what it was like to be stuffed up a chimney.

Ah, but he'd let that go. Still, he was longing for sunshine and warm air. For different lands and words and choices. That was one reason he hadn't put up an argument when Long Molly told him they were to spend another night on the road. He was in no hurry to return to London. He could happily drive this landaulet anywhere Miss Pagett with the sweet brown eyes and the wonderful mouth told him to.

He prided himself on being a practical man, a pragmatic one. He'd had that dammable romantic streak beaten out of him when he was young, for all that Scorpion liked to tease him. There was just something about her eyes....

He drained his ale, setting the mug down with a snap. As always he was the last man standing, alone in the taproom. She would have gone to bed by now, wouldn't she? He could make a little bargain with himself. He'd go check on the private dining room. She was more than likely gone, in which case he'd go on out to his bed in the stables with no one the worse for wear. If she was there he'd stay and talk with her, flirt with her just a little bit. It was up to the fates.

The private dining room was up a few steps, and he stumbled, cursing. He was old enough to know better, he told himself, and reached for the cast-iron door latch.

The room was empty, the fire banked down to coals. It was a clear night, and the moon shone in brightly, illuminating the empty parlor. He closed the door and leaned against it, telling himself it was relief that he felt and nothing more.

And then he saw the stairs.

It was a very small inn. There was only one bedroom for the quality. Their servants, including Long Molly, were housed around back of the kitchens. He'd known that when he'd stopped for the night, hoping that the place would already be bespoken, and they could push on for the night, relieving him of temptation that much sooner.

But that had worked against him. The place was deserted except for the landlord, his good wife and the barmaid, and now all were abed. Everyone but the wicked, randy King of Thieves masquerading as a coachman, in search of . . .

He didn't want to think about what he was in search of. In truth, his brain was too foggy to clarify exactly what he wanted, though his lower half was leaving him in no doubt. And he headed for the stairs.

Would she be asleep? Would her door be locked? Any sensible woman would lock her door in a public house, but he wasn't convinced of Jane's sense. She'd let him kiss her, hadn't she? She'd invited him to join her by the fire. She hadn't a whole lot of sense when it came to protecting herself from wolves like him.

Though those were two different men she'd invited, he reminded himself. Perhaps he was completely wrong about the girl. Beneath her startled eyes and soft mouth was the heart of a wanton, who took whatever was offered.

No. She hadn't known how to kiss, and he could tell by the racing of her heart and the trembling of her body that she would have kissed him back quite hungrily had she known how. As it was, her attempts had only whetted his appetite.

No, she was an innocent, all right and tight. Most likely very tight, he thought dreamily. The women he tupped had had so many men that if he weren't a good-sized man he might have fallen out.

Ah, but virgins were the very devil. He'd had his share of them, going through scores of them when he first discovered sex, and they'd discovered things together. As he grew more experienced he avoided them. They cried, they hurt, they didn't know where to put their legs or their hands, they especially didn't know where to put their mouths, they believed your lies and they wanted to be held when all was said and done.

He looked at the staircase. There was a window on the landing, and the moon illuminated the way. Clearly that was a sign.

He started up the stairs, thinking about what lay ahead of him. If the door was locked would he force it? Would he knock, and if she said go away, would he? If she screamed would he put his hand over her mouth until she liked it? Just how big a bastard was he?

He reached the top landing. Her door was there, the only door, and he contemplated it. What if he opened the door and she smiled and bade him come in? What if she was frightened?

He stood very still. Tomorrow she'd be out of his life for good. Tonight was his last chance, and he had to be hog-whimpering drunk to even risk coming up these stairs.

He was at her door, and he leaned his forehead against the warm wood, closing his eyes. He thought he could smell the faintest trace of violets through the door, but that had to be his imagination. The imagination that had become his worst enemy.

He whispered her name, so softly it could be the sound of the wind through the fresh leaves outside the moon-shadowed window. And then he laughed soundlessly, at what an idiot he was being. Moon-mad indeed.

He pushed back from the door. The first thing he was doing after he dropped her off at her family home was head straight back to Beggar's Ken, grab Grace by the hand and take her up against the nearest hard surface.

And then he'd find Lady Blanche and do the same. And then see if he could get the two of them together—right now he felt as if he could take on half a dozen hungry women at once, he was so fucking randy.

He turned, silent, letting out his pent-up breath, not sure if it was relief or regret. And he started back down the stairs.

Jane lay in her bed, breathless and unmoving. She heard the footsteps, slow and faintly unsteady, coming up her stairs, and she knew who it was. He'd been drinking a fair amount, Mrs. Grudge had said with a cluck of disapproval, excusing herself early to see to him. So Jane had eaten her dinner in solitary splendor, waiting to see if anyone would come by. She'd even opened the door, just a crack, and waited, long into the evening, but there was no noise from the taproom beyond but the muffled sound of a few voices, and then eventually silence.

So she'd closed the door again and headed upstairs for her usual struggle with her gown and undergarments. Never in her life had she been without her maid, and she appreciated her absent servants' efforts more than ever.

Speaking of which, what did her maid Hester and Miranda's abigail make of their mistresses' sudden disappearance? She hadn't even stopped to think of that.

She'd find out soon enough. Tomorrow, in fact. Tomorrow, when she'd be back in her old life and Jacobs the womanizer would be long gone, ensuring her safety. Safety.

If she let Jacobs seduce her, she thought with a snort of amusement, at least he'd know how to get her blasted clothes off without much effort.

Or maybe he'd simply push her down on the bed and pull up her skirts. She could certainly manage her drawers on her own—it was the rows of tiny buttons at her sleeves and her back, and the corset ties that annoyed her, but in the end she managed. No need for a lover after all, she thought wearily.

She'd be so happy to get into fresh clothes again. Back to her own bed, the comfort of her maid and her family, her future mapped out in front of her.

She heard him in the room beneath her, and she muttered a polite curse under her breath. If she'd just stayed down there a little longer she could have seen him, talked to him. Harmless enough. Though she wasn't quite certain why she wanted to do that.

Anyway, it would have been a great deal longer. She'd been in bed for hours, tossing and turning. She'd even slept for a bit, then woken again, from a strange dream in which her mysterious jewel thief had kissed her once again, picked her up in his arms and carried her into the light, and she'd looked up into his handsome face and seen Jacobs.

Ridiculous. If a man was clever enough and well-spoken enough to be a jewel thief then he'd hardly be driving a carriage to dispose of an unwanted female.

For that's what she felt like. Unwanted, awkward, in the way. Not that her parents ever made her feel that way. They loved her dearly, and her older brother doted on her, as well. But she knew the way her parents looked at each other, the deep passion that still ran between them, the kind of passion that wasn't to be her fate. And she knew she needed to let them be on their own.

When she heard the booted footstep on the first stair her heart slammed to a stop. And started again on the second step. There was nothing up here but her bedroom, no one up here but her. Lying in bed in the nightgown Mrs. Grudge had brought her, along with a few other necessities. And she heard another step, and she sat up, her hand to her throat.

She hadn't locked her door. There'd been a key all right and handy, and she hadn't used it. Hadn't she heard tales of robbers who came upon lonely inns and slaughtered the guests asleep in their beds?

But she knew those footsteps. It could only be Jacobs. Though why in the world would she suppose the handsome coachman would have an eye for someone like her?

He was far beneath her in every way, she reminded herself. One didn't speak to servants; one didn't even look at them. Though in truth her parents were far more casual than that, and treated the vast number of servants who kept Montague House going with kindness and respect.

And the Rohans as well weren't particularly starchy. Not that anyone would consider hopping into bed with a coachman, no matter how handsome he was. It simply wasn't done.

Not that a betrothed, virginal young lady should consider hopping into bed with anybody but her husband, and only that well after the marriage ceremony. It was too bad she couldn't view the inevitable ceremonial de-flowering with the excitement that was rising with each of his footsteps on the narrow, twisty stairs.

He reached the top, and she let out a squeak of excitement and dismay, one she quickly smothered as she clapped both hands over her mouth. It took but another step or two to reach her door, and she waited, holding her breath, for the door handle to move.

She heard a soft thump, and she considered calling out. Good sense kept her silent. The door handle remained still. He would knock, so as not to scare her. He wouldn't want to frighten her, after all. Particularly since, if he didn't know she was hoping, expecting him to follow her up those stairs, and she'd be likely to scream the house down at the first sign of an intruder.

She wouldn't scream. She closed her eyes, and she could feel him on the other side of the door, and she waited, breathless.

Until she heard him turn around and start back down the stairs again, leaving her alone in her virginal bed. Safe and sound. And weeping.

20

The sun came out on the sixth day Miranda was at Pawlfrey House, and for a moment she simply stared at the window in shock. The bright beams turned the lingering raindrops on the windows into diamonds, and it was suddenly warm.

She would have dressed in her old pelisse but Lucien had given word, high-handed creature that he was, that all her clothes were to be burned, as if she were a victim of the plague, so she had no choice but to take the fur-trimmed one and the thoroughly enchanting bonnet that went with it.

She'd been circumspect with her bonnets since the incident, when before she'd indulged in the most outrageous confections. This was much more to her style than the subdued hats she'd grown accustomed to, and she set it atop her head with real pleasure.

Which was nothing compared to what she felt when she stepped out onto the front portico and looked around her.

The air was warm, too warm for the pelisse, and she unfastened it, draping it over her arm. The ground was still wet beneath her feet, but as she walked past the tangled growth that surrounded the old house and got her first glimpse of blue, blue sky she suddenly felt as if she could breathe again.

There was a broad expanse of overgrown lawn in front of the house, with the driveway twining around it and beyond, to her astonishment, was the vast stillness of a lake, quiet and empty, with mountains looming behind it. She shouldn't be surprised. After all, it was the Lake District, was it not? But Lucien seemed to have his own private body of water. Of course he would—he had more money than God, he'd told her, blasphemous as always. The field leading down to it was a mass of yellow, thousands upon thousands of daffodils, their familiar scent a perfume in the air. Everything sparkled from the brightness of the sun, and when she looked back at Pawlfrey House she realized it was even larger than she'd thought. She was pleased to see the roof looked in decent shape, as did the windows, and as for the wretched condition of the front of the house, it was nothing a small army of gardeners couldn't whip into shape in no time.

Mrs. Humber would scream, she thought placidly. She'd fought hiring the maids, insisting there was no one available, until she discovered that Miranda planned to make her do the hard work alone. Eleven strong and healthy young women were immediately produced.

She looked at the house. Her house. She could be happy here, which would drive Lucien mad. She would be happy if he were there, to joust with, to sleep with. At the oddest moments she would remember those moments in her bed, and her body would react in the strangest ways, tightening, blossoming.

If he stayed away it would be even better. Sleeping with him upset her. It threw her mind into disarray, it made her want to laugh and cry and dance and scream. It was disturbing, and she preferred calm. She didn't want to long for his kiss, his touch, his mouth on her body. The very thought made her start to tremble again, and she pushed it out of her mind. There must be a rose garden somewhere. She could put some of her energies into that.

She walked down to the lake, an easy hike with the overhead sun bright above her. The water was clear and cold to the touch, and there was an old dock leading far out into the lake.

She dropped her pelisse onto a large stone and headed for it. She could hear the cry of the birds overhead, wheatear and mountain blackbirds and ravens as they wheeled and darted, and she smiled up at them, before she began to climb up onto the dock.

It was slippery from being in the water so long, and there was no railing, but she couldn't see the contours of the lake from the shore, and from her vantage point there wasn't even a farm in sight. She wanted to see how far the lake extended, and whether there were any neighbors. Just in case she had the need for a midnight escape.

She started down the wooden dock, showing a reasonable amount of care, when the voice she dreaded most, longed for most, broke her concentration.

"What the bloody hell are you doing?" he shouted, startling her so that she whipped around, and promptly slipped on the slimy wood decking.

She went down on one knee, catching herself before she tumbled into the icy cold waters, and then she brought her other knee down, staying there, motionless, trying to regain her breath.

Her pounding heart was beyond her control. The combination of the fright he'd given her and her inevitable reaction to his return made calm just about impossible.

She looked up at him, and froze.

She'd never seen him in sunlight before. He was dressed in black, as always, his black hair tied back, and she could see the scarring quite clearly. He had his cane with him, but apart from that his body was tall, lean, and yes, she must admit it, beautiful. She found everything about him beautiful, even more so in the bright sunlight, with him glowering at her.

"You nearly scared me to death!" she called back.

"Must you sneak up on one?"

"Must you risk your life on a slimy, rotting piece of dock? Come back here at once. No, on second thought, don't move. I'll have someone bring a boat out to get you."

"I fancy the water is only waist deep if I happened to take a tumble, and while I wouldn't like it I doubt I'd be in much danger."

"It's well over your head. Don't look!" he added impatiently. "You might fall."

"I'm not that poor a creature," she replied, leaning over the dock to peer into the clear water. And pulled back, immediately, feeling dizzy. "You're right, it's very deep."

"Of course I'm right!" he said crossly. "Why would I lie about it?"

"You have a habit of lying to me, and you're very good at it. I have every reason to doubt your veracity."

Bloody hell, she suddenly thought. She wasn't going to show her annoyance. She let out a trill of laughter.

"Ah, but listen to me! How silly I'm being. Welcome home, my most adored…what shall I call you? My lover? Future husband? If I'm a kept woman does that make you my keeper? Like something in a zoo?"

His expression was sardonic. "That sounds accurate."

"You're very droll." She rose to her feet and started toward him.

"Stay right there!" he said again.

"I know it would devastate you if I happened to fall and drown myself, but I'm hardly going to wait here until you fetch someone with a boat. I dispensed with my pelisse and the wind is cool off the water. I'm ready to come in and welcome my darling…keeper properly."

"I'm coming out to get you."

She arched her brow. "Why? Won't two be more dangerous than one on this wretched thing?"

"I'm more afraid of you slipping on the rotten decking." He mounted the steps, his cane clicking on the wood.

"But if you tried to catch me we'd both fall in," she pointed out.

"Do you swim?"

"No."

"I do. If we both fall in I should probably manage to save us both. While the water is very deep you're not far from shore, and even when it's this cold I should still manage to suffice."

"And if I'm too much for you?"

"Then I'll save myself and let you drown," he said

with callous good humor. He was moving down the walkway with slow, measured steps, barely limping.

"You're already dressed in mourning. That should make things easier. Though perhaps I'll push you aside and watch *you* drown."

"Not if *you* can't swim."

"Something that needs to be remedied this summer when the water gets warmer," she said firmly, moving toward him.

She must have hit a plank that she'd missed before. The ominous crack was the first warning, and then it splintered beneath her foot, and this time she was falling, falling toward the icy depths, when he was there, catching her, yanking her across the space and pulling her against him. His other arm came round her and his cane clattered to the dock and over into the water as he held her.

She looked up at him, breathless again. "Thank you," she said, unable to find her saucy voice. "I don't think I would have liked a ducking."

He didn't move: he just held her, his pale eyes watching her, an odd expression in them. And then he released her, looking around him. "Damn, I've lost my best cane."

It was floating out of reach, an ebony stick with polished gold top. "We could get one of the servants to go after it."

He grimaced. "They can try. In the meantime that presents us with another problem. I came down on my bad leg when I was trying to rescue you from the results of your folly. I doubt I can make it back to the house on my own." He looked at her. "I'm afraid I'll have need of your assistance."

It was an odd moment, she thought, surrounded by sparkling water that nonetheless held danger and death. Facing a man who was everything she hated and everything she longed for. And then she moved. "Of course," she said finally. "Put your arm around my shoulder and we should do quite well."

"We'll make our way off the dock first. I won't risk having you drown because of me."

She gave him her sauciest smile. "You won't? Pray, why not? Have you fallen madly in love with me and forgotten all about your precious revenge?"

"I never forget about revenge," he said in a cool voice.

"Of course you don't." She took his arm and placed it around her shoulders, and when he tried to remove it she jabbed her elbow into his stomach. Gently. "Behave yourself or we'll both go over. Slowly now."

He couldn't very well fight her. He let her help him down the rest of the dock, managing to climb down the stairs with his usual grace. The walk up to the house was more difficult, and she realized he'd been withholding his weight on her while they were still in danger. It gave her something to concentrate on, rather than how big he was, how warm he was, pressed up against her body.

She could feel his heart beating. She glanced up at him, but his face was averted. She was on the side that was less grievously scarred, and for a moment she faltered in astonishment.

He stumbled, glaring down at her. "What's the problem?"

"You're quite beautiful," she said ingenuously. And then realized what she had said. "But la, of course a fiancée, if that is what I am, would you think so. I'm sorry you're in such a foul mood, my love. Did you have a bad time in the city?"

"My leg hurts like the very devil," he said. And then he must have realized he was admitting a weakness to her, even worse than accepting her help. His sardonic smile reappeared. "But my time in the city was well-spent, so I am hardly likely to complain. We'll be leaving for my friend's house party tomorrow. His estate is just outside of Morecambe, and it shouldn't take us more than a few hours to get there. We'll formalize our wedding vows there, and I promise you an absolute orgy of delight."

"It sounds delightful." *Bloody hell.* Lucien didn't use words without great thought, and "orgy" was not a good one. "I'll look forward to meeting your friends."

"I'm sure they'll find you...delicious, just as I do."

"Just as you do, Lucien?"

His cool smile was his only reply.

By that time the servants had seen them coming, and they were surrounded, with Bridget clucking over the stains on her dress where she'd fallen and Lucien borne off in another direction. She continued on into the house with Bridget, trying to shake off the uncomfortable sense of foreboding.

Mrs. Humber met her in the hall. "He's back, you know."

"Yes, I noticed," Miranda said briefly. "He joined me down at the lake." If it wasn't quite the joyous reunion she wasn't about to clarify it. "Do you think he'd be happy with your manner of addressing me?"

Bridget made a muffled choking sound, but fortunately for her Mrs. Humber was too infuriated to notice.

Miranda watched as a panoply of emotions swept over her, but the woman managed to get herself under control. "I have no idea what you're talking about, my lady," she said in a tight voice.

"Better," Miranda murmured. "Come along, Bridget."

Lucien went directly to his study, using the walking stick his valet had quickly provided. He walked into the room, closing the door behind him, shutting everyone out, and then took the stick and smashed the Chinese porcelain vase on the mantelpiece, the delicate silver candelabrum, the crystal clock on the desk. And then he threw himself into a chair, cursing.

His room felt stuffy, dank. He'd told them to let no one, including his curious fiancée, into his study, though he'd left the library unlocked. He wasn't ready for her to go mad from boredom, not yet. He had another act for this drama yet to be played.

If he'd been close enough he would have smashed a window with his cane in order to let in some fresh air. He hated his leg, hated the weakness. The scars he bore with a perverse pride, but when his leg, his body betrayed him he became infuriated. Miranda was lucky he hadn't drowned her simply out of bad temper.

And then he laughed at his own absurdity. He was like a little boy having a tantrum, and he'd best get over it, quickly. He hated showing weakness, particularly in front of her, and anger was weakness.

Damned foolish woman! What the hell did she mean by wandering out on that slippery, rotting dock all by herself? She could have gone in, been rapidly taken by the freezing water and no one would have ever known what had happened to her.

The very idea made his temper rise again, and he made an effort to control it. It wasn't as if he actually cared about her, he told himself. But if she died in an accidental drowning it would blunt the pain of her family's suffering. They would mourn her and move on with their lives, knowing she was at peace.

He had gone to a great deal of trouble for just the right revenge—he didn't want to have it foreshortened. He wanted them to suffer, knowing she was trapped up here, subject to his every whim, and he wanted them knowing just how twisted his whims could be. He wanted them to spend years worrying about her, wondering about her, and have no recourse.

That, and only that, would equal the pain of Genevieve's death, the death that Rohan's carelessness had caused. It mattered not that a grievous instability had run through Genevieve and her mother. She had been all that he had, and she had died because of Benedick Rohan.

No revenge was too cruel for that family, even if his young wife had to be the instrument of it. Once he was satisfied he would leave Miranda in peace, to live out her days in this gloomy old place.

Except that it didn't feel as gloomy. He hadn't paid much attention as he limped into the great hall, but there was a sense of…lightness, that hadn't been there before. Damn her, what had she done? Next thing he knew he'd find flowers all over the place. He shuddered at the thought.

He stayed in his study all afternoon, barking at anyone who knocked at his door or tried to speak with him, including his valet. While Pawlfrey House had little business to cover, having no tenant farmers or discernible income, there were still servants to be paid, and that number seemed to have suddenly swollen in size, as well as the concomitant costs of food, housing, uniforms and cleaning supplies, and his factor brought everything before him, which was tedious in the extreme. It wasn't that the money was a problem—he'd told Miranda the truth. He had more money than God, and not enough things to spend it on. He just begrudged spending it on something he didn't particularly want, and the dark, gloomy confines of Pawlfrey House suited his dark, gloomy soul. It had been less than a week she could hardly have made much of an inroad against years of neglect.

He looked around him suspiciously. He did typically allow Essie Humber in to dust and clean, but the room looked brighter, as well. It could be simply because the sun was shining, but as he glanced past the heavy curtains to the small amount of glass showing he realized that the window was now very clean.

He'd told Miranda she could do anything she wanted on the house except touch his study, but he'd assumed she'd be too traumatized to do more than lie in bed and weep. Clearly he'd underestimated her. It was a good thing he hadn't left her alone much longer. She'd probably attack the overgrown gardens next, and the tangled jungle suited him.

He worked steadily, refusing to think about the ceremony set two days from now at midnight. He'd allowed others to plan it, saying he had no particular interest in what form his bride's humiliation would take, just that it would torment the Rohans once they heard of it. By the time he rose to dress for dinner his knee was better. He could manage to move around the place with the help of his cane, and his insipid fiancée need never realize what kind of pain he'd been in.

Well, not *insipid*, no matter how hard she was trying to convince him otherwise. His life would be a great deal simpler if she were.

His leg wasn't paining him too badly by the time he reached the first floor and the wing that held his rooms, at a goodly distance from his future wife's. He wasn't sure in retrospect how wise an idea that was, but he could always move her closer if he felt like enjoying her on a more consistent basis for a while. He could also have her moved to an attic if she annoyed him.

His valet was coming down the hall when he approached the door to his rooms, and he looked up, his face pale. "Your lordship," he said in his habitually nervous tone of voice. "I wanted to inform you—"

"It can wait," he said brusquely, pushing past him. "I trust you've got a bath awaiting me?"

"I...I wasn't certain..."

"Wasn't certain I would want a bath? How long have you served me? I always want a bath after a day of traveling. See to it immediately."

"Indeed, sir. There will be but the slightest delay, my lord, and..."

Lucien stopped, his hand on the doorknob. "And why should there be a delay at all?" he asked in the voice meant to strike terror into whoever heard it. "I'm unused to my orders being ignored, as I'm certain you recall."

If his valet was pale before, now he looked positively deathly. "Her ladyship has ordered a bath, and the servants are bringing her water."

"Indeed?" He could afford to be generous, he thought.

Knowing he was waiting, the servants would make all haste to finish filling Miranda's bath, and the delay would be minimal. "Tell them to hurry."

And he pushed open his door and walked in.

21

Jacob Donnelly knew how to hold his liquor, and he had barely a trace of a hangover the next day, despite the amount of alcohol he'd consumed. After coming back down the stairs he'd gone back into the taproom, helped himself to the whiskey and finished off the night thoroughly and cheerfully bosky.

The morning came a bit too soon, but he was up and about at dawn, making certain the horses were fed and ready, the carriage pulled out into the courtyard. The sooner he got rid of Miss Jane Pagett the better.

It was a good way to think of her. As long as he called her Miss Jane Pagett in his mind it kept her at a distance. He'd come dangerously close to her in the last few days, and he needed to get the hell away from her, back to Beggar's Ken, the one place he could call home. He needed to mind his own business, not everyone else's, and as soon as Long Molly emerged he started badgering her to get young miss ready.

Miss Jane came out, still eating a piece of toast. He should have felt guilty at making her hurry. This was the last bit of the trip—they shouldn't have to stop before they reached London, and he wasn't inclined to wait.

The hostler was holding the head of the lead horse, and Long Molly climbed up into the carriage, leaving Jane to follow. For all that she was a tall girl she wasn't used to climbing up those steps without a groom to hand her up, so he simply came up behind her, put his hands on her waist and lifted her up into the carriage.

She tried to turn around, and ended up falling onto the seat in an ungainly heap. "Sorry, miss," he said, bobbing his head in his most obsequious manner. "Didn't mean to scare you."

She was staring at him like she'd seen a ghost. She was white-faced, speechless, and Long Molly pulled her back into the seat and put a blanket over her, even though it promised to be a warm day.

"Come now," she said in her perfect Yorkshire accent. "Tha' mustn't let yon laddie frighten you."

Jane managed to find her voice as he swung the door shut. "He doesn't," she said in an odd voice.

He was still thinking about it as he swung up into the driver's seat and nodded at the boy to release the horses. She'd looked at him in shocked recognition, but that was impossible. She couldn't know who he was, just from the feel of his hands on her waist. For Christ's sake, she was wearing forty layers of clothes and he'd had on his leather gloves. No way could she recognize him.

But she'd looked at him as if she had.

Long Molly was a smart enough woman—she'd do her best to distract her charge from any untoward suspicion. And there were four more hours, at the most, and by the time they reached the outskirts of London she would have forgotten any ridiculous suspicions she might have had. They'd reach her house not long after, and he'd be free of her. Thank God.

She wasn't for the likes of him. He knew it, and always had. But it had been too easy to forget, looking into her sweet eyes, letting the smell of violets dance around him.

The sooner they got there, the better.

Jane sat back in the seat, feeling numb. Mrs. Grudge was tucking a cover over her, a cover she didn't need, and she sat there, her face turned toward the window as the carriage started with a jerk.

A good coachman would start more fluidly, but then, the man seated above was no more a driver than she was. He was a jewel thief, she had absolutely no doubt.

The knowledge had been dancing around in her subconscious ever since she saw him, but it seemed too incredible to even contemplate.

Incredible or not, she knew it to be true. The feel of his hands on her had been like an electric shock, like lightning from the sky. She'd known him, and nothing could convince her otherwise.

Not Mrs. Grudge, who immediately went on a long and lively story about Jacobs the womanizer and his adventures in the household of the Scorpion. The stories were vastly entertaining and she laughed at all the right moments and she didn't believe a word of it.

Jacobs, if that was even his name, was no one's servant. There was a good chance that neither was Mrs. Grudge, given the tales she was actively spinning. If she lied so well about one thing she was doubtless lying about everything else. Jane kept her hands beneath the soft wool throw, turning the diamond on her finger, slipping it on and off. What would Miranda do in this situation? Would she say nothing, keep her head down, wait for life to revert to its usual quiet rhythm?

Or would she confront the so-called coachman, tell him she knew who he was and see what he did about it? She might even kiss him, just to see if it was still as powerful.

Jane would have loved to kiss him again. That night in the dark bedroom seemed so long ago, and she knew she had to have imagined the power of that embrace, the magic that had suffused her body as his hot, wet mouth covered hers. If he kissed her again it would be proof that it was nothing more than a very bad man having a very good time, and she'd been momentarily caught in his toils.

But she wasn't going to kiss him again. She wasn't Miranda, she was ordinary Jane Pagett, and she was going to keep her head down and pretend she hadn't noticed anything. When they left her at her parents' house she would walk inside without looking back, and she would forget all about him.

She pulled the ring completely off her finger, letting it rest in one open palm. She could toss it out on the street, but that seemed a wasteful thing to do. After all, he'd gone to so much trouble to steal it.

Then again, he'd given it up so easily, slipping it on her finger as he kissed her, and she'd been too blind and besotted to notice.

She pulled her handkerchief out of her reticule and tied it around the ring, all under the enveloping cover so Mrs. Grudge, if that was even her name, wouldn't notice.

The older woman had been kind to her, even if she'd

lied. She could give her the ring, leave it up to her to
return to the thief. She probably wouldn't, but that wasn't
her concern. Her concern was facing Mr. Bothwell after
running off so precipitously. He wouldn't be pleased
with her. Though with luck he might be totally ignorant
of her clandestine trip. She just wasn't sure that was what
she wanted.

She felt a faint tremor of resentment. In truth, she
wasn't pleased with Mr. Bothwell. And if he were the
one to break off their engagement she'd consider herself
well-rid of him.

No, he wouldn't break it off, no matter what she did.
He was much too conscious of his reputation and his
consequence. A gentleman didn't jilt a lady.

He was her best chance at a life of her own, and it
was a poor chance at best. But if he was willing to forgive her she supposed she'd have no choice but to bow
her head and be grateful.

She hadn't slept well the night before, and she drifted
in and out of sleep, Mrs. Grudge's soothing monotone in
her ears. The last time she awoke, with a small jerk, she
looked out the window and realized they had stopped.
They were at the front door of her parents' London
home.

She saw the door open and relief swept through her.
Her parents must be in town—she could throw herself
in her mother's arms and not have to think about a thing.
Lady Evangelina Pagett would see to everything. They
might be angry with her, but were more likely to simply
be worried.

The coach rocked as the driver jumped down, and to
her dismay he beat her footman to the door, opening it
and letting down the steps.

"Miss Pagett," His voice was the voice of that midnight dark room, smoky and sensual. No Yorkshire accent anymore, and she didn't know if that was by accident or design.

She hadn't bothered to replace her gloves, and in a moment of sheer bravado and anger she put out her left hand, so that he had no choice but to look at it. At Mr. Bothwell's stingy engagement ring back in place where it belonged, with no sign of the massive diamond.

His hand closed around hers, and she knew a moment's nervousness, as he reached in and lifted her down onto the cobbled streets. Her boot heel slid on one of the cobbles, and she started to lose her balance, and he caught her, easily, his hand beneath her elbow.

And that brief spurt of bravery blossomed. *What would Miranda do?* came lilting through her mind again, and she squared her shoulders, looking him straight in the eye. "You've been very kind, Jacobs," she said in a formal voice, "though your driving skills leave a bit to be desired. For your trouble." And she handed him the handkerchief, wrapped around the ring.

He grinned at her, tucking it into his pocket without looking. Would he have guessed what it was? It didn't matter—by the time he looked at it, it would be too late. Clearly the sight of her hand hadn't distressed him, not the missing diamond or the replaced engagement ring.

But she wasn't going to pretend to herself that she was wrong. She knew him as surely as if she'd seen him in the light of day that first time.

She started up at the front steps, and her face broke out in a smile that died as quickly as it was born. It wasn't her parents standing there, ready to welcome her return.

It was her affianced husband, his handsome face dark with disapproval.

She faltered for a moment. Jacobs glanced at the door, then back at her. "Don't let him see your fear, love," he whispered, so softly she almost didn't believe he'd dare. And then he turned away from her, letting her go.

"I don't suppose anyone is going to bother to assist me out of this contraption?" Mrs. Grudge demanded in a loud voice. "I really don't want to sit here all day."

"Beggin' your pardon, missus," Jacobs said, his voice suddenly three rungs down on the social ladder. "I was seeing to the lady."

But Jane was no longer looking back, and she was barely conscious of the words. She climbed up the steps like Marie Antoinette climbing onto the scaffold, her back straight, a tentative smile on her face.

"Why, Mr. Bothwell, how kind of you to welcome me home," she said, her voice strained.

"Inside, Miss Pagett," he ordered in a thunderous voice. "Now."

The servants were watching them curiously, and she had little doubt that Jacobs would be amused by it all. The sad little scarecrow of a girl and her bullying fiancé. She couldn't hope for much, but she prayed he hadn't entertained his friends with the story of the midnight kiss and the way she'd trembled in his arms.

She followed Mr. Bothwell into the house, fully aware that he was deliberately not showing her the courtesy of letting her precede him. He must be very angry indeed to exhibit that much rage in front of the servants.

"The front parlor," Mr. Bothwell had very large, very white teeth, and they were clenched together. They made her nervous. This time he let her precede him, and she'd barely made it into the middle of the room before he began his tirade.

She sat.

"Shouldn't you be going in there, Molly?" Jacob said as she climbed down from the coach. "You're her guarantee of respectability, after all, and her fiancé looked ready to bite her head off."

"Afraid I can't, love. I recognize the gentleman. He's one of my customers, and he's got very nasty habits, that one has. I've had to give him warning a time or two, and he'll remember me for it. I hope the lass isn't going to marry him—he's a mean one. Anyway, you've done your job, Jacob me darling. What're you waiting for?"

"She recognized me."

"Don't be ridiculous. And even if she suspected for a moment I spun her such tales that she has to be convinced she was wrong."

He shook his head. "She knew." He pulled out the piece of cloth she'd given him and opened it, though he knew what would lay in its bunched-up folds. He shoved the ring in his pocket, then brought the cloth to his nose. Violets.

He glanced up at the elegant house, the door closed against intruders. "I've got more business here," he said abruptly.

"Jacob…"

"Shall I call you a hackney, Molly lass? I may end up in Newgate or I'd offer you a ride home when I'm done."

She looked at him for a long, frustrated moment. And then she smiled and shook her head. "You're a fool, Jacob. Who would have thought to see King Donnelly laid low by love? It would fair turn one's stomach if it weren't so sweet." She stretched. "I'll walk. It's not far and my bum is fair killing me after all that jolting around. The girl's got the right of it—you weren't born to be a coachman."

"God only knows what I was born to be," Jacob muttered. "Mind if I borrow yon trunk?" He nodded toward the smallish trunk that was bound up behind the black coach.

"Will I get it back? You could always give me yon ring in return for it if no one has a use for it."

"I have a use for it. And you know I'm good for whatever the cost. You'd never wear one of those dresses again if you could help it."

"Aye," Long Molly said. "Have at it, yon Romeo. Go rescue the damsel in distress."

He'd hoisted the heavy trunk on his shoulder with relative ease. "You've got your stories mixed up."

Molly shrugged. "You're the one who can read, not me. Let me know what happens."

"I expect you'll hear about it," he said, half to himself. And he mounted the front steps.

Her family's servants didn't want to let him in, of course. Not in the front door. And the footman tried to take the trunk from him, but since he towered over all of them they didn't have much recourse. "Where's thy mistress?" he demanded. "I promised her I'd see this into no one's hands but hers."

"I don't believe that is Miss Paget's trunk," the superior-looking butler began, but Jacob, recognizing the opposing commander in this particular battle, went straight toward him, towering over the man.

"I promised Miss Paget I'd be bringing her trunk

"directly to her," he said in his best Irish. "Would you like to try an' stop me?"

The butler moved out of the way hastily, and Jacob continued on into the house.

It smelled of beeswax and lemon oil and old money, and he took a deep breath, resisting the impulse to curl his lip. He didn't need to ask the way—he could hear Jane's fiancé lecturing her in an upraised voice, and he headed in that direction.

He took the steps lightly, two at a time, the heavy trunk on his shoulder. They were in a small *parlor* near the top of the first flight, and he paused in the doorway.

Jane was sitting in a chair, her shoulders bowed, her head down, as her fiancé loomed over her, bullying her, yelling at her.

"I cannot *believe* you would be so *lost* to all sense of propriety that you would simply take off, with nothing but a note from one of the most notorious men in London to set their minds at ease. And that you would accompany a strumpet of Lady Miranda's reputation goes beyond *all understanding.* For all her titled family I would have disallowed the connection the moment we were married, but I thought you had the delicacy to keep your association with such a *reckless* and *unacceptable* personage quiet. But no, you must needs go haring off to the ends of the earth with her, sending word back to your parents that you were 'assisting' her in a marriage by special license *to a man whose name with which I shall not soil my lips.* Are you so lost to all sense of propriety—*to what is due to my consequence as your affianced husband*—that you would do such a thing?

Your understanding must be pathetic indeed, not to have considered what this must look like."

"Mr. Bothwell, I beg pardon. I'm sorry…" Her voice was thick with choked-back tears, and Jacob's rage momentarily blinded him.

"Silence!" Mr. Bothwell thundered. "Do you have any idea what kind of people you spent the last few days with? That…that man is a member of the Heavenly Host, and you know what they are, Miss Paget? Satanists. Devil worshippers, who sacrifice children and practice the most obscene behavior, and he's arranging for them to join him in what I can only term an—" he lowered his voice for a moment in whispered disgust "—an *orgy*, to celebrate his marriage to that doxy! God knows what will happen to her, but she is only reaping the result of her own unspeakable behavior. Behavior that you have chosen to emulate! I cannot think how I was fool enough to affiance myself to someone *so lost to all sense* of what is fit and proper. I cannot cry off, but I will speak to your father, and I don't doubt we can make some kind of arrangement to sever this distasteful association without causing harm to my reputation. Yours, I'm afraid, is beyond repair, and I—"

"Excuse me," Jacob said, having had enough of this, striding into the salon. "Where were you wanting me to put this, Miss Paget?"

Jane looked up, her face streaked with tears, and he would have clocked Bothwell and had done with it, until he looked at the joy in her eyes as she looked at him, and everything fell into place like a puzzle. He knew what he wanted, what he needed, and it was suddenly very simple.

"How dare you interrupt your betters?" Bothwell

shouted at him, clearly happy to bully anyone he thought would have to take it. "Get out of here, or I'll have you turned off immediately." He turned back to Jane. "As for you, Miss Pagett, I'll have my ring back. You…"

"Excuse me," Jacob said again, turning on his heel, calculating it perfectly. The trunk on his shoulder slammed into Bothwell's head, and he went down like a stone.

Jacob lifted the trunk down and set it on the floor, leaning over Bothwell's motionless body. He gave him a none-too-gentle nudge with his boot, but the man didn't move, knocked cold.

"Pity," he said in his normal voice. "I didn't mean to knock him out."

Jane had leaped up. "You didn't?"

He looked over at her, grinning. "No. I was hoping for the chance to hit him a few more times." He tilted his head, observing her. "I think, lass, that you gave the wrong man back his ring."

She looked flustered, uncertain, but she pulled off the pitiful jet ring Bothwell had given her and threw it at his unconscious form. No blood coming from his head, Jacob noticed with no particular concern. He'd been in enough fights to know when someone was badly injured, and being wanted for the murder of an upstanding gentleman wouldn't have suited him. But Bothwell would live to bully another young woman, more's the pity.

"That's the girl. Now where do you fancy you'd like to go?"

She wiped the tears from her face with the back of her ringless hand. "I need to go to Miranda."

It wasn't the answer he could have hoped for, but it

was better than some he might have feared. "I can do that." He held out his hand for her.

She didn't move. "First, tell me who you are. What your name is."

Ah, here it goes, he thought. It was one thing when he was a mystery, a kiss in the dark. The truth was less palatable. "You know who I am. Or at least what I am. I'm Jacob Donnelly—called King Donnelly in some parts of London, due to my leadership of a group of in- dividuals who are, for want of a better word, thieves."

She didn't flinch. "And who is Mrs. Grudge?"

Sparing her would get them nowhere; he had a mind for the truth now. "She runs a brothel over in Brunton Street, but she likes a bit of adventure every now and then, does Long Molly, and she was willing to help out. She has a special fondness for Scorpion."

She took it well, did Miss Jane Pagett. "And you'll take me to Miranda?"

"Aye. You'll have to give me leave to check on my people first, but then we can be off. If you don't mind the traveling."

"I like to travel," she said firmly. "What are we wait- ing for?"

22

Miranda slid into the warm bath, closing her eyes and breathing in the scent of roses that surrounded her. There were dried rose petals floating in the water, and she could almost imagine it was summer. She would continue her explorations tomorrow, this time through the gardens behind the house. It was spring, daffodils were blooming everywhere and the fresh canes of rose-bushes would be spiking through the damp earth. She couldn't wait.

She closed her eyes, sliding down. If she tried really hard perhaps she could forget that he was back. He hadn't made any move to touch her, to kiss her. He'd had her—perhaps that was all he intended.

It was easy enough to be sensible about it when she was dressed and walking around. But lying naked in a hot tub of rose-scented water aroused too many of her senses, and a host of memories returned. His mouth on her breast, sucking. His thick, hard invasion that had been uncomfortable at first, and then quickly became quite…wonderful.

She shouldn't want it again. Most of the time she

didn't. She simply pushed it out of her mind. But he'd returned, and it was no longer so easy. Suddenly she was wanting it, wanting him, again.

She heard his bellow from a distance, and she smiled to herself. He must have discovered his rooms. She'd been waiting for this moment all day, been loath to leave the house for fear she'd miss it. Every spare inch of his bedroom, dressing room and adjoining sitting room had been painted the loveliest shade of powder pink. She hadn't had enough time to find a matching shade of fabric for the curtains, but the white cotton lace had a nice, cheery touch, as did the coverlet and pillows. She'd even managed to paint several old chairs to go with the overall effect.

If he were a seventeen-year-old girl he would love it.

She chuckled. She ought to see about painting her own rooms. They were currently a faded green, and her dressing room, without windows, was very dark unless the adjoining door was open.

She knew exactly what he would do. He would storm around, have his valet find him another set of rooms in this huge old place and not say a word to her. It was part of the battle plan, her stealth attack, and he would never let her know she'd scored a hit.

She was wrong. Her door was slammed open, and he stood there, a furious expression on his face. Bridget, who'd been laying out her clothes for the evening, looked up, frankly terrified.

"Get out," he said.

Bridget fled.

He advanced on Miranda. The water was cloudy from the soap, and she slid down farther, watching him warily, half expecting him to spring on her. And then she gave him a wide smile. "Do you like your rooms? I wanted to redecorate them first—a good wife always sees to her husband before she attends to her own needs, and I fancy I did quite an excellent job. There were a few things I wasn't able to get done, but I think it very peaceful, don't you? I've always found pink to be such a calming color."

Apparently not. "Get out of the tub."

"I'm not finished my bath yet, my dearest. Come back in half an hour if you want to talk. I can tell you're ever so slightly cross with me, and I vow I can't imagine why, unless you tell me that by some strange circumstance you don't like pink."

"I don't like pink."

"Well, how was I to know that?" she demanded, all fluttery exasperation. "Perhaps you would prefer a pale lavender?"

"Get. Out. Of. The. Tub."

He was very angry indeed, and she wanted to chortle with glee. Lucien de Malheur, Earl of Rochdale, the Scorpion, the untouchable, who never showed any emotion, was furious.

"Would you perhaps prefer a baby blue?"

She knew the moment she said it that she'd gone too far. He came up to the tub, reached down into the water, up to his elbows in his elegant coat of superfine and hauled her out of the tub with such force that water sloshed everywhere.

Instinctively she fought him, but he was very strong. He simply picked her up, carried her into her dressing room and dropped her on the floor. A moment later the door slammed, plunging her into darkness.

She'd ended up on the rug, and she quickly pulled herself into a sitting position, huddling on the floor in the darkness, hugging herself in the rapidly chilling air as she waited for the sound of the lock.

It didn't come, and she started to get to her feet. Why did she toss her into her dressing room if she could simply walk out?

And then she heard the sound of a coat being tugged off and tossed on the floor, and she knew she wasn't alone in the darkness.

"Lucien," she said in a conciliatory tone from the ink-dark shadows. "I'm sorry I annoyed you. Really, my darling, you have no sense of humor..." She ended with a little shriek, as he hauled her up, pushing her wet body against the wall, his own pressing her there.

He said nothing, and she could feel his heart beating through the thin cloth of the shirt he wore. His long legs were against hers in the darkness, breeches against bare legs, and she squirmed, accidentally allowing him to move one leg between hers, pinning her there.

He slid his hands behind her head, moving her face forward to his. "Vixen," he said pleasantly. "You're lucky I don't beat you."

She held herself very still. She was awash in the feel of him up against her body, between her legs, his mouth so close. She was frightened of feeling that depth of reaction again. She wanted him. She was terrified of the way he made her feel.

"You wouldn't beat me," she said in a hushed voice, trying to keep it light. "You know you adore me."

"Vixen," he said again. And kissed her.

She knew he would. Knew this was going to happen, no matter what she said or did. If she pretended she wanted it he would do it anyway. If she pretended she hated it he could still continue. Because he told her he knew her body better than she did, and her body couldn't lie.

His mouth was hard, angry, and for a moment it hurt. She put her hands on the wall behind her, bracing herself as he kissed her, wanting his hard mouth on hers despite the pain. And then it softened, opened, and his tongue touched hers, and it felt as if all the anger had drained away, and she lifted her hands to his shoulders, clinging to him.

He kissed like an angel; he kissed like the very devil. His mouth was dark and sweet, a memory that roused her in ways that should have shamed her. She didn't care. His long sleeves were wet against her body, and she reached for the hem of his shirt, pulling it free from his breeches.

He pulled it over his head, and then it was his bare chest against hers, for the first time, her breasts pressed against hard muscle and wiry hair. In the darkness he was all around her, and he kissed her again, pushing her back against the wall, and she slid her arms around him.

She could feel the ridges on his back, the cording of scar tissue, and for a moment he froze, his mouth just above hers, and she was afraid, so afraid that he would pull away, that he would leave her.

And then he moved. "I'm a scarred monster," he whispered in her ear. "And you're trapped."

She pulled her arms from around him, and he stayed very still, waiting, she knew not for what. For her to push him away in horror?

She found his face in the darkness, cradling it with

her hands. "You aren't a monster," she whispered against
his lips. "And you're trapped, as well." She kissed him,
on his mouth, his jaw, his neck.

He claimed the kiss then, holding her still for it, pushing her mouth open once more, and she kissed him back,
inexpertly, to be sure, but with her whole heart.

He moved his hand down, between her legs, and she
could feel the dampness there that hadn't come from the
bath, a dampness he spread around, sliding his fingers
inside her, moving up to circle her with the moisture,
rubbing, sliding. She wanted him to keep on touching
her, and she spread her legs, giving him better access,
her hands on his shoulders now, clinging to him.

He made a low, growling sound in the back of his
throat, a sound of pure animal need. He reached up and
took one of her hands, sliding it down his chest to the
front of his breeches.

She hadn't touched him the other night, had only felt
his invasion. He placed her hand on his erection, and
she let her fingers move along its length, astonished by
how hard, how thick, how big he was.

"Release me," he whispered in a hoarse voice. "Unfasten my breeches."

She wanted to. The more his hand slid and touched
and danced between her legs the more she wanted him
there, the hardness that was maddeningly out of reach,
and she slid her hands around the waist of the breeches,
looking for some kind of fastening, buttons, whatever,
but her hands were shaking, and she felt like a clumsy
idiot.

"I don't know how," she finally confessed, trying to
drop her hand.

He caught it, moved it to the side where she felt

hidden buttons, and with his hand guiding her she unfastened the buttons, four of them. "Now push my breeches down."

She took her other hand from his bare shoulder, placing them both on his hips, and shoved the breeches down his thighs, and she felt him spring up against her, thick and hard.

He kicked his clothes away, and then he was just as naked as she was, in the dark, his body pressed up against her.

She reached down and touched him, gasping at the silken smoothness, letting her fingertips learn him. "This is ridiculous," she said in a choked whisper. "This can't possibly fit."

She felt his laugh more than heard it. "Trust me."

And he put his arm under one of her legs, lifting her, bracing her against the wall. With his other hand he took the head of his sex and slid it against her, against that place that seemed so powerful to her overwrought nerves, and he was wet as well, smearing the dampness all around her, sliding down her cleft, and then up again. Her quiet moan of disappointment was unstoppable, and he laughed again.

"Hold on to me, Miranda," he said, and she did, putting her arms around his neck as he lifted her, and she could feel him at the entrance of her sex. He thrust inside her, a thick, wet slide, and she cried out, not in pain but in sheer, guttural pleasure. He hoisted her higher, using both arms to support her under her thighs, bracing her against the wood paneling behind her bare back, and he began to move.

She let out a strangled cry, dropping her face onto his shoulder, letting her hands slide down his heavily scarred back, clinging tightly. He no longer seemed to mind, he was too intent on the sinuous movement of his hips, thrusting in, withdrawing as her body cling to him, then moving in deeper still, and each time she cried out, in blind, helpless pleasure.

She felt the first convulsion begin to sweep over her, and she clutched him more tightly, trying to speed him, needing more, needing harder, faster, but he must have felt the fluttering contractions, and instead he shoved all the way in, holding her completely still as wave after wave washed over her. She fought him then, fought his iron control. She needed more, but he was adamant, refusing to move, in so deep she could feel his leathery sac against her, and all she could do was dig her fingernails in as her body trembled.

As the first wave passed he started to move again, and she murmured a strangled protest, one he refused to listen to, and this time when her climax came it was even stronger, and she cried out, begging him in strangled tones, but once more he held himself in deep, impaling her.

She was sobbing by then, unable to control herself, and when he began to move again she begged him. "No more," she gasped, her body shaking apart. "I can't take any more."

"Yes," He thrust deeper still. "You can." He was moving faster now, and her body was accepting his rhythm, his dominance, in this at least, and she knew she was past fighting. She surrendered, letting her fingertips caress the corded scars on his back, her legs tight around his hips, and she told herself this was for him, now. The last of her had burned up in a storm of desire and there was nothing left.

Nothing left but his thick, heavy thrusts as she clung to him, nothing left but his final, powerful slam into her, and she could feel him, feel his climax, feel him fill her with his seed, and out of the darkness something took over, some dark, terrible, wonderful place, and she buried her face against his neck to muffle her scream as she was lost once more.

He was trembling, every nerve and muscle in his body suddenly weak, and he could only be glad he had the wall to brace her against, or they would have both collapsed on the floor in a comical welter of limbs. He could feel her face against his shoulder, the heated puffs of her breathing, the wetness of her tears, and he vaguely wondered how he was going to disentangle them. When he didn't really want to.

He wanted to stay buried deep inside her. His cock was still twitching, still semierect, and he knew if he stayed that way he'd get hard again. Because no matter how thoroughly he'd fucked her, he still seemed to want more of her. He couldn't imagine ever having enough.

But he pulled free, because he didn't want her to know how much he needed her. Not that she would guess—for a ruined woman she seemed to have the sophistication of a nun. But he liked that. He liked that she seemed to know almost nothing about the intricacies of pleasure. He could thank St. John for his ineptitude after all.

He let her legs down onto the floor, carefully, then caught her as her knees gave way. He took her down onto the padded floor with him, letting her fall against his body, and he found he was cradling her in his arms as she wept silently. Her tears were hot against his already heated flesh, and he found he was stroking her back in wordless comfort, though he wasn't quite sure why. Why she needed comfort after what had had to be as soul-shattering for her as it had been…*almost* had been for him.

No, he could understand. The power of it, the vulnerability. She was trembling slightly, just an errant shiver that ran over her body and had nothing to do with cold.

He was sorry there wasn't some kind of shawl in here to pull over them. He hadn't been thinking, at least, not much. He'd been so angry with her. He'd spent the entire day trying not to think about her body pressed up against his, about the smell of her in the fresh spring air, and then the sight of his appalling rooms had simply set something off. He'd come storming in, to find her soft and sweet and rosy in her hot bath, and all he knew was he needed to be naked with her. Immediately.

He'd had enough presence of mind to know that it was still light outside. And he didn't let anyone see his back, the damage that had been done.

It was bad enough that she could feel it, and he'd wanted to pull away from her then, when he'd felt her hands on him. Almost. But her touch had been so gentle, her mouth so sweet, that instead he'd let her stroke him, hold him as he pumped into her body, let her dig her fingernails into him as she reached her final climax.

He could barely feel it—the scar tissue so thick that the top layers of his skin were numb. Though oddly enough, her gentle caresses had been unmistakable.

He tucked her head against his shoulder, wrapping his arms and his body around hers. He didn't tend to fall asleep after sex; he was always too intent on escaping.

But right now he felt he could close his eyes and drift off quite easily.

That wasn't going to happen. He could feel her tears slow, feel her body relax into sleep, and he carefully pulled away from her, stifling his groan. He didn't want to. Her dressing room was big enough, perhaps he'd have the servants tuck a small bed in here. Most dressing rooms had a place for a lady's maid to sleep. Though he didn't necessarily want to disport on a servant's bed.

It took him a while to find his abandoned clothes in the dark, even though his eyes had become accustomed to it. He dressed quickly and quietly, then opened the door to her bedroom, letting in a shaft of twilight.

She was pretending to be asleep, but the tears on her face were fresh. He didn't stop to consider the ramifications, he simply went and scooped her up in his arms, thanking God she wasn't that big and his leg wasn't that weak. He carried her over to her bed, setting her down as he pulled away the covers, then placing her under them, tucking her in. She was still crying. Pretending to be asleep, but he'd felt the heat and wetness on his skin.

He stared down at her, not certain what he should do. He could mock her—she would rise up and fight back, the tears forgotten. Perhaps.

But what if she simply cried more? He was usually impervious to crying women. Any women who spent time with him usually ended with tears, because he simply wasn't interested in the little games they tended to play.

Miranda's game was anything but little. And for some odd reason her tears bothered him, perhaps because the rest of the time she was so fearless. He opened his mouth to chide her, then closed it again, and for some damnable reason he stretched out his hand and pushed the damp strands of her hair away from her tears.

Christ, if he stayed any longer he'd probably climb into bed and start comforting her!

He turned, quickly, wondering where the hell he'd left his cane. He couldn't see it in the twilight, and it was too dangerous to wait. Limping, he made his way out of her rooms as fast as his aching leg would let him, closing the door silently behind him.

23

Jane let him hand her back up into the carriage, closing the door behind her. He hadn't done anything but offer her his hand when needed, and she knew a sudden lowering of spirits after the exhilaration of seeing Mr. Bothwell felled like a stone, and she sat back in her seat, her hands folded neatly in her lap as the carriage moved forward with a jerk. A faint, melancholy smile danced across her lips. He really *wasn't* a very adept coachman.

He was, however, far more of a gentleman than her erstwhile fiancé. He wouldn't stand by and let a lady be bullied, and he'd brought her safely home in the first place, when a king of thieves would certainly have more important things to do. Of course, he probably wanted to retrieve the ring that he'd quixotically put on her finger. But that was in the dark, when he hadn't had a good look at her. Ever since he'd seen her clearly he'd been the soul of propriety, no doubt regretting that soul-searing midnight kiss.

Well, soul-searing for her, Jane amended with great

practically. Midnight kisses were most likely de rigueur for thieves.

She had to get to Miranda. If her husband was truly planning to bring her to a meeting of the Heavenly Host, then Miranda could be in grave danger. Everyone had heard the stories, the black masses, the drinking of blood, the orgies and devil worship and human sacrifice. It was of far greater importance than mooning after a man who was so inappropriate he wasn't beneath her, he may as well be on the moon.

What would her parents say if she told them she'd fallen in love with a thief? Not that she had, of course! She would admit to a mild infatuation, but nothing more. Still, it was an interesting question. What would they do?

Most parents would beat their rebellious daughters and lock them up on a diet of bread and water. But her father had been a man of much experience, a reformed rake and gamester, a vicar before acceding to the title, a man of great compassion and understanding. He would listen calmly, and pass no judgments.

And her mother, who'd lived her own scarlet life before she'd met her father, would doubtless keep an open mind. She'd always said, "You never know where love might find you, but when you see it, grab it with both hands and hold on tight."

But of course, she wasn't in love. It was simply an interesting supposition to while away the time, the endless time she'd spent in one carriage after another. She'd be far better off worrying about what she'd do for clothing. It had been bad enough spending two days on the road with two dresses, clean undergarments and a bowl of cool water to freshen in. Another three days or however long it might take was lowering. She wanted to run away, to travel, to see different and glorious places and things. She simply wanted the occasional change of clothes, as well.

Was it so wrong for an aspiring adventuress to be fond of the small elegancies of life? Like cleanliness?

Would Mrs. Grudge accompany them this time? How was she going to respond to a former whore known as Long Molly? Well, presumably the same way she responded to a cheerful widow named Mrs. Grudge, she decided. No matter what else she did with her life, Mrs. Grudge was a good and affectionate traveling companion. Not to mention good at making up stories about Jacob the philandering house-servant turned coach driver.

The coach came to its usual abrupt stop, throwing her forward, and she caught the strap just in time to keep from hurtling onto the opposite seat. There was a great deal of conversation outside, most of it unintelligible, and then the door opened and Jacob Donnelly appeared.

She had automatically started for the door when he shook his head. "Not here, Miss Jane. I've got a couple of men watching the horses and at least four keeping an eye on the carriage to make sure no one disturbs you. But I'm not having you out among these rogues." There was no mirth in his eyes. Clearly the term rogue was an understatement. "This is Beggar's Ken, home to vagabonds and thieves for the last seventy-five years and no place for a lady. I'll do my best to get my business done quickly, and then we'll be on our way."

"Yes, but..." She stopped, not wanting to complain.

"Yes, but what?"

"Is there any way we could get some clothes for me? And perhaps something to eat?"

He looked amused, some of the grimness fading from his eyes. "It'll be seen to." He paused. "I can have you safely back at your parents' house in the countryside if you wish it. You don't have to stay with me. I promise I won't let your former fiancé anywhere near you." His lip curled in contempt.

He was looking for a way to get rid of her, she thought, her heart dropping. "You don't have to take me anywhere," she said, doing a creditable job of sounding unmoved. "I can find a hackney back to my house—by now Mr. Bothwell will have removed himself and I can simply leave orders that he's not to be admitted. You don't need to feel you have any responsibility for me. I'm certain there are a great many things you'd rather do than…"

He put one foot on the step, vaulted up and leaned into the dark carriage interior, and she let out a little squeak of nervousness. One that was swallowed by his mouth, closing over hers as he slid one big hand behind her neck, holding her there.

It was a brief, thorough kiss, and when he pulled back she simply sat there, dazed. "There's nothing I'd rather do. And you needn't worry I'll be all over you. I'll be taking you to Ripton Waters, all right and tight, and leave the rules up to you. But you'll be treated like a lady. I just wanted to make my point."

She was still stunned by his kiss, but she tried to gather some of her shattered intellect. "Ripton Waters? Is that where they are?"

He nodded. "In the Lake District. So it'll take us two

days to get there if we push hard, maybe three. But I'm game if you are, lass."

She had no reason why she adored it when he called her "lass," but it made her stomach warm and her heart smile. "I'm game," she said. "If it's not too much trouble."

He grinned at her, that same, cheerful, slightly wicked grin. "No trouble at all, Miss Jane."

Lucien ate dinner in solitary splendor in the dining room. It was damnably clean, and he'd been right. There were flowers, vases and vases of fresh daffodils, and he could only be glad the greenhouses were in disrepair, or she'd have even worse throughout the house. The daffodils were bad enough, their sunny yellow at war with his mood. He was tempted to take his cane and smash all the vases, but resisted the impulse. He was feeling guilty, and it was making him childish and petulant, and he wanted Miranda to come downstairs with her sunny smile and bait him once more.

But she didn't. He didn't see her until the next day, when she sailed into his study wearing a gown of cherry sarcenet with paler trim and he immediately wondered how difficult it would be to get her out of that particular gown. And which dark place he could take her.

"Good morning, Lucien," she said in that mock-cheerful voice. "My, my, you do tend to immure yourself in your study, do you not?"

"I find it soothing." He ran his eyes over her. "Don't you?"

She glanced around her. "I find it gloomy. We could paint it a charming shade of…"

"Touch this and I'll beat you."

"Empty threats, my dear," she said, sinking into the chair. "I wanted to find out more about the visit you mentioned. What clothes will I need to bring with me? You were more than generous with my wardrobe, and I'm certain I have everything I need, but Bridget will want to know what to bring ahead of time. Will anyone I know be attending?"

"So many questions!" He leaned back in his chair. "I'll answer them in order. Clothes are of little importance at our little gatherings. I've ordered something suitable from a dressmaker who specializes in such things."

"A different dressmaker?" she said, her voice faltering. Then she smiled. "Oh, lovely! More new clothes! You really are the most thoughtful of lovers!"

"I'm happy to have pleased you, my love. And whether you know any of the other guests or not, I should most sincerely doubt it."

"You forget, I've been on the town for a number of years, and I've met a great many people."

"Not these. Even a soiled dove such as Lady Miranda Rohan would be warned against these particular men."

"Only men are at this party?" she asked with a barely audible gulp. "Is it a gaming party?"

"Some will bring mistresses. Some will even bring sisters and wives if they're particularly perverse. For the most part, though, Long Molly will send a dozen of her finest ladybirds up to entertain them."

"I am to assume you mean whores?"

"Who else to entertain the Heavenly Host?"

She didn't flinch, he had to grant her that. But then, she was an intelligent woman, perhaps a bit too intelligent. She had probably figured that much out already.

"And we are to be married in front of this particular group of your friends?" she said in a tranquil voice.

"Not that I object—they sound perfectly delightful. But don't weddings have to be held in churches in order to be legal?"

"You're talking about matches made in heaven, my love. Or at least, in drawing rooms. Our match was made in hell, and the ceremony planned will reflect that. With appropriate revelry afterward." He was watching her closely, looking for a reaction. "An absolute orgy of rejoicing."

She didn't fail to understand him. Her smile remained firmly in place, but she rose, her body graceful, and he remembered the feel of her beneath him. He'd only taken her in the dark and now wondered what color her nipples were, dark or light? And her triangle of hair—did it match the rich brown of her head or was it darker, lighter? The problem with keeping to the dark was that in ensuring she couldn't see his scars, in return he couldn't see her. And he wanted to.

He would when the Host convened. He and everyone else would see a great deal of her, and he refused to feel guilty about it. If she objected he would send her safely back to her room, defeated.

But she wouldn't object. She wouldn't cry off. And he was looking forward to it.

"And when may I look forward to this exceptional treat?" she inquired in a dulcet voice.

"We'll leave tomorrow. It's not a long drive—not more than a few hours. We'll leave in the afternoon."

She had her share of courage, he could grant her that.

"I imagine you have a very great many things to do, having been gone so long. Shall I see you for dinner?"

"Perhaps," he murmured, watching her closely for signs of distress. There were none. "Good morning, my love."

He sat very still when he was alone once more, staring at her empty chair, abstracted. He was feeling oddly melancholy. It was most likely the advent of spring. He always tended to brood when spring arrived, though he'd been unable to understand why. Perhaps it was simply his determinedly evil disposition. Sunshine was no good for a villain. He was much more disposed to darkness and shadows.

He laughed. Now he was acting like an adolescent, like that ass Byron she'd compared him to. Posturing and moping. Things were moving along quite well, and he had no reason to brood. For all Miranda's resourcefulness, all he had to do to silence her was to take her to bed. In truth, things were coming together just as he planned. The bizarre ceremony was in place, and once the revels were over he would bring her before a priest in a church and finish it off legally, just to close her last avenue of escape. And let the Rohans suffer. The only drawback was that the grandsons of Francis and the sons of Adrian Rohan didn't partake of the Heavenly Host. It would have been perfect if they were in attendance when their sister was brought in.

Then again, they'd probably stop things. No, this way they'd hear about it once it was fait accompli, and they would suffer.

He simply wondered why he wasn't feeling more pleased about the whole thing.

* * *

A light rain began to fall on the carriage roof, and the day was growing darker. Jane reached for the heavy shawl, huddling under it. She'd forgotten her pelisse in her precipitous flight, forgotten everything when he'd held out his hand to her.

She'd simply put her hand in his and gone, without a backward glance. She hadn't even stopped to consider whether Mr. Bothwell might be dead. If he was, then Jacob was in grave trouble, and the sooner they got out of London the better. Even so, striking a gentleman of Mr. Bothwell's stature was a highly dangerous thing to do as well, and he could have the Bow Street Runners out after them. Mr. Bothwell was the kind of man who would hound a person, and she couldn't bear to think of her jewel thief endangering himself for her sake. The longer it took him the more nervous she became, at one point opening the carriage door to go look for him.

A bad idea. She'd had the shades pulled down on the carriage, but the sight of the area was shocking. The filth, the poverty, the sheer number of people milling around. A huge man appeared at her door immediately, and while he didn't look particularly savory his smile was quite sweet, despite the number of teeth missing.

"You'll need to stay in the carriage, miss. The king says that no one's to go near you and you're not to set foot outside. Too dangerous for the likes of you, if I do say so myself. There are some bad people around here."

"And you're one of them, Neddie," a woman's cheerful voice came through, and Jane looked behind the man to see a pretty woman standing in the rain, a basket on her arm. "I've brought food for her."

"The King said no one was allowed in."

"Do you really think he was worried about me?" she woman countered, pushing past him. "The girl's bored and hungry, aren't you, miss? I've brought you food."

Neddie wasn't looking any too happy with this, but he decided not to argue. He moved out of the way, and the woman climbed up into the carriage. "You call me if you feel the need, miss. I'll be right here."

"I'll be fine," Jane said, hoping she was right. The woman had plumped herself down on the seat opposite her, and when Neddie closed the door behind her the carriage was plunged into gloomy darkness.

Not for long. The woman rifled in her basket and a moment later came up with a tinder box. The two candles on the walls were lit, and she sat back to survey Jane.

"You're a plain little thing," she said frankly. "Oh, you've got pretty eyes and a nice mouth, and your skin and teeth are good, but in fact you're quite ordinary, and the king has had some of the most extraordinary women in England. What does he see in you?" Before Jane could come up with an answer the woman thrust a basket in her hands. "I'm Gracie, by the way. I run yon ken—at least, the parts that they let me. And I'm wondering what would make King Donnelly give up everything, hand it over to an upstart like Jem Beesom with not so much as an argument. Mind you, Jem was making moves to take it over anyway, and he'll be a good enough master around here. But for Jacob to simply hand it over fair makes one think, and I had to see the lass what made him do it."

Jane just stared at the voluble creature across

from her. "I didn't make him do anything," she said, bewildered.

"No, I 'spose not. He's been restless for the last year or so. I've seen signs of it meself, and so has Jem, which is why he was ready to make his move. You should have seen his face when Jacob told him he was leaving and giving the leadership over to him. He looked ready to cry. Nothing like girding your loins for battle and having your enemy surrender. Not that Jacob and Jem are enemies, though let's hope Jacob doesn't change his mind, because Jem doesn't give up what's his easily. And of course you made him do it. He's got a thing about you. He guards you like some precious treasure—he'll be that mad when he finds out I came out here...."

Jane blinked while the girl continued to talk. Gracie had a thick accent, and for a moment she wondered if she was misunderstanding what she was saying. Gracie leaned forward and patted her hand. "Not much for conversation are you, Miss Pagett?" she said, ignoring the fact that she didn't allow much room for it. "That's all right—Jacob will get you to talking, right and tight. There's food in yon basket—Jacob said you were that hungry. And I've packed some of me own dresses for you, though you'll hardly fill them out. You're a skinny little thing, aren't you—though Jacob says you're tall. Are you in love with him?"

Jane was following all this silently, and she wasn't expecting the sudden question. "I beg your pardon?"

"You heard me, Miss Pagett. Are you in love with him? Ah, it's a daft question—most women are. All he has to do is look their way and they fall at his feet, me included."

Jane was tempted to tell the woman that it wasn't

any of her business, but there was only so far her courage could take her. "I don't know what you're talking about," she said faintly.

"Ah, you do indeed, Miss Pagett." She reached out and grasped Jane's wrist in a painfully tight grip. "Are you in love with him?" She squeezed tighter. "The truth now. I'll know if you're lying."

"You're hurting me!" She couldn't bring herself to meet Gracie's eyes. "Of course I'm not in love with him. I barely know him. He's simply been very kind to me, but he doesn't care about me and I certainly am not in love with him."

Gracie released her wrist, and Jane rubbed it. There was a dawning smile on Gracie's face, and she nodded. "You'll do. I told you I'd know if you lied, and you just lied to me. You never once said he was beneath you. I think he'll do right well with you." Before Jane could say anything Gracie opened the carriage door and scrambled down the steps. She looked back. "Mind you, if you break his heart you'll have me to answer to."

"But he doesn't love..." But Gracie was already gone.

She'd left the food behind, and the candles expelled some of the gloom. There was always a chance that Gracie was a madwoman who'd poisoned her, but at that point Jane was so hungry she didn't care. The bread and cheese weren't what she was used to—the bread was dark and dense, the cheese strong, and she ate every bit, loving it all.

It was getting darker outside, and when she heard someone at the door she drew back, afraid of another visit from Gracie, when Jacob Donnelly put his head in. "We're ready to go, lass, if you've still a mind to."

He smiled up at her, that rakish, charming smile that matched his kiss. She shouldn't be thinking of that. "Yes," she said in a steady voice. "I have to save Miranda."

"Well, as to that I'm not sure her ladyship is going to need saving, but I'm at your service." He held out his hand, the strong, well-shaped hands that had once touched her quite indecently in the darkness, and she wondered if they'd touch her again. "I've got a smaller, lighter carriage waiting for us, and since you've expressed such doubts about my driving ability I've got a professional to drive us. If you'll come with me."

She would go anywhere with him, she knew that to her everlasting shame. Gracie had seen the right of it: sensible or not, she'd fallen in love with the man, and she should just stop fighting it and spend her energy learning how to deal with it. How to keep from showing it, how to live without him. Because that was the way it was going to be. She wasn't for the likes of him. She wasn't for the likes of anyone.

But for a few brief days she could turn her back on common sense and self-respect. She would be with him, and that was enough.

She put her hand in his, and went.

24

All right, so this wasn't working out as well as she'd planned, Miranda thought, sitting at the newly polished and tuned piano, her hands motionless on the keys early the next morning. The house was too big to drive Lucien crazy—if she was being bright-eyed and amenable, he could always simply walk away. She'd kept him from her bed last night by the simple expedience of asking when he was coming back and that she'd enjoyed it "oh, ever so much!"

She wasn't quite sure if he knew the truth. He said he knew women's bodies, knew her body better than she did, and from his astonishing mastery over her she suspected he was right. She could try to work harder on her flippant attitude. If he decided he wanted her again, which seemed unlikely considering the wide berth he was giving her, she would try telling him she found it tiresome. If he persisted she could keep talking as he touched her, even sing in her unfortunately off-key voice as he...as he...

No, maybe she couldn't manage that. It was far too overwhelming. In fact, she hadn't quite made up her mind about the whole thing. With Christopher St. John it had simply been nasty. With Lucien it was...demoralizing. Upsetting. All-consuming. It stripped her soul even as he stripped her body, leaving nothing left. Both times she'd somehow had to pull herself back together, and each time it had been harder.

It had nothing to do with the emptiness she'd felt after Christopher St. John had taken her to bed.

With Lucien, she felt too full, too overwhelmed, in a very real sense. She could shrug off St. John's clumsy pawings, the hurt he'd dealt her.

Lucien would be a different matter entirely.

She ran her fingers over the keys, launching into a Bach prelude she'd memorized last year. She loved Bach, the mathematical precision of him, the joy and lightness. She played with great force, hoping to annoy Lucien wherever he was in the house. It was a challenging piece, and she tended to miss notes, but she still enjoyed herself tremendously.

"Please stop."

She let out a shriek, crashing her hands onto the piano and turning to glare at him. "You frightened me," she accused him. "Must you sneak up on one like that?"

"You were playing so loudly I doubt you would have heard a dragoon of soldiers if they marched in. If you must torture a composer why don't you choose one of his more lugubrious pieces—perhaps a fugue? Surely your repertoire must include pieces that don't have to be played quite so loudly? One that you might, perhaps, know better?"

He was dressed in black, as always, and sunlight shone in on his scarred face. His pale eyes were unreadable as he watched her, and she could only hope she was equally inscrutable. Because she looked at his ruined beauty and her heart ached.

"I'm afraid it's not the level of skill," she managed to say sweetly, pulling herself together. "People say I play with great abandon."

"Yes. Abandoned to all sense of musicality."

"I suppose you can do better?"

"I can. I won't. Please yourself, but a little more quietly, if you will. I have the headache."

She hit a chord on the piano, quite loudly, one note deliberately off, watching him wince before she left off and rose from the bench. "So tell me, at what time are we leaving for our visit?"

That soon. "As soon as you're ready. I assume you're longing to get away from here and back into company—you should enjoy yourself extremely."

"Actually I've been very happy here," she said brightly. "I like having my own house, and I enjoy having it to myself. But I'm perfectly happy to go wherever you wish. I'm looking forward to meeting your friends." She summoned her dazzling smile, the one that didn't reach her eyes. "My darling, I'll do absolutely anything you wish me to."

His expression, cynical as always, did little to ease her anxieties. "I was hoping you'd say so, my dearest. I have great plans for you."

She could stab him, she thought dreamily. If he thought she was going to have anything to do with his nasty little friends she would have to disabuse him of the notion, but she didn't quite believe he meant to go through with it. He was a man who valued his possessions, and a wife was, unfortunately, a possession, assuming he still meant to marry her. She couldn't see him lending her out to his friends.

Could she? For the sake of the revenge he held so dearly?

She would stab him.

She smiled sweetly. "Will we arrive in time for dinner? Otherwise I'll have Mrs. Humber make us up a basket."

"We don't eat formal meals. Don't worry your head about such things—Mrs. Humber will take care of it. All you need to do is smile and be pretty." After a moment he lifted a well-shaped eyebrow. "What was that, my love? Did I hear you growl?"

Miranda's fingers had curled into claws, and she quickly relaxed them. "Not at all, my darling. I'm looking forward to this." Bloody hell, he was good at this. What was the line? "That one may smile and smile and be a villain." He wasn't Richard the Third, he was Hamlet, out for revenge.

Except it had been Hamlet speaking, had it not? She looked at him, wondering just how villainous he truly could be. Stab him, she thought, marshalling her courage.

"What are you thinking, my pet? Your lovely brow is now furrowed."

"I was thinking about Hamlet," she answered with absolute truth.

"My lovely classical bride! Of course you were. 'O smiling, damned villain,'" he said, and she jerked at how close he was to her thoughts. But then, that had been the way during the short, sweet time they had been friends. They had been curiously in tune with each other. He went on, "But even Claudius repents. I've already told you, the closest I can come is Richard the Third."

On impulse she reached up and touched the scarred side of his face. "Caliban," she said softly. "Are you going to tell me how this happened?"

He didn't move for one breathless moment. And then he flinched, pulling away from her. "I don't think it would entertain you, my lady," he said, suddenly formal. "There are far more interesting ways to spend our time."

She looked at him for a long moment. "You try so hard to convince me how evil you are," she said softly, dropping her overbright smile. "Don't you tire of it?"

"Trust me, my love, it's effortless." He was cold, withdrawn, his pale eyes wintry. "We'll be leaving within the hour. I've left instructions with your so-called maid. Be ready."

If Jane had thought the pace of her first trip north had been *ventre à terre* it was nothing compared to this one. Jacob Donnelly's driver was far more skilled, though in fact no one could make such high speeds on the rough roads easy, and she held on to the strap as they traveled into the darkness, trying to keep from being bounced around.

They rode in grim silence. Jacob had changed his clothes, and apart from asking her if someone had brought her some food he said nothing, leaning back on the opposite seat, his long legs propped on the floor beside her, and he slept.

She wished she could do the same. She felt as if she'd spent her life in a carriage, and while she still loved the idea of travel, she wouldn't have minded a more leisurely pace or time off between trips in the best of all situations.

This was far from the best. She glanced over at her companion, frustrated. She was frightened for Miranda, who seemed surrounded by enemies. Her closest friend had accepted her dismissal and in fact had been so busy becoming enamored of a thief she'd forgotten all about her. After all, Jane had seen the way Rochdale had looked at her. She knew what love looked like—she'd seen it often enough between her parents, and she was sure she'd recognized it without question.

But it seemed as if she was wrong. Not if he was going to offer her up to the Heavenly Host as some sort of gift, or sacrifice, or plaything. She shuddered.

Jacob Donnelly slept on, impervious to worry and the racketing of the carriage, impervious to everything. She might just as well be alone in the coach, she thought, much aggrieved. If he didn't wake up and set her mind at ease she would be tempted to go into strong hysterics.

They hit a bump, and she almost flew off the seat. Her companion barely moved, and enough was enough. They'd been in the carriage almost twelve hours, stopping only to change horses, and the morning sun was coming up. If her companion was really that sound a sleeper then she pitied the poor woman who married him.

Of course she did, she mocked herself. Poor, shy, pitiful Jane. She reached out and kicked him.

He didn't move, continuing to sleep soundly as the coach tore onward. She wondered what would happen if she pinched him. She reached out to kick him again when his quiet voice reached out through the dawn-lit carriage.

"Don't kick me, lass," he said quietly.

"Mr. Donnelly," she said, hating the sound of her high and nervous voice. "Do you think we're going to get there in time to dissuade Lord Rochdale from taking Miranda to his evil friends?"

He opened his eyes, looking at her with a lazy appreciation that startled her. What was there about her skinny, plain figure that was worth appreciating? "Now, Miss Jane," he said, "you'll find that most things aren't quite as bad as they seem. The Heavenly Host are no more than a bunch of spoiled, gormless aristocrats with more money than sense, and they try to keep themselves entertained by playing at being wicked. It's mostly harmless, if not particularly sanctioned by the church, and some of the things that go on there might be against the law, but I always hold with the fact that if the two or three or more people involved want to do it then it's no one else's business."

"Two or three or more...?" That was something she didn't care to think about. "So there's no blood sacrifice or anything?"

"The only thing that gets sacrificed is some fools' dignity."

Jane concentrated on making pleats in her poor abused traveling dress. "And have you ever been to one of these gatherings?"

"Oh, they're not for the likes of me. For one thing, I've never been particularly interested. For another, only a favored few are allowed to join, and those are of the upper crust. Your fiancé was rejected."

"What?" she stared at him in shock. "My boring, stiff-necked, straitlaced fiancé wanted to be part of their disgusting group?"

"Maybe he wasn't so boring as you thought."

"Trust me, he was," she said. "One can be perverse and still be boring."

He laughed. "Very true. And being a member doesn't mean you've lost your soul. Your own…" He stopped abruptly, as if realizing he'd said too much.

But Jane, for all her shyness, had never been particularly slow. "My own…' what? Never mind, I know the answer to that. My father told me he spent many years as a total wastrel. It shouldn't surprise me in the least that he was part of them". She looked at his impassive face. "You did mean my father, didn't you?"

"Ask him if you dare," he suggested affably. "I've said too much."

"You don't know my father, do you? I can ask him anything." She sat back on her seat, fidgeting. "Do you think we'll get there in time to keep them from going?"

"Don't worry, lass, we'll get to Ripton Waters in plenty of time, but it wouldn't do to underestimate Scorpion. He'll more than likely realize he's a flaming idiot and stop before he goes through with it."

"A flaming idiot?"

"You and I both know he's mad for her, something I never thought I'd see. I'm more than happy to take you up there, just to set your mind at ease, but he's in love with her, and I suspect she feels the same way."

"And yet he's serving her up to the Heavenly Host," Jane said with some asperity.

"You've seen Scorpion, Miss Jane. You've spent time with him. Do you really think he's the kind of man who'd share the woman he's fallen in love with? His problem is he doesn't seem to realize it just yet, and he won't listen when I tried to point it out to him. But he'll come to it soon enough when he sees another man put a hand on her."

"If she's really safe then why are you willing to race up north to rescue her?" she said, unconvinced.

His smile was slow and charming. "Maybe I just wanted the chance to spend time with you."

She allowed herself an inelegant snort. "I own a mirror, Mr. Donnelly."

His smile vanished. "Perhaps you do, lass," he said finally. "But you must be half blind. And the name's Jacob."

And before she realized what he'd intended, he'd moved across the carriage and sat beside her, his warm, big body pressed up against her, and he'd taken her nervous hand in his.

Miranda curled up in the corner of the coach, her cloak wrapped tight around her. They would be gone for three or four nights, Lucien had said, and yet he refused to let her bring Bridget. The trunk that had been packed for her was both ominously small and mysterious. She had no idea what was inside it, but clearly there wasn't much.

She'd done her best, played her cards well, but she had to face facts. She had lost. Lucien always held the stronger hand, and there was only so much skill could do against a master player. He was taking her to his degenerate friends, the final proof of how little she truly mattered. Any hopes she'd had of a real connection had finally died.

He rode outside, a good thing. She would have had a hard time keeping up her bubbly conversation during the ride, which he'd told her would take most of the day. Instead she could try to think if there was any way of escape.

He'd told her it would never be rape. Perhaps he only meant with him. He would offer her up to his friends, and she had no idea what would happen if she struggled. Perhaps it would only sweeten the game for them. She'd refused to struggle with St. John—she would hardly give a bunch of jaded aristocrats that pleasure.

She could escape, perhaps. She'd given Lucien every sign that she was cowed—if he glanced away for even a minute she could run.

Her chances of success would be slim. She had no money, and he would find her easily enough, and then all he had to do was lie if someone tried to help her. Tell them she was a runaway bride. Or a madwoman. Or he could simply kill anyone who offered to assist her—she had no real knowledge of the depths his infamy could go. So the only people who could truly help her would be her family, and they had no idea where she was.

Even Jane didn't know exactly where they were headed. She could direct her family north, but Lucien had taken back roads, and Jane would have little information.

Oh, they would find her eventually. But not soon enough.

If he'd joined her in the coach she might have been able to make him change his mind. Perhaps he knew that, and stayed outside for that very reason. It was just as well. Pulling up her skirts, she took out the knife that was strapped to her calf.

It was a nasty-looking weapon, part of a display of armory used during the Civil War, though she wasn't sure if it was by the Roundheads or the Royalists. Either way, it was about a foot long with a nice point, even if the blade was sadly dull. She'd slipped it out of the display in the third-floor hallway. It hadn't been dusted in what looked like decades, and there were so many weapons adorning the walls that Lucien would never realize something was gone.

If worse came to worst, she'd stab him.

Oh, no place on his body that would actually kill him. In the arm or leg or something, just enough to shock him and hurt like hell and give her time to get away. She'd considered smashing a ewer on his head as she had with St. John but Lucien probably had too hard a head to make that work. But he could bleed if she stabbed him, she had no doubt.

She tucked the blade back in the garter. Getting into the carriage had been tricky, as dismounting was bound to be, but the groom had handled the honors and Lucien would be busy with other things. Like planning her total subjugation by deviates.

The Heavenly Host! Heaven spare her. She had no fear of blood sacrifice or black masses. She'd heard the stories, much expurgated, from her own family. Both her father and grandfather, the notorious Francis Rohan, had been active in the Heavenly Host, and unless they'd greatly changed in the last twenty years they were nothing but a group of bored aristocrats playing games with God and sex, dressing in outlandish costumes and cavorting. She had no quarrel with their silly doings, as long as they kept their grubby hands off her.

She considered the vain hope that her brothers had lied to her, that they had followed in the family footsteps and joined that group of degenerates, and would, upon discovering her identity, rescue her, but she doubted it. She knew them too well, and none of them would have any patience with that kind of playacting. The Heavenly Host would hold no interest for them. Benedick and Charles were happily married, and Brandon was such a prig he'd be horrified.

So she could fight, she could run, or she could stab Lucien. While that was definitely the most appealing, she somehow doubted she'd have the courage in the end. Because, appalling, toad-sucking, slime-dwelling bastard that he was, she…

She what? Didn't want to hurt him? That certainly wasn't true—she'd like to bash him in the head. She was fond of him? Hardly. One couldn't be fond of someone who skulked around like a Shakespearean villain. Pitied him? Not likely. He was much too strong to be pitied.

Lusted after him? Perhaps she would say yes, if she were to be honest with herself, but she was fighting it, fighting her own weaknesses. So he was good at making a woman shiver and tremble and dissolve. It was a skill and nothing more. She needed to remember that.

But she could also remember the way he held her as she cried. The expression on his face when he thought she wasn't looking. The way they were so oddly in tune, when they weren't at war.

If he'd just stop being such an arrogant bastard she might start to care for him. Might stop wanting his head on a platter.

But she was much too wise a woman to fall in love with a man who was only intent on vengeance against her family and thought of her as nothing but a weapon.

She was too smart to love a man who couldn't love her back, no matter how easy it was to fall under his spell. Wasn't she?

25

The rain had begun to fall by midafternoon, but Lucien made no effort to join his bride in the carriage, despite the cold chill. He wasn't particularly happy with himself, which was nothing new. Happiness wasn't something he tended to consider—it was far too ephemeral, and, in fact, he wasn't sure he'd ever really known it.

His mother had died in childbirth, taking his baby brother with her. And his father, inheriting nothing but debts and a fatal propensity for gaming, had had no choice but to decamp to the remaining family estates in the new world, taking his four-year-old son with him.

He'd married again, another émigré, more to warm his bed and his coffers than to provide a mother for his neglected son.

Lucien could remember, if not happiness, at least a form of hope. Cecily was kind to him, and she gave him a sister, Genevieve, before his father had died of cholera.

He must have recognized the darkness that lay within Cecily, that stopped him from giving his child's heart to the only mother he had ever known.

Because it wasn't long before the madness was on her.

In truth, he was much more familiar with solid, long-lasting things like justice and revenge. Happiness is an illusion.

Though there were moments, when he'd been with Miranda Rohan, that he thought he might have caught a glimpse of it.

Why the hell had he ever thought marrying her was a good idea? He never would have tolerated a milksop, never have considered it. But Miranda was a woman with fire and determination, and he'd been reluctantly entranced with her from the moment she stepped inside his carriage in Hyde Park. Before that she'd simply been a catspaw, a tool to bring him what he wanted. He thought he could play with her and then discard her, immure her in Pawlfrey House and not have to think about her again.

He'd greatly underestimated her. She drew him in ways he didn't want to think about. She infuriated him, made him laugh, filled him with lust.

And she weakened him.

This was the greatest danger. He looked at her and something inside him softened, just as his cock hardened. He should have realized what a risk she was and come up with another plan. He was fiendishly inventive—it would have been simple enough to have orchestrated some other design that would leave the Rohans in the dust, sparing Miranda. He'd already had to regroup once when St. John had failed so miserably. He could have done so again.

And there it was again, his ridiculous desire to spare

her, to protect her. When his life's work aimed at using her to hurt the people who loved her most.

It was no wonder he was happier riding in the rain. It suited his gloomy preoccupation.

The current members of the Heavenly Host were ensconced in Bromfield Manor, a house in the countryside beyond Morecombe, their revels already commenced. He'd joined in a number of times, watching their futile black masses with amusement, helping himself from the banquet of sexuality offered. He told himself he would have nothing to feel guilty over. No one, woman or man, was coerced or forced at the revels. All Miranda need do was say no and she would be left alone. She was the mistress of her own fate.

She was also infuriatingly stubborn, and not one to back down. Well, neither was he. In the end it would be up to her, her choice.

It was evening when they arrived at Bromfield Manor. If Miranda had any trepidation she hid it perfectly, keeping up a steady stream of inconsequential chatter as they were shown to their rooms. She only balked when the maid opened her trunk and laid out her outfit for the night.

At first glance it was suitably demure—a Grecian style gown in black, with gold sandals of a classic design, as well. It took but a moment to realize the dress was diaphanous to the point of transparency, and all of his future wife's charms would be revealed to the Host.

He even had Bromley work up a black mass wedding, and he'd done so with his usual enthusiasm. That ceremony included consummation by whomever she accepted, thereby sealing their vows of a nonmonogamous relationship and an openness to indulgences of every kind. If Miranda accepted this absurdity her subjugation would be complete, and the Rohans would have lost her. A few days with a fortune hunter were one thing. A willing participant in what would quickly become an orgy was a different matter.

"You expect me to wear that?" she said, picking up the sheer fabric and dropping it. Her voice was a bit higher and tighter than usual, but apart from that there was no sign of her uneasiness. "I'll catch my death of cold."

"They keep the rooms heated," he said, not moving from his seat by the fire. "And you'll have a domino in the beginning to keep you warm."

She cast him an acerbic look. "How nice." Finally her sarcasm was beginning to leak through the cheeriness. "It will be *so* delightful to enjoy new experiences. But did you not say there would be a wedding ceremony with your friends in attendance? I see no wedding dress or anything remotely suitable."

He took a sip of wine, keeping his face impassive. "It's not precisely a wedding ceremony. The Heavenly Host are intellectuals with inquiring minds. They investigate the existence of God and his counterpart. I believe our wedding is to be in the service of the latter, assuming there is such a thing. We'll have a legal ceremony after we return home."

She was holding very still. "Indeed," she said after a moment. "A Satanic wedding. How original! It's a rare bride who can say she was wed in front of God *and* the devil."

He set his wineglass down with a snap. "During which, instead of promising your eternal fidelity and devotion, you'll be swearing to keep an open mind. And open legs," he added with deliberate crudeness.

She didn't flinch, damn her. "Fascinating," she said faintly. "And will I then be called to act upon this oath?"

"It generally works that way." A patently ridiculous thing to say, since the Heavenly Host had never held a wedding before.

"Did you know my father and grandfather were members of the Heavenly Host?" she murmured, plucking at the gown she was to wear.

"I did. I thought it made the irony particularly appealing."

She looked up, and her smile was the one that made him want to smash things. The smile that said "you shan't touch me, no matter what you do." "Indeed. Well, I shall look forward to tonight's festivities. It will be most instructive to compare other men to you. Clearly you're far superior to a poor creature like Christopher St. John, but I do wonder if you're not oddly made. Surely most men can't be as large as you are."

For the first time in what seemed like days he wanted to laugh. At this point his darling fiancée was innocent enough not to realize that was a far cry from an insult.

But that would change. "I'll be most interested to hear your observations."

She came back to the table, poured herself a glass of wine and drained it in one, unappreciative gulp. "When are they expecting us?"

"At any time."

"Then perhaps you might summon one of the

maids and allow me some privacy in which to prepare myself."

He'd rather hoped to sit and watch her strip down and attire herself in her Grecian whore's outfit. But she was looking just the slightest bit dangerous, and he hadn't forgotten how she'd managed to dispatch with Christopher St. John. There were no water ewers available, though a wine bottle could make a fairly effective weapon.

He rose, languidly, and he expected that he looked like the very devil in the flickering firelight. "As you wish, my love. Take your time. Perhaps you might like a bath?"

She cocked an eyebrow at him. "I expect I'll be in need of one even more after the festivities," she drawled. "But yes, if you could procure me one it might settle my nerves."

"Nerves, my love?"

"All brides are nervous, my dearest." There was a real edge to the endearment. "And I don't want to disappoint your friends."

He found he was grinding his teeth. He stopped, immediately. "As you wish." And he bowed himself out of the room.

Miranda watched him leave, a composed expression on her face. The moment the door clicked behind him she would have been tempted to run and lock it, but there were no keys in the doors at Bromfield Manor. The truth was plain but unpalatable. He really didn't care for her, not in the tiniest bit.

She glanced toward the windows. She could try to escape, but they were on the second floor, and she'd already checked. There was no balustrade or terrace to afford her an easy exit.

She could pull on the plain black domino, Lucien's cloak, eschewing the golden monstrosity he'd brought for her, and she could probably manage to sneak out of the house that way. The only problem being that they were on the edge of the moors, and she was far too pragmatic to court death before dishonor.

She'd hidden the ancient dagger beneath the pillow on the bed, and she pulled it out to look at it. How many men had it killed? Could she bring herself to stab him?

Yes. If he handed her over to his friends, and then brought her back to this bed, then yes, she could stab him before she left. And stab him she would.

She sat silently while they brought a bath and filled it. The maid assigned to her was thankfully subdued, presumably having been accustomed to the foul goings-on between Lord Bromley's friends, and she helped her in silence, washing her back, drying her, helping her dress like a sacrificial vestal virgin in the embarrassing costume. She even plaited and arranged her hair in a pseudoclassical style, bent down and fastened the gold sandals on her feet, and then stood back.

"Will there be anything else, my lady? Some of our ladies prefer to start the evening with a bit of assistance."

Miranda managed to emerge from her welter of abstracted misery. "Assistance?"

"We're told to offer laudanum, if you prefer it, or brandy to settle the nerves, or the evening's punch, which tends to animate guests most effectively," the maid said with a blank expression.

Miranda seriously considered, then rejected the idea. She would follow this night through with whatever it held. "No, thank you. I shall be fine."

The maid opened her mouth to speak, then shut it again, and Miranda suspected why. She probably didn't look fine. She probably looked as devastated and broken as she felt.

"Would you please inform his lordship that I'm ready?"

She waited until the girl was gone, then went over to look at the pier glass, curious how she looked as a whore.

She gasped. She might as well be standing naked. She could see the thrust of her small breasts, the dark nipples clear through the wispy fabric. The line of her body, the darker triangle of hair, the outline of her legs. All was revealed and yet disguised in a gown made for sexual titillation.

She closed her eyes for a moment, then looked at her face. It was pale and ghostly, and her eyes were nothing but dark holes. They hadn't offered her makeup, but she bit her lips to bring color back to them, pinched her cheeks. She smiled brightly, and to her discerning eyes the effect was ghastly.

Lucien wouldn't even notice.

The door opened behind her and she turned. A great many candles lit the room, brightening it, and he could see her quite clearly. He froze for a moment, staring at her, and she wanted to weep, to scream at him, to beg him to stop this.

And then he moved forward, calm and urbane. "You look quite magnificent, my love. You'll be the perfect blushing bride. Unless you've changed your mind?"

Why was he asking her this? He was the one who'd brought her here; he was the one who was asking this of her. She smiled at him, her face muscles feeling stiff and tight. "I will do whatever you ask of me, my darling. If you desire this, then I desire this."

He stared at her for a long moment. "So be it," he said in a tight voice. He picked up the domino and draped it around her shoulders, fastening it at her neck. His hands were surprisingly gentle, caressing at her throat as he fastened the cape, and she wondered what he would do if she lowered her face to rub against his hands. She kept her head still.

Instead he lifted his hand to brush her cheek, gently, and she would have broken, if he hadn't turned away, starting toward the door and opening it. He paused there, holding out his arm. "Shall we join the others, my love?"

She took his arm, and went.

The halls he led her down were dark and shrouded, but he seemed to know where he was going. "Have you been here before?" she asked in a calm tone.

In answer he said, "Bromley holds these gatherings every few months. If I have nothing better to do I join them."

"You have a taste for degeneracy?"

He looked down at her and smiled grimly. "Haven't you noticed?"

She subsided. She could pull back, cry off. What was the worst thing that would happen?

She would lose. She hated to lose, but most particularly she hated the thought of losing to him. She was gambling on the hope that he wouldn't go through with this, and she just might lose. He cared for her, whether he could admit it or not. She was certain of it, though she couldn't say why. He would pull back himself, take her away from this terrible place.

But he continued moving forward, and she kept up with him. He was walking swiftly, not bothering with a cane this evening, as if he were in a hurry to get to the dark heart of the night.

She heard the noise from a distance, the soft murmur of voices growing louder until they approached a wide set of doors. Impassive servants stood on either side, and they waited for a nod from her terrible, beautiful lover. The doors were opened, and they were greeted with a roar.

26

He was holding her bare hand, Miranda realized belatedly. He would be able to feel the cold sweat on her palms, the faint tremor. She pulled her hand away, surveying the room with a critical eye.

At one end of the huge hall there was a dais, which one might purport to be an altar, albeit one dedicated to the darker arts. She was marginally relieved to see that instead of a sacrificial stone there was a low bed. Not that she'd ever believed the stories about sacrifice. Her father and grandfather had been far from proper gentlemen but their wickedness didn't go the way of murder.

She glanced around her. People were wearing all sorts of strange garments, from nuns' habits and priests' robes to the simple, enveloping dominos that left one with no idea who they were. Little wonder, if the members of the Heavenly Host were as august as she'd heard.

A short, slightly rotund man approached, and she could only guess he was the host of this particular gathering. He, too, was wearing classical costume, with a laurel wreath on thinning hair styled à Brutus and the mask of a goat on his face.

"We call you all to witness the marriage made in hell of our dear brother Lucien the Scorpion and his chosen lady, and we ask you all to partake of the chalice that will sanctify this unholy union…"

He was carrying some kind of glass vessel, and it took her a moment to identify it. It was a goblet shaped like a phallus, though admittedly more like Lucien's impressive appendage and less like St. John's tiny stub. She supposed before the night was over she would have knowledge of any number of penises, and would be able to judge what was normal and what was not. A grim shiver of amusement ran over her.

It was cold in the room, even though she could see the sweat stand out on the foreheads of some of the people who pressed around them. Or perhaps she was simply nervous. Lucien stood beside her, silent. Damnably silent.

She reached up, unfastened the domino and let it fall to the floor. She could feel Lucien's start, as the assemblage roared in approval.

The man, whom she presumed was Lord Bromley, held the obscene glass up to her. "Take of our communion, my dark lady, and we shall…"

"I think not," she said in a cool voice. "It looks most unsanitary, and I have grave doubts as to what's inside."

The room was struck silent, as if the devil himself had suddenly appeared. The goat lord seemed nonplussed. "Er…all right." He handed the goblet to a waiting minion, then turned back to her, trying to regain his concentration. "We call upon the powers of darkness, Beelzebub and his angels, to curse this union..."

Miranda rolled her eyes. "Oh, please. You don't seriously expect to conjure up the devil, do you? I doubt you even believe in the devil. This is all extremely tiresome—could we get on with it?" Cheery good humor was beyond her at this point, but she could manage bored annoyance quite well. Even if she thought she heard a muffled snort of laughter from the man who brought her.

The man in front of her looked aggrieved, but he wasn't to be deterred from his course. "First you must be judged worthy. Take your chosen bride to the marriage bed."

At least he didn't call him the Scorpion again. It would have made her giggle. Perhaps she shouldn't have indulged in the glass of wine, but she could have barely faced all this sober, could she?

For a moment Lucien didn't move. And then he put his hand beneath her arm and led her toward the altar. She might have thought his hand was like ice beneath her skin, but she was too cold to be certain. She allowed herself one brief glimpse at him. He looked like a wax figure, expressionless, emotionless.

He stopped in front of the bed. The portly goat-man had been following, and as Lucien turned her to face the crowd the man said, "Do you join us of your own free will, my lady? Is it your wish to be one of us?"

The silence in the room was so complete one could have heard a stray mouse. She glanced at Lucien, his cold, pale face. "Not exactly," she allowed in a carrying voice. "It appears to be my lord's wish, and my wish is to make my lord happy." It felt like it was the last smile she would ever have the strength to summon, and she flashed it toward him, hoping he would miss the bleak misery in her eyes.

Another murmur of conversation from the crowd, but apparently it was agreement enough. "My Lord Scorpion, you may retire," said the man, and took her cold hand away from the man she was fool enough to love.

For a moment she lost sight of him, as the avid crowd pushed closer, and the pudgy man led her toward the bed. Bloody hell, she thought. Clearly she'd played this wrong. At every minute she'd expected Lucien to renege, to pull her back, but he'd done nothing. This was his will.

And she was half tempted to go through with it, just to spite him.

She glanced down at the bed. Did they really expect her to disport in public? Clearly they did. Would Lucien watch, unmoved? Clearly he would.

And what would happen if she suddenly screamed no and smacked the little toad beside her? And what was keeping her from doing so?

Hope? Surely that was long gone. Pride? That couldn't be worth this kind of shame, to stand here practically naked in front of all these people. Why the hell had she dumped her domino? She was a fool and a half to put up with this nonsense. It was past time to put an end to it.

The toad was intoning something about the bonds of submission but she was paying no attention, and she opened her mouth to tell them all to sod off, when a velvet scarf was yanked around her mouth, effectively silencing her, just as someone else tied her wrists together.

She panicked then. She'd waited too long. They placed a hood over her head, and she felt herself lifted and placed on the bed, and no matter how hard she struggled there seemed to be hands everywhere, holding her down.

"Do not worry about her struggles," she heard the voice say, as she tried to scream against the gag. "It is simply part of the ceremony. She has given us her word free and clear that she wishes to participate, and we will..."

"Get your hands off her."

She heard those words, loud and clear, and she fell back against the bed, no longer struggling. The hands were still holding her down, hands on her shoulders, hands on her legs. "You heard me." Lucien's voice was cold and clear, murderous. "If anyone touches her I'll kill them."

All the hands immediately left her, and she tried to sit up. She felt dizzy, her terror making her light-headed in the muffled darkness, and she felt Lucien approach her, knew him by the feel of him, the warmth of him. He took her bound hands in his and cut the ties, so that they fell apart. He pulled the hood from her head and she blinked in the now bright candlelight as he reached behind her and unfastened the gag, letting it drop to the floor.

"I find I'm more possessive than I realized," he said, and took her arm and pulled her to her feet. He whipped off his own black domino and covered her with it, shielding her from the avid eyes.

She was trembling, afraid she wouldn't be able to stand, but she refused to show weakness in front of these pathetic creatures. He put his arm around her waist, ostensibly out of affection, but she could feel his silent support, just as she'd helped him up to the house a few short days ago. And she wanted to weep.

But she kept her face stony cold as he led her down the long walk to the door. He paused, for one brief moment as he glanced into the crowd, and she could feel shock vibrate through his body. And then he moved on, leading her from the hall in grim silence.

There were curious eyes on them as they descended the staircase, but he simply scooped her up in his arms and she instinctively put her head against his shoulder, hiding her face. He didn't pause, didn't speak to anyone, and she could feel his body tremble as he carried her. She wasn't sure if it was from anger or her weight, and she didn't care. She wished she weighed five stone more. It would serve him right.

To her astonishment he placed her in a waiting carriage, settling her gently on the seat, and for a moment she dazedly wondered whose carriage he was stealing. And then she recognized his own, from the softness of the squabs, the faint scent of sandalwood and Lucien, a dark, spicy scent that had once seemed like everything she had ever wanted.

She knew it, now that it was too late. She'd loved him, and he betrayed her. It made no difference that in the end he'd recanted. He could have a thousand reasons for that.

He'd thrown her away, and he'd lost her.

She would have hoped he had the decency to let her ride alone. He had little decency, if any. He climbed in beside her and tried to pull her into his arms.

She kicked him to get away, ending up on the opposite seat in a far corner. He wouldn't be able to see her face. He should have known that she wasn't to be touched.

But he said nothing. The carriage moved forward a moment later in the cool night air, and she felt the rich fur throw tossed over her in the darkness, without a word.

She would have liked to have thrown it on the floor and stomped on it, but she was too cold in the ridiculous clothes he'd made her wear. So she simply wrapped it around her, pulling it up around her ears, and closed her eyes, shutting him out completely.

Still, she thought. The carriage had been ready and waiting this entire time.

Well, how extremely interesting, Christopher St. John thought, moving away from the crowd. The future countess of Rochdale had certainly told off the Heavenly Host quite nicely. And Rochdale himself had been as cold-blooded as ever, offering up his future wife as if she were a decent bottle of port to be shared.

But even more interesting was the fact that he'd changed his mind, stopped them, carried her out of there like some noble knight.

He'd gone out of his way to make certain Rochdale would see him, standing at the edge of the crowd, and his reaction was all St. John could have asked for. He would have thought he was still on the continent, where he'd fled after the debacle with Rochdale's mistress. But he was back, and it was clear from the expression on the earl's face that the woman had no idea he'd hired him in the first place.

And if it was something he'd kept secret then he'd most likely continue to do so. And be willing to pay a comfortable sum of money to ensure St. John's discretion.

Life certainly took the damnedest turns.

He would find where Rochdale was staying and pay him a little visit, when his mistress was nowhere around. Blackmail was always better than revenge, but he'd take the latter if Rochdale refused to pay. Rochdale had always had the ability to terrify him, but this time he held all the cards.

In the meantime, he was going to enjoy himself. And he turned back and moved into the crowd.

Jacob wouldn't have woken Miss Jane Pagett if he could have helped it. When the carriage came to an unexpected stop he carefully disentangled himself from her sleeping body and opened the door as quietly as he could, jumping down into the cool night air. After consulting with Simmons, the best driver in half of London, if not all, he tried to climb back in as quietly as he had left, but she was already wide-awake, staring at him out of sleepy eyes.

"What's happened?" she asked.

God, he loved the look of a woman as she was just waking up. There was something so blissfully erotic about it, the softness of her mouth, the vulnerability in her eyes. A vulnerability that suddenly disappeared as her eyelashes swept down.

He'd been hoping not to have to tell her, but his Jane was just a bit too sharp. "The left leader's thrown a shoe. We're almost at the next posting house, but we may be facing a bit of a delay."

There was no missing the alarm that swept through her. "But what if we're too late?"

"Hush, lass," he said in a soothing voice as the carriage started forward, this time at a snail's pace. "Scorpion's more than capable of seeing after his woman. He's more dangerous than you might think, and he's not about to let anyone touch her. He'll have changed his mind, you'll see."

She didn't look reassured. He started to cross the carriage, to sit beside her again, when she held up a restraining hand. "You don't need to comfort me, Mr. Donnelly. I'm not a child. I'm simply worried about my friend."

"I know you are, lass. And I..."

"You m...may call me Miss Pagett." Her voice was high and nervous, and she didn't meet his eyes. "And I don't care how angry that makes you."

He cocked his head. "It doesn't make me angry, *Miss Pagett,*" he said with faint ironic emphasis. "It just puzzles me. Have I done something to offend you?"

"Of course not," she said in an aggrieved voice, and it was a good thing she couldn't see in the dark, because his smile widened.

Women really were the damnedest creatures. He'd been so very careful not to frighten her, simply holding her carefully in the crook of his arm while she slept. He knew the rules of decent behavior, even though he seldom chose to follow them. For all that he wanted nothing more than to push Miss Jane Pagett down on the narrow seat of the carriage and find his way beneath her skirts, he knew that sort of thing wasn't done. Any more than visiting her room at the inn, or taking her on the floor in her own salon by the side of her unconscious fiancé, even though he'd briefly considered all those things.

He wasn't quite sure when or how or if he could have her. She was a proper young lady, despite what that bastard had yelled at her, and she deserved a proper husband. If he'd ruined things for her by taking her off like this then maybe he stood a chance.

But if she somehow managed to squeak through with her reputation intact then he'd stand aside. The kind of life he offered was much too rough for the likes of her, though she was more resilient than she seemed. And for her to have a chance at that proper life she needed her virginity intact, as well.

Of course he'd agreed to take her on the hope that Bothwell had talked and she was already ruined. That he would end up being the best of bad choices, and he'd never let her regret it.

But now it didn't seem to matter, since for some reason she was so angry with him she probably wouldn't ever want to see him again.

There was a faint sliver of moonlight shining in the carriage as they turned a corner, and he thought he saw the sheen of tears in her eyes. "What's wrong, lass?" he said in a gentle voice. "Are you that worried about your friend?"

"Of course I am," she said, and now he could hear the tears in her voice. "Why else would I be here, with you, in the middle of the night...?"

Enough was enough. He crossed the rocking carriage and took her into his arms, half expecting a struggle. Instead she burst into tears, burying her face against his shoulder, and he held her, whispering soft, meaningless phrases until she slowly calmed.

"You don't need to do this," she said in a damp, sulky voice.

"Don't need to hold a girl in my arms? It's a sore trial to me, but I'm willing to make the effort."

He heard a watery giggle and was encouraged. Her hair was starting to come down, and he stroked the back of her neck beneath it, gently massaging the tension away. Her quiet sound of pleasure had the expected effect on his body, and he wished he had a free hand to adjust himself, but with luck she wouldn't notice. She probably wouldn't even recognize the problem.

He let his hand slide down her neck, his thumb brushing against the softness of her throat, feeling the hammering of her pulse. It would be so easy to move his head down, put his mouth against hers and kiss her the way he had that night so long ago, kiss her with the full and glorious longing that could lead to so much more.

But if he did he'd have to pull her onto his lap, possibly ruining himself for any future pleasure. And even if he did manage to rearrange himself properly before she landed, what was the likelihood he'd be able to stop if she'd prove to be the slightest bit acquiescent?

And she'd be more than that. He knew women, and he knew his Jane. She was in love with him, dazzled by him, and if there were the slightest chance he could have her then he'd make her a good husband. He'd already given over Beggar's Ken to Jem and Gracie, and he had more than enough money to keep them in whatever style she wanted.

But she'd be shunned, he thought, absently stroking the side of her neck, his fingers gently touching her collarbone. And he wouldn't ask it of her.

So no kisses, no matter how badly he wanted them. He'd hold her chastely, like the saint he wasn't, and——

"Get your hands off me," snapped his gentle beloved.

He didn't, of course. He simply shifted her around to face him, thankfully adjusting his own rebellious body at the same time. "Enough is enough, Janey. Tell me what's gotten you in such a swivet."

"I'm not…" He put his hand across her mouth silencing her.

"Don't lie to me, darlin'. You'd fair like to cut my throat, and I'm wanting to know why."

"I don't…I don't like being touched."

He grinned, and he was close enough for her to see it. "Now that's not true. You fair purr like a little cat when I touch you."

"Not true. So there's no need for you to…to…feel sorry for me. I'm perfectly fine. I don't need you to hold me like a child till I feel better."

Realization was beginning to dawn. "I don't feel sorry for you," he said in a practical voice. "And I wasn't precisely holding you like a child."

"Please, don't." There was real misery in her voice.

It was so patently ridiculous that he wished he didn't have to spin this particular bit of idiocy along. He was about to reach for her when the carriage pulled to a stop, and he realized they'd come to an inn.

He practically leaped out of the carriage, knowing that in another minute he would have said everything he was determined not to say. Not until he had to.

When he turned to help her down from the carriage he saw that she'd already managed it herself, wincing slightly at her stiff muscles, and he told himself he wasn't going to think about how he could rub those muscles, loosen them right up and then make them all tense again in the best possible way.

"Does the lass want something to eat?" the innkeeper inquired.

Jane shook her head. "Just a bed, thank you," she said in her small, polite voice, not looking at him.

"I'll have Simmons bring your trunk, Miss Pagett," Jacob said politely.

"Of course you will," was her odd reply as she disappeared up the winding stairs.

He stood and watched her go. He'd mortally offended her, that much was sure. Or maybe she'd just realized how very foolish she'd been, running off with a thief. One guess was as good as another, and the last thing he was going to do was ask her. That could get them both into too much trouble, and besides, he might not like the answer.

Simmons dropped the small trunk down to him, and Jacob caught it easily. It was about the same size as the one he'd used to clock her fiancé, and he relived that glorious moment for an instant before dropping it at the foot of the stairs for the landlord to deliver.

"I'll see to the horses, Jacob," Simmons said. "A poultice and a good night's rest should help matters, and then we can hire new ones at the next posting house if you're still in such a bloody hurry."

Jacob glanced toward the stairs. She'd disappeared behind a closed door now, shutting him out of her life, and he told himself he was glad.

He turned back to Simmons. "Maybe you'd best give the horse another day and night," he said, wanting to kick himself as he did.

"Yon lass giving you trouble?" Simmons said sympathetically.

"No more than I can handle."

"The day Jacob Donnelly finds a woman more than he can handle is the day I give up on women altogether myself. We'll have all lost hope then," Simmons said with a heartfelt sigh.

Jacob resisted the impulse to tell him to prepare for a life of celibacy. Jane Paget was a rare handful, and he still wasn't sure how it was all going to end.

Dutch courage was the order of the day, and mine host had some fine Irish whiskey. Two shots and he was ready for his own bed, which, unfortunately, was up those stairs, too close to Miss Jane Paget for comfort. He considered a chair by the fire again, but the night was warm and he was restless and told himself he needed a bed

He did. He needed her bed.

He made his way up the stairs, trying to keep quiet. There were three doors on the upper landing, and two of them were open. He chose the smaller one, closing the door quietly behind him before opening the window to the soft night air. He groaned as he sat down on the narrow bed and began to remove his boots. God was out to torment him, sure and proper. Here he was, trying to be a decent human being for a change, and he got to share the floor of a tiny bloody inn with the love of his life. If he were a hard-drinking man and she was a glass of whiskey, just out of reach, he'd feel the same way. Ready to cut his own throat.

He dumped his coat and vest on the floor, then used the cold water to wash up as best he could before putting his loose shirt back on. The bed sagged in the middle, and he lay down in the middle of it. It was lumpy, but he'd slept in worse, and as long as he didn't think about Miss Jane…

He heard her. She was crying. There were any number of things he could resist, and he'd never been overly fond of weeping women, but Jane was different. He could no more lie there and listen to her cry than he could fly to the moon.

He climbed out of bed, calling himself every kind of name. He opened his door, and there was sudden silence from behind the closed one, as if she'd heard him.

He should go back in his own room and close the door.

And he knew he wasn't going to.

He didn't even bother to knock. He simply pushed open her door and stepped inside, closing it behind him.

She was a shadow in the bed in the middle of the room. She'd opened her window as well, and he could feel the soft spring breeze. She froze, looking at him, and he couldn't see more than the glitter of her tear-filled eyes in the moonlight.

Ah, to hell with noble plans. Even if she'd come through this with her reputation unscathed he wasn't going to give her up and he knew it. He crossed the room to her, caught her face in his hands and kissed her. She let out a quiet sob.

"Miss Jane Pagett. I've been trying my damnedest to be a gentleman, when I've been wanting to kiss you so badly my hands shake with it, but I knew if I kissed you I'm going to end up doing far worse to you, and…"

"Far worse?" she echoed.

He couldn't smother his laughter. "Well, I'd be trying

to make it something glorious, but either way, it's nothing I should be doing to you at all, and you know it. I'm not for the likes of you." He could at least try to do the right thing. Sitting down on the bed beside her wasn't a very good start, but he did so anyway.

"I don't believe you," she said flatly. "You don't want me."

"Oh, Lord, love," he said, taking her hand and placing it on his erection. "Do you have any idea what this is?" She jumped, and he expected her to pull her hand away as if she'd touched a poisoned snake, so to speak. But she didn't. Her lovely little fingers danced along the stiffening ridge in his breeches, and he let out a choked gasp.

"Christ, Janey!" he said, removing her hand himself. "Don't do that! It's dangerous to a man's behavior."

She sat very still in the bed, as if she were considering all this. "I know what that is. So you do want to kiss me. And you want to put that inside me."

Bloody hell. "Lass, you can't imagine the things I want to do to you. I want to take you to bed and not let you out for days. I want to take you every way I can, so hard that neither of us can walk. I want you in my bed and in my life, for the rest of my life, and if you don't want to believe it you can check your hand."

"My hand?" she echoed, confused. She looked down, and saw the huge, winking diamond on it. "When did you do that?"

"Just now, love. You're mine, Miss Jane Pagett, and you know it, too. I was just trying to be polite about it."

She appeared to consider this for a moment. Her cheeks were tear-stained, and he hated to think he'd caused her pain. He held still, but her hand was still on his John Thomas, and she was absently stroking it.

"Prove it."

"Prove what?" he said, confused, doubtless as much by what her hand was doing as by what she said.

"Prove that you really want me." She moved her hand then, and he wanted to beg her to put it back. Instead she pushed down the covers, and she was lying there in nothing but her shift. "If you want me, ruin me. And then we won't have any other choice."

He hadn't had a better offer in his entire life, but he still hesitated. "I don't know as I'd call it ruined, lass...."

She reached up, grabbed his shirt in two fists and pulled him down to her. "Please," she said.

"Now how can I refuse you when you ask so politely?" he said, covering her body with his, letting her see what she was getting into. She didn't flinch, and he caught her mouth and kissed her, as slow and as deep and as hard as he had that night so long ago.

He went slowly, giving her time to get used to things. When he put his hands on her breasts she was shy, but he was so lavish in his praise and his touch that she became braver, letting him strip the chemise over her head so that she lay there in her lacy drawers and nothing else.

The drawers were a little harder to talk her out of, but she knew they had to go, and he managed to slip them off while he was kissing her breasts, so that she didn't even notice until they were gone.

But then she made him take off his clothes, and he was certain he'd frighten the wits out of her, but she'd taken one long, assessing look at him and then held out her arms, and he was helpless to resist.

He made it as easy for her as he could. He kissed her and stroked her and gave her ripples of pleasure with his clever hands, he used his mouth on her to make certain she was slick enough to make it easy, and he went slowly, but he knew that sooner or later he was going to have to hurt her, and when he did, finally thrusting in deep, breaking through her maidenhead and giving her all of him, he held her, waiting for her tears and anger.

"Is that all there is?" she whispered.

"Now, lass, I'm considered fairly well-sized…"

"No, I mean is that all the pain?"

He looked down into her lovely, thoughtful face. The face that foolish girl didn't think was beautiful. "I expect so."

"Oh," she said, and a small smile curved her lips. "That wasn't bad at all. Go ahead and do your worst."

"My worst?"

"That's what you warned me, Jacob," she said, looking up at him lovingly, using his name for the very first time.

He kissed her, hard. "I'll give you my very best, lass."

And he did.

Miranda would have hoped she'd sleep during those endless hours back to Pawlfrey House, but her body betrayed her. Despite the wine she'd drunk she was wide-awake, alert, and in a torment of anger, confusion, relief and hope. She kept her mind a deliberate blank, concentrating on the gentle rocking of the carriage, the sounds of the night birds, the smell of the air, the strong sure sense of the man sitting across from her in the dark. As she'd first met him, unseeable in a darkened carriage, spinning his webs of intrigue and revenge. He was no scorpion; he was a spider, with a slow web and no instantaneous sting. And she was caught, struggling, fighting, refusing to give in.

It was just before dawn when they finally arrived back at Pawlfrey House, and the huge old building looked cold and deserted. Lucien stepped down from the carriage, then held up a hand to assist her, a hand she blatantly ignored as she climbed down on her own, doing her best to hide the weakness in her legs. The front door had opened, and one of the new footmen stood there, sleepy-eyed and surprised, ready to assist his lord and lady.

"I'll leave you here, madam," Lucien said formally, not making the mistake of trying to touch her again. "I'm going for a ride."

She didn't signify that she heard him, or that his words made the slightest bit of difference as she sailed past him, into the house. With luck he'd fall and break his bloody neck, or simply never return. She could be quite happy alone in this house, as long as she could get rid of Mrs. Humber.

There was even a remote chance that she might be carrying his child. Some women conceived the moment a man looked at them, others waited years with nothing but empty wombs. She wasn't sure which she wanted, and she wasn't going to waste her time thinking about it. All she wanted was to get this poisonous gown off her and find her own bed.

Bridget must have been warned of their abrupt return, for she was waiting in the room, fully dressed. She took one look at Miranda's outfit when she stripped off the black domino and then immediately closed her mouth.

"Get this off me," Miranda said in a tight voice, already yanking at the golden ties that threaded around her waist.

Bridget immediately began to work at it, but her hands weren't deft enough or swift enough, and Miranda's unnatural calm finally broke. "Get it off me," she said again, her voice rising into hysteria as she tore at it, desperate, making the knots even worse, "I can't stand it. I don't care what you do, cut it, tear it…"

Bridget did just that, slicing through the gold leather cord that bound it so that it pooled on the floor around her, and Miranda began to cry, deep, ugly sobs that racked her body as Bridget pulled her into her strong arms and comforted her as if she were a young child.

"There, there, my lady. Don't weep so. He brought you back, didn't he? I knew he couldn't go through with it. Mrs. Humber said you wouldn't even be returning, but I knew different, and I kept up here, waiting for you, and now here you are." She held Miranda's shivering, naked form against her comfortable bosom. "The master's no so bad as he says he is, and if you ask me he cares for you, whether he likes it or not."

"I didn't ask you," Miranda said in a small, miserable voice as Bridget pulled a fresh white chemise over her head. "I don't care what he likes or doesn't like, I don't care about anything."

"Of course you don't, mistress," Bridget said in her soothing voice. "Let me get a nightgown for you and you can get some sleep…"

Miranda shook her head. "This is fine for now," she said in a watery voice. "I just want to sleep."

"Yes, mistress." Bridget helped her between the snowy-white sheets. Everything was clean and white and safe. The hands that had touched her might as well have never existed, and Lucien had run away. She would survive.

The cool linen covered her, and she lay back, closing her eyes. Closing out everything but the sleep that finally, mercifully claimed her.

27

Lucien rode hard and fast in the early morning light, pushing himself and his horse beyond reason. He'd gone mad, stark, staring mad, and he ought to be hauled off to Bedlam with the other lunatics. What the hell had he done? The perfect revenge had been just within his grasp, and all he'd had to do was turn and walk away.

Instead he'd scooped her up like some bloody romantic hero, carried her back here and abandoned her.

And all he'd had to do was see Christopher St. John standing at the edge of the crowd, watching them, to know just how far along the road to disaster he'd come.

If he thought he could make it he'd head straight for London. He even started in that direction, when the ugly truth hit, and hit him hard.

He'd fallen in love with her. He, who didn't believe in love, had been seduced by a slip of a girl, his wings clipped, his locks shorn, his entire life now centered on a woman. Bloody hell.

Clearly he'd been a fool to underestimate her. But now that the illness was diagnosed, the cure was simple.

He'd get rid of her. Send her back to London, or off to the continent. Maybe even to his estates in Jamaica, where he could forget all about her existence. He certainly couldn't continue on like this. He'd marry her first, just to ensure she was taken care of, and then he'd do his best never to see her again. She'd like that.

He wheeled around, heading back toward Pawlfrey House. He was a lot of things, a lot of terrible things, but he wasn't a coward. By the time he reached home the sun was bright overhead, glinting off the lake like the diamonds Jacob had stolen. If he didn't get rid of her there'd be no more of that, he thought morosely, handing the reins to the groom and charging him to give his hard-used roan an extra measure of grain. No more skulking around in the darkness, no more Heavenly Host, thank God. They'd always been tedious, though he'd enjoyed the sex. But all the determined depravity had begun to pall, and their little rituals were ridiculous.

Right now he wanted sex with no one but Miranda, and he had the depressing feeling that it was always going to be the case. Sending her across the ocean was the only cure.

He took the steps two at a time, determined to find her before he could think better of it, heading straight for her rooms on the third floor. To his astonishment the door was actually locked.

This moldy old place had more than its share of antique armaments, and a complete suit of arms stood at the end of the hall. He strode down to it, picked up the battle-ax and headed back to Miranda's door. One solid whack and the door splintered, the doorknob crushed at his feet.

He pushed inside, then slammed it behind him.

Without a latch it immediately swung back and hit him in the bum, so he grabbed a chair and shoved it against it.

Then turned to advance on her.

Miranda woke up with a start, pulling the covers up to her neck like some silly virgin as she stared at Lucien. He stood inside her doorway, holding a battle-ax, and she wondered for a moment if he was going to kill her. She didn't care.

He dropped the ax, trying to be casual, and came toward the bed. "Your door was locked," he said unnecessarily.

"Against you," she pointed out in an even tone.

"Well, you see how much good that did."

She should simper and smile, but that ability had vanished the moment he'd left her to that horrid little man in the goat mask. She glared at him. "What do you want?"

"To talk."

"Well, I don't wish to." There was none of the cloyingly flirtatious lover now. The mask had dropped.

"I thought I was your darling, your true love?" he said, taking one of the delicate chairs and lounging in it, for all the world like a man in his mistress's bedchamber. Well, she wasn't his mistress and she never would be.

Her face stayed grim. "You're an evil, treacherous, degenerate monster, just as you always told me you were. Go away."

"I saved you," he pointed out.

"God knows why. By the way, I'm afraid you've lost

one of your prize pieces of armament. I stole a dagger from the Roundhead collection and left it behind."

He looked amused. "No, you didn't. I took it from beneath the pillow and had it placed in the coach ahead of time."

Her eyes narrowed. "You knew I had it?"

"Of course."

"I should have stabbed you when I had the chance."

He smiled at that. Bad move.

"If you don't go away I'll scream."

"It won't do you any good, my angel. This is my house, remember. No one will come."

"Not if Mrs. Humber has anything to say about it. She hates me."

"Don't be ridiculous—Essie doesn't hate anyone."

"I don't care about Mrs. Humber. I just want you out of here."

"The coach was waiting to take us away," he pointed out.

"It was doubtless waiting to take *you* away. I think you had every intention of abandoning me there and going on your way."

He didn't deny it. "Why do you think I changed my mind?"

"God only knows. You must have come up with something even more foul and evil to do to my family, using me to do it, no doubt."

He rose, coming up to the bed. The midday light filtered in the windows, leaving strange shadows on the pure white sheets, and he loomed over her like the monster she knew he was. "In fact, I have."

"The truth for a change. Well, pray, enlighten me."

"Well, I had considered that your family would be

driven mad by the thought of you married to me, being kept away from them, made miserable by my neglect and misbehavior."

"I hope and pray for your neglect," she said spitefully.

"Let me finish." He held up a restraining hand. "And then I thought of an even better revenge. What if I made you blissfully happy, so happy that you never wanted to leave me? They would be helpless. If I mistreated you they could always ask the Crown to intervene. If I loved you they'd be helpless."

She stared at him. "You're out of your mind. That's impossible."

"I'm afraid it's too late," he said. And he began to take off his coat.

She didn't move. "And you think I'm going to lie still and let you touch me again?"

"I hope you won't be lying still. It's much better when you participate." His vest followed, onto the floor.

"So you expect me to get out of this bed and follow you into my dressing room so I can't look at you? Your insanity knows no bounds."

"Only when it comes to you." He sat in the chair and began to pull off his boots, dropping them on the floor. And then he rose, reached for the hem of his shirt and pulled it over his head so that for the first time she could actually see him in the bright sunlight that poured in her windows. No pitch-black darkness this time.

He was beautiful. Muscled and lean and strong, with wide shoulders and powerful arms and a flat waist. And then he deliberately turned around, and she stared at the ruin of his back.

She couldn't control her horrified intake of breath. It

was astonishing that someone could have gone through that kind of torture and lived. The stripes crisscrossed his back, some so deep they had to have hit bone, others lighter, less vicious. It looked to her untrained eye that the beatings had happened over an extended length of time—some of the scars had widened as his body grew, others were still narrow. And then he turned back, tossing his head so she could get a clear look at the same damage to his face, reaching into his scalp.

"So," he said in a flat voice. "Richard the Third or Caliban?"

She knew she was crying, crying for him, for the pain he'd endured. Crying when she never cried.

Except that she did, for him. Always. She managed a smile. "'O brave new world,'" she quoted Miranda's speech, "'that hath such people in it.' Come here, my love."

And he came.

It was late afternoon as they dozed, sleepy and sated. He'd won another wager: she had used her mouth on him, of her own accord, though he had to stop her before the afternoon ended too soon. She lay now in a state of bliss, looking out into the afternoon sunlight.

Lucien lay beside her, on his stomach, and she slowly traced the scars along his back with gentle, loving fingers. "Do these still hurt?"

"Not for a long time," he said, his face half in the pillow.

She leaned over and kissed one of the deeper stripes, and then another, featherlight, and he groaned with pleasure. "It's a waste of time," he muttered. "I'm going to need at least an hour to recover."

She laughed, falling back on the mattress but keeping her hand on his, wanting, needing to hold him. "Who did this to you?"

She was afraid he'd tense up, push her away. But he didn't. It was as if he'd finally given up fighting her, fighting his own feelings for her. The feelings she'd somehow known he had, buried deep inside.

"My stepmother," he said after a moment. "She was mad. That's why Genevieve was brought up here. Her family didn't want to leave her with her mother. I was no kin of theirs, so I was fair game." His voice was calm, emotionless.

"And your father?"

"Already dead. We were in Jamaica, but I don't think I would have fared much better here." He turned his head to look at her. "Don't cry, love. It was over long ago." He reached up and brushed the tears away with his thumb.

"What happened to her? Your stepmother? What finally stopped her?"

"I expect she would have killed me before she stopped, but fortunately she drowned herself one night. With no help from me, I might add. I was only twelve at the time. I would have killed her if I could, but at that point I was small for my age. No one ever fed me."

"Oh, Lucien," she cried.

He moved to cover her, so quickly she didn't realize what he was doing. "No more tears, vixen. You unman me."

"Well, that's the last thing I'd want to do."

He laughed, then pulled himself out of bed, reaching for his clothes, and she saw for the first time that the scarring went over his buttocks as well, down to his thigh.

"It's not a pretty sight," he said without turning around, knowing she was looking.

"Actually it's a very pretty sight," she said, doing an excellent job of keeping the tears from her voice.

"Saucy wench. Do you realize the door's been open all this time? I don't know if it will close again. You'll have to move into the pink room with me."

She giggled, unable to help herself, and at that he turned and smiled at her. She had the oddest feeling it was as if he was saying goodbye, but she knew that was impossible. He loved her; he was no longer fighting it. There was nothing to be afraid of.

She wriggled back down in the covers. "Where are you going?"

"I have things to do. Much as I'd love to spend the entire day despoiling you I think you need to rest. I promise to wake you by dinner time."

"And how are you going to awaken me?"

"As wickedly as possible."

She smiled sleepily. There was nothing to worry about. She was simply unused to being happy. "Come back sooner," she said in a sleepy voice. And before he could even leave the room she fell back into a sound, sated sleep.

Lucien left his pink rooms, having bathed and changed, a rueful smile on his face. She really did have an unholy nerve. He wondered if that was the god-awful moment when he'd fallen in love with her? Or had it been earlier than that, when she'd wept in his arms and then turned around and burbled cheerfully at him.

Or had it been, as he suspected, the moment she kneed Gregory Panelle in his privates?

She was fearless, and he'd been a fool to try to resist her.

"You've got a visitor, my lord." One of the new footmen was waiting for him by his door, and Lucien froze. They were too remote for casual visitors, and he knew exactly who it was. He thought he'd have more time, time to admit to Miranda the wretched truth about Christopher St. John. He'd told her he was a villain. What more could she expect of him? But the thought of St. John's vapid face in the crowd at Bromfield made him a little ill.

"Where is he?" He couldn't remember the servant's name, but it hardly mattered.

"He's in the green drawing room, my lord. He said to tell you his name is——"

"I know what his name is. Tell him I'll be with him in a few moments." And he went back inside his room to find his pistol.

Christopher St. John had changed very little in the last years. He was still a handsome man, if one didn't notice the weak chin, now slightly softer than before with the hint of a second one beneath it. His clothes were the sort that looked expensive at a casual glance but were made of poorer quality fabrics and inferior tailoring. He'd fallen on hard times, which pleased Lucien.

What didn't please him was the fact St. John no longer seemed terrified of him. Perhaps he needed Leopold's stern presence to keep him in line. He gave St. John his calm, icy smile. "Don't rise," he murmured as he came in the room, leaning more heavily on his cane than he needed to. "What a delight to see you, old friend. Though I'm afraid I was under the misapprehension that you were to stay out of England. In fact, I thought I paid you a very great deal of money never to return. But perhaps I'm mistaken."

"Money runs out, Rochdale," he said with a faint sneer. "I find I'm in need of more. Which I'm certain you'll be more than happy to provide, given that you've taken that piece of crumpet for your own."

"Blackmail?"

Oh, let's not call it blackmail, old man," he said. "Call it insurance. You don't want her to know you paid for me to kidnap and deflower her and I'm more than happy to be discreet. I just require a little loan."

He could shoot him, Lucien thought dreamily. He'd derive great pleasure from it, but the sound would alert Miranda, and that was the last thing he could afford. "And just how great a loan are we talking about, dear boy?"

St. John eyed him carefully. He would want to come up with the perfect number, Lucien thought. Too little and he'd appear a fool, too much and Lucien would balk.

"Let me make this easier for you," Lucien purred. "I would think five thousand pounds would keep you out of England and living quite well for the rest of your life." He didn't for one moment believe that. St. John would be back within the year, wanting more. He was a man with expensive tastes.

St. John looked torn. On the one hand that was clearly more than he'd been planning to ask for, on the other, if that was the offer then more was always possible.

"I suggest you take it," Lucien said gently. "Before I change my mind and put a bullet in you."

"You wouldn't do that. How would you explain me to your lady?"

"With great difficulty, I have no doubt. However, do you really think I wouldn't be able to bend her to my will?"

St. John was looking uncertain. Fear was beginning to gather in his shallow eyes once more, and Lucien knew he'd won. At least for now.

St. John tried bluster. "Well, there's no guarantee of that, now is there, my lord? And I'm thinking..."

"I'm thinking you should stop thinking, take it and be gone, before I change my mind."

"And you're going to tell me you have five thousand quid in cash just sitting around?"

"In fact, I do. Small change, my boy." He tossed the small satchel at him, and St. John fumbled for a moment, then clung tightly.

He rose, and there was a faint sheen of sweat on his brow. "Pleasure doing business with you, my lord," he said with a final show of bravado.

"I don't think so," Lucien said gently.

St. John fled.

28

Jacob awoke, wrapped in Jane's sweet arms, and groaned. He wanted to lie in bed with his darling girl, kiss her into arousal, take her again, very gently given that he'd already had her twice and she was doubtless tender, but he couldn't resist. Except some bloody idiot in the taproom below thought normal conversation was carried on in a modified bellow, and there was no way he could woo his beloved with those voices echoing through the small inn.

Her eyes opened sleepily, and he smiled down at her. "Go back to sleep, love," he said softly, kissing her eyelids. "I'll see about some tea and breakfast for you."

"And a bath?" she murmured sleepily. "Or is that too much to ask for?"

"Nothing's too much to ask for, my girl," he said. If the innkeeper didn't have the means to provide a hip bath for his patrons he'd scour the neighborhood until he found one.

Fortunately it didn't have to come to that. The host most certainly did have a hip bath, and it wouldn't take

above ten minutes to get it up to the young miss, full
of hot water.

Satisfied his job was momentarily done, he headed
into the taproom and a morning mug of ale.

There were three young men there, toffs by the look
of them. Old money, old blood—he knew the type well.
He'd need to warn Jane to stay out of sight, just in case
she knew these three young bucks, but the chances of
that were so slim he stayed put.

The moment he entered the room they lowered their
booming voices, talking amongst themselves like con-
spirators, and he smothered a snort of disgust. The fools
didn't realize their voices carried throughout the inn,
or they would have kept their bloody voices down earlier and let him enjoy his first morning in bed with his
heart's love.

"We'd best be going," the oldest of the three said,
and he realized they must be brothers. Not so much by
the look of them, though there was some similarity, but
they way they held themselves. "But remember, if this is
to be a killing matter then it's on my head as the eldest.
The grudge is against me, and it's my responsibility to
deal with it."

Shit, Jacob thought, taking another lazy drink of
ale. If they thought someone needed to be killed it was
doubtless Scorpion—he had only to meet people to turn
them murderous. The question was, how was he going
to distract them without compromising his time with
Jane.

"She was mad, Benedick," the youngest one said.
"She threatened you with a gun. She said she was going
to kill our parents—you could scarcely be expected to
marry a madwoman."

"I should have seen to her, Charles. At least made certain she was no danger to herself and others. I'll never forgive myself for that."

Damn it all to hell. Apparently his Jane wasn't the only one bent on rescue. These could only be Lucien's future brothers-in-law, and future family gatherings were not looking promising.

He was just trying to decide what to do when Jane came down the stairs, looking rumpled and decidedly well-tupped.

"Good God, Jane, what are you doing here?" The youngest of the three who addressed his Jane, *his Jane*, in a peremptory manner was running a very great risk, until Jane put a calming hand on his arm. He didn't like that much better but he bided his time, rather than rip the lad's arm off.

"I imagine the same thing you are, Brandon," she replied calmly. "Trying to save your sister. Hullo, Benedick, Charles."

The other two were staring at her in disbelief. The eldest one pulled himself together. "Surely you're not out here alone, Janey?" he said, his voice a rumble of disapproval, and Jacob's irritation spilled into possessive rage. Who was he to call Jane, his Jane, Janey? And to set himself up as protector? He heard a soft, growling noise and realized, to his astonishment, that it had come from his own throat as he pushed away from the bar.

But Jane, his Jane, smiled at him, her dear, sweet face mischievous. "I'm very well taken care of indeed. My dear Benedick, allow me to introduce you to my fiancé, Mr. Jacob Donnelly. Mr. Donnelly, these are Miranda's brothers and my childhood friends. Benedick, Charles and Brandon Rohan."

There was a dead silence as the three surveyed him, knowing from one glance that he wasn't of their world. Finally the youngest spoke. "Your fiancé, Jane? That's not Mr. Bore-well?"

"No, it isn't, is it?" Jane said in a tranquil voice.

"Well, thank God for that," the young one said. "Your servant, Mr. Donnelly."

"King Donnelly?" the eldest, Benedick, inquired in an icy voice.

"The same." Was he going to have to fight these three? Well, at least two of them. The youngest was looking at him with approval.

Lord Benedick was glaring at him. "And why, may I ask...?"

"No, you may not ask," Jane said with more courage than he'd heard from her before. "We may have grown up like brother and sister but my marriage is none of your business."

"I thought you said you were only engaged."

"That won't be for long," Jacob said quietly. "Do you want to make something of it?"

Benedick appeared more than ready to, when Jane once more intervened. "Stop it, you two. I'm not some bone for you two to fight over. We need to be rescuing Miranda, not arguing. At least, I presume that's why you're here."

"Lord, Janey, why else would we be at the back end of nowhere?" the middle one demanded, and Jacob decided he really didn't like strange men, even if they'd grown up with her, calling her Janey. "It's been more than ten days since she was taken, and I don't know how long the family can keep it quiet."

"There's no need for you all to go racing up to Ripton

Waters," Jacob said in a calm voice. "Jane and I were headed there ourselves. But I don't think we're going to be needed. I expect they'll be happily married by now and not wanting their honeymoon interrupted."

Benedick Rohan cast him a long, speculative look. "Ripton Waters, is it? And how do we get there?"

"Oh, Christ," *his* Janey said. "Jacob is right. And I don't imagine Miranda wants you three great loobies bursting in on them. We could send word…"

"We're not going anywhere until we're certain our sister is all right," Benedick said, still eyeing Jacob with profound distrust.

There was a reason he'd spent his adult life robbing the peerage. They were a royal pain in his backside. "I can take you to Ripton Waters. I'm the only one around here who knows where the house is." He smiled politely. "If you promise to leave them alone once you've satisfied yourself that she's happy."

"I find that unlikely. Our sister has a profound distrust of men, for very good reason. She's hardly likely to relax her guard with someone known as the Scorpion," Benedick said.

"Will you leave her be if she tells you to?" Jacob said.

Benedick glanced at his brothers for agreement, then nodded. "Agreed." He started for the door, turned back and gave them all a peremptory look. "Well? What are we waiting for?"

The quality, Jacob thought wryly. If this was the price he had to pay for Jane, then he'd do it. But he didn't have to like it.

Jacob sighed, glancing down at Jane. "We'll be with you in a moment."

He waited until they were alone, and then he pulled her to him and kissed her, full on the mouth, not caring if any of the Rohans came storming back into the inn. "She's all right, you know? Scorpion wouldn't hurt her. He might come close, but in the end he's not nearly as bad as he likes to think he is."

"I hope you're right," she said doubtfully.

"I've known him for more than twenty years, love. I know what he will and will not do. They'll be happily romping in their marriage bed and he won't thank me for dragging her three brothers up there to interfere."

"I need to see her as well," she said in a quiet voice. "It's not that I don't take your word for it. But I want to say good-bye before we head for Scotland. I want her to meet you."

"Then we'll go," he said, kissing her again. And he only hoped his faith in his old friend wasn't misplaced.

The late afternoon sun was shining brightly, casting long shadows on the wide front lawns. They were going to have to be cut, Lucien thought absently, staring out through the Palladian windows on the landing.

He could see her walking out there, the sun gilding her rich brown hair he'd once thought quite ordinary. She was walking toward the dock, and he knew a moment's disquiet. She wouldn't make the mistake of walking out there again, would she? Not when she'd almost fallen through.

But no, she walked on, her arms filled with daffodils, down to the old boat that had been pulled up on the shore, and sat. Waiting for him.

His relief was so strong he was almost weak with

it. He should have known a leech like St. John would be easy enough to deal with. The kind of money he'd asked for was merely a pittance in the scheme of things, and he'd happily pay ten times that amount to know that Miranda need never discovered the depths of his perfidy.

Sooner or later he'd probably have to have the man killed. Once a blackmailer started he never stopped, and it went against Lucien's grain to let a little worm like St. John think he'd gotten the better of him. But for now he was gone, and when the time came Jacob would know someone who could handle it, neatly and quietly. It wasn't as if St. John was any boon to this world.

No, everything was going to be fine after all. Whether he liked it or not he was tied to the woman who was waiting for him down by the lake. The Rohans had gotten their revenge instead of the other way around, and he no longer cared. As long as he had Miranda, then nothing else mattered.

It was a beautiful day, Miranda thought absently. The kind of day to fall in love. Scarcely the kind of day to discover that the man you were going to marry was even more of a toad-licking, worm-kissing, putrescent arse of a skunk. Scarcely the kind of day to commit murder, but one had to start somewhere.

There were daffodils everywhere, and she began to pick them for lack of something better to do. She'd dressed once he left her, and gone looking for him. He wasn't in his very pink rooms, and she'd been half tempted to take off her clothes and climb into his bed to await him. He'd find her soon enough.

But she didn't have the patience for it. So instead

she went looking for him, finding him closed up in the green parlor, in low conversation with someone. She was about to push open the doors when she recognized the second voice, and she froze.

Silly, of course, she was imagining things. She put her hand on the doorknob, about to push it open, and then she heard the word "blackmail" in the voice she'd once hated most in the world.

No, Christopher St. John's voice wasn't the one she hated most. It was the drawling, mocking voice of the man who lay in her bed just hours ago and told her he loved her. The man she had every intention of killing.

Stabbing was too good for him. She'd done a frenzied search for pistols among the walls of weapons that made the gloomy old house so cozy, but apparently the de Malheurs gave up war when guns were introduced. And no wonder. They were much better at stabbing people in the back.

She looked at the lake. The old rowboat sat there, no longer seaworthy but with a good solid seat, and she headed toward it, her arms filled with daffodils. She dumped them on the ground, crushing them beneath her feet as she climbed into the beached boat and picked up the oar. It was still solid and heavy, and she climbed out, carrying it up and onto the dock. The sun had dried some of the slime, but she could see the broken board where she'd nearly gone through. He'd saved her then. She almost wished he hadn't.

She was halfway down the length of the dock when he began shouting at her, but she kept her back to him, pretending she couldn't hear. Her face was set in stone. Swill-sucking bastard. To think that she'd loved him.

After all the things he'd done, he'd threatened to do, and she'd forgiven him.

Not anymore. She gripped the oar more tightly, keeping her back to him, and waited.

The weak old dock bounced when he climbed up, and he was starting toward her. She turned, and she knew her face was cold and terrible.

Unfortunately he didn't. He was too busy haranguing her for being foolish enough to put her life at risk by going out on the dock again, after the close call last time. She didn't move, waiting as he negotiated the missing plank. He hadn't brought a cane with him. Good thing—it would make his balance even more precarious. It wouldn't take much to make him go over.

She waited until he was almost in reach. Not close enough to grab her, but close enough for the old oar. "Stay there, my darling," she said in a silken voice.

Finally he caught on. He jerked his head up, looking at her. "What are you doing out here?" he asked in a steady voice.

"Waiting for you. The water is ice-cold, you said."

He watched her warily. "Yes."

"And very, very deep?"

"Yes." She could see the tension radiating through him, the same tension that ran through her. "You must have run into St. John."

"Not exactly. I listened at the door."

"Curiosity killed the cat," he said lightly.

"No, it didn't. It killed you."

And she swung the old oar at him with all her strength.

It hit with a great *thwack*, splintering in two, and he

went over the side, into the dark, cold waters of the lake, sinking like a stone.

It took her two seconds. And then she let out a scream for help, tossing the broken oar away from her, and jumped into the water after him.

It was very cold, numbingly so, and as it closed over her head she grabbed for him, wrapping her arms around his body, ready to sink to the bottom with him.

Instead he kicked, pushing them up so that they broke the surface, his arm clamped around hers as she struggled. "Jesus, woman!" he snapped. "When did we have to become Romeo and Juliet?"

"You liar!" she screamed, hitting him. "You filthy, evil, degenerate piece of garbage, you slimy, unspeakable pile of offal, you worm-ridden dung heap of a human being, I hate you I hate you I hate you." Her struggles were pulling them down again, and water filled her mouth, stopping her mid-tirade.

Unfortunately, even with a bleeding head he was still stronger than she was, and it seemed to take him no effort at all to disable her, clamping her arms together as he dragged her toward shore, doubtless helped by her angry kicks. By the time it was shallow enough for them to walk he released her, collapsing on the stone beach.

She followed him a moment later, her sodden dress clinging to her heavily. She looked down at him, then started looking around for another weapon. There was another abandoned oar in the weeds, and she started toward it, but he rolled over and caught her ankle and she went sprawling. A moment later he covered her, holding her down as she fought him, fury in every inch of her body.

He let her fight, doing nothing to shield himself from

her blows, simply pinning her with his weight so she couldn't get away. It seemed like hours later when she finally grew too tired. Her arms ached, her hands were sore and he seemed to realize she was spent. He let her shove him off her, and she rolled onto her stomach in the dirt, sobbing.

They stayed like that for a long time. The sun was sinking lower, and finally she looked up at him. "Your head is bleeding," she said in a raw voice. Indeed, it was bleeding a great deal, pouring down the side of his face and staining his shirt bright red. Maybe she'd killed him after all.

"I know."

She got to her feet slowly, slapping away his hand when he tried to help her. "Come back to the house," she said wearily. "I may as well bandage you. It will bring me little enough satisfaction if you die of blood poisoning."

He very wisely said nothing, following her up to the house. She gave orders for clean rags and warm water as well as bandages and lint, and then ordered him into the salon. "Not the green one," she snapped, as he started toward it.

The red one was on the other side of the hall. He paused, looking at her. "Why did you jump in after me?"

"I wanted to make sure you'd stay down and wouldn't bob up again."

He laughed, and something inside her, some cold hard rock of fury split and melted. She turned her back on him, placing more orders so he wouldn't see. He knew her too well.

His head wound was hardly serious, and she dabbed

at it with enthusiasm, hoping to inflict a little more pain, but he bore it stoically enough, saying nothing as she continued a muttered litany of his many character defects. She'd almost finished when she heard a huge commotion in the front hall, and she looked up from her ministrations, in no very charitable mood.

"What the bloody hell is going on out there?" she shouted.

The door burst open, and she groaned. In came her three brothers with swords and pistols drawn, accompanied by a panic-stricken Jane and a tall stranger. A man, she decided, who looked like a jewel thief prone to midnight kisses. He had a protective arm around Jane's shoulder, and then her brothers started shouting.

She was used to them. "Be quiet!" she thundered, and Lucien, who probably had a monumental headache, winced.

"Damn it, Miranda," Brandon began in a plaintive voice.

"Brandon!" Benedick said in a shocked voice. "Remember there are ladies present."

"She's got the mouth of a sailor and always has had," Brandon muttered. "And it's your fault—you taught her those words."

"Just be quiet, all of you," she snapped. "Can't you see I have a wounded man here?"

"What happened to him?" her quiet brother Charles asked curiously.

"I hit him with an oar."

"Good," Benedick said.

Miranda rinsed out the rag, then dabbed it a little too enthusiastically at the wound. Lucien looked at her sideways, cursing beneath his breath, but had the good sense not to say anything out loud.

"Why'd you do that?" Jane asked, curious.

"He probably deserved it," the strange man.

"I was trying to kill him."

"Oh, he definitely deserved *that*," said the man.

"I can take care of that," Benedick said in a threatening voice.

She glanced down at Lucien's impassive face. "It's tempting," she said in a thoughtful voice. "But first let me stop the bleeding."

"But why bother if Benedick's just going to kill him?" Brandon demanded.

"You idiot," Jane said. "She's not letting Benedick anywhere near him."

"I'm calling you out, Rochdale," her oldest brother snarled. "You may choose your weapons. I know you're a dead shot, but you'll find…"

"Oh, go away, Benedick. I'll let you have him after I finish bandaging him." Miranda poked Lucien again, just for good measure, and he muttered "vixen" under his breath.

"I'll have your bags packed," her brother suddenly announced. "Our horses need to rest, or otherwise I'd take you out of here immediately."

Jane put a gentle hand on the pugnacious brother's arm. "Let's leave them for a bit, Benedick," she said soothingly to her childhood friend. "I'm sure she's perfectly safe."

Benedick made a disgusted noise, but Jane was undeniable, and a moment later all was quiet with their departure.

"Is that the one who was going to marry my sister?" Lucien said after a moment.

"It is."

"She's better off dead," he said morosely.

She almost wanted to laugh. "He's a bit high-handed. So are you." She took a clean cloth, dipped it in the second bowl of water and finished washing the rest of the blood off, making sure to be as rough as possible.

"Are you going with them?"

She'd found some gauze, and she was busy concentrating on wrapping it around his head. "You'll likely get blood poisoning or a fever and die a painful, miserable death," she muttered.

"You can only hope. However, I think with such gentle nursing I'm bound to survive," he said. He caught her hand, forcing her to look at him. "I'm..."

"Don't you dare say it. Don't even try," she warned him in a fierce voice.

"I'm everything you've said I am. A worthless, pig-sucking bastard. You can go if you want. I wouldn't blame you."

She stared at him in furious disbelief. "You stupid, fatheaded, pig-livered, mutton-larded pond scum. I didn't put up with all this for nothing. Do you love me?"

His pale eyes were like ice. "I love no one."

She rolled her eyes. "You can be very tedious, you know that? Do you love me?"

"No."

"You don't want to see me when I get really mad. Do you love me?"

He looked at her warily. "Yes, damn it."

"A good thing," she said. And she bent over to kiss him.

A moment later she was beneath him on the sofa, his bandaged head giving him no trouble whatsoever, as he kissed her, pressing her down into the cushions, and she could feel him growing hard against her.

"You can get an erection less than an hour after I've tried to kill you?" she said in disbelief. "Just how perverse are you?"

"Let me show you."

* * * * *